Prosdocimo de' Beldomandi, *Plana musica* and *Musica speculativa*

Prosdocimo de' Beldomandi, professor of arts and medicine at Padua in the early fifteenth century, brought to his eight treatises on music an originality, a scientific rigor, and an aesthetic sensitivity that made him one of the preeminent music theorists of his time. Both treatises presented here respond to Marchetto of Padua's famous *Lucidarium*. Though Prosdocimo disdained works that confused "the theoretical part with the practical part of ... plainchant"—with the *Lucidarium* evidently in mind—, he recognized Marchetto's authority in plainchant practice and borrowed extensively from the *Lucidarium* in his *Tractatus plane musice* of 1412. As to Marchetto's radical theories of tuning, Prosdocimo hoped that his *Tractatus musice speculative* (1425) would help "Italy be purged of such errors."

Critical editions and translations of both treatises are long overdue. The *Tractatus plane musice* has never before been published, and the *Tractatus musice speculative* is available only in a scarce and inadequate early edition of 1913. Based on a collation of the three sources of the *Tractatus plane musice* and both sources of the *Tractatus musice speculative*, the present edition includes an annotated translation on pages facing the Latin text; a critical introduction placing Prosdocimo and the treatises in their historical context; and indices of terms, names, and subjects.

Jan Herlinger is Derryl and Helen Haymon Professor of Music at Louisiana State University. He is the editor and translator of *The Lucidarium of Marchetto of Padua* and Prosdocimo's *Contrapunctus, Brevis summula proportionum* and *Parvus tractatulus de modo monacordum dividendi*; and author of articles in the leading journals and the *Cambridge History of Western Music Theory, New Oxford History of Music, Medieval Italy: An Encyclopedia*, and *Oxford Dictionary of the Middle Ages*.

Studies in the History of Music Theory and Literature

Thomas J. Mathiesen,
General Editor

volume 4

Prosdocimo de' Beldomandi

Plana musica

Musica speculativa

New Critical Texts, Translations,
Annotations, and Indices by

Jan Herlinger

University of Illinois Press
Urbana and Chicago

University of Illinois Press
1325 South Oak Street
Champaign, IL 61820-6903
www.press.uillinois.edu

Complete Cataloging-in-Publication information
is on file at the Library of Congress.

ISBN-10: 0-252-03259-4
ISBN-13: 978-0-252-03259-2

Music   MUX

CONTENTS

PREFACE AND ACKNOWLEDGMENTS

Prosdocimo de' Beldomandi, professor of arts and medicine at Padua in the early fifteenth century, brought to his eight treatises on music an originality, a scientific rigor, and an aesthetic sensitivity that made him one of the preeminent music theorists of his time. The two treatises presented here respond to the plainchant treatise of Marchetto of Padua, the *Lucidarium*. Though Prosdocimo disdained works that "make a useless confusion of the theoretical part with the practical part of ... plainchant"—a characterization evidently made with the *Lucidarium* in mind—, he recognized that when Marchetto addressed plainchant practice he wrote "correctly ... and most excellently"; so it is not surprising that Prosdocimo borrowed extensively from the *Lucidarium* in his own *Tractatus plane musice* (1412). But Prosdocimo saw Marchetto's radical theories of tuning, involving division of the whole tone into fifths and the construction of not two but four intervals smaller than the tone, as based on unorthodox arithmetic procedures; considering that these theories had "spread through Italy and beyond," Prosdocimo hoped that with his *Tractatus musice speculative* (1425) the "evils, lies, and mistakes concerning music that had been brought forth and disseminated by one Paduan might be removed by another, and thus Italy be purged of such errors."

Critical editions and translations of both treatises are long overdue. The *Tractatus plane musice* is the only musical treatise of Prosdocimo of which an edition has never been published, and the *Tractatus musice speculative* is available only in the edition of Baralli and Torri, based on a single source, published in an Italian journal in 1913 and held only by specialized libraries.

The present edition is based on a collation of the three sources of the *Tractatus plane musice* and both sources of the *Tractatus musice speculative*. It includes an annotated translation on pages facing the Latin text; a critical introduction placing Prosdocimo and the treatises in their historical context; and indices of terms, names, and subjects.

I thank the Series Editor, Professor Thomas J. Mathiesen, Distinguished Professor of Music and Director of the Center for the History of Music Theory and Literature at Indiana University, for his careful reading of the text, his judicious advice, and his splendid editing of this volume. Professor Mathiesen also deserves great credit for conceiving and directing the *Thesaurus Musicarum Latinarum* project, which has so greatly facilitated the study of medieval and Renaissance music theory. Professor Margaret Bent, Fellow of All Souls College, Oxford, read a draft of the book and made penetrating suggestions, for which I am very grateful.

Work on the project was funded in part by the National Endowment for the Humanities and the Louisiana State University Council of Research. Librarians of the Civico Museo Bibliografico Musicale, Bologna; the Biblioteca Governativa, Cremona; and the Biblioteca Statale, Lucca, provided exemplary assistance. In particular, I wish to thank the Civico Museo Bibliografico Musicale (Museo internazionale e biblioteca della musica), Bologna, and the Biblioteca Statale, Lucca, for permission to reproduce images from their manuscripts.

I would also like to thank my friend and colleague Professor Linda Page Cummins of the University of Alabama for her support throughout the genesis of this book, and especially for significant assistance during the preparation of final copy.

INTRODUCTION

Prosdocimo and His Treatises

Information on Prosdocimo's life is scant. Antonio Favaro in his study on Prosdocimo's life and works quotes documents that call him a student in arts at Padua in 1400 and 1402;[1] in the colophon to the copy Prosdocimo made in 1409 of the *Canones super tabulas Alphonsi* of Johannes de Saxonia, he called himself a student of arts at Bologna.[2] He took the doctorate in arts at Padua on 15 May 1409 and was probably the Prosdocimo who received the license in medicine on 15 April 1411.[3] He was a professor at Padua from 1422 at the latest until his death in 1428. Documents list him as professor of astrology or astronomy, among the doctors of "astrology, mathematics, and experimental philosophy," or among the "artists and

---

[1] Antonio Favaro, "Appendice agli studi intorno alla vita ed alle opere di Prosdocimo de' Beldomandi, matematico padovano del secolo XV," *Bullettino di bibliografia e di storia delle scienze matematiche e fisiche* 18 (1885): 420. The present account includes information previously published in the introductions to Prosdocimo de' Beldomandi, *Contrapunctus: A New Critical Text and Translation*, ed. and trans. Jan Herlinger, Greek and Latin Music Theory, vol. 1 (Lincoln: University of Nebraska Press, 1984); and Prosdocimo de' Beldomandi, *Brevis summula proportionum quantum ad musicam pertinet and Parvus tractatulus de modo monacordum dividendi: A New Critical Text and Translation*, ed. and trans. Jan Herlinger, Greek and Latin Music Theory, vol. 4 (Lincoln: University of Nebraska Press, 1987).

[2] "Scriptum per me prosdocimum de beldemandis de padua in artibus Bononie studentem"; Florence, Biblioteca Medicea-Laurenziana, Ashburnham 206, f. 19r. For a description of the manuscript, see my introduction to Prosdocimo de' Beldomandi, *Brevis summula ... Parvus tractatulus*, 30–39; a facsimile of the colophon appears on p. 155.

[3] *Acta graduum academicorum gymnasii patavini ab anno 1400 ad annum 1450*, 2d ed., ed. Gasparo Zonta and Giovanni Brotto, 3 vols. (Padua: Antenore, 1970), 1:6–7 (document no. 31: "1409 maii 15. Examen et conventus art. mag. Prosdocimi de Beldemando") and 62–63 (no. 155: "1411 apr. 15. Licentia privati examinis in scientia med. mag. Prosdocimi [*other MS:* Prosdocimi de Padua]"). Prosdocimo is a patron saint of Padua, and the name was common in the city. In Prosdocimo's day, a private examination (*examen*) for the license to teach was prerequisite to the public examination (*conventus*) for the doctorate; see Nancy G. Siraisi, *Arts and Sciences at Padua: The Studium of Padua before 1350*, Studies and Texts, no. 25 (Toronto: Pontifical Institute of Mediaeval Studies, 1973), 31.

physicians" and record his presence at convocations on 26 July 1420, 15 July 1426, and 16 June and 21 August 1427.[4]

Italian universities were organized into two colleges, one for law, one for arts and medicine. As a consequence, many doctors of arts, like Prosdocimo, were physicians as well. Of sixty members of the Paduan college of doctors of arts and medicine in the late fourteenth century, twenty-eight are known to have taken degrees in both arts and medicine as compared to thirteen in medicine alone and seven in arts alone; of the five sponsors at Prosdocimo's examinations in arts and medicine (if the second document cited in n. 3 indeed refers to him), four were doctors of both.[5] In the catholicity of his interests, then, Prosdocimo was a typical Paduan doctor of his day.

Prosdocimo's musical treatises fall into three groups. Three date from his student years:

1. *Expositiones tractatus practice cantus mensurabilis Johannis de Muris* (Padua, 1404 [?])

2. *Tractatus practice cantus mensurabilis* (1408)

3. *Brevis summula proportionum quantum ad musicam pertinet* (1409).

Four, as well as his first revision of treatise 2, may be regarded as the fruit of his maturity:

4. *Contrapunctus* (Montagnana, 1412)[6]

5. *Tractatus pratice cantus mensurabilis ad modum Ytalicorum* (Montagnana, 1412)

6. *Tractatus plane musice* (Montagnana, 1412)

7. *Parvus tractatulus de modo monacordum dividendi* (Padua, 1413).

---

[4] Antonio Favaro, "Intorno alla vita ed alle opere di Prosdocimo de' Beldomandi, matematico padovano del secolo XV," *Bullettino di bibliografia e di storia delle scienze matematiche e fisiche* 12 (1879): 29–31 and 34–38; *Acta graduum academicorum gymnasii patavini*, 1:220–24 (nos. 658, 685, 693).

[5] "At Padua the Faculty of Arts, instead of being, as in the university centers of northern Europe, merely a preparatory stage through which aspirants to the higher faculties must pass, was itself indissolubly linked with a higher faculty, that of medicine" (Siraisi, *Arts and Sciences at Padua*, 9; she counts the doctors of arts and medicine on p. 30). The association of arts and medicine in Italy goes back to the archetypical medical school of Salerno (Hastings Rashdall, *The Universities of Europe in the Middle Ages*, 3 vols., new ed. by F. M. Powicke and A. B. Emden [Oxford: Clarendon Press, 1936], 1:83). Isidore of Seville (*Etymologiae* 4.13.1–5) and Peter of Abano (*Conciliator*, Differentia 1) stressed the importance to the physician of studies in the arts.

[6] Montagnana is a walled town some 40 km southwest of Padua.

Late in life he wrote a treatise on speculative music that is, in substance, an attack on Marchetto of Padua:

8.   *Tractatus musice speculative* (1425).

To this same period belong Prosdocimo's revisions of the *Contrapunctus, Cantus mensurabilis ad modum Ytalicorum, Monacordum*, and probably *Plana musica* as well, plus a second revision of *Practica cantus mensurabilis*,[7] all of them preserved uniquely in the Lucca manuscript. The revisions in the Lucca versions of *Plana musica* and *Musica speculativa* will be discussed below.

Prosdocimo's eight treatises on music constitute a systematic survey of the main departments of the art; several of them became quite influential. The *Expositiones tractatus practice cantus mensurabilis Johannis de Muris* is a commentary on the seminal treatise on French mensural notation, a topic to which Prosdocimo devoted his own *Tractatus practice cantus mensurabilis*. The *Brevis summula proportionum quantum ad musicam pertinet* surveys the ratios that figure in music theory, though without detailing their

---

[7]Modern publications of Prosdocimo's treatises on music:

1.   *Expositiones tractatus pratice cantus mensurabilis magistri Johannis de Muris*, ed. F. Alberto Gallo, Antiqui musicae italicae scriptores, no. 3: Prosdocimi de Beldemandis opera, vol. 1 (Bologna: Antiquae Musicae Italicae Studiosi, 1966). The treatise is dated 1404 in Bologna, Civico Museo Bibliografico Musicale, A.56 (henceforward: **B**), 1412 in the less reliable Catania, Biblioteche Riunite Civica e Antonio Ursino-Recupero, Ursino-Recupero D.39.

2.   *Scriptorum de musica medii aevi nova series a Gerbertina altera* (henceforward: CS), 4 vols., ed. Edmond de Coussemaker (Paris: Durand, 1864–76; reprint, Hildesheim: Olms, 1963), 3:200–228.

3.   CS, 3:258–61; Prosdocimo de' Beldomandi, *Brevis summula ... Parvus tractatulus* (ed. Herlinger), 46–63.

4.   CS, 3:193–99; Prosdocimo, *Contrapunctus* (ed. Herlinger), 26–95.

5.   CS, 3:228–48; revised version, Claudio Sartori, *La notazione italiana del Trecento in una redazione inedita del "Tractatus practice cantus mensurabilis ad modum ytalicorum" di Prosdocimo de Beldemandis* (Florence: Olschki, 1938); English translation of the revised version, Prosdocimus de Beldemandis, *A Treatise on the Practice of Mensural Music in the Italian Manner*, trans. Jay A. Huff, Musicological Studies and Documents, no. 29 ([Rome]: American Institute of Musicology, 1972).

6.   Edition and translation below.

7.   CS, 3:248–58; Prosdocimo, *Brevis summula ... Parvus tractatulus* (ed. Herlinger), 64–117.

8.   Revised version, D. Raffaello Baralli and Luigi Torri, "Il *Trattato* di Prosdocimo de' Beldemandi contro il *Lucidario* di Marchetto da Padova per la prima volta trascritto e illustrato," *Rivista musicale italiana* 20 (1913): 731–62. Complete edition and translation below.

musical applications, topics with which Prosdocimo would deal elsewhere. The *Contrapunctus* provides a succinct statement of the most common counterpoint precepts of the time, each supported by an explanation of the principle that lies behind it; its discussion of *musica ficta* has proven particularly fruitful for scholars and editors.[8] The *Tractatus pratice cantus mensurabilis ad modum Ytalicorum* is the final major theoretical discussion of the Italian system of mensural notation. The *Parvus tractatulus de modo monacordum dividendi* provided for the first time in Italy a monochord division with five sharps and five flats, in addition to the natural degrees of the scale. It became the prototype for a number of monochord divisions that use accidentals tuned as flats and thus have thirds that are virtually pure. According to Mark Lindley, such divisions "whetted that Renaissance appetite for sonorous triads which only meantone temperaments could fully satisfy on keyboard instruments";[9] put another way, it was Prosdocimo's *Monacordum* that opened the door to the construction of non-Pythagorean monochords that was to preoccupy theorists for several centuries. The *Tractatus plane musice* and the *Tractatus musice speculative* are discussed below.

In addition to the music treatises, Prosdocimo wrote at least two on arithmetic:

9. *Canon in quo docetur modus componendi et operandi tabulam quandam* (Padua, 1409 [1419?])

10. *Algorismus de integris sive pratica arismetrice de integris* (Padua, 1410);

perhaps nine on astronomy:

11. *Brevis tractatulus de electionibus secundum situm lune in suis 28 mansionibus* (Montagnana, 1413)

---

[8]Margaret Bent cites Prosdocimo frequently in her groundbreaking articles on musica ficta, e.g., "Musica Recta and Musica Ficta," *Musica disciplina* 26 (1972): 73–100 (reprinted with annotations and an introductory essay in her *Counterpoint, Composition, and* Musica Ficta, Criticism and Analysis of Early Music [New York: Routledge, 2002], 61–93); "Diatonic Ficta," *Early Music History* 4 (1984): 1–48 (reprinted, with annotations and an introduction that revisits the issues, in her *Counterpoint, Composition, and* Musica Ficta, 115–59); "Ciconia, Prosdocimus, and the Workings of Musical Grammar as Exemplified in *O felix templum* and *O Padua*," in *Johannes Ciconia: musicien de la transition*, ed. Philippe Vendrix, Collection «Épitome musical», no. 16 (Turnhout: Brepols, 2003), 75.

[9]Mark Lindley, "Pythagorean Intonation and the Rise of the Triad," *Royal Musical Association Research Chronicle* 16 (1980): 4–61.

12. *Scriptum super tractatu de spera Johannis de Sacrobosco* (Padua, 1418)

13. *Canones de motibus corporum supercelestium* (Padua, 1424)

14. *Tabule mediorum motuum, equationum, stationum et latitudinum plane-
    tarum, elevationis signorum, diversitatis aspectus lune, mediarum con-
    iunctionum et oppositionum lunarium, feriarum, latitudinum climatum,
    longitudinum et latitudinum civitatum*

15. *Stelle fixe verificate tempore Alphonsi*

16. *Canon ad inveniendum tempus introitus solis in quodcumque 12 signo-
    rum in zodiaco*

17. *Canon ad inveniendum introitum lune in quodlibet signorum in zodiaco*

18. *Compositio astrolabii*

19. *Astrolabium*;

and one on geometry:

20. *De parallelogramo.*[10]

Prosdocimo's works on arithmetic and astronomy are also those of an
expert, and at least several made their mark. His *Scriptum super tractatu de
spera Johannis de Sacrobosco* found its way into print (Venice, 1531), and
his *Algorismus de integris sive pratica arismetrice de integris* was printed
twice (Padua, 1483; Venice, 1540). Luca Pacioli placed Prosdocimo in the
distinguished company of authorities on which he drew for his *Summa de
arithmetica, geometria, proportioni, et proportionalita* (Venice, 1494): "the
most perspicacious Megaran philosopher Euclid and Severino Boetio, and,
among our moderns, Leonardo the Pisan, Giordano, Biagio of Parma, Giovan
Sacrobusco, and Prosdocimo the Paduan." Leonardo of Pisa, better known as
Fibonacci, was a pioneer in the use of Hindu-Arabic numerals and the first
great mathematician of Western Christendom. The *Arithmetica* of Jordanus
de Nemore became the standard medieval source book for theoretical arith-

---

[10]For manuscript sources of treatises on arithmetic, astronomy, and geometry, see
Favaro, "Intorno," 41–74 and 115–221. For treatise 9, **B** gives the date 1409; three other
manuscripts have 1419. I provisionally accept the former because of the relative reliability
of **B**. Published in Favaro, "Intorno," 143–45. Treatise 10 was printed in Padua, 1483, and
in Venice, 1540; the latter gives the date of composition as 1460, obviously impossible.
The date 1410 appears in **B**. Treatise 11 is dated in **B**. Three of the four manuscript sources
for treatise 12 give the date 1418; the other has 1348, obviously impossible. It was printed
in Venice, 1531. Seven manuscripts agree on the date of treatise 13. It is possible that
titles 18 and 19 refer to a single work. Treatise 20 was published by Favaro, "Intorno,"
170.

metic; its author is generally regarded as the greatest medieval student of statics. Biagio Pelacani of Parma was instrumental in transmitting current scientific ideas from Paris to Italy and was, incidentally, one of Prosdocimo's sponsors for his examination in arts. Works of Johannes de Sacrobosco became standard medieval textbooks on both arithmetic and astronomy.[11]

The Tractatus plane musice, *the* Tractatus musice speculative, *and* Marchetto's Lucidarium in arte musice plane

The two treatises by Prosdocimo presented in this volume are those in which he addressed aspects of music theory he had encountered in the *Lucidarium in arte musice plane* (1317/18) of Marchetto of Padua. *Musica plana*, as Marchetto conceived it, encompassed all aspects of music aside from mensuration: the philosophy of music, including its history, origin, definition, and nature; music fundamentals, including letters, syllables, registers, solmization, and mutation; intervals and their ratios; simple counterpoint and *musica ficta*; tuning (in particular the tuning of intervals smaller than the tone); and the theory of ecclesiastical modes. In the preface to his own *Tractatus plane musice*, Prosdocimo made clear his low opinion of such comprehensive works:

> I have opened volumes by many different authors on the art of plainchant practice ... in which is made a useless confusion of the theoretical part with the practical part of that plainchant, although there ought to have been different volumes for these because the parts are entirely distinct one from the other. On this basis, I think those authors err most gravely—to such an extent that while intending to discuss plainchant practice alone, they are distracted from their intent by contemplating the exceedingly difficult theoretical foundations of their volumes. Accordingly, ... I intend ... to undertake ... a brief little treatise on this art of plainchant practice, treating ... only those things that pertain to this practice.

Thus, in the *Tractatus plane musice* of 1412, Prosdocimo restricted himself to music fundamentals and the theory of ecclesiastical modes, while in the *Tractatus musice speculative* of 1425, he addressed the matter of tuning.

Tractatus plane musice

Despite Prosdocimo's stated aversion to theoretical works (presumably including Marchetto's *Lucidarium*) that tackle too broad a range of subjects and despite the scathing criticism to which he would subject Marchetto's

---

[11]Pacioli's list of mathematicians appears on f. 4v of the dedication of his *Summa*; information about them comes from the *Dictionary of Scientific Biography*, 16 vols. (New York: Scribner, 1970–80).

theory of tuning in the *Musica speculativa,* he indicated in the preface to the latter work the high esteem he held for Marchetto's theory of mode:

> Turning [in the latter part of the *Lucidarium*] to the simple practice of plainchant, he wrote correctly, in an orthodox fashion, and most excellently, so much so that I have thus far seen nothing more orthodox in what I have read on this subject.

That Prosdocimo borrowed a great deal from Marchetto's theory of mode is, then, not surprising; I shall survey Prosdocimo's theory, finally pointing out significant discrepancies between his and Marchetto's approaches.

In the First Book of the *Tractatus plane musice,* Prosdocimo surveys the fundamentals of *musica plana,* beginning with its definition as a theory that deals with music in which the melodies are delivered without rhythmic differentiation (1.1) and proceeding through accounts of the six solmization syllables ut, re, mi, fa, sol, la (1.2), the twenty letters Γ-ut through E-la and their representation on the hand (1.3), and their division into low, high, and very high registers (1.4). He describes the staff (1.5); expounds on mutation, the process of exchanging one syllable for another from a different hexachord on a single note while retaining the same pitch (1.6); and distinguishes between the tone and the semitone, explaining that the latter is not a true half tone but an incomplete tone (1.7). He differentiates the three properties (as others have called them), reporting that melodies in which ut is placed on C are said to be sung "through nature," those in which ut is placed on F "through round (or soft) b," and those in which ut is placed on G "through square (or hard) ♮" (1.8–9), and he describes three clefs: the letters C, F, and round b (1.10). Finally (1.11), he raises and answers several hypothetical questions. Why does the gamut begin with G, the last of the seven musical letters, rather than the first? Why do some letters have one syllable, some two, and others three; and why are the syllables placed precisely where they are? Why are the degrees of the gamut placed on the left hand rather than the right, and why are they arranged in a circular fashion?

Many of the topics in the First Book are among the most common in late medieval theory, so common that it would be hard to trace any of them to a particular source. Two of Prosdocimo's points, however, are unique to this treatise, so far as I am aware. In an aside in the chapter on clefs (1.10), he rails against certain moderns—"not musicians but destroyers of music"— who write melodies without clefs, use arithmetic symbols for clefs, or even write whole melodies with arithmetic symbols instead of notes. His reference to clefless compositions antedates the earliest such piece of which I am aware, Binchois's "Mon seul et souverain desir"; and his last point seems to attest to the existence of numeric tablature in Italy by the early fifteenth century, much earlier than it is otherwise known to exist.

In the Second Book, Prosdocimo turns to the doctrine of mode, or "tone," in plainchant, defining tone quite comprehensively as "a certain manner of ordering notes or figures of some chant, that manner found in the total progression of the chant, that makes us recognize the difference of one chant from another through its beginning, middle, and end, as well as through ascent and descent in pitch" (2.1). He reports that the "original" four tones had finals on the syllables re, mi, fa, and sol (2.2), and he presents two accounts of the excessive ranges of the four tones leading theorists to divide them into four pairs, the tones of each pair sharing a final but differing in range and designated as authentic or plagal (2.3–4). All this is perfectly straightforward doctrine, common in late medieval theory.

Prosdocimo goes on to explain the classification of tones as perfect, imperfect, pluperfect, mixed, or intermixed (2.5). A perfect tone is one that "fills its measure" above and below the final: for the authentics, ascending an octave above the final and descending a tone (for fifth mode, a minor third) below it; for the plagals, ascending a sixth or seventh (and in the Lucca revision a sixth only) above the final and descending a fifth below it.[12] An imperfect tone is one that does not fill its measure, either above or below the final.[13] A pluperfect (literally, "more than perfect") tone ascends more than an octave above its final if authentic or descends more than a fifth below its final if plagal.[14] A mixed or intermixed tone is one that "adopts the nature" of another tone and "composes a third nature from its own and the other's." Fivefold classification of tones like this one originated with Marchetto and were widespread in Italy by the end of the fifteenth century. Prosdocimo's classification differs from Marchetto's, however, not only in the alternative definitions given in the Lucca revision (see nn. 12–14) but also in that, for Prosdocimo, "mixed" and "intermixed" are simply synonyms, regardless whether the tones belong to the same pair or not. For Marchetto, on the other hand, "mixed" tones combine aspects of a tone and its authentic or plagal partner, while "intermixed" tones combine aspects of two tones that are not partners. I shall return to this last difference later in this introduction.

---

[12]Alternatively, according to the Lucca revision, "filling the measure" is recognized in authentics only through ascent to the octave above the final, in plagals only through descent to the fifth below it.

[13]Alternatively, according to the Lucca revision, the imperfect tone is that which, if authentic, does not rise to the octave above the final or, if plagal, does not fall to the fifth below it.

[14]Alternatively, according to the Lucca revision, the pluperfect tone is that which, whether authentic or plagal, ascends or descends more than the requisite maximum.

Prosdocimo then enumerates nine (or in the Lucca revision, seven) factors that distinguish one tone from another: ascent, descent, the chord, initials, finals, *differentiae* of the *Seculorum amen*, species, neumes, and distinctions (2.6; the last two are omitted in the Lucca revision). Extent of ascent and descent can define the tone (2.7) provided the melody rises to the octave above its final if authentic or descends to the fifth below it if plagal (as in the "perfect" tones described above). If not, the "chord," the note a third above the final, can be invoked (2.8): one counts notes lying above the chord and below it; if more notes lie above, the tone is authentic; if more lie below, it is plagal; if the same number lie above and below, other means must be used to judge the tone. Judgment in terms of the "chord" seems also to have originated with Marchetto—at least, I have found no mention of it in the *Thesaurus Musicarum Latinarum* database earlier than his—and, like the fivefold classification of mode, it became common in Italy by the end of the fifteenth century; so far as I know, however, Prosdocimo is unique in introducing, in addition to the "principal chords" lying a third above the finals, "secondary and consequent chords" lying above the cofinals (this in the Lucca revision), probably to accommodate chants located exceptionally on the cofinals rather than the finals.[15]

Initial notes—those on which melodies of a particular tone tend to begin—constitute the fourth factor (2.9). Prosdocimo's list of initial notes for the various modes agrees almost entirely with Marchetto's, though Prosdocimo did not follow Marchetto in qualifying certain notes as appropriate only for pluperfect, mixed, intermixed, or "improper" forms of the tones, or as "not in use in the melodies of Gregory." Final notes are the fifth factor (2.10), and Prosdocimo lists three systems of defining them. In one system, the first and second tones together have as their finals low D and high A; the third and fourth together, low E and high square ♮; the fifth and sixth together, low F and high C; and the seventh and eighth together, the second low G and high D. In each case, the higher finals are called cofinals or "finals by relation" to the proper finals. In another system, the first and second tones together have as their finals D and A, the third and fourth, E and ♮; the fifth and sixth, F and C; and the seventh and eighth, G and D. In each case, the finals are given without regard to register, though here low D, E, F, and G are said to be the "most proper" finals and the notes a fifth higher are said to be cofinals. The third system, reported only in the Lucca

---

[15]Marchetto accommodated the tones of melodies located on cofinals rather than finals by classifying them as "irregular" (*Lucidarium* 11.4.30; Jan W. Herlinger, *The Lucidarium of Marchetto of Padua: A Critical Edition, Translation, and Commentary* [Chicago: University of Chicago Press, 1985], 406–7).

revision, places the final of the first and second tones on any letter carrying the solmization syllable re, that of the third and fourth on any letter carrying mi, that of the fifth and sixth on any letter carrying fa, and that of the seventh and eighth on any letter carrying sol; this is a fairly common way of defining modes in medieval music theory and seems particularly appropriate for singers who had learned the chants they sang by rote and might have to identify a mode by the arrangement of tones and semitones around the final without being aware of that final's letter name.

The *Seculorum amen differentiae* constitute the sixth factor (2.11): if, for instance, the *differentia* begins a third above the final of the preceding antiphon, the antiphon belongs either to the second tone or to the sixth; if it begins on low F, the tone is the second; if on high A, it is the sixth. Prosdocimo continues through intervals of the fourth, fifth, and sixth, subdividing according to the first notes of intonations where necessary. He also shows ways in which similar considerations can help determine the tones of introits and responsories, depending on the note on which the introit or responsory itself ends and its relationship to the first note or opening gesture of its verse.

Species of the diatessaron (tetrachord) and diapente (pentachord) constitute the seventh factor (2.12). The former has three species, the latter four, depending in either case on the location of the semitone among steps that are otherwise whole tones (in the following list the patterns of tones and semitones are to be read ascending):

	diatessaron	diapente
first species	T S T	T S T T
second species	S T T	S T T T
third species	T T S	T T T S
fourth species		T T S T

When the first species of the diapente is built on the final of a melody and the first species of the diatessaron lies conjunctly above it, the melody belongs to the first tone; when the first species of the diapente is built on the final and the first species of the diatessaron lies conjunctly below it, the melody belongs to the second. Similar arrangements of the second and third species of the diapente and diatessaron indicate the third, fourth, fifth, and sixth tones; arrangements of the fourth species of the diapente and the first species of the diatessaron indicate seventh and eighth tones. But inasmuch as these considerations apply only if melodies fill the octave above their finals, Prosdocimo offers another criterion for other cases: a melody that does not ascend beyond the sixth above its final and that several times "takes the diatessaron" between its final and the note a fourth above is to be judged plagal.

Prosdocimo lists two further factors in the original version of the *Plana musica* but omits them in the Lucca revision. Whenever a melody ascends a fifth above its final very often and descends no further than a tone below it, or if it takes the diapason above its final, it is judged authentic. When it frequently ascends a diatessaron above its final, it is judged plagal forthwith; if it leaps up from the final to the note a fifth above, it is judged authentic forthwith; if it leaps up to the note a fourth above the final, it is judged plagal (2.13). Finally, the endings of phrases ("distinctions") should lie no higher than the first note of its *differentia*, and most phrases should end on the final of the melody (2.14).

Following the presentation of these nine factors, Prosdocimo presents a rule for determining whether to use B-flat or B-natural in a particular instance (2.16): "if ... uncertainty ... strikes you whether to sing through round b or through square ♮, examine where the fewer mutations fall and take that manner in which the fewer mutations were found, whether that manner of singing involves round b or square ♮." The rule seems at first sight quite restrictive and very much at odds with the highly inflected musical examples in his treatises on counterpoint and the monochord, each of which would require several mutations; it seems, as well, to question the belief common among scholars of *musica ficta* that hexachords were not determinants of accidental inflection (or lack thereof) but that medieval singers, rather, first decided what inflections were appropriate through various considerations (melodic, harmonic, contrapuntal) and only then chose the hexachords appropriate to those inflections. Actually, Prosdocimo's is perhaps the extreme statement of a longstanding theoretical tradition limiting mutation in plainchant. The gamut's two inflections of B had bothered theorists almost from the time they were able to notate pitches precisely. The author of the anonymous *Dialogus de musica* of ca. 1000 circumvented the problem by simply assigning B-natural to modes 1, 3, 7, and 8, B-flat to modes 2, 4, 5, and 6.[16] Within a few decades, Guido of Arezzo prohibited the placement of B-natural and B-flat within the same *neuma*, a term I take to mean "melodic gesture."[17] Prosdocimo's pronouncement reflects rather closely

---

[16]*Scriptores ecclesiastici de musica sacra potissimum* (henceforward: GS), 3 vols., ed. Martin Gerbert (St. Blaise: Typis San-Blasianis, 1784; reprint, Hildesheim: Olms, 1963), 1:252–64. Gerbert's badly garbled text conceals the assignment of B-natural and B-flat to different modes, but it is clearly stated in (among other sources) Monte Cassino, Biblioteca abbaziale, 318.

[17]*Micrologus* 8.12; *Guidonis Aretini Micrologus*, ed. Joseph Smits van Waesberghe, Corpus scriptorum de musica, vol. 4 ([Rome]: American Institute of Musicology, 1955), 124; trans. Warren Babb in *Hucbald, Guido, and John on Music: Three Medieval Trea-*

that of the (13th-century?) *Introductio musicae planae secundum magistrum Johannem de Garlandia*—a statement that ends by stressing mutation's occasional necessity (a qualification Prosdocimo omitted):

> To whatever extent we can sing, in all music, entirely through these syllables, *ut re mi fa sol la*, we should avoid mutations and be on guard concerning them, unless they can totally be avoided or guarded against. *But when the necessity arises of effecting a mutation, then it ought to be made,* and not otherwise, because mutation was invented for the sake of necessity.[18]

Even the highly nuanced treatment of B-flat vs. B-natural in Marchetto's *Lucidarium* is couched in terms that suggest that frequent alternations of the two inflections are unwelcome.[19] Though Prosdocimo had warned in the *Contrapunctus* that *musica ficta* "is never to be applied except where necessary," he explained in detail the necessity of each of the accidentals in the musical examples in that treatise.[20] In each of these cases, the necessity arose through contrapuntal considerations; in plainchant, of course, considerations would be purely melodic but might involve range or inflection or both. Prosdocimo, though he indicates what to do "if uncertainty strikes," glosses over rules that would obviate uncertainty.[21]

---

tises, ed. with Introductions by Claude V. Palisca, Music Theory Translation Series (New Haven, CT: Yale University Press, 1978), 64.

[18]"Et sciendum est quod quantumcumque possumus operari cantum per has voces uniuersales ad omnem musicam, scilicet *ut re mi fa sol la*, debemus mutationes vitare et eas precauere nisi quia totaliter possint euitari uel precaueri. Sed dum venerit necessitas mutationem agendi, tunc debet fieri et non aliter, quia causa necessitatis inuenta fuit mutatio" [emphasis added]. *Musica plana Johannis de Garlandia*, ed. with Introduction and Commentary by Christian Meyer, Collection d'études musicologiques, no. 91 (Baden-Baden: Éditions Valentin Koerner, 1998), 72; cf. CS 1:160. The statement is echoed in the fifteenth century by the anonymous *Quaestiones et solutiones*, ed. Albert Seay, Critical Texts, no. 2 (Colorado Springs: Colorado College Music Press, 1977), 10.

[19]*Lucidarium* (ed. Herlinger) 11.4 *passim*; the passages that seem to discourage frequent alternation of the inflections are 11.4.12–16 and 149–59 (pp. 398–401 and 458–67).

[20]The warning, *Contrapunctus* (ed. Herlinger) 5.2, Lucca revision (pp. 72–73); the example and explanations, 5.6 (pp. 84–87).

[21]A set of solmization exercises from Bergamo, Biblioteca Civica "Angelo Mai," Manoscritti antichi bergamaschi, 21 (*olim* Σ.IV.37) suggests that, at least by the late fifteenth century, Bergamo monks were learning to mutate rapidly between hexachords involving B-natural and those involving B-flat. I reported on these exercises in my paper "Singing Exercises from a Bergamo Convent," presented at the 41st International Congress on Medieval Studies, Western Michigan University, 4–7 May 2006; and in revised versions at the Medieval and Renaissance Music Conference, Cambridge, 17–20 July 2006, and the Annual Meeting of the American Musicological Society, Los Angeles, 2–5 November 2006.

Finally, Prosdocimo provides paradigms for the psalm (and Magnificat) tones for each mode, providing separate models for solemn days and ferias and including in the first category the *tonus peregrinus* (2.17).

Comprehensive as Prosdocimo's theory of *musica plana* is, it betrays very clearly the interests of a university man surveying plainchant theory as one branch of the discipline *musica* rather than those of a member of the clergy, a large part of whose life would have been devoted to singing.[22] No singer, for instance, would have needed Prosdocimo's exhaustive account of why the syllables ut, re, mi, fa, sol, and la needed to be distributed on the hand precisely where tradition has placed them (*Plana musica* 1.11). And Prosdocimo's combination of Marchetto's mixed and intermixed tones into a single category is also quite revealing in this regard. When a tone is mixed with its authentic or plagal partner, its final is preserved and only questions of range come into play; mixing a tone with one *not* its partner is quite a different matter, because it calls into question which note *is* the final and, thus, renders ambiguous the characteristic array of intervals around that final. The difference, again, would have been quite obvious to any singer. Indeed, given the patent similarities between Marchetto's and Prosdocimo's approaches to plainchant theory, the dissimilarities tend to stand out strikingly. Both theorists included species of diatessaron and diapente as key elements of their modal theory. Prosdocimo's species of diapente, however, involve only B-naturals, ignoring the possibility of using B-flats even in fifth and sixth tones; Marchetto, on the other hand, discussed diapente species involving B-flat or B-natural in those tones, and his treatments of first, second, and fourth tones also accounted for the option of B-flat, even though it was not explicitly represented in the species paradigms. Indeed, in contrast to Marchetto's rich treatment of the use of B-flat or B-natural in various modes, Prosdocimo recommends choosing only the inflection that demands the fewer mutations. And Prosdocimo's *Musica plana* entirely lacks any treatment of accidentals *other* than B-flat, a subject Marchetto expounded in

---

[22]This observation is very much in line with Prosdocimo's disdain for performers, expressed most characteristically in his dismissal of Marchetto (*Musica speculativa*, preface, quoted p. 14 *infra*). One might, indeed, suspect that Prosdocimo was not a trained singer, in light of his comment on the deficiencies of his first two methods of dividing the monochord (*Monacordum* 8.2; "deficiencies" that involve the differences in tuning [i.e., commas] between the flats of one method and the sharps of the other): "these deficiencies are perhaps so slight that they cannot be perceived by the sense of hearing" (*Brevis summula ... Parvus tractatulus* [ed. Herlinger], 110–11). Any singer could be expected to realize that discrepancies of intonation on the order of a quarter semitone would not only be perceptible but intolerable. In "Around the Performance of a 13th-Century Motet," *Early Music* 28 [2000]: 343–57), Christopher Page argues that medieval singers were expected to discriminate between pitches differing by intervals much smaller than a comma.

detail. On the whole, Prosdocimo's survey is very much oriented toward the most conventional aspects of the theory.

Conventional as Prosdocimo's plainchant theory is in general, he is one of very few theorists of his time to state unequivocally that modal theory applies to polyphony as well as plainchant: "Any manner of singing, whether in plainchant or in measured song, is of some one of those eight manners or tones named above" (2.3). It is well known that the Berkeley treatise does so,[23] but Frans Wiering in his *The Language of the Modes* reads Amerus and Jacques de Liège, too, as treating mode in polyphony.[24] Reinhard Strohm in his "Modal Sounds as a Stylistic Tendency of the Mid-Fifteenth Century" has argued that as theorists of the late Middle Ages had discussed mode in works on plainchant, they did not need to duplicate the discussion with respect to polyphony but concentrated instead on counterpoint and mensuration; "it could be claimed," he concludes, that "the relevance of modes for polyphony was simply an accepted norm."[25] This last point recalls Prosdocimo's statement in *Contrapunctus* 2.3 that "the art of counterpoint presupposes the art of plain chant practice, without which nothing of this science will be understood."[26] On plainchant as the basis of counterpoint, further important statements appear in Franco, *Ars cantus mensurabilis*, Prol. 1; *Cum notum sit*; Ugolino, *Declaratio musicae disciplinae* 2.4.2; and *Ratio contrapuncti est ista.*[27] Surely it is time for scholars to reconsider the question of modal theory in polyphony.

---

[23]*The Berkeley Manuscript: University of California Music Library, MS. 744 (*olim *Phillipps 4450): A New Critical Text and Translation*, ed. and trans. by Oliver B. Ellsworth, Greek and Latin Music Theory, vol. 2 (Lincoln: University of Nebraska Press, 1984), 84–85.

[24]Frans Wiering, *The Language of the Modes: Studies in the History of Polyphonic Modality*, Criticism and Analysis of Early Music (New York: Routledge, 2001), 49–56.

[25]Reinhard Strohm, "Modal Sounds as a Stylistic Tendency of the Mid-Fifteenth Century: E-, A-, and C-Finals in Polyphonic Song," in *Modality in the Music of the Fourteenth and Fifteenth Centuries*, ed. Ursula Günther, Ludwig Finscher, and Jeffrey Dean, Musicological Studies and Documents, no. 49 (Neuhausen-Stuttgart: Hänssler Verlag for the American Institute of Musicology, 1996), 152–53.

[26]Prosdocimo, *Contrapunctus* (ed. Herlinger), 32–33.

[27]*Franconis de Colonia Ars cantus mensurabilis*, ed. Gilbert Reaney and André Gilles, Corpus scriptorum de musica, vol. 18 ([Rome]: American Institute of Musicology, 1974), 23; CS, 3:60; *Ugolini Urbevetanis Declaratio musicae disciplinae*, ed. Albert Seay, 3 vols., Corpus scriptorum de musica, vol. 7 ([Rome]: American Institute of Musicology, 1959–62), 2:8; and Milan, Biblioteca Ambrosiana, I.20.inf., ff. 27v–28r (cited in Klaus-Jürgen Sachs, *Der Contrapunctus im 14. und 15. Jahrhundert: Untersuchungen zum Terminus, zur Lehre und zu den Quellen*, Beihefte zum *Archiv für Musikwissenschaft*, vol. 13 [Wiesbaden: Steiner, 1974], 53).

Tractatus musice speculative

Prosdocimo opens the *Musica speculativa* of 1425 by reporting that when he and his friend Luca di Lendinara had been reading music theory treatises,

> we discovered one extremely erroneous and dissonant with the truth, named *Lucidarium*, which a certain person—Marchetus, by name, my fellow Paduan citizen—had compiled.... Its earlier parts treat certain theoretical or speculative aspects of music theory falsely, but in the subsequent part, turning to the simple practice of plainchant, he wrote correctly, in an orthodox fashion, and most excellently, so much so that I have thus far seen nothing more orthodox in what I have read on this subject.[28]

Prosdocimo had a simple explanation for Marchetto's errors:

> In the science of music, you see, this man was a simple performer, totally lacking in its theoretical or speculative side, which, mistakenly, he thought he understood most perfectly; and thus he presumed to address that of which he was totally ignorant.

He resolved to remedy the situation:

> Considering ... that the errors of this Marchetus had been circulated throughout Italy, and beyond, and had been held as most true by singers (yet not by theorists), my aforesaid brother entreated me, for his love, to compose a little work against these errors so that the evils, lies, and mistakes concerning music that had been brought forth and disseminated by one Paduan might be removed by another, and thus Italy be purged of such errors....

But since Prosdocimo had devoted works to the individual aspects of music, his intention here was to

> touch only on some things that seem to me necessary for the explanation of the errors of the aforesaid Marchetus, adding to these the methods by which anyone learned in ratios and the practice of arithmetic might be able to discover and recognize the ratio of any interval.

Prosdocimo lays his foundation carefully, beginning in the First Book with descriptions of the musical intervals. Even in this cursory list, he touches on two favorite themes, the lesser dissonance of the perfect fourth in comparison to other dissonant intervals (*Musica speculativa* 1.8) and the fact that the number of intervals is infinite (1.18).[29] He ends the discussion

---

[28] Cf. the opening of the preface to the *Plana musica* of 1412, quoted above.

[29] On the fourth, cf. *Contrapunctus* 3.3 (ed. Herlinger, 41): "The fourth and its equivalents are less dissonant than the other dissonant intervals; in a certain way, indeed, they hold the middle place between true consonances and dissonances—to such a degree that certain of the ancient writers were ready to say that they should be counted among the conso-

(still in 1.18) by naming several intervals that "can be found through artificial means [but] cannot be found in the musical hand": the "third of two semitones" (our diminished third), the "fourth of three semitones" (our doubly diminished fourth), and the "fifth of four semitones" (our triply diminished fifth). His point seems to be that the elementary discussion in *Musica speculativa* will exclude such intervals from consideration.

In the Second Book, Prosdocimo presents basic information on dealing with the intervals and their ratios. He presents the ratios of the four basic intervals as discovered by Pythagoras: the tone (9:8), the diatessaron (4:3), the diapente (3:2), and the diapason (2:1); and states the principles: two intervals are equal if their ratios are equal to each other, and all intervals of the same specific name are equal to each other (*Musica speculativa* 2.1). He computes ratios for the other intervals described in the First Book, from the unison to the diminished and augmented octaves (2.2–13):

unison	the ratio of any two equal numbers
[minor][30] semitone (m2)	256:243 and its compounds
ditone (M3)	81:64 and its compounds
semiditone (m3)	32:27 and its compounds
tritone (A4)	729:512 and its compounds
diatessaron with semitone (d5)	1024:729 and its compounds
diapente with tone (M6)	27:16 and its compounds
diapente with semitone (m6)	128:81 and its compounds
diapente with ditone (M7)	243:128 and its compounds
diapente with semiditone (m7)	16:9 and its compounds
diapente with tritone (A8)	2187:1024 and its compounds
double diatessaron with semitone (d8)	4096:2187 and its compounds

In the course of these computations, Prosdocimo provides a trove of rules for working with intervallic ratios: how to find the ratios of their sums and differences, given the ratios of two intervals; how to find the numbers that will represent a succession of intervals of the same type (both of these are discussed in *Musica speculativa* 2.3); how to determine which of two ratios is larger; how to determine whether a ratio is given in lowest terms; and how to find the lowest terms if it is not (these three are discussed in *Musica speculativa* 2.16).

---

nances." In the Lucca revision of the *Contrapunctus*, Prosdocimo added that they "seem to approximate somewhat the consonant fifth and its equivalents—to such a degree that those not much practised in singing frequently take this fourth for the consonant fifth," wording that accords with the text of *Musica speculativa* 1.8. In *Contrapunctus* 3.2 (ed. Herlinger, 37), Prosdocimo concluded his list of intervals with the words "... proceeding in this way to infinity, if the syllables or instruments could be extended to infinity."

[30] As Prosdocimo noted in *Contrapunctus* 3.9 (ed. Herlinger, 55), "All semitones found in intervals are minor semitones."

With these principles stated and basic calculations accomplished, Prosdocimo refutes in *Musica speculativa* 2.15 Marchetto's division of the whole tone into fifths: the whole tone cannot be divided into any number of equal parts, he shows, because to divide an interval into equal parts is to divide it into smaller intervals represented by equal ratios, or to insert geometric means between the terms of the ratio of the interval to be so divided; the whole tone cannot be so divided because it is represented by the sesquioctave ratio (9:8; or 18:16, 27:24, etc.) and a geometric mean or means cannot be placed between the terms of any superparticular ratio using integers, the numbers operational in the "Pythagorean" arithmetic of Prosdocimo's day.[31] Prosdocimo shows, essentially, that the insertion of integers between the terms of a superparticular ratio yields arithmetic means rather than geometric ones; thus, 18:17:16, 27:26:25:24, 36:35:34:33:32, 45:44:43:42:41:40, etc. all involve arithmetic means, dividing the whole tone respectively into two, three, four, five, etc. *unequal* intervals. He concludes, "Therefore, in no way is it to be said that the sesquioctave ratio is divisible into equal parts, and consequently neither the tone .... From this, it follows that if the tone is divided into two parts, they will necessarily be unequal; and because universally among musicians the tone is divided into two parts, they will necessarily be unequal."

Prosdocimo next shows that two minor semitones are indeed smaller than one tone and calculates the ratios of the major semitone and the comma, or the difference between the major and minor semitones (*Musica speculativa* 2.16–18):

major semitone (A1)	2187:2048 and its compounds
comma	531441:524288 and its compounds

Finally, he shows that every major interval exceeds the corresponding minor interval by a major semitone, with the exception of the "major" and "minor" octaves (our augmented and diminished octaves),[32] as he calls them here. As a consequence, he shows that when the rules of counterpoint require making a minor interval major or a major interval minor so that it lies as close as possible to a following perfect consonance, the change is effected by adding or subtracting a major semitone, which is indicated by the application of a

---

[31] On this subject, see Richard L. Crocker, "Pythagorean Mathematics and Music," *Journal of Aesthetics and Art Criticism* 22 (1964): 189–98 and 325–35 (reprinted in his *Studies in Medieval Music Theory and the Early Sequence*, Variorum Collected Studies [Aldershot: Variorum, 1997]).

[32] In *Contrapunctus* 3.5 (ed. Herlinger, 46–49), Prosdocimo had called the three sizes of octave *minor*, *major*, and *maxima*; in *Musica speculativa* 2.22, he calls them *minor*, *media*, and *maior*.

square ♮ or round b to the note to be inflected, rather than being effected by adding or subtracting one-, two-, three-, or four-fifths of a whole tone, which is indicated by the ♯ sign or its equivalent among the moderns who follow "the false teaching of the Paduan Marchetus." "Let us exclude these moderns, then," he concludes, "along with their Marchetus .... We stick with our ancients, who knew the true science of music; and so we shall be able to acquire the true science of music" (2.22).

It is in the Third Book that Prosdocimo addresses Marchetto's other errors and, in his view, they are legion. Marchetto called Pythagoras the first discoverer of music, whereas credit for that discovery should go to Jubal-Cain; Macrobius, moreover, whom Marchetto cites as his source, actually reported that Pythagoras had discovered not music but the ratios of intervals (*Musica speculativa* 3.2). Marchetto described "enharmonic," "diatonic," and "chromatic" semitones, whereas these terms should designate species of tetrachord, not semitone (3.3). Marchetto claimed to *prove* that the tone consists in the ratio 9:8, whereas that is a principle to be presupposed, not a proposition to be proven (3.4), and he claimed to show "why the tone consists in the novenary number," whereas the tone consists not in a number but in a ratio (3.5); "how the tone is related to the octonary number," when it is impossible to compare a ratio (as here, of an interval) with a number (3.6);[33] and that the tone consists in the ratio 9:8 *and not in the ratios of other numbers*, whereas the tone consists in the ratio of any two numbers related in a sesquioctave ratio, e.g., 9:8, 18:16, 27:24, etc. (3.7). Marchetto's "logical" demonstrations concerning division of a continuum to produce the tone are no more valid "than this would be: a man is an ass and a goat is a lion; therefore, God exists" (3.8–9). Marchetto claimed that the tone has "five parts and neither more nor fewer," whereas it can have an infinite number of parts; that the tone consists "in the ratio of the novenary number," when 9 is not a ratio; that 9 cannot be divided into equal parts; and that 9 can be divided into five parts only (3.10).

In *Musica speculativa* 3.11, Prosdocimo addresses what he calls Marchetto's "*principal* falsehoods," falsehoods that he says Marchetto had "disseminated throughout all Italy": that the whole tone is divisible into five equal parts, whereas its indivisibility into any number of equal parts was shown in *Musica speculativa* 2.15; that each of those parts is called a *diesis*, a term that properly refers to either the minor semitone or one-half the minor semitone; that five dieses constitute the tone while two, three, and

---

[33] In *Brevis summula proportionum* 2 (ed. Herlinger, 49), Prosdocimo had stated that "ratio as properly so called is the mutual relationship of several quantities of the same proximate genus"; a number and a ratio do not belong to the same proximate genus.

four dieses constitute respectively the "enharmonic," "diatonic," and "chromatic" semitones, whereas (reiterating *Musica speculativa* 3.3) in fact these terms properly refer to tetrachords, not semitones. Derivative from these are a series of subsequent errors, in Prosdocimo's view (*Musica speculativa* 3.12): Marchetto's claim that when F♯ proceeds to G over D moving to C, the F♯ lies a "chromatic semitone" (4/5 tone) above the unsharped F and that the interval between F♯ and G is a "diesis" (1/5 tone), whereas in actuality these intervals do not exist; his use of a special sign to indicate the division of the tone into 4/5 and 1/5; his calling this sign a "diesis"; and his array of four intervals smaller than the tone, when only two of these exist.

Prosdocimo closes with criticisms of Marchetto's claim that there are only six species of consonance and six ratios in which consonances exist— whereas there is an infinite number of each—and his calling the number 4 epitrite and the number 3 hemiolic, when these terms refer not to numbers but to ratios (*Musica speculativa* 3.13). He also criticizes Marchetto's claim that there are only three ratios of "members of consonances," whereas these, like sesquioctave ratios, are infinite (3.14); his "proof" that the number 3 is perfect, when 6 is the first perfect number (3.15); his statement that "no ratio is found between the duple and the triple," whereas there are many (3.16); and the statements that the ditone and semiditone do not consist in any ratio, when every interval has a ratio (3.17).

I have traced the intricacies of Marchetto's arguments elsewhere,[34] showing that they can be seen as imaginative attempts to reconcile a non-Pythagorean conception of tuning with Pythagorean orthodoxy, arguments that necessarily lead to illogical conclusions. Most of Marchetto's statements to which Prosdocimo objects in *Musica speculative* 3.13–17 are based on received wisdom that was evidently outside Prosdocimo's ken.[35] For instance, when Marchetto stated that the ternary number is perfect (*Lucidarium* 6.3.9 [ed. Herlinger, 234–35]), he was quoting Remigius's commentary on Martianus Capella:[36] "the number three is perfect, because the system of numbers dispenses, orders, and disposes beginning, middle, and end." Some of these Prosdocimo himself hedged, claiming for instance that the number 4 could be called epitrite *in relation to the number 3*, the number 3 hemiolic *in relation to the number 2*—expressions very close to

---

[34]"Marchetto's Division of the Whole Tone," *Journal of the American Musicological Society* 34 (1981): 193–216; introduction to *The Lucidarium of Marchetto of Padua*, 14–21, and notes to relevant sections of the treatise.

[35]The sources are indicated in footnotes to the translation.

[36]Remigius, *Commentum in Martianum Capellam*, 2 vols., ed. Cora E. Lutz (Leiden: Brill, 1962–65), 44.5.

what Marchetto actually wrote: "Hemiolic numbers are three *in comparison to* two and the like" (*Lucidarium* 3.2.5 [ed. Herlinger, 172–73; emphasis added]).

But Prosdocimo was certainly correct in claiming that Marchetto's theories of tuning had spread throughout Italy. They are traceable, for instance, in the works of Bonaventura da Brescia, Johannes Tinctoris, Nicola Vicentino, and a host of anonymous works from the fifteenth century.[37] Indeed, Marchetto's terms for the semitones even invaded a copy of Prosdocimo's *Contrapunctus* (Einsiedeln, Benediktinerkloster, 689), the very version of the treatise that Coussemaker was to present to the world.[38] Christopher Page, a scholar experienced in the performance of medieval music, treats Marchetto's more sharply differentiated chromatic semitone and diesis as a representation of the musical reality of the time, implicitly recommending them to performers of early music.[39] Prosdocimo may have had logic on his side, but Marchetto's pronouncements proved to have the greater durability.

---

[37]Herlinger, "Marchetto's Division of the Whole Tone"; introduction to *The Lucidarium of Marchetto of Padua*; "Marchetto's Influence: The Manuscript Evidence," in *Music Theory and Its Sources: Antiquity and the Middle Ages*, ed. André Barbera, Notre Dame Conferences in Medieval Studies, vol. 1 (Notre Dame, IN: Notre Dame University Press, 1990), 235–58. Since publication of the latter study, many additional echoes of Marchetto's theories have come to light in manuscript sources; I shall report on them in another publication.

[38]Prosdocimo, *Contrapunctus* (ed. Herlinger), 23.

[39]Christopher Page, "Polyphony before 1400," chapter 5 of *Performance Practice: Music before 1600*, ed. Stanley Sadie and Howard Mayer Brown (New York: Norton, 1990), 79–81.

The Manuscripts

B

Bologna, Civico Museo Bibliografico Musicale,
A.56 (Martini, 4)

Paper; 268 pages, ca. 32.5×23.0 cm
Sabbioncello (near Ferrara), 1437

The manuscript consists of thirteen quinions (pp. 1–260) and a final binion (pp. 261–68; this may have originally been another quinion from which the internal three bifolia were lost, since Prosdocimo's *Tractatus musice speculative* breaks off abruptly just at the middle of the gathering); it is bound in boards, ca. 33.5x23.0 cm, with a leather spine. There are four paper flyleaves at the front, three at the rear.

Two columns of 24x7 cm are marked off on each page, separated by a space of 1.5 cm with margins of 2.5 cm at the top, 6 cm at the bottom, 4.5 cm at the outside edge, and 3 cm at the inside edge (measurements are approximate, as there is ca. 0.5 cm variation in size from one sheet to another). The text was written by a single hand, with forty-three to fifty lines per column. According to a colophon on one of the sheets now missing from the last gathering, the manuscript was copied by Antonius de Obizis of Lucca and completed at Sabbioncello (district of Ferrara) on 21 August 1437.[40] The text is in light brown ink with ornate initials (many decorated with fine vertical lines) in red and blue. The pages were numbered 1–268 in their upper outside corners after the loss of the center sheets of the last gathering.

The manuscript contains only treatises by Prosdocimo, including all those on music plus the most important ones on arithmetic and astronomy and the sole surviving work on geometry. The treatises on music appear chronologically by year of composition, with the three of 1412 (here as in **L**) in the order *Contrapunctus, Cantus mensurabilis ad modum Ytalicorum*, and *Plana musica*.

---

[40]The colophon is recorded by Giacomo Filippo Tomasin, *Bibliothecae patavinae manuscriptae publicae et privatae quibus diversi scriptores hactenus incogniti recensentur ac illustrantur* (Udine, 1639), 128, and quoted by F. Alberto Gallo, "La tradizione dei trattati musicali di Prosdocimo de Beldemandis," *Quadrivium* 6 (1964): 57–84: "Et ego Antonius quondam Roberti de Obizis de Luca totum hunc librum scripsi, atque complevi Sablonzelli districtus Ferrariensis die Mercurii xxi Augusti 1437."

1. *Expositiones tractatus pratice cantus mensurabilis magistri Johannis de Muris*. *Inc*. "ROgasti me amice dilecte | Vt in arte musicali tui amore aliqua in Vno opusculo colligere ..." *Exp*. "... et per hoc infallanter in notitiam mensure cuiuscunque cantus sibi propositi devenire poteris | si laborare uoles. Et sic sit finis totius huius opperis per musicorum minimum prosdocimum de Beldemandis patauum anno domini .1404. padue compilati. Deo gratias. Amen. Expliciunt expositiones tractatus pratice cantus mensurabilis. Magistri Iohanis de Muris a Magistro Prosdocimo de Beldemandis de Padua compilate. Deo gratias. Amen." (pp. 1a–72b)

2. *De parallelogramo*. *Inc*. "Item Magister Prosdocimus de Beldemandis. Dato trigono paralollogramum equale describere. Sit datus trigonus abc. cui equale parolollogramum describere intendimus ..." *Exp*. "... diuisa linea nobis intensiorem qualitatem denotante per medium et etiam linea nobis uniformem interessionem super subiecto [?] denotante similiter per medium diuisa [*diagrams*]." (Favaro, "Intorno," 170) (p. 73a–b)

3. *Tractatus pratice cantus mensurabilis*. *Inc*. "QVoniam multitudo scripture lectoris animo sepius fastidium non parum infert ..." *Exp*. "... et per hoc infallanter in notitiam mensure cuiuscunque cantus tibi propositi deuenire poteris | si laborare uoles. Et hec de modo cognoscendi mensuras cantuum | atque de totali tractu [*sic*] anno domini .1408. padue compillata | pro nunc suffitiant uolentibus sub breuitate colligere ea que diffusius dillataui in quodam meo oppere quod scripsi super tractatu pratice cantus mensurabilis Iohanis de muris. Si uero quis dubia aliaque prolixa hic recitata atque ibi pertractata uidere uellet illuc recurrat et ibidem uidebit si quid boni erit. Amen. Explicit tractatus pratice cantus mensurabiblis a prosdocimo de Beldemandis de padua compositus deo gratias. AMEN." (pp. 74a–91b; p. 92 blank)

4. *Brevis summula proportionum quantum ad musicam pertinet*. *Inc*. "Tibi dillecte frater tuus Prodocimus [*sic*] de Beldemandis patauus de nocte laborauit ..." *Exp*. "... qui terminus siue prepositio sub denotat comparationem minoris quantitatis ad maiorem. Hec ergo sunt que breuiloquus summaui tibi de proportionibus musice aplicabillibus anno domini .1409 multaque istis sinonoma sunt propter breuitatem dimittendo. sume ergo ea | et ipsa corrige prout tibi opportunum uidetur. Amen. Explicit breuis sumulla proportionum quantum ad Musicam pertinet per Magistrum prosdocimum de

beldemandis patauum taliter ordinata. Amen." (pp. 93a–95a; pp. 95b, 96 blank)

5. *Contrapunctus. Inc.* "SCribit aristotiles secundo ellencorum capitulo ultimo facile fore inuentis addere ..." *Exp.* "... et hec omnia comprehendere poterit quilibet boni ingenij si ipsa subtiliter speculabitur. Sufficiant ergo ista de contrapuncto per musicorum minimum prosdocimum de Beldemandis patauum anno domini .1412. in castro montagnane paduani districtus breuiter compilata. Deo gratias. Amen. Explicit contrapuntus Magistri prosdocimi de Beldemandis paduani in castro montagnane paduani districtus anno domini .1412. compilatus. Deo gratias. Amen." (pp. 97a–100b)

6. *Tractatus pratice cantus mensurabilis ad modum Ytalicorum. Inc.* "ARs pratice cantus mensurabilis duplex reperitur ..." *Exp.* "... cum quelibet figura que in proportione ad alteram cantatur | in proportione ad figuram in eodem cantu existentem cantari habeat | quod non sic esset in tali figuratione. Et sic sit finis huius tractatus | per musicorum minimum Prosdocimum de Beldemandis patauum anno domini .1412. in castro Montagnane paduani districtus compilati. Deo gratias. Amen. Explicit tractatus pratice cantus mensurabilis ad modum ytalicorum | per prosdocimum de Beldemandis de padua in castro montagnane paduani districtus compilatus. deo gratias. AMEN." (pp. 101a–113a; pp. 113b, 114 blank)

7. *Tractatus plane musice. Inc.* "MUltorum diuersorum auctorum artis pratice cantus plani musica plana nominate volumina reuolui ..." *Exp.* "... et hoc quando carmina componere intendunt. Sit ergo finis huius parui opperis plane musice | per prosdocimum de Beldemandis patauum Montagnane paduani districtus anno .1412. taliter ordinati. Deo gratias amen. Explicit tractatus plane Musice a Prosdocimo de Beldemandis patauo in castro montagnane paduani districtus anno domini .1412. conpilatus Deo gratias AMEN." (pp. 115a–133b; p. 134 blank)

8. *Brevis tractatulus de electionibus secundum situm lune in suis 28 mansionibus. Inc.* "[*in later hand:* questo non appartiene alla musica] NIchil prestantius in humano regimine apud quemlibet censeri uidetur ..." *Exp.* "... Cauendum est ergo tunc a cuiuslibet operis initio. Et sic sit finis huius breuissimi tractatuli de ellectionibus secundum situm lune in suis .28. mansionibus per Prosdocimum de Beldemandis patauum ab ellectionibus Indorum anno domini .1413. in castro montagnane paduani districtus taliter extracti. Deo gratias Amen.

Explicit breuis tractatulus de ellectionibus secundum situm lune in suis .28. mansionibus per Prosdocimum de Beldemandis patauum ab ellectionibus Indorum taliter extratus. Deo. Gratias. Amen." (pp. 135a–137b; p. 138 blank)

9. *Parvus tractatulus de modo monacordum dividendi. Inc.* "Et si facile sit inuentis addere | addenda tamen negligenda existere non uidentur ..." *Exp.* "... ex ipsis in noticiam superius dictorum facile deuenire poteris. Et sic sit finis huius parui tractatuli de modo monacordum diuidendi quem prosdocimus de Beldemandis patauus padue anno domini .1413. compillauit. Amen. Explicit paruus tractatulus de modo monacordum diuidendi quem prosdocimus de Beldemandis patauus padue anno domini .1413. compilauit ad laudem et honorem omnipotentis dei atque tocius eius superne curie. Amen [*diagram*]." (pp. 139a–145b; p. 146 blank)

10. *Scriptum super tractatu de spera Johannis de Sacrobosco anglici. Inc.* "BOnum enim quanto comunius tanto melius ..." *Exp.* "... et in posterum baptizatus uitam suam in fide xpistiana finiuit ad dominum. Et sic sit finis huius opperis per prosdocimum de beldemando de padua | anno domini nostri yhesu xpisti 1418 padue compilati ad laudem omnipotentis dei ac totius supernorum curie. Amen. Explicit scriptum super tractatu de spera Iohanis de sacrobusco Anglici per prosdocimum de Beldemando de Padua compilatum. Deo gratias Amen." (pp. 147a–229b)

11. *Canon in quo docetur modus componendi et operandi tabulam quandam. Inc.* "QVia opperantibu circa artem calculatoriam | et maxime in ipsa arte non multum expertis siue praticis sepe error contingit ..." *Exp.* "... Et ut suprascripta magis patefiant | describo in margine sequenti tabulam exemplarem quam inspitias et melius intelliges suprascripta. Et sic sit finis huius canonis anno domini 1409 padue compilati. Amen. Explicit canon in quo docetur modus componendi et opperandi tabulam hanc sequentem | per prosdocimum de Beldemandis patauum compilatus. Amen [*table*]." (Favaro, "Intorno," 143–45) (pp. 230a–233)

12. *Algorismus de integris sive pratica arismetrice de integris. Inc.* "INueni in quampluribus libris pratice arismetrice algorismi nuncupatis | modos circa numeros opperandi satis uarios atque diuersos ..." *Exp.* "... Et hec de extractione radicum in cubicis numeris | ac de totali tractatu per prosdocimum de Beldemandis de padua anno domini .1410. de mense iunij compillata | suffitiant uolentibus alium

modum in hac arte opperandi quam contineatur in algorismo Iohanis de sacrobusco exercere. Amen. Explicit algorismus de Integris siue pratica arismetrice de Integris secundum Prosdocimum de Belde-mandis de Padua." (printed Padua, 1483; Venice, 1540) (pp. 234a–247b)

13. *De progressionibus. Inc.* "Idem Prosdocimus de Beldemandis de Padua. Progressionis ubi non seruatur similis excessus sed similis proportio siue progressionis geometrice et non arismetrice quod idem est suma sic cognoscitur ..." *Exp.* "... in progressione uero sexqui-quarta | subtrahendus est primus terminus quadruplatus ab ultimo quincuplato | et sic ultra | et tunc patebit summa tue progressionis | ex eo quod post subtractionem remanebit." (p. 247b)

14. *Tractatus musice speculative,* incomplete at the end. *Inc.* "DUm quidam michi carus ac uti frater intimus | Lucas nomine | de castro Lendenarie ..." *Exp.* "... Item in capitulo de coniunctionibus uocum dicit | quod diptonus et semidiptonus non consistunt in proportione aliqua | quod falsum est | eo quod omnis sonorum combinatio in ali-qua proportione consistit | ut clare patet ex supradictis. Multasque etiam alias ..." (pp. 248a–264b; pp. 265–68 blank)

The text of **B** is excellent, both for *Plana musica* and *Musica speculativa.* It is marred by rare misspellings (e.g., *precessores* for *predecessores*); several omissions of phrases, most occasioned by *saut du même au même*; and the loss of the last few lines of *Musica speculativa,* along with several folios of the manuscript's final gathering (see p. 21 above).

C

Cremona, Biblioteca Governativa, 252

Parchment; 41 folios, ca. 20.0×14.5 cm
Italy, fifteenth century

The manuscript consists of four quinions preceded by a single leaf, with the leaves numbered 1–41 in the lower left corners of their recto sides. An earlier numbering used the letters c–f to represent the four complete gatherings presently in the manuscript. In each gathering, the five bifolia are numbered in the lower right corners of the rectos of their front halves: c1 ... c5, d1 ... d5, e1 ... e5, f1 ...f5. The single leaf at the front of the manuscript shows the letter b; its number has been trimmed.[41] The first and last treatises are incomplete; hence we can infer that there were originally two additional gatherings at the front of the manuscript and one or more at the end. The binding (21.0×15.0 cm) is pasteboard.

A writing block of 14.5×9 cm is marked off on each leaf, leaving margins of 2 cm at the top 3.5 cm at the bottom, 4 cm at the outside edge, and 1.5 cm at the inside edge. The text was written by a single hand, with thirty lines of text per page. Starting on f. 24, the writing seems more hurried and less regular. The main text is in light brown ink, with initials—decorated with fine vertical lines—in red and blue. The vertical lines and the uncrossed tironian *et* sign (𝒴) attest to the Italian provenance of the manuscript. The scribe's spelling is characterized by the use of double *l* between vowels (e.g., *regulla, volluerunt, tallis*) and the frequent use of *sc* for *s* (e.g., *muscica, uscitantur*).

The manuscript as it stands contains only works of Prosdocimo:

1. *Tractatus plane musice*, incomplete. *Inc.* "… prima tribuerunt | que sunt hec. protus. deuterus. tritus. et tetrardus …" *Exp.* "… A vero accutum quinti et sexti toni pro corda reputatur. sed ♮ quadrum." *Inc. cum notis* "[ca]thedra pestillencie non sedit. Seculorum amen. Secundus tonus sic incipit et sic mediatur | et sic finitur …" *Exp.* "… et hoc quando carmina componere intendunt. Sit ergo finis huius parui operis plane musice | per prosdocimum de beldemandis patauum | montagnane paduani districtus anno 1412. talliter ordinata. Deo. Gratias. Amen. Explicit tractatus plane musice per prosdocimum de beldemandis patauo in castro montagnane paduani districtus anno domini 1412 compilatus. Deo gratias amen." (ff. 1r–v [internal fragment], 2r–9r [end]; f. 9v blank)

2. *Contrapunctus. Inc.* "SCribit aristotiles secundo ellencorum capitulo ultimo facile fore inuentis addere …" *Exp.* "… et hec omnia comprehendere poterit qui[liq]libet bonj ingenij si ipsa subtilliter specullabitur Sufficiant ergo ista de contrapuncto per musicorum minimum prosdocimum de beldemandis patauum anno domini 1412 | in castro montagnane paduanj districtus breuiter compillata. deo gratias amen. Explicit contrapunctus prosdocimj de beldemandis de padua." (ff. 10r–15v)

3. *Tractatus practice cantus mensurabilis. Inc.* "QVoniam multitudo scripture lectoris animo sepius fastium [*sic*] non parum infert …"

---

[41] In the introduction to my edition of the *Contrapunctus* (ed. Herlinger, 16), I misread the "b" as a "6" and drew unwarranted conclusions concerning the original structure of the manuscript.

Exp. "... quoniam sicut in talli collore retorico fit pluries repetitio eiusdem dicti | ita in collore musico | fit pluries repetitio figurarum simillium | siue simillium uocum | siue simillium figurarum et uocum simul | secundum quod uarie sunt iste oppiniones | hoc possito uenio ad recitationem oppinionum iam dictarum | quibus recitattis [*reclamans*: et intellectis]." (ff. 16r–41v)

These are Prosdocimo's treatises on the three most fundamental topics of music: plainchant, counterpoint, and French mensuration. The letters representing gatherings (see above) make it clear that the compiler intended these three treatises to appear in this order, which is not their order of composition. Perhaps he placed plainchant first as a sort of foundation, counterpoint next as the doctrine that most clearly builds on it (see p. 14 above), and mensuration last as the most abstruse. One naturally wonders about the contents of the two gatherings missing at the front of the manuscript and the one or more missing at the end. The text of *Plana musica* is incomplete due to the loss of all but one folio of the first two gatherings of the manuscript. The text that remains commences in 2.4 with the words *prima tribuerunt* (86.20) and breaks off in 2.8 after the words *pro corda reputatur* (96.7), resuming in the musical examples for the second tone with the second syllable of the word *cathedra* (126.7) and continuing to the end.

L

Lucca, Biblioteca Statale,[42] 359

Paper; 98 folios, ca. 29.5×21.5 cm
Italy; ff. 2–93 not earlier than 1425; ff. 106–10 and 115 not later than 1477

The manuscript consists of nine quinions numbered (in light brown ink, in the upper right corners of the recto sides) 2–91 plus eight sheets in a gathering of uncertain construction numbered 92, 93, 106–10, 115.[43] It is contained in a modern brown leather binding, 30×22.5 cm.

The pages are marked off in double columns of 17.3×5.7 cm separated by ca. 1.1 cm, with margins of ca. 4.5 cm at the top, 7.5–8 cm at the bottom, 5.5–6 cm at the outside edge, and 2.5–3 cm at the inside edge. The text was copied in light to medium brown ink in a very beautiful gothic book hand,

---

[42]The library was formerly known as the Biblioteca Governativa.

[43]Gallo ("Trattati di Prosdocimo," 79) and other scholars have read the last folio number as 119.

with forty lines of text per column. The treatises begin with elaborate initials in red, blue, green, and gold; otherwise, initials are in red and brown ink.

Contents of the manuscript are as follows:

1. Prosdocimo, *Tractatus pratice cantus mensurabilis*, revised version. *Inc.* "QVoniam multitudo scripture lectoris animo sepius fastidium non parum infert ..." *Exp.* "... et per hoc indubitanter in noticiam mensure cuiuscunque cantus tibi propositi deuenire poteris si intelectum tuum ad hoc diligenter appones et laborem non timebis. Et hec de modo cognoscendi mensuras cantuum atque de totali tractatu anno dominj .1408. per musicorum minimum prosdocimum de beldemando patauum padue compillata | pro nunc sufficiant | uolentibus sub breuitate colligere ea que diffusius dillataui in quodam meo opere quod scripsi super tractatu pratice cantus mensurabilis iohannis de muris. Si uero quis dubia aliaque prolixa hic dimissa atque ibi pertractata uidere uellet illuc recurrat | et ibidem uidebit si quid boni erit. Ad laudem et gloriam omnipotentis dei Amen. Explicit tractatus pratice cantus mensurabilis a prosdocimo de beldemando de padua compilatus deo gratias Amen." (ff. 2ra–27vb)

2. Prosdocimo, *Contrapunctus*, revised version. *Inc.* "SCribit Aristotiles secundo elencorum capitulo ultimo | facile fore inuentis addere ..." *Exp.* "... Scire autem ubi hec signa dulcius cadunt auri tui dimitto quia de hoc regula dari non potest | cum hec loca quodammodo infinita sint. Sufficiant ergo ista de contrapuncto per musicorum minimum prosdocimum de beldemando patauum anno domini .1412. in castro montagnane paduani districtus taliter compilata ad gloriam omnipotentis dei amen. Explicit contrapunctus Prosdocimi de beldemando de padua. (ff. 28ra–33va; f. 33vb blank)

3. Prosdocimo, *Tractatus pratice cantus mensurabilis ad modum Ytalicorum*, revised version. *Inc.* "ARs pratice cantus mensurabilis duplex reperitur ..." *Exp.* "... in hac ultima huius tractatus corectione aliqua mutaui que consequenter in hac arte procedendo michi uisa sunt fore mutanda aliquantulum discrepantia a figuratione ytalica ad presens usitata et ista extraxi ex pomerio marcheti paduani Si tamen figuratio ytalica ad presens usitata magis tibi grata foret recurre ad huncmet tractatum quem primitus de arte ytalica ante eius corectionem compilauj et ibi tuum inuenies intentum. Et sic sit finis huius tractatus per musicorum minimum Prosdocimum de beldemando patauum anno dominj .1412. in castro montagnane paduanj districtus compilati ad laudem et honorem omnipotentis dei totiusque curie supernorum.

Amen. Explicit tractatus pratice cantus mensurabilis ad modum ytalicorum per Prosdocimum de padua compilatus." (ff. 34ra–48ra; f. 48rb, f. 48v blank)

4. Prosdocimo, *Tractatus plane musice*, revised version. *Inc.* "MVltorum diuersorum autorum artis Pratice cantus plani Musica plana nominate uolumina reuolui ..." *Exp.* "... et hoc quando carmina sua componere intendunt. Sit ergo finis huius parui operis plane musice per Prosdocimum de beldemando patauum in castro montagnane paduani districtus Anno domini .1412. taliter ordinati. Ad laudem et gloriam omnipotentis dei ac totius curie supercelestis Amen. Explicit Tractatus plane musice. Prosdocimi de beldemando de Padua." (ff. 49ra–71rb; f. 71v blank)

5. Prosdocimo, *Parvulus tractatulus de modo monacordum dividendi*, revised version. *Inc.* "ET si facile sit inuentis addere addenda tamen negligenda non sunt ..." *Exp.* "... ex ipsis in noticiam superius dictorum facile deuenire poteris Et sic sit finis huius parui tractatuli de modo diuidendi monacordum quem Prosdocimus de beldemando patauus anno domini .1413. padue compilauit Ad laudem et honorem omnipotentis dei atque tocius eius superne curie. Amen. Explicit paruus tractatulus de modo diuidendi monacordum quem Prosdocimus de beldemando de padua compilauit. Deo gratias Amen [*diagram*]." (ff. 72ra–78rb; f. 78v blank)

6. Prosdocimo, *Tractatus musice speculative*. *Inc.* "DVm quidam michi carus ac uti frater intimus lucas nomine de castro lendenarie ..." *Exp.* "... Multasque etiam alias falsitates scripsit supradictus Marchetus | quas scribere dimisi propter breuitatem et etiam quia intelectis que suprahabita sunt poterit quilibet omnes eius cognoscere falsitates. Et sic sit finis huius tractatus per Prosdocimum de beldemando patauum anno dominj nostri yhesu xpisti .1425. padue compilati. Ad laudem gloriam et honorem omnipotentis dei Amen. Explicit tractatus Musice speculatiue | quem Prosdocimus de beldemando paduanus contra Marchetum de padua compilauit. Deo gratias Amen. [*in later hand:* Ab anno 1600, usque ad 1603 Praesul huius Monast(erii) S. Jo(hannis) in Virid(ari)o extitit R(everendus) D(ominus) Benedictus Veranus. Vir uita ac moribus irreprehensibilis]" (ff. 79ra–93rb; f. 93v blank)

7. *Ars musice plane optima et perfecta*, incomplete (unedited). First part *inc.* "Incipit ars musice plane | optima | et | perfecta. AD euidentiam tam mensurabilis musice quam immensurabilis ..." *Exp.* "... fa.la.fa.

sit tibi quintus ..." (ff. 106ra–110vb). Second part *inc.* "... ordinatum. Sciendum est quod Antiqui quatuor tantum toni terminationes in quatuor finalibus litteris grauibus. scilicet .D.E.F.G. habebant...."
Exp. "... Multos autem cantus inuenimus qui sub finalibus non descendunt | et supra fines raro ascendunt Diatessaron | uel Diapente et tales dicuntur Plagales. Amen. [*in later hand:* Hunc librum dono dedit Canonicis regularibus Commorantibus in monasterio S. Ioannis in Viridario dominus Petrus Montagnana bonarum artium cultor quare pro eius anima quisque precari (?) meminerit]" (f. 115ra–b; f. 115v blank)[44]

Claudio Sartori has suggested that ff. 106–10 and 115 did not originally belong to the same manuscript as ff. 2–93.[45] If so, the compiler of its (present) first part most likely planned to devote it to Prosdocimo's musical works (though it does not include the *Expositiones* and the *Proportiones*[46]) with the works presented, as in **B**, chronologically by year of composition. Whether or not the two parts originally belonged together, the same scribe appears to have copied both, and their decorated initials are very similar in style—indications not that they belong to the same manuscript but that they came from the same scriptorium. Ff. 2–93 cannot have been copied earlier than 1425, inasmuch as they contain the *Musica speculative* of that year; the end of that treatise is missing, as is, of course, whatever colophon might have closed it. Ff. 106–10 and 115 were copied no later than 1477, the death year of Pietro Montagnana, who, according to the note at the end of item 7, donated the book of which they were a part to the Paduan monastery of San Giovanni in Verdara. If the two parts were together when that note was added, 1477 also serves as a *terminus non post quem* for ff. 2–93.

The Edition

Prosdocimo's *Tractatus plane musice* has never been published; the *Tractatus musice speculative* exists only in the edition of Baralli and Torri, based on **L** alone;[47] this edition is inaccurate and is not readily available. The

---

[44]It is impossible to rule out the possibility that what are referred to here as two parts of a single treatise might actually come from separate treatises.

[45]*Notazione italiana del Trecento*, 30–31.

[46]The compiler might have omitted the *Expositio* as a commentary on the work of another and the *Proportiones* because it discusses ratios without relating them to musical phenomena.

[47]See p. 3, n. 7, item 8 *supra*.

present edition is based on a collation of all three sources of the *Plana musica* and of both sources of the *Musica speculativa*. The text is presented at the top of each verso page, with variant readings at the bottom.[48] Medieval orthography is retained (following the spellings of **B**), but with i/j, u/v, c/t before i plus vowel, single vs. double consonants, assimilation, and the like normalized. Prosdocimo's revisions of the treatises, transmitted in **L**, are presented between the main text and variants.[49] The illustrations of hands on pp. 38–39 and 70–71 represent the readings of **B**; no significant variants appear in **L** (the portion of text including the hands is missing in **C**).

Comments at the bottom of the rectos explain the text, trace quotations, and link Prosdocimo's ideas with those of other theorists, principally Boethius and Johannes de Muris, both of whom he quotes, and Marchetto of Padua, whom he variously praises and derides.

---

[48] Variants are reported by line. Generally the *lemma* from the text is given, the variant reading, and the siglum of its source. Where the *lemma* is obvious, it is omitted. Subsequent variants in the same line are separated by a single vertical line, subsequent lines but a double vertical line.

[49] It is sometimes impossible to know whether a particular variant in **L** is inadvertent or conscious on the part of Prosdocimo (or of the scribe). Accordingly, only those that significantly alter the meaning are reported between main text and variants; the others are relegated to the variants at the bottom of the page.

CONSPECTUS CODICUM, EDITIONIS ET NOTARUM

Manuscripts

B   Bologna, Civico Museo Bibliografico Musicale, A.56 (Martini, 4), I-Bc

C   Cremona, Biblioteca Governativa, 252, I-CR

L   Lucca, Biblioteca Statale, 359, I-Lg

Earlier Edition

D. Raffaello Baralli and Luigi Torri, "Il Trattato di Prosdocimo de' Beldomandi contro il Lucidario di Marchetto da Padova per la prima volta trascritto e illustrato," *Rivista musicale italiana* 20 (1913): 731–62 (the revised version of *Musica speculativa*)

Notes

ante corr.	before correction	*m. sec.*	in the second hand
fort.	perhaps	*om.*	omitted
in marg.	in the margin	*scripsi*	I have written
in ras.	over an erasure	*rub.*	in red
inter coll.	between the columns	*sub lin.*	below the line
m. pr.	in the first hand	*sup. lin.*	above the line

⟨ ⟩ enclose words added by the editor's conjecture
[ ] indicate deletion by the scribe
{ } indicate a passage in the paradosis that should be deleted

With the exception of the full variant musical example on p. 142, variants in the musical notation are indicated in the critical apparatus by pitch letters corresponding to each note (excluding clefs, ♭ and ♮, and phrase division marks), individually numbered within the line. Individual puncta are separated by hyphens (e.g., a-g-a); notes in ligature are given as groups (e.g., ga-g); and phrase divisions are marked with a comma.

⟨TRACTATUS PLANE MUSICE A PROSDOCIMO DE BELDEMANDIS⟩

⟨Prefatio⟩

⟨1.⟩ Multorum diversorum auctorum artis pratice cantus plani, musica plana nominate, volumina revolvi, ab ipsismet auctoribus taliter intitulata, in
5   quibus partis theorice cum parte pratice ipsius cantus plani inutilis fit permixtio, cum ipsorum diversa deberent esse volumina, eo quod partes omnino abinvicem distincte sunt, et ob hanc causam ipsos errare gravissime puto, in tantum quod ob hoc soli pratice ipsius cantus plani intendentes, ab ipsorum intento distrahuntur primitias suorum voluminum theoricales sibi difficilli-
10 mas intuentes, qua de re, motus amore michi fratris dilecti necnon viri scientifici, spectabilis, et egregii magistri Antonii de Pontevico de civitate Brixiensi, hanc artem pratice cantus plani capere cordialiter affectantis, intendo, cum cause prime subsidio, brevem tractatulum huius artis pratice cantus plani etiam cordialiter agredi, solum ad hanc praticam pertinentia,
15 iuxta mei parvi intellectus imbecilitatem, pertractando.

Tit.: ad finem tractatus || 2 *scripsi* || 3 Multorum … nomina (86.20) *om.* C || 9 theoricales *om.* L || 12 Brixiensi]Antonius de Pontevico de Civitate Brixiensi *in marg. man. sec.* B || 12 hanc artem … affectantis *om.* L || 14 etiam *om.* L ||

Treatise on *Musica Plana* by Prosdocimus de Beldemandis

Preface

1. I have opened volumes by many different authors on the art of plainchant practice, named *musica plana* and thus titled by those authors, in which is made a useless confusion of the theoretical part with the practical part of that plainchant, although there ought to have been different volumes for these because the parts are entirely distinct one from the other. On this basis, I think those authors err most gravely—to such an extent that while intending to discuss plainchant practice alone, they are distracted from their intent by contemplating the exceedingly difficult theoretical foundations[1] of their volumes. Accordingly, moved by the love of my esteemed brother, the most knowledgeable, admirable, and illustrious Master Antonius de Pontevico[2] of the city of Brescia, who aspires with his whole heart to acquire this art of plainchant practice, I intend with the aid of the First Cause to undertake with my whole heart a brief little treatise on this art of plainchant practice, treating to the feeble extent of my small intellect only those things that pertain to this practice.

---

[1] *Primitiae* is glossed as "rudimenta fidei" in *Glossarium mediae et infimae latinitatis Regni Hungariae*, ed. Antal Bartal (Leipzig: B. G. Teubner, 1901; reprint, Hildesheim: Olms, 1970). I borrow the idea of rudiments but render the word "foundations."

[2] I have not been able to identify Antonius.

36

⟨1.⟩   Musica ergo plana est musica notas sive figuras absque ulla determinata mensura considerans, modum cantus planos componendi ac ipsos
abinvicem per tonos autenticos et plagales distinguendique demonstrans; et
5   ut hec descriptio melius intelligatur, est sciendum quod ideo hec musica
plana musica nominatur quia eius cantus uniformiter quantum ad eorum
notas sive figuras, et modo plano, sive absque ulla variatione, proferuntur, et
propter hoc tales cantus etiam cantus plani nominantur. Nominantur et etiam
cantus firmi et cantus immensurati; cantus firmi quia firmiter absque ulla
10   variatione proferuntur, immensurati vero quia absque ulla mensura determinata pronuntiantur.

⟨2.⟩   Ulterius sciendum quod figure sive note musicales sunt signa in
libris reperta per que debitam elevationem vel depositionem vocum apprehendimus, et talia signa sive note sunt solum sex, talibus diversis nominibus

---

7 *Huc pertinet emendatio quae in L invenitur:* … absque ulla determinata
variatione …

9–11 *Huc pertinet emendatio quae in L invenitur:* … firmiter et absque ulla
variatione determinata …

12–14 *Huc pertinet emendatio quae in L invenitur:* … signa in libris reperta
per lineas et spatia{que} dispersa, per que debitam ellevationem vel depositionem vocum aprehendimus, et dicuntur figure quoniam sic figurate note
autem appellantur, quasi nobis notificantes qualiter voces variare debemus
in cantando, et talia signa sive note sunt solum sex …

---

7 modo]quodammodo L ‖

1

1. *Musica plana*, then, is the theory of music that considers notes or figures without any determinate measure, demonstrating the manner of composing plainchants and of distinguishing them from one another in accordance with authentic and plagal tones. So that this description be better understood, one must know that this theory of music is named *musica plana* because its chants are delivered uniformly with respect to their notes or figures and in a plain manner—or without any variation. On account of this, such chants are named plain chants. They are also named both stable chants and unmeasured chants—"stable" chants because they are delivered stably, without any variation, but "unmeasured" because they are pronounced without any determinate measure.

2. Further, one must know that musical figures or notes are signs, found in books, by means of which we apprehend the requisite elevation or deposition in pitch.[1] There are only six such signs or notes, named by the fol-

---

8 ... without any specified variation ...
10–11 ... stably and without any specified variation ...
13–15 ... signs, found in books and scattered on lines and in spaces, by means of which we apprehend the requisite elevation and deposition in pitch. They are called figures inasmuch as, thus drawn,[2] they are also called notes, as if notifying us how we ought to vary pitches in singing. There are only six such signs or notes ...

---

[1]In *Contrapunctus*, Prosdocimo generally uses the term *vox* to refer to solmization syllable, e.g., *Contrapunctus* 3.1: "by 'syllables' I understand the musical syllables, of which there are six, ut, re, mi, fa, sol, la [intelligo per voces, voces musicales, que sunt sex, scilicet ut, re, mi, fa, sol, la]." Prosdocimo de' Beldomandi, *Contrapunctus: A New Critical Text and Translation*, ed. and trans. Jan Herlinger, Greek and Latin Music Theory, vol. 1 (Lincoln: University of Nebraska Press, 1984), 34–35; previously edited in CS, 3:193–99. In *Plana musica*, his term for solmization syllable is more typically *nota* or *signum*, as in the present chapter, or *nomen note*, as in the next; and *vox* generally means "pitch," e.g., *Plana musica* 1.6 (46–47): "Mutation is the variation of one of the six names into another in the same part of the hand with the same pitch retained [Mutatio est unius sex nominum in aliud eiusdem partis manus eadem voce retenta variatio]." Accordingly, I generally translate *vox* as "pitch" except in those cases where Prosdocimo obviously means syllable, e.g., *Plana musica* 2.2 (82–83): "of the six syllables named above—*ut, re, mi, fa, sol, la* ... [de sex vocibus superius nominatis, scilicet ut, re, mi, fa, sol, la ...]." Where necessary, I distinguish *vox* from *sillaba* (an element in a word) by translating the former as "solmization syllable," e.g., *Plana musica* 1.6 (46–49).

[2]"Drawn," *figurate*.

nominate, scilicet ut, re, mi, fa, sol, la; unde per ista sex signa sive notas taliter ordinatas nobis paulatina elevatio denotatur si ab ut incipiamus et ad la per omnia signa sive notas medias ordinate ut superius nominate sunt accedamus, et e converso per ipsas nobis paulatina depositio denotatur si a
5 la incipiamus et ad ut per omnia signa sive notas intermedias ordinate accedamus, sic quod per unum istorum sex nominum parvam apprehendimus elevationem vel depositionem respectu nominis sibi immediate sequentis vel precedentis. Quomodo autem per talem musicam planam modum cantus planos componendi et quomodo etiam per ipsam modum hos cantus per
10 tonos autenticos et plagales distinguendi doctrinam suscipiamus inferius in propriis locis clarissime patebit.

⟨3.⟩ Sed quia per hec sex nomina notarum superius nominata, scilicet ut, re, mi, fa, sol, la, non possemus omnem debitam ac opportunam elevationem vel depositionem vocum habere absque ipsorum nominum reiteratione,
15 ordinaverunt predecessores nostri viginti dictiones a primis septem literis alphabeti, ut ipsas distinctius haberemus, ordinate incipientes, in quibus dictionibus talia sex nomina pluries ordinate reiterata reperiuntur, et tales dictiones sunt iste, scilicet gamaut, Are, ♮mi, Cfaut, Dsolre, Elami, Ffaut, Gsolreut, Alamire, bfa♮mi, Csolfaut, Dlasolre, Elami, Ffaut, Gsolreut, Alamire,
20 bfa♮mi, Csolfa, Dlasol, Ela. Et ut melius ista que dicta sunt memorie commendarentur et clarius haberentur ut moris ipsorum antiquorum erat has viginti dictiones taliter super manu sinistra ordinaverunt, ut hic patet inferius.

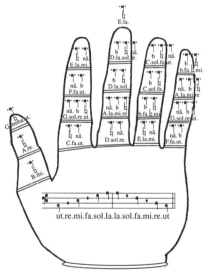

ut.re.mi.fa.sol.la.la.sol.fa.mi.re.ut

---

3 medias]intermedias L ‖ 8 precedentis]immediate precedentis L ‖ 12 notarum *om.* L ‖ 15 precessores B | a]et L ‖ 19–20 Csolfaut … bfa♮mi *in marg.* B ‖ 21 ipsorum *om.* L ‖

lowing specific names: *ut, re, mi, fa, sol, la.* Accordingly, these six signs or notes thus set in order denote for us a gradual elevation if we begin from *ut* and approach *la* through all the intermediate signs or notes in order as they were named above. Conversely, they denote for us a gradual deposition if we begin from *la* and approach *ut* through all the intermediate signs or notes in order. So, by one of these six names we apprehend a little elevation or deposition with respect to the name immediately following or preceding it. Moreover, it will become very clearly evident below in the proper places[3] how, through *musica plana*, we are to adopt the manner of composing plain chants and, through the same discipline, the manner of distinguishing these chants as well in accordance with authentic and plagal tones.

3. But because through these six names of notes named above—*ut, re, mi, fa, sol, la*—we could not obtain every requisite and appropriate elevation or deposition in pitch without reiteration of their names, our predecessors set in order twenty expressions beginning with the first seven letters of the alphabet in order (so that we might grasp them more distinctly), and in these expressions, these six names are found reiterated several times in order. The expressions are these: *gamma-ut,* A-*re,* ♮-*mi,* C-*faut,* D-*solre,* E-*lami,* F-*faut,* G-*solreut,* A-*lamire,* b-*fa-*♮-*mi,* C-*solfaut,* D-*lasolre,* E-*lami,* F-*faut,* G-*solreut,* A-*lamire,* b-*fa-*♮-*mi,* C-*solfa,* D-*lasol,* E-*la.* So that those things that have been said might be better committed to memory and more clearly grasped, as was the custom of those ancients, they set them in order thus on the left hand, as is evident here below:

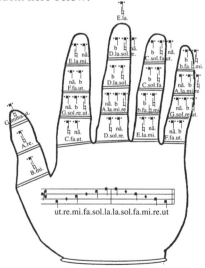

ut.re.mi.fa.sol.la.la.sol.fa.mi.re.ut

---

[3]In *Plana musica* 2 (80–155 *passim*).

Unde mos erat antiquorum multa que ab ipsis sciebantur manibus adaptare, ut patet de compotistis, qui quasi omnes suas regulas manibus adaptant,
ut de modo inveniendi epatam, pasca, aureum numerum, indictionem, literam dominicalem, et sic de aliis. Si ergo manum suprascriptam bene consi
5 deraveris, reperies in predictis viginti dictionibus superius numeratis sex
nomina notarum superius nominata, scilicet ut, re, mi, fa, sol, la, pluries reiterari; incipiunt enim primo in gamaut et terminantur in primo Elami; postea
incipiunt in Cfaut et terminantur in primo Alamire; postea incipiunt in primo
Ffaut et terminantur in Dlasolre; postea incipiunt in primo Gsolreut et termi
10 nantur in secundo Elami; postea incipiunt in Csolfaut et terminantur in
secundo Alamire; postea incipiunt in secundo Ffaut et terminantur in Dlasol;
postea incipiunt in secundo Gsolreut et terminantur in Ela.

Et ut hoc melius intelligas scire debes quod quelibet sillaba dictarum
viginti dictionum primis literis ipsarum abstracti est nomen alicuius note,
15 preterquam in gamaut et bfa♮mi, nam in gamaut hoc totum quod dico, gama,
stat pro litera una, scilicet pro G, eo quod gama grece idem est quod G
latine, et ideo bene dicendo ita possemus dicere Gut sicut dicimus gamaut et
ita scribere etiam in principio manus. Ymo sunt aliqui, qui in principio
manus loco istius dictionis bisillabe gama ponunt unum G grecum, quod
20 taliter scribitur, Γ, et bene, iam quod unum et idem important, sic quod
primam dictionem taliter scribunt, Γut. In bfa♮mi vero binum reperitur B,
primum in principio dictionis et secundum in medio de fa et mi, et scribi
habent diversimode, eo quod diversis nominibus notarum famulantur, nam
primum B famulatur huic nomini fa ipsum immediate sequenti, et debet
25 scribi sub forma rotunda, ita quod habeat corpus rotundum, ut sic, b, et
propter hoc illud fa dicimus cantari per b rotundum; secundum vero B

1 multa que]multa multaque L ‖ 4 aliis]multis aliis L | suprascriptam]supradictam L ‖ 5
numeratis]nominatis L ‖ 6–7 reiterari (-ri *in ras.* B) ‖ 14 viginti [quinque] B ‖ 16 pro *sup.
lin.* B ‖ 17 ideo adhuc L ‖ 18 etiam scribere L ‖ 26 B]♮ L ‖

It was the custom of the ancients to adapt to hands many things that were known by them, as is evident from users of the *computus*, who adapt almost all their rules to hands, such as the manner of discovering the epact, Easter, the golden number, the indiction, the dominical letter, and so forth.[4] Therefore, if you will have properly considered the hand written above, you will find in the aforesaid twenty expressions (enumerated above) the six names of notes named above—*ut, re, mi, fa, sol, la*—reiterated several times, for they begin first in *gamma-ut* and end in the first E-*lami*; then, they begin in C-*faut* and end in the first A-*lamire*; then, they begin in the first F-*faut* and end in D-*lasolre*; then, they begin in the first G-*solreut* and end in the second E-*lami*; then, they begin in C-*solfaut* and end in the second A-*lamire*; then, they begin in the second F-*faut* and end in D-*lasol*; and then, they begin in the second G-*solreut* and end in E-*la*.

So that you might better understand this, you should know that any syllable of the twenty expressions stated (their first letters having been detached) is the name of some note except in *gamma-ut* and b-*fa-♮-mi*, for in *gamma-ut* the whole "gamma" that I say stands for one letter, namely for G, because "gamma" in Greek is the same as G in Latin. Thus, in speaking properly, we could have said "G-*ut*" just as we say "*gamma-ut*" and also could have written it thus at the beginning of the hand. More precisely, there are some who at the beginning of the hand in place of that bisyllabic expression "gamma" place one Greek G, which is written thus, Γ (and properly, because the two convey one and the same thing). So, they write the first expression thus, Γ-*ut*. In b-*fa-♮-mi*, on the other hand, B is found twice, first at the beginning of the expression and second between *fa* and *mi*, and the Bs must be written differently because they serve different names of notes, for the first B serves that name *fa* immediately following it and ought to be written in a round form so that it have a round body thus: b. For this reason, we say that that *fa* is to be sung "through round b." The second B, on the

---

[4]*Computus* was the medieval method of reckoning time. The epact is the number of days in the age of the moon on the first of the year; the dominical letter corresponds to the first Sunday when the days are assigned letters A–G, starting on the first of the year. Both are useful for finding the date of Easter, the first Sunday after the first full moon after the vernal equinox. The golden number is the number of the year in the nineteen-year solar cycle; the indiction is the number of the year in one of the consecutive fifteen-year cycles that commenced in 312. See Joseph R. Strayer, ed., *Dictionary of the Middle Ages*, 13 vols. (New York: Charles Scribner's Sons, 1982–89), s.v. "Calendars and Reckoning of Time," "Computus," and "Indiction"; and Bonnie Blackburn and Leofranc Holford-Strevens, *The Oxford Companion to the Year* (Oxford: Oxford University Press, 1999), 791–832. On the use of hands in the *computus*, see Karol Berger, "The Hand and the Art of Memory," *Musica disciplina* 35 (1981): 87–120, esp. 105–11.

famulatur huic nomini mi ipsum immediate sequenti, et debet scribi sub
forma quadra ad differentiam primi, ita quod habeat corpus quadrum, ut sic,
♮, et propter hoc illud mi dicimus cantari per ♮ quadrum. Et sic habes quomodo nullum istorum B est nomen alicuius note, sed quodlibet ipsorum
5 notis famulari habet. Quare autem primum B potius scribi habeat sub forma
rotunda quam secundum, quod scribitur sub forma quadra, et quare non ita
fit e converso, inferius patebit.

⟨4.⟩ Notandum ulterius quod hee viginti dictiones superius nominate
tripartite sunt, quoniam quedam sunt graves, uti sunt octo prime, scilicet a
10 gamaut inclusive usque ad primum Alamire exclusive; quedam vero acute,
uti sunt septem sequentes, scilicet ab Alamire primo inclusive usque ad
secundum exclusive; relique vero quinque sequentes sunt superacute; et
dicuntur hee viginti dictiones graves, acute, et superacute solum in comparatione ipsarum ad semetipsas, quoniam, si bene consideramus, in grada-
15 tim voces ellevando per sex nomina iam dicta, ipsa sex nomina totiens reite-
rando donec ad finem dictionum omnium perveniatur; a gamaut incipiendo
et semper per omnes intermedias dictiones usque ad finem ipsarum, cum
dicta reiteratione gradatim ascendendo, inveniemus nos in primis octo dictionibus respectu sequentium vocem gravitare et in septem intermediis
20 ipsam vocem acuere et in extremis quinque ipsam superacuere, et ideo
prime octo graves vocantur, secunde vero septem acute, et tercie quinque
ultime superacute, ipsis adinvicem semper comparatis. Et fuerunt graves

4 B]duorum B diversarum figurarum in bfa♮mi positorum L ‖ 5 Quare autem]Sed quare L ‖
8 Notandum ulterius]Preterea sciendum L ‖ 11 ab Alamire primo]a primo Alamire L ‖ 16
perveniantur B ‖

other hand, serves that name *mi* immediately following it and ought to be written in a square form for differentiation from the first so that it have a square body thus: ♮. For this reason, we say that that *mi* is sung "through square ♮." Thus you grasp how neither of those Bs is the name of any note, but each of them must serve a note. Moreover, why the first B must be written in a round form rather than the second, which is written in a square form, and why this is not done the other way round will become evident below.[5]

4. One must note further that these twenty expressions named above are divided into three parts inasmuch as certain ones are low, as are the first eight, from *gamma-ut* up to but excluding the first A-*lamire*; certain ones, on the other hand, are high, as are the seven following, from the first A-*lamire* up to but excluding the second; but the remaining five following are very high.[6] These twenty expressions are called low, high, or very high only in comparison to one another inasmuch as (if we properly consider it) in elevating the pitches stepwise through the six names already stated, reiterating these six names a number of times until we come to the end of all the expressions, beginning from *gamma-ut* and ascending stepwise with the said reiteration always through all the intermediate expressions up to the end of them, we shall discover that we lower the voice in the first eight expressions (with respect to the following ones), raise the voice in the seven intermediate ones, and raise it further in the five extreme ones. For that reason, the first eight are called low, the second seven high, and the third (and last) five very high, always compared one with another. The first expressions, eight in

---

[5]*Plana musica* 1.9 (58–59).

[6]Similar classifications of the low, high, and very high notes appear in Jacobus Leodiensis, *Speculum musice* 5.16.10 (*Jacobi Leodiensis Speculum musicae*, ed. Roger Bragard, 7 vols., Corpus scriptorum de musica, vol. 3 [n.p.: American Institute of Musicology, 1955–73], 5:52); Ugolino, *Declaratio musicae disciplinae* 1.9–10 (*Ugolini Urbevetanis Declaratio musicae disciplinae*, ed. Albert Seay, 3 vols., Corpus scriptorum de musica, vol. 7 [(Rome): American Institute of Musicology, 1959–62], 1:28–30); and Franchino Gaffurio, *Practica musice* 1.1 (Milan: Ioannes Petrus de Lomatio, 1496; reprint, Farnborough: Gregg, 1967). More commonly, theorists chose not to include Γ among the low notes, e.g., Guido d'Arezzo, *Micrologus* 2 (*Guidonis Aretini Micrologus*, ed. Joseph Smits van Waesberghe, Corpus scriptorum de musica, vol. 4 [(Rome): American Institute of Musicology, 1955], 93–95; trans. Warren Babb in *Hucbald, Guido, and John on Music: Three Medieval Treatises*, ed. with Introductions by Claude V. Palisca, Music Theory Translation Series [New Haven, CT: Yale University Press, 1978], 59–60; Guido omits the high E as well); *Introductio musice secundum magistrum de Garlandia* (*Scriptorum de musica medii aevi nova series a Gerbertina altera* [henceforward: CS], 4 vols., ed. Edmond de Coussemaker [Paris: Durand, 1864–76; reprint, Hildesheim: Olms, 1963], 1:158); *Quatuor principalia* 2.5 (CS, 4:208); Marchetto, *Lucidarium* 14.10–21 (Jan W. Herlinger, *The Lucidarium of*

numero octo prime dictiones, eo quod omnis vox ab eius loco infimo ad
ipsius octavam locum obtinet gravem, cum tenorum locus existat; fueruntque acute sequentes septem dictiones, eo quod omnis vox ab octava sui
infimi loci usque ad quintam decimam locum obtinet acutum, cum discan-
5 tuum locus existat; fueruntque ultime quinque dictiones superacute, eo quod
vocem humanam comunem que ad quintam decimam vocem terminatur
excedunt, et ideo merito superacute nominate sunt, quia super voces acutas
hominum comuniter cantantium elevate sunt.

⟨5.⟩   Sed ut melius per sex nomina superius pluries nominata agnoscere
10 possemus debitam elevationem et depositionem vocum, ordinaverunt antiqui nostri predecessores quasdam lineas per quas et earum spatia note collocarentur, secundum quod exemplariter scriptum est in palma manus
superius depicte, et ex hoc diviserunt ipsi antiqui viginti dictiones superius
recitatas, quasdam ipsarum in lineis ponendo et quasdam in spatiis, que
15 qualiter cognoscantur habere potes per hanc regulam que talis est, quod

---

13 *Huc pertinet emendatio quae in L invenitur:* ... superius depicte et in
voluminibus cantuum ecclesiasticorum, et ex hoc ...

---

1 numero]solummodo numero L ‖ 3 septem]solummodo numero septem L ‖ 4 quitam B ‖ 9
nominata [melius] B ‖ 11 precessores B ‖ 12 exemplariter collocarentur L ‖ 13 hoc *sup. lin.*
B ‖

number, were low because every pitch from its lowest position to its eighth occupies a low position, since the position is that of tenors; the seven expressions following were high because every pitch after the eighth from its lowest position to the fifteenth occupies a high position, since the position is that of discants; and the last five expressions were very high because they exceed the common human voice, which ends at the fifteenth pitch. Thus, they were named "very high" with good reason because they are elevated above the high voices of men as they commonly sing.

5. So that we might be able better to recognize the elevation and deposition in pitch required by the six names named several times above, our ancient predecessors set in order certain lines by means of which (with their spaces) notes might be assigned a position[7] according to what was written as an example in the palm of the hand depicted above. For this reason, those ancients apportioned the twenty expressions recited above, placing certain of them on lines and certain of them in spaces. How these are recognized you can know through this rule, which is as follows: every expression that is

---

13 ... depicted above and in volumes of ecclesiastical chants. For this reason ...

Marchetto of Padua: A Critical Edition, Translation, and Commentary [Chicago: University of Chicago Press, 1985], 540–43); Walter Odington, *De speculatione musice* 5.1.14–17 (*Walteri Odington Summa de speculatione musicae*, ed. Frederick F. Hammond, Corpus scriptorum de musica, vol. 14 [(Rome): American Institute of Musicology, 1970], 92–93; Walter also omits the high E); Johannes Gallicus, *Ritus canendi* 2.1.2.1–3 (Johannes Gallicus, *Ritus canendi*, ed. Albert Seay, 2 vols., Critical Texts, nos. 13–14 [Colorado Springs: Colorado College Music Press, 1981], 2:2; cf. CS 4:346); Johannes Tinctoris, *Dictionary of Musical Terms*, ed. Carl Parrish (Glencoe: Free Press, 1963), 6–7, 34–35, 60–61); Tinctoris, *Expositio manus* 1.20 (*Johannis Tinctoris Opera theoretica*, ed. Albert Seay, 3 vols. in 2, Corpus scriptorum de musica, vol. 22 [(Rome): American Institute of Musicology, 1975–78], 1:35; Tinctoris calls Γ "lowest" [*gravissima*]); Burzio, *Florum libellus* 1.16 (*Nicolai Burtii Parmensis Florum libellus*, ed. Giuseppe Massera, "Historiae Musicae Cultores" Biblioteca, vol. 28 [Florence: Olschki, 1975], 86; cf. Nicolaus Burtius, *Musices opusculum*, trans. Clement A. Miller, Musicological Studies and Documents, no. 37 [Neuhausen-Stuttgart: Hänssler Verlag for the American Institute of Musicology, 1983], 51). Cf. Prosdocimo, *Contrapunctus* (ed. Herlinger), 47–49, n. 10.

[7]For early descriptions of the staff, see Guido d'Arezzo, *Regule rhythmice* 214–61 and *Prologus in antiphonarium* 54–107 (*Guido d'Arezzo's* Regule rithmice, Prologus in antiphonarium, *and* Epistola ad Michahelem: *A Critical Text and Translation*, ed. Dolores Pesce, Musicological Studies, vol. 73 [Ottawa: Institute of Mediæval Music, 1999], 372–83 and 418–31; cf. *Scriptores ecclesiastici de musica sacra potissimum* [henceforward: GS], 3 vols., ed. Martin Gerbert [St. Blaise: Typis San-Blasianis, 1784; reprint, Hildesheim: Olms, 1963], 2:30–31 and 35–36).

omnis dictio in pari numero existens spatialis esse dignoscitur; omnis vero dictio in impari numero existens linealis esse discernitur. Unde quia gamaut, ♮mi, Dsolre, et sic ultra in numero impari existunt, puta in unitate, ternario, quinario, et sic ultra, ideo dicuntur in lineis collocari; et quia Are, Cfaut,
5 Elami grave, et sic ultra in numero pari existunt, ut in binario, quaternario, senario, et sic ultra, ideo in spatiis collocari dicuntur.

⟨6.⟩ Item sciendum quod antiqui huius artis magistri, volentes modum reiterandi sex nomina notarum superius pluries nominata, que ab aliis sex voces nuncupantur, nobis tribuere, quendam invenerunt modum permutandi
10 unum sex nominum in aliud, per quem fit postea facilis modus talia sex nomina reiterandi, et iste talis modus permutandi apud musicos comuniter mutatio nominatur, que mutatio sic describi potest: Mutatio est unius sex nominum in aliud eiusdem partis manus eadem voce retenta variatio, ut inde voces magis quam per sex continuas varias elevationes vel depressiones
15 elevari vel deprimi possint. Ad cuius descriptionis declarationem est sciendum quod auctores musice septem acceperunt primas literas alphabeti, scilicet A, B, C, D, E, F, et G, et ab istis ordinate incohaverunt quamlibet viginti dictionum superius nominatarum, ut supradictum est atque patere potest cuilibet manum musicalem inspicere volenti; et solum istas septem acceperunt
20 literas, quoniam voluerunt in qualibet parte manus locum octavum ad quamcumque partem precedentem obtinente similem precedenti sumere literam, eo quod octava similis unisono reputatur.

16–17 *Huc pertinet emendatio quae in L invenitur:* … auctores musice ad maiorem claritatem et noticiam faciliorem huius artis septem acceperunt primas alphabeti literas, scilicet …

---

1 numero pari L ‖ 2 numero impari L ‖ 3 ♮mi]bmi L ‖ 7 Item sciendum]Sciendum ulterius L ‖ 12 mutatio (*sec.*)]mutatio ut musico spectat L ‖ 14 continuas atque L ‖ 17 B]b L | et (*pr.*) *om.* L ‖

in an even number is distinguished as lying in a space, whereas every expression that is in an odd number is discerned as lying on a line. Accordingly, because *gamma-ut*, ♮-*mi*, D-*solre*, and so forth are in odd numbers (in unity, the ternary, the quinary, and so forth), they are said to be assigned positions on lines; and because A-*re*, C-*faut*, low E-*lami*, and so forth are in even numbers (in the binary, the quaternary, the senary, and so forth), they are said to be assigned positions in spaces.

6. Again, one must know that the ancient masters of this art, wishing to apportion to us a manner of reiterating the six names of notes named several times above (which are called six solmization syllables by others),[8] discovered a certain manner of exchanging one of the six names for another, through which then arises an easy manner of reiterating these six names. Among musicians, this manner of exchange is commonly named "mutation," and mutation can be described thus: mutation is the variation of one of the six names into another in the same part of the hand with the same pitch retained[9] so that pitches could then be elevated or depressed through more than six varied adjacent elevations or depressions. For an explanation of this description, one must know that authors of music took the first seven letters of the alphabet—that is, A, B, C, D, E, F, and G—and they began any of the twenty expressions named above with these letters in order (as has been said above and can be evident to anyone willing to inspect the musical hand). They took only these seven letters inasmuch as they maintained that in any part of the hand, the eighth place in relation to any preceding part should take a letter similar to that occupying the preceding part because the octave is held to be similar to the unison.

18–19 ... authors of music, for greater clarity and easier knowledge of this art, took the first seven letters of the alphabet—that is, ...

---

[8]On use of the term *vox* for syllable, see *Plana musica* 1.2 (n. 1 *supra*).

[9]The definition is standard in late medieval theory. Cf. Marchetto, *Lucidarium* 8.2.2 (ed. Herlinger, 280–81): "Mutation is a change in the name of a syllable or note lying in the same space or on the same line and with the same pitch [Mutatio est variatio nominis vocis seu note in eodem spacio, linea, et sono]"; and Nicolaus de Capua, *Compendium musicale*: "Mutation is a change in the name of a syllable or note lying in the same space or on the same line, with the same pitch, and under the same sign, that is, under the same letter [Mutatio est ... variatio nominis vocis sive notae in eodem spatio vel linea sub uno sono et etiam sub uno signo, id est sub una littera]" (in Adrien de La Fage, *Essais de diphthérographie musicale* [Paris: Legouix, 1864; reprint, Amsterdam: Knuf, 1964], 315).

Item notandum quod in qualibet dictarum viginti dictionum, prima litera excepta, quelibet sillaba pro nomine alicuius note sumitur, et vox comuniter apud musicos nominatur, ut supradictum est, et de istis nominibus sive vocibus reperiuntur aliquando tres in unica dictione, et in nulla possunt plures
5 reperiri; aliquando vero reperiuntur solum due et aliquando una, modo ubi una sola vox seu nomen note reperitur nulla potest esse ibi mutatio, cum ibi deficiat aliud nomen in quod possit fieri nominis variatio, ut gratia exempli in gamaut, Are, ♮mi, et Ela, in quibus una sola vox pro qualibet dictione reperitur.

10 In qualibet vero dictione in qua due voces sive duo nomina notarum reperiuntur, due reperiuntur mutationes preterquam in bfa♮mi, et fit prima mutatio de primo nomine in secundum et secunda e converso; ut gratia exempli in Cfaut prima mutatio est de fa in ut et secunda est e converso, scilicet de ut in fa, et sic de aliis dictionibus solum duas voces habentibus.
15 Et dixi preterquam in bfa♮mi, quoniam dato quod in bfa♮mi unum reperiatur nomen in quod aliud mutari possit, non tamen hoc fieri potest eadem voce retenta, ut patebit inferius, quod ponit descriptio mutationis superius posita.

In qualibet vero dictione in qua tres voces sive tria nomina notarum reperiuntur sex reperiuntur mutationes, et fit prima mutatio de primo nomine
20 in secundum et secunda fit e converso; tercia vero mutatio fit de primo nomine in tercium et quarta fit e converso; quinta vero mutatio fit de secundo nomine in tercium et sexta fit e converso, ut gratia exempli in Gsolreut prima mutatio fit de sol in re et secunda fit e converso, scilicet de re in

---

1–4 *Huc pertinet emendatio quae in L invenitur:* Preterea voluerunt isti antiqui quod in qualibet dictarum viginti dictionum, prima litera excepta, quelibet sillaba pro nomine alicuius note sumeretur, que vox comuniter apud musicos nominatur, preterquam in utroque bfa♮mi, et de istis nominibus sive vocibus ...

10–11 *Huc pertinet emendatio quae in L invenitur:* In qualibet vero dictione in qua due voces sive duo nomina notarum reperiuntur, due tantum reperiuntur mutationes preterquam in utroque bfa♮mi ...

15 *Huc pertinet emendatio quae in L invenitur:* ... preterquam in utroque bfa♮mi, quoniam ...

---

5 una]solum una L | ubi]ubicunque L ‖ 6 nulla potest esse ibi]ibi nulla penitus potest esse L ‖ 7 possit]*fort.* posset L | nominis *om.* L | gratia exempli]verbi gratia L ‖ 12–13 gratia exempli]verbi gratia L ‖ 15 in (*sec.*) *om.* B ‖ 16 nomen *in marg.* B ‖ 22 gratia exempli]verbi gratia L ‖

Again, one must note that in any of the said twenty expressions, any syllable (the first letter excepted) is taken as the name of some note, and among musicians, it is commonly named "solmization syllable" (as was said above). Of these names or syllables, sometimes three are found in a single expression, and in none can more be found. But sometimes only two are found and sometimes one. Where one syllable or name of a note is found alone, there can be no mutation, since there is lacking in that place another name into which a variation of name could be made, as for example in *gamma-ut*, A-*re*, ♮-*mi*, and E-*la*, in which one syllable alone is found for whichever expression.

On the other hand, in any expression in which two syllables or two names of notes are found, two mutations are found, except in b-*fa*-♮-*mi*. The first mutation is made from the first name to the second and the second vice versa: for example, in C-*faut* the first mutation is from *fa* to *ut* and the second vice versa from *ut* to *fa*, and thus for the other expressions having only two syllables. I said "except in b-*fa*-♮-*mi*" inasmuch as, granted that in b-*fa*-♮-*mi* one name is found into which the other could be mutated, this cannot be done with the same pitch retained (as will become evident below),[10] which the description of mutation stated above specifies.

But in any expression in which three syllables or three names of notes are found, six mutations are found. The first mutation is made from the first name to the second and the second is made vice versa; the third mutation is made from the first name to the third and the fourth is made vice versa; the fifth mutation is made from the second name to the third and the sixth is made vice versa. For example, on G-*solreut* the first mutation is made from *sol* to *re* and the second is made vice versa from *re* to *sol*; the third mutation

---

1–4 Moreover, those ancients of ours maintained that in any of the said twenty expressions, any syllable (the first letter excepted) might be taken as the name of some note (except in b-*fa*-♮-*mi*), and among musicians, it is commonly named "solmization syllable." Of these names or syllables, ...

11–12 On the other hand, in any expression in which two syllables or two names of notes are found, only two mutations are found, except in either b-*fa*-♮-*mi*, ...

16 ... "except in either b-*fa*-♮-*mi*" inasmuch as, ...

---

[10]*Plana musica* 1.7 (50–55).

sol; tercia vero mutatio fit de sol in ut et quarta fit e converso, scilicet de ut in sol; quinta vero mutatio fit de re in ut et sexta fit e converso, scilicet de ut in re, et sic de aliis dictionibus tres voces habentibus.

⟨7.⟩ Sciendum ulterius quod in qualibet gradata elevatione vel deposi-
5 tione vocum per illa sex nomina causatur elevatio quedam vocis vel deposi-
tio que tonus nominatur preterquam in elevatione vel depositione vocis que fit a mi ad fa vel e contra, scilicet a fa ad mi, ex quibus quedam imperfecta elevatio vel depositio vocis causatur que apud musicos semitonium nominatur, non quod sit medietas toni sed quia imperfectus, semus, vel
10 incompletus tonus, unde non dicitur semitonium in hoc loco a semi grece quod est medium latine et tonus, sed a semi grece quod aliquando est imperfectum, semum, sive incompletum latine et tonus, sic quod in hoc loco

2 fit (pr.) sup. lin. B ‖ 4 Sciendum ulterius]Preterea sciendum L ‖ 5 nomina pluries dicta L | vel]sive L ‖ 6 nominatur apud musicos L ‖ 9–10 quia est imperfectus, vel semus, vel incompletus L ‖ 11 sed dicitur L ‖ 11–12 imperfectum, vel semum, sive incompletum L ‖

is made from *sol* to *ut* and the fourth is made vice versa from *ut* to *sol*; the fifth mutation is made from *re* to *ut* and the sixth is made vice versa from *ut* to *re*; and thus for the other expressions having three syllables.

7. One must know further that in any stepwise elevation or deposition in pitch through those six names, a certain elevation or deposition in pitch is caused that is named a tone, except in the elevation or deposition in pitch that is made from *mi* to *fa* or vice versa from *fa* to *mi*. From these, a certain imperfect elevation or deposition in pitch is caused that among musicians in named a semitone, not because it is half of a tone but because it is an imperfect, deficient,[11] or incomplete tone. Accordingly, semitone in this instance is derived not from the *semi* in Greek that is *medium*[12] in Latin and *tonus*, but from the *semi* in Greek that is sometimes *imperfectus*, *semus*, or *incompletus* in Latin and *tonus*.[13] So, in this instance semitone means as much as

---

[11]"Deficient," *semus*. Cf. *Musica speculativa* 1.4 (162–63)

[12]*Medium*, middle. Cf. *Musica speculativa* 1.4 (162–63)

[13]Similar statements are common in medieval theory, e.g. Johannes de Muris, *Musica ⟨speculativa⟩*, conclusio septima ("the semitone is unanimously so named by musicians, not from that *semi* which is half but from that *semi* which is imperfect [a musicis semitonium unanimiter appellatur, non a semis, id est dimidium, sed a semis, id est imperfectum]"; *Johannis de Muris Musica ⟨speculativa⟩*, ed. Susan Fast, Musicological Studies, vol. 61 [Ottawa: Institute of Mediæval Music, 1994], 114); Philippe de Vitry, *Ars nova* ("the semitone is named not from that *semi* which is half, as some hold, but from *semi*, *-ma*, *-mum*, an imperfect sound, as it were [non enim dicitur semitonium a semis, quod est dimidium, ut quidam putant, … sed dicitur a semus, -ma, -mum, quod est imperfectum, quasi imperfectus sonus]"; *Philippi de Vitriaco Ars nova*, ed. Gilbert Reaney, André Gilles, and Jean Maillard, Corpus scriptorum de musica, vol. 8 [(Rome): American Institute of Musicology, 1964], 21); Johannes Ciconia, *Nova musica* 1.23 ("Guido: For the semitone is called, as it were, 'semis tonus,' that is, 'not a full tone' [Guido: Semitonium enim dictum est quasi semis tonus, id est non plenus tonus]"; Johannes Ciconia, *Nova musica and De proportionibus: New Critical Texts and Translations*, ed. and trans. Oliver B. Ellsworth, Greek and Latin Music Theory, vol. 9 [Lincoln: University of Nebraska Press, 1993], 104–7). Cf. Prosdocimo, *Monacordum* 4.1 (Prosdocimo de' Beldomandi, *Brevis summula proportionum quantum ad musicam pertinet and Parvus tractatulus de modo monacordum dividendi: A New Critical Text and Translation*, ed. and trans. Jan Herlinger, Greek and Latin Music Theory, vol. 4 [Lincoln: University of Nebraska Press, 1987], 82–85).

tantum valet semitonium quantum imperfectus, semus, vel incompletus
tonus. Et sic habes quod in constitutione semitonii tonus per medium non
dividitur sed per partes inequales, et inde postea procreantur semitonia inequalia, quorum unum maius semitonium nominatur et reliquum minus; et
5 qualiter hoc proveniat non est presentis speculationis, sed hoc tanquam
verum et probatum ab huius artis theorico habere debemus. Et intelligo per
gradatam elevationem quando in elevatione vocis ab uno sex nominum in
aliud nullum intercipitur nomen nec linea nec spatium, et similiter per gradatam depositionem intelligo quando in tali depositione vocis ab uno sex
10 nominum ad aliud nullum intercipitur nomen nec linea nec spatium, et ex his
talem potes sumere descriptionem toni: tonus est elevatio vel depositio
vocis nullo intervallo lineali vel spatiali interposito, ex qua elevatione vel
depositione debita, plena, et perfecta insurgit resonantia. Sumere potes
etiam descriptionem semitonii talem: Semitonium est elevatio vel depositio
15 vocis nullo intervalo lineali vel spatiali interposito, ex qua elevatione vel

---

1–5 *Huc pertinet emendatio quae in L invenitur:* ... incompletus tonus.
Impossibile nanque est tonum in partes equales dividi, quia nec in duas
medietates nec in tres tercias nec in quatuor quartas nec in quinque quintas
et sic de aliis, dato quod Marchetus Paduanus in suo Lucidario, et aliquantulum in suo Pomerio, voluerit tonum in quinque quintas dividi, quarum
quelibet apud ipsum nominabatur dyesis, ignorans de hoc quid loqueretur.
Multa nanque scripsit in suo Lucidario que ignorabat et falsa. A principio
nanque Lucidarii usque circa medium tangere voluit aliqua in theorica
musice, quam theoricam totaliter ignorabat; sed a circa medium usque ad
finem, ubi se transtulit ad praticam musice plane, scripsit egregie, sic quod
ibi in nullo fit reprehensione dignus. Tonus ergo quantum ad eius primam
divisionem in duas partes inequales partitur, quarum quelibet semitonium
apud musicum nuncupatur, et ergo, ut apparet, per consequens tonus in duo
semitonia inequalia dividitur, quorum unum maius semitonium nominatur et
aliud minus semitonium appellatur; et qualiter hoc proveniat ...

---

1 imperfectus, sive semus, sive incompletus L || 8–10 et similiter ... nec linea nec spatium
om. L || 13 debita, et plena, et perfecta L ||

"imperfect, deficient, or incomplete tone." And thus you grasp that in the construction of the semitone, the tone is divided not in the middle but into unequal parts, and thus unequal semitones are then created, one of which is named the major semitone and the remaining one the minor. How this arises is not for the present speculation, but we must grasp it as true and as proven by a theorist of this art.[14] By "stepwise elevation," I understand an elevation in pitch from one of the six names to another when no name, line, or space intervenes; and similarly by "stepwise deposition," I understand a deposition in pitch from one of the six names to another when no name, line, or space intervenes. From this, you can take such a description of the tone: the tone is an elevation or deposition in pitch with no interval on a line or in a space interposed, from which elevation or deposition a proper, full, and perfect resonance arises. You can also take this description of the semitone: the semitone is an elevation or deposition in pitch with no interval on a line or in a space interposed, from which elevation or deposition an improper, par-

---

1–4 ... incomplete tone"; for it is impossible for the tone to be divided into equal parts—neither into two halves nor into three thirds nor into four fourths nor into five fifths, and so forth—granted that Marchetus the Paduan, in his *Lucidarium* and to some extent his *Pomerium*, maintained that the tone is divided into five fifths, any of which was named diesis by him,[15] ignorant about that of which he spoke. To be sure, he wrote many things in his *Lucidarium* of which he was ignorant and that are false. From the beginning of the *Lucidarium* to about the middle, he wished to touch on some matters in the theory of music, of which theory he was totally ignorant; but from about the middle to the end, where he turned to the practice of *musica plana*, he wrote surpassingly; so, there he deserves no censure. The tone therefore is divided (for its first division) into two unequal parts, either of which is called a semitone by the musician; therefore, then (as is evident), the tone is divided into two unequal semitones, one of which is named the major semitone and the other is called the minor semitone. How this arises ...

---

[14]For instance, Johannes de Muris, *Musica ⟨speculativa⟩* 1. Conclusio sexta (ed. Fast, 90–113). Prosdocimo will prove it himself in *Musica speculativa* 2.15 (194–201). Inequality of semitones is a common topos in medieval theory, deriving perhaps from Boethius, *De institutione musica* 1.16 (A. M. S. Boethius, *De institutione arithmetica libri duo, De institutione musica libri quinque*, ed. Godofredus Friedlein [Leipzig: B. G. Teubner, 1867], 201–3; translated with introduction and annotations by Calvin Bower as *Fundamentals of Music*, Music Theory Translation Series [New Haven, CT: Yale University Press, 1989], 22–26).

[15]Marchetto, *Lucidarium* 2.5–8, 5.6, 8.1 (ed. Herlinger, 130–57, 206–23, and 270–81) and *Pomerium* 13–14 (*Marcheti de Padua Pomerium*, ed. Ioseph Vecchi, Corpus scriptorum de musica, vol. 6 [(Rome): American Institute of Musicology, 1961], 68–70). Prosdocimo addresses the matter at greater length in the *Musica speculativa*.

depositione indebita, non plena, et imperfecta insurgit resonantia. Ex his
ergo que de tono et semitonio dicta sunt patere potest quomodo fa et mi in
bfa♮mi acuto sive superacuto existentia non sunt in eadem voce, ut superius
dicebatur, quoniam minor est elevatio que fit a mi immediate precedente
5　posito in Alamire acuto ad ipsum fa existens in bfa♮mi acuto quam elevatio que fit a re existente in predicto Alamire acuto ad ipsum mi existens
in bfa♮mi acuto, cum ex prima harum elevationum semitonium causetur et
ex secunda tonus, ut statim dictum est.

〈8.〉　Sciendum ulterius quod antiqui auctores variationem maximam
10　invenerunt in ordinatione sex nominum notarum pluries superius nominatorum, quoniam in quibusdam locis invenerunt in mutando unum nomen
note in aliud voces nichil penitus variari et in quibusdam aliis locis in talibus
nominum mutationibus voces magnam sumere variationem, ut dictum est
supra de utroque bfa♮mi tam accuto quam superacuto, et propter hoc, secun-
15　dum quod in diversis partibus manus musicalis tales ordines manus reperie-
bantur, voluerunt ipsos ordines alio et alio modo cantari debere. Unde voluerunt quod ordo nominum in mutationibus quorum in eadem parte manus
musicalis nulla penitus fiebat vocum variatio per naturam cantari diceretur,
cuius causa potest duplex assignari. Prima quarum est quia ipsa nomina in
20　suis mutationibus non assuescunt alias sumere voces quam illas quas prius
habebant, et ideo hoc est sibi naturale, et merito eius ordo per naturam cantari dicitur, cum illud naturale sit quod non aliter assuescit. Secunda causa

---

7–8 *Huc pertinet emendatio quae in L invenitur:* ... et ex secunda tonus, ut
statim dictum est; et similiter minor est descensus qui fit a fa C acuti vel
superacuti ad mi B acuti vel superacuti 〈quam descensus qui fit a sol C acuti
vel superacuti〉 ad fa B acuti vel superacuti, cum ex primo descensu semitonium causetur et ex secundo tonus, ut statim dictum est.

---

1 indebita et L ‖ 2 semitono B | in]de L ‖ 3 existentia *om.* L ‖ 5 acuto (*pr.*)]acuto vel supera-
cuto L | ipsum *om.* L | acuto (*sec.*)]acuto vel superacuto L ‖ 6 a re]Are B | acuto *om.* L |
ipsum *om.* L ‖ 7 in predicto L | bfa♮[acu]mi　B | acuto *om.* L | [ex] ex B ‖ 9 Sciendum
ulterius]Ulterius etiam sciendum L | auctores huius artis L ‖ 14 tam ... quam]scilicet ... et L
‖ 17 manus *sup. lin.* B ‖ 20 prius *om.* L ‖

tial, and imperfect resonance arises.[16] From what has been said of the tone and the semitone, it can be evident how the *fa* and the *mi* in high or very high b-*fa*-♮-*mi* are not on the same pitch, as was said above,[17] inasmuch as the elevation that is made from the *mi* immediately preceding, placed in high A-*lamire*, to the *fa* in high b-*fa*-♮-*mi* is less than the elevation that is made from the *re* in the aforesaid high A-*lamire* to the *mi* in high b-*fa*-♮-*mi*, since a semitone is caused from the first of these elevations and a tone from the second, as has just been stated.

8. One must know further that ancient authors discovered a very great variation in the ordering of the six names of notes named several times above inasmuch as they discovered that in mutating one name of a note into another in certain positions, pitches are not varied at all, and in such mutations of names in certain other positions, the pitches undergo a great variation, as was said above concerning either b-*fa*-♮-*mi*, high or very high. For this reason, following those orders of the hand as they were found in different parts of the musical hand, they maintained that these orders ought to be sung in different manners. Accordingly, they maintained that the order of names was said to be sung "through nature" in the mutations of which no variation of pitch whatever was made in that same part of the musical hand.[18] Two causes can be assigned for this, of which the first is that these names are not accustomed in their mutations to take pitches other than those they earlier had. Thus, this is what is "natural," and for good reason its order is said to be sung "through nature," since the natural is that to which one does not become accustomed in some other way.[19] The second cause is

---

7–8 ... and from the second a tone, as has just been stated. Likewise, the descent that is made from the *fa* of high or very high C to the *mi* of high or very high B is smaller than the descent that is made from the *sol* of high or very high C to the *fa* of high or very high B, since a semitone is caused by the first descent and a tone by the second, as has just been stated.

---

[16]Cf. Philippe de Vitry, *Ars contrapunctus* (CS, 3:24): "the tone is a combination of two pitches producing a full and whole ascent or descent without any interval intervening; the semitone is an interval of two pitches producing a partial ascent or descent without any interval intervening [tonus est coherentia duarum vocum plenam et integram elevationem reddens seu depositionem sine aliquo intervallo; ... semitonium ... est conjunctio duarum vocum semiplenam elevationem reddens atque depositionem sine aliquo intervallo]."

[17]*Plana musica* 1.6 (48–49).

[18]That is, in the part of the musical hand (the C hexachord) that excludes the position (b-*fa*-♮-*mi*) where a change of syllable results in a change of pitch.

[19]The force seems to be that what is natural does not have to be established through custom.

est quia humane voci multum facilius est in talibus mutationibus eandem vocem retinere quam ipsam ita paucum variare, ut potest quilibet in se experiri, et sibi ergo naturalius et per consequens naturale, cum illud voci naturalius et pro naturali reputatur quod sibi facilius esse discernitur, nimi-
5 rum ergo si ordo talium nominum in quorum mutationibus nulla penitus fit vocum variatio per naturam cantari dicatur; et merito propter hoc ergo voluerunt huius artis magistri quod ut repertum in Cfaut et similiter in Csol-faut cum omnibus suis nominibus eum sequentibus, scilicet re, mi, fa, sol, la, per naturam cantaretur, eo quod in eorum mutationibus nulla penitus
10 fiebat vocis variatio. Et dixi cum omnibus suis nominibus, eo quod reliqua quinque nomina sequentia ipsum ut, scilicet re, mi, fa, sol, la, dicuntur eius nomina, cum ab ipso ut tanquam ab eorum principe et principio habeant gubernari, eo quod naturam ipsius ut semper insequuntur.

Voluerunt ulterius antiqui auctores quod ordo nominum in quorum ali-
15 quo etiam ipsum in aliud nomen mutando fiebat vocis variatio non per natu-ram sed alio modo cantaretur, et quia talis vocis variatio in talibus mutatio-nibus nullibi in manu musicali reperiebatur nisi in hac dictione bfa♮mi que per B sumit exordium, ideo voluerunt ipsi talem ordinem nominum in quo-rum aliquo in aliud nomen mutando fiebat vocis variatio in eadem parte
20 manus musicalis cantari dici per B, et ulterius quia in bfa♮mi binum reperi-tur B diversimode figuratum, ut visum est superius, scilicet b rotundum et ♮ quadrum, voluerunt aliquem ordinem per b rotundum cantari dici et aliquem per ♮ quadrum, et illum cantari dici per b rotundum qui in se fa de bfa♮mi assumebat, illum vero per ♮ quadrum qui in se mi de bfa♮mi possidere vide-
25 batur, hac ergo de causa dixerunt ipsi antiqui quod ut repertum in utroque Ffaut, tam gravi quam acuto, cum omnibus suis nominibus per b rotundum cantabatur, eo quod in tali ordine fa de bfa♮mi positum reperiebatur. Item dixerunt quod ut repertum in utroque Gsolreut, tam gravi quam acuto, cum omnibus suis nominibus per ♮ quadrum cantabatur, eo quod in tali ordine mi
30 de bfa♮mi mixtum reperiebatur, unde primus ordo per b rotundum cantari dicitur, quia eius fa a quo indicationem sumere videtur b rotundum ipsum b rotundum famulatur, ut dictum est supra; secundus vero ordo per ♮ quadrum cantari dicitur, quia eius mi a quo indicationem sumere videtur ♮ quadrum famulatur ipsum ♮ quadrum, ut etiam dictum est superius.

7–8 et similiter in Csolfaut *om.* L ‖ 9 cantaretur et universaliter omne ut in C repertum cum suis nominibus ipsum sequentibus L ‖ 10 varitio B ‖ 11 dicuntur [quinque] B ‖ 14 antiqui huius artis L ‖ 15 etiam]in L ‖ 18 sumit exordium]principiatur L ‖ 19 aliquo in ipsum B ‖ 29 quadrum *in marg.* B ‖ 31–32 ipsum b rotundum *om.* B ‖ 33–34 ♮ quadrum famulatur ipsum ♮ quadrum]famulatur ♮ quadrum B ‖

because it is much easier in such mutations for the human voice to hold the same pitch than to vary it a little, as anyone can try for himself. This is therefore more natural and consequently said to be "natural," since the more natural for the voice—and held to be "natural"—is that which is discerned as being easier. No wonder, then, if the order of those names in the mutations of which no variation of pitch whatever is made was said to be sung "through nature." With good reason, the masters of this art maintained on this ground that the *ut* found in C-*faut* and similarly in C-*solfaut* with all its names following it—*re, mi, fa, sol, la*—was sung "through nature" because no variation of pitch whatever was made in the mutations of these. And I said "with all its names" because the remaining five names following *ut*—*re, mi, fa, sol, la*—are called "its" names, since they must be governed by it, as if by their chief, their beginning, because they always follow the nature of that *ut*.

The ancient authors maintained further that the order of names in any of which a variation of pitch was made in mutating that name to another was sung not "through nature" but in another way. Because such a variation of pitch in such mutations was found nowhere in the musical hand except in the expression b-*fa*-♮-*mi*, which begins with B, they maintained that the order of names in any of which a variation of pitch was made in mutating to another name in that same part of the musical hand was said to be sung "through B." Furthermore, because in b-*fa*-♮-*mi* two Bs are found differently drawn (as has been seen above)[20]—round b and square ♮—, they maintained that one particular order was said to be sung "through round b" and another "through square ♮": the one was said to be sung "through round b" that took the *fa* of b-*fa*-♮-*mi*, while the other was said to be sung "through square ♮" that seemed to possess in itself the *mi* of b-*fa*-♮-*mi*. On this basis, then, those ancients said that the *ut* found in either F-*faut*, low or high, with all its names, was sung "through round b" because the *fa* of b-*fa*-♮-*mi* was found placed in that order; again, they said that the *ut* found in either G-*solreut*, low or high, with all its names, was sung "through square ♮" because the *mi* of b-*fa*-♮-*mi* was found mixed in that order. Accordingly, the first order is said to be sung "through round b" because the round b serves its *fa*, from which round b seems to take its designation, as was said above, but the second order is said to be sung "through square ♮," because the square ♮ serves its *mi*, from which square ♮ seems to take its designation, as was also said above.[21]

---

[20]*Plana musica* 1.3 (40–43).

[21]*Plana musica* 1.3 (40–43).

58

⟨9.⟩ Scias tamen, ne in nominibus tibi insurgat difficultas, quod istud binum B, scilicet b rotundum et ♮ quadrum, solet duobus aliis diversis nominibus nominari, scilicet b molle et ♮ durum, et merito, quod satis discernitur in voces elevando, quoniam per primum b, scilicet rotundum, vox

5 molliter atque dulciter elevatur cum inde semitonium causetur, quod dulcius tono reputatur, et ideo b molle nominatur; per secundum vero ♮, scilicet quadrum, vox duriter atque aspere elevatur, cum inde tonus causetur, qui respectu semitonii quodammodo durus reputatur, et ideo ♮ durum nuncupatur, et propter hoc primum b scriptum fuit sub forma rotunda et absque ullo

10 angulo, et secundum ♮ sub forma quadra et angulis involutum, quoniam anguli asperitatum causa, ut asserunt naturales esse dicuntur, et defectus angulorum pro lenitatum causa apud ipsos reputatur, qua de causa dicunt celos sub forma rotunda fore procreatos; nec mireris si ista magis per elevationem quam per depositionem vocis agnosci habeant, cum naturalius sit

15 voci ab infimo incipere et ad supremum ascendere quam e contra, eo quod sibi facilius esse videtur, ut potest quilibet in se experiri; item quia nobilior est ascensus quam descensus.

Habes ergo in suma sex nomina notarum triplici variatione cantari posse, scilicet per naturam, per b rotundum sive molle, et per ♮ quadrum sive

20 durum, ad cuius variationis maiorem noticiam tale solet assignari carmen:
C naturam dat,
F b molle,
G quoque ♮ quadrum;
quod carmen sic intelligi habet, quod omne ut in dictione per C incipiente

25 repertum cum omnibus suis nominibus cantari habet per naturam, et propter hoc habes quod ut de Cfaut et de Csolfaut cum omnibus suis nominibus cantari habent per naturam; omne vero ut in dictione per F incipiente repertum cum omnibus suis nominibus cantari habet per b rotundum sive molle; quapropter habes quod ut utriusque Ffaut, tam gravis quam acuti, cum

30 omnibus suis nominibus cantari habet per b rotundum sive molle; omne vero

16–17 *Huc pertinet emendatio quae in L invenitur:* ... ut potest quilibet in se experiri quoniam facilius est cuilibet graviorem vocem quam facere possit assumere et ad acutiorem quam facere possit ascendere quam e contrario; item quia nobilior est ascensus ...

13 fore]fuisse L ‖ 23 ♮ *om.* L ‖ 26 et etiam ut L ‖

9. Know, nevertheless, lest a difficulty arise with names, that these two Bs, "round b" and "square ♮," are in common practice named with two other different names, "soft b" and "hard ♮," and with good reason. This is discerned adequately in elevating pitches. Inasmuch as through the first, the round b, the pitch is elevated softly and sweetly since, then, a semitone is caused, which is held to be sweeter than the tone, it is thus named "soft b." Inasmuch as through the second, the square ♮, the pitch is elevated in a hard and harsh manner, since, then, a tone is caused, which is held to be hard in a certain way with respect to the semitone, it is thus called "hard ♮." For this reason, the first b was written in a round form, without any angle, and the second ♮ in a square form, enveloped by angles, inasmuch as those ancient authors (as they asserted was said to be natural) hold angles to be the cause of harshness and the lack of angles the cause of softness. On this basis, they say that the heavens were created in a round form. Do not wonder if these things must be recognized more in elevation of pitch than in deposition, since it is more natural for the voice to begin from the lowest and ascend to the highest than vice versa because that seems to be easier, as anyone can try for himself, and because ascent is nobler than descent.[22]

In summary, then, you grasp that the six names of notes can be sung with three variations: "through nature," "through round or soft b," and "through square or hard ♮." For greater knowledge of this variation, this verse is customarily affixed:

> C indicates nature,
> F soft b,
> and G square ♮.[23]

This verse must be understood thus: every *ut* found in an expression beginning with C, with all its names, must be sung "through nature." For this reason, you grasp that the *ut* of C-*faut* and of C-*solfaut*, with all its names, must be sung "through nature"; that every *ut* found in an expression beginning with F, on the other hand, with all its names, must be sung "through round or soft b." For this reason, you grasp that the *ut* of either F-*faut*, low or high, with all its names, must be sung "through round or soft b"; every *ut* found in

---

17–18 ... as anyone can try for himself, inasmuch as it is easier for anyone to take the lowest pitch he can make and ascend to the highest he can make than vice versa; and because ascent is nobler ...

---

[22]Prosdocimo will return to this point in *Plana musica* 2.3 and 2.4 (84–85 and 86–87).

[23]Similar verses are common in fourteenth- and fifteenth-century theory. See for instance Philippe de Vitry, *Ars nova* 9 (ed. Reaney et al., 19); Nicolaus de Capua, *Compendium Musicale* (ed. La Fage, 311).

ut in dictione per G incipiente repertum cum omnibus suis nominibus cantari
habet per ♮ quadrum sive durum, et propter hoc habes quod ut de gamaut et
utriusque Gsolreut, tam gravis quam acuti, cum omnibus suis nominibus
cantari debet per ♮ quadrum sive durum, nec te molestet ut de gamaut cum
5 omnibus suis nominibus in quorum mutationibus nulla penitus fit vocis variatio, quapropter dicere habeas ipsum cantari debere per naturam, et non per
♮ quadrum sive durum, quia hoc non est nisi ratione defectus nominis in
quod aliud nomen mutari possit, scilicet in ♮mi tercia dictione, unde si in
tali dictione essent ita duo nomina que inter se mutari possent sicut in
10 utroque bfa♮mi tam accuto quam superacuto, ita in ipsa fieret vocis variatio
in tali mutatione sicut in aliis; cantari ergo ita habet per ♮ quadrum sive
durum ut de gamaut cum suis nominibus sicut alia ut in aliis dictionibus per
G incipientibus reperta.

⟨10.⟩   Sed quia nomina notarum in lineis vel spatiis positarum absque ullo
15 ullo signo agnoscere non possemus, ut verbi gratia que nota ut nominaretur
et que re et que mi et que fa et que sol et que la, invenerunt antiqui quedam
signa que in principiis linearum vel spatiorum ponebant et que nomina notarum sparsim per lineas et spatia positarum clare manifestabant, et hec signa
fuerunt tria, secundum quod triplex est modus nomina notarum proferendi
20 superius recitatus, scilicet natura, b rotundum, et ♮ quadrum, que signa sunt
tres litere, scilicet b rotundum, C, et F; unde b rotundum acceperunt ut modo
cantandi qui b rotundum nominatur famularetur, sed quia in b tali nullum
reperitur nomen note quod per b rotundum cantari habeat nisi hoc nomen fa,
voluerunt ipsi antiqui, et bene, invenire literas in quarum dictionibus reperi-
25 retur fa aliorum duorum modorum, scilicet nature et ♮ quadri, et hoc ut ars
facilior redderetur, quia facilius est memorie commendare quod ubicunque
ponitur aliquod istorum trium signorum, sive in linea sive in spatio, habeamus dicere hoc nomen fa quod sic est, quam quod ad quodlibet ipsorum
trium signorum dicere habeamus unum nomen per se et ab alio diversum, ut
30 gratia exempli ad b fa, ad C mi, et ad F re, vel aliqua alia nomina ab his
diversa; et ob hoc invenerunt predicti antiqui has duas literas, scilicet C et F.
Invenerunt nanque C ut ♮ quadro famularetur, quia in ipso solo C fa ♮ quadri
reperitur; hanc vero literam F invenerunt ut nature famularetur, quia in ipso
solo F fa de natura reperitur. Habes igitur quare antiqui has tres literas
35 superius nominatas, scilicet b rotundum, C, et F, pro signis acceperunt, et
quomodo intentio ipsorum fuit quod ubicunque poneretur aliquod istorum
signorum, sive in linea sive in spatio, ibi diceretur hoc nomen fa, quia vole-

an expression beginning with G, with all its names, must be sung "through square or hard ♮." For this reason, you grasp that the *ut* of *gamma-ut* and of either G-*solreut*, low or high, with all its names, must be sung "through square or hard ♮." Do not let the *ut* of *gamma-ut*, with all its names, bother you in the mutations of which no variation of pitch whatever is made—for which reason, you might say that it ought to be sung through nature and not through square or hard ♮—because this is only by reason of a lack of a name to which another name could be mutated, that is, in ♮-*mi*, the third expression. Accordingly, if in this expression there had been two names between which a mutation could have been made, as in either b-*fa*-♮-*mi*, the high or the very high, so a variation of pitch could have been made in it in such mutations as in the others. Therefore, *ut* of *gamma-ut*, with all its names, must be sung through square or hard ♮ like the other instances of *ut* found in the other expressions beginning with G.

10. But because we would not have been able to recognize the names of notes placed on lines or in spaces—as for instance which note might be named *ut*, which *re*, which *mi*, which *fa*, which *sol*, and which *la*—without some sign, the ancients discovered certain signs that they placed at the beginning of lines or spaces and that manifested clearly the names of notes placed here and there on lines and in spaces. These signs were three, just as there are three manners of delivering the names of notes recited above, nature, round b, and square ♮. The signs are the three letters, round b, C, and F. Accordingly, they took round b so that it would serve the manner of singing that is named "round b," but because on this b no name of a note is found that must be sung through round b except the name *fa*, those ancients wished, and properly, to discover letters in the expressions of which the *fa*s of the two other manners, those of nature and of square ♮, might be found. They wished this so that the art might be rendered easier because it is easier to commit to memory that wherever any of these three signs is placed, whether on a line or in a space, we should have to say the name *fa* (which is so) than that we should have to say one name for whichever one of these three signs and a different name for another: for example, to say *fa* at b, *mi* at C, and *re* at F, or any other names different from these. On that account, the aforesaid ancients discovered the two letters C and F. They discovered C, to be sure, so that it would serve square ♮ because in C alone is found the *fa* of square ♮; they discovered the letter F, on the other hand, so that it would serve nature because in F alone is found the *fa* of nature. You grasp, then, why the ancients took these three letters named above (round b, C, and F) as signs and how it was their intention that wherever any one of these signs might be placed, whether on a line or in a space, there the name *fa*

bant, et bene, ut ars facilior redderetur, quod illud nomen note quod per unum illorum signorum importatur per omnia tria signa importaretur.

Voluerunt ulterius isti antiqui quod duo supradictorum trium signorum essent in linea, scilicet C et F, sic quod voluerunt per hoc signum C nos
5 intelligere C accutum, quod in Csolfaut reperitur, et per hoc signum F F grave, quod in Ffaut reperitur, et ratio huius est, et primo de hoc signo C, quoniam si per hoc signum C voluissent intelligere C spatiale et non lineale, statim fuisset dubium an istud C fuisset C de Cfaut an de Csolfa, que ambo spatialia esse ponuntur, et propter hoc dubium removere, voluerunt, et bene,
10 C lineale, quod unicum reperitur, scilicet in Csolfaut, sumere, et non spatiale, quod saltim in duobus locis reperitur, ut visum est. De hoc vero signo F dico quod si ipsum spatiale accepissent et non lineale, tunc nullum habuissemus signum per quod agnoscere potuissemus nomina notarum in dictionibus gravibus existentium, que dictiones, ut supradictum est, locum tenorum
15 tenere videntur. Tercium vero signum, scilicet b rotundum, ab istis antiquis aliquando ponebatur in linea et aliquando in spatio; si in linea, per ipsum b rotundum intelligebant b rotundum in bfa♮mi superacuto existens et non B in ♮ gravi existens, quia illud est quadrum et non rotundum, et sic scribi habet in manu musicali, dato quod ut plurimum apud ignorantes sub forma
20 rotunda scribatur; si vero in spatio ponebatur, per ipsum b rotundum intelligebant ipsi antiqui b rotundum in bfa♮mi acuto existens.

Scias tamen, ne in deceptionem incurras, quod moderni propter maiorem decorationem has tres literas, que sunt nobis signa, aliter figurant, ut sic, ◗,
◗ , ✗; unde secundum intentionem horum modernorum primum signum
25 ponitur pro b rotundo, secundum vero pro C, et tercium pro F; et sic habes quomodo signum b rotundi potest multipliciter figurari, ut sic, b, vel sic, ◗; et similiter signum ♮ quadri, ut sic, C, vel sic, ◗ ; et similiter signum nature, ut sic, F, vel sic, ✗, vel adhuc sic, ◗ , secundum alios. Et vocant isti moderni hec signa methaforice claves cantus, uti etiam sua signa voca-

23–24 *Huc pertinet emendatio quae in L invenitur:* … has tres literas, que sunt nobis signa, scilicet b rotundum, C, et F, aliter figurant, ut sic, ◗◗✗◗; unde secundum intentionem …
25 *Huc pertinet emendatio quae in L invenitur:* … et tercium et quartum pro F …

2 importeretur *fort.* L ‖ 5 intelligere debere L | signum F]signum F nos intelligere debere L ‖ 9 ponuntur ut notum est L ‖ 17 B]♮ L ‖ 18 ♮]♮mi L ‖

should be said because they wished (and properly, so that the art would be rendered easier) that the name of the note that was conveyed by one of those signs would be conveyed by all three signs.

Those ancients wished, further, that two of the aforesaid three signs, C and F, would be on a line; so, they wished that we should understand by the sign C high C, which is found on C-*solfaut*, and by the sign F low F, which is found on F-*faut*. The reason for this is (first, for the sign C): inasmuch as if by the sign C they had wished to understand C in a space and not on a line, the problem would have arisen forthwith whether the C were the C of C-*faut* or of C-*solfa*, both of which are placed in a space. In order to remove this problem, they wished, and properly, to take the C on a line, which is found once, on C-*solfaut*, and not C in a space, which at all events is found in two locations, as has been seen. Of the sign F, I say that if they had taken it in a space and not on a line, we would then have had no sign through which we could have recognized the names of the notes in the low expressions, expressions that, as was said above, seem to hold the position of tenors.[24] But the third sign, round b, was placed by the ancients sometimes on a line and sometimes in a space. If on a line, they understood through that round b the round b in very high b-*fa-♮-mi* and not the B in low ♮ because that B is square and not round and it must be so written in the musical hand (granted that among the ignorant, it is most often written in a round form). But if they placed it in a space, the ancients understood through that round b the round b in high b-*fa-♮-mi*.

Know, nevertheless—lest you go astray—that the moderns, for the sake of greater ornament, draw these three letters—which for us are signs—differently, like this, ▞, ▞, ✸. Accordingly, following the intention of these moderns, the first sign is placed for round b, the second for C, and the third for F. So, you grasp how the sign of round b can be drawn in many ways, like this, b, or this, ▞; similarly the sign of square ♮, like this, C, or this, ▞; and similarly the sign of nature, like this, F, or this, ✸—or even this, ▞, according to others. Those moderns metaphorically call these signs the "keys"[25] of chant, as the ancients also called their signs, and properly. The

---

25–26 ... draw these three letters (round b, C, and F)—which for us are signs—differently, like this, ▞ ▞ ✸ ▞ . Accordingly, following the intention ...

27–28 ... and the third and fourth for F ...

---

[24]*Plana musica* 1.4 (42–45).

[25]From *clef*, the French derivative of Latin *clavis* (key), comes our English *clef* for the sign at the beginning of the staff showing where C, G, or F are located.

verunt antiqui, et bene, et dicunt tam moderni quam antiqui primum signum
esse clavem b rotundi sive mollis, secundum vero esse clavem ♮ quadri sive
duri, et tercium esse clavem nature; et sumitur hec methafora hoc modo,
quoniam sicut per claves hostia apperiuntur, ut inde pateat introitus cuilibet
5   manifestus, ita per hec signa apperitur nobis introitus ad quemlibet cantum
pronuntiandum, eo quod cognito quod in linea vel spatio ubi est clavis
dicere habeamus hoc nomen fa, scimus qualiter alias notas superiores vel
inferiores nominare habeamus, cum ista sex nomina sciamus sic gradatim
ascendere vel descendere, ut re mi fa sol la, la sol fa mi re ut, per debitas
10 lineas atque spatia. Si bene tamen consideramus, perpendere possumus hec
signa modernorum satis assimilari signis antiquorum prius acceptis, scilicet
tribus literis superius nominatis, licet pauci ad hoc advertant.

    Sunt tamen aliqui moderni, non musici sed musice destrutores, qui
putantes se magnum miraculum operari, eorum figurant cantus absque ullo
15 signo sive clavi, et pessime, pulcrius in musica dimittentes, quoniam tunc
nullam rationem habere possunt quare in aliquo ipsorum cantuum potius
dicere habeant ut quam re, et potius mi quam fa, et potius sol quam la, vel
aliquod aliud nomen; ymo ubi putant quid laboriosum fecisse nichil operati
sunt, cum valde difficilius sit invenire quam inventa dimittere, ymo proprius
20 loquendo unum facillimum et reliquum difficillimum fore comuniter experi-
mur. Ponunt et etiam isti moderni in eorum cantibus aliquando pro clavibus
cifras arismetricales, ymo quod plus est, totum cantum cum istis cifris aris-
metricalibus figurant, saltim in cantu mensurato nullam notam musicalem
ibidem apponendo, ex qua figuratione se super alios putant supermilitari,
25 quod totum pessime operatum est, cum diversarum artium diversa debeant
esse signa, quod bene apud antiquos notum est, qui alia et alia signa arismetrice et musice applicaverunt, cum signa nobis numeros denotantia arismetrice et signa debitam elevationem vel depositionem vocum nobis denotantia musice tribuerunt.

---

3 *Huc pertinet emendatio quae in L invenitur:* ... et tercium et quartum esse
clavem nature; ...
16 *Huc pertinet emendatio quae in L invenitur:* ... quare in aliquo loco
ipsorum cantuum ...

---

1 et dicunt *in marg.* B ‖ 10 tamen bene L ‖ 24 supermilitari]militari L ‖ 26 est]fuit L ‖ 27–
28 arismetrice assignaverunt L ‖

moderns and ancients alike say that the first sign is the key of round or soft b, the second is the key of square or hard ♮, and the third is the key of nature. This metaphor is taken in this manner: inasmuch as it is by keys that doors are opened so that an entrance is made manifest to whomever, so it is by these signs that an entrance to the pronunciation of some chant is opened to us because when it is recognized that on the line or in the space where there is a key we must say the name *fa*, we know how we must name the other, higher or lower, notes,[26] since we know that these six names ascend or descend stepwise thus, *ut re mi fa sol la, la sol fa mi re ut*, through the requisite lines and spaces. If we consider it properly, we can assess these signs of the moderns to be sufficiently assimilated to the signs of the ancients that were taken earlier, the three letters named above, although the moderns attend to this but little.

Nevertheless, there are some moderns—not musicians but destroyers of music—who, thinking that they work a great marvel, draw their chants without any sign or key (and most unacceptably), excluding the more beautiful in music inasmuch as they can then have no reason why in some one of their chants they must say *ut* rather than *re*, *mi* rather than *fa*, and *sol* rather than *la*, or any other name. Rather, where they think that they have made something involving a lot of work, they have accomplished nothing, since it is much more difficult to discover than to exclude what has been discovered; or rather, speaking more properly, we commonly ascertain that one is very easy and the remaining one very difficult. These moderns sometimes even place arithmetic symbols in their chants for keys. What is more, they draw an entire chant with these arithmetic symbols, even to the point of placing no musical note in a metric chant;[27] and with this sort of figuration they think themselves supermen above others. All of this is done most unacceptably, since there ought to be different signs for the different arts, as the ancients properly knew; they applied one set of signs to arithmetic and another to music, since they apportioned to arithmetic the signs that denote to us numbers and to music the signs that denote to us requisite elevation and deposition of pitch.

2–3 ... and the third and fourth are the key of nature ...
17–18 ... why at some position in their chants ...

---

[26]On the metaphor of the key, cf. Marchetto, *Lucidarium* 14.1.4 (ed. Herlinger, 538–39). Marchetto, however, considers only two clefs, F and C.

[27]Though many sixteenth-century lute and keyboard tablatures use numerals, *Plana musica* is an important witness for the use of numeric systems of notation by the early fifteenth century.

⟨11.⟩ Sed pro maiori ac ultimata istius manus musicalis declaratione ad solutionem quorundam dubiorum circa ipsam manum musicalem oriri potentium accedamus, unde primo posset aliquis querere, et bene, quare est quod hec manus musicalis potius incepta est per G, quod est ultima litera
5   septem literarum alphabeti per quas incepte sunt omnes viginti dictiones in hac manu musicali reperte, quam per A, quod est ipsarum septem literarum, ac totius alphabeti, in ordine litera prima, cum hac de causa rationabilius fuisset ipsam manum musicalem incepisse per A quam per G. Pro solutione huius dubii est sciendum quod sex nomina notarum superius pluries nomi-
10 nata non fuerunt ab uno et eodem inventore ac eodem tempore reperta, sed prius inventa fuerunt quatuor nomina intermedia, scilicet re, mi, fa, sol, quam duo extrema, scilicet ut, la, et prius la quam ut, sic quod tunc temporis re primum nomen note erat in ordine, et propter hoc ipsi nomini re, quod tunc primum nomen existebat, A, quod erat septem literarum in hac manu
15 acceptarum, ac totius alphabeti, in ordine primum, associaverunt, et primam dictionem composuerunt, scilicet Are, que tunc temporis prima dictionum in manu existebat, et ipsam in principio manus apposuerunt, sed postquam hoc nomen ut per successores subtili investigatione fuit inventum, et pro duce sive principio aliorum nominum constitutum, voluerunt ipsum nomen ut
20 nomini quod prius principatum obtinebat, scilicet re, tanquam eius subdito, preponere, et unam septem literarum sibi tribuere, sed eorum predecessores, qui alia quinque nomina invenerunt, in honorem habere volentes, eo quod ad ulterius speculandum viam eis tradiderant, mutare nolluerunt ea que ab ipsis predecessoribus acta fuerant, et ob hoc A ipsi re dimiserunt, et G ipsi ut tri-
25 buerunt, quia in reiteratione septem literarum superius acceptarum, semper post G sequi immediate debet A, et sic semper ipsum G precedere A, ut notum est, et sic aliam dictionem, que nunc prima in ordine manus existit, scilicet Gut sive gamaut, quod idem est, ut dictum est supra, composuerunt, et sic manum per G et non per A inceperunt, quod est solutio dubii. Memo-
30 rantes tamen gramaticam nostram ex greca gramatica originem sumpsisse, pariterque musicam, ut hoc ostenderent in principio manus musicalis G gre-cum apposuerunt, quod sic scribitur, Γ, ut visum est supra, atque gama apud ipsos grecos nominatur, secundum quod etiam scripsi superius.

---

7 litera prima in ordine L ‖ 15 ac etiam totius L | in ordine primum]litera prima in ordine L | primam]prima B ‖ 18 inventum fuit L ‖ 19 ut nomen L ‖ 21 precessores B ‖ 22 invenerant nomina L ‖ 24 precessoribus B | acta]apta B ‖ 26 debet inmediate sequi L | ipsum *om.* L | precedere]debet precedere L ‖ 27 et sic]quare L | manus *om.* L ‖ 28 scilicet *sup. lin.*B ‖ 30 tamen isti antiqui predecessores nostri L ‖ 32 supra visum est L ‖

11. But for a greater and definitive explanation of the musical hand, let us approach the solution of certain formidable problems concerning the musical hand. First, someone could have asked (and properly) why it is that this musical hand was begun with G, which is the last letter of the seven letters of the alphabet with which all twenty expressions found in this musical hand were begun, rather than with A, which is the first letter in order of those seven letters and of the entire alphabet, since on this basis, it would have been more reasonable for the musical hand to have begun with A rather than with G. For the solution of this problem, one must know that the six names of notes named above several times were not found by one and the same discoverer and at the same time; rather, the four intermediate names, *re, mi, fa, sol*, had been discovered before the two extreme ones, *ut, la*, and *la* before *ut*. So, at one time *re* was the first name of a note in order, and for this reason, with that name *re*, which at that time was the first name, they associated A, which was the first in order of the seven letters taken for this hand and of the entire alphabet. They composed the first expression, A-*re*, which at that time was the first of the expressions in the hand, and they placed it at the beginning of the hand. But after the name *ut* had been discovered by successors through careful investigation and had been constituted the leader or the beginning of the other names, they wished to place that name, *ut*, before the name that had earlier occupied the principal place, *re* (now its subordinate, as it were) and to apportion one of the seven letters to it. But wishing to hold their predecessors in honor, who had discovered the other five names (because the predecessors had handed down to them a way of speculating further), they did not wish to mutate those things that had been accomplished by their predecessors. On that account, they left A to the *re* and attributed G to the *ut*, because in the reiteration of the seven letters taken above, A ought always to follow immediately after G, and thus G ought always to precede A, as is known. So, they composed another expression that now exists as first in order of the hand, G-*ut*—or *gamma-ut*, which is the same thing, as was said above.[28] So, they began the hand with G and not with A, and this is the solution to the problem. Nevertheless, remembering that our grammar had taken its origin from Greek grammar, and music likewise, so that they might show this, they placed at the beginning of the musical hand the Greek G, which is written thus, Γ, as was seen above, and is named *gamma* among the Greeks, as I also wrote above.[29]

---

[28]*Plana musica* 1.3 (40–43).

[29]*Plana musica* 1.3 (40–43).

68

Scias tamen quod postquam inventum fuit hoc nomen ut, apposuerunt inventores ipsum ut in quibusdam aliarum dictionum sequentium, secundum quod eis visum est fore opportunum; unde ubi primitus dicebatur Cfa apposuerunt hoc nomen ut et composita est hec dictio Cfaut; similiter ubi prius
5 dicebatur Ffa appositum est hoc nomen ut et composita est hec dictio Ffaut; similiter ubi prius dicebatur Gsolre appositum est hoc nomen ut et composita est hec dictio Gsolreut; similiter ubi prius dicebatur Csolfa in C acuto appositum est nomen ut et composita est hec dictio Csolfaut; et isto modo non variatis literis post inventionem ipsius ut prolungaverunt inventores
10 ipsius ut quasdam dictiones, eis addendo solum hoc nomen ut, secundum quod visum est.

Ulterius posset dubitare aliquis de ordinatione sex nominum pluries superius nominatorum, scilicet ut, re, mi, fa, sol, la, in suprascriptis viginti dictionibus repertorum, quare scilicet in quibusdam illarum viginti dic-
15 tionum unicum solum ponitur nomen, in quibusdam vero duo, et in quibusdam tria, cum solum in tribus locis, scilicet in E gravi, C acuto, et A superacuto, appareat duo posse sufficere, scilicet la, ut, et sic solum ibidem posse fieri mutationem; in aliis vero unicum solum, et per consequens ibi nullam mutationem fieri posse, ut sic viginti una dictiones ordinate sint, sci-
20 licet Gut, Are, bmi, Cfa, Dsol, Elaut, Fre, Gmi, Afa, Bsol, Claut, Dre, Emi, Ffa, Gsol, Alaut, Bre, Cmi, Dfa, Esol, Fla; hoc ultimum F ipsis viginti dictionibus addendo, ut ordo sex vocum totaliter compleatur, sic quod non pos-

2 inventores ipsius ipsum L ‖ 3 Cfa in C gravi L ‖ 5 dicebatur *in marg.* B | Ffa in utroque F, gravi scilicet et acuto L ‖ 6 prius]primo L | Gsolre in utroque G, gravi scilicet et acuto L ‖ 8 nomen]hoc nomen L ‖ 15 ponatur L ‖ 18 in aliis vero]et in aliis L | solum sufficere posse L | 19 viginti una]viginti B ‖ 20 bmi]Bmi L | Gmi]Cmi B ‖ 21–22 ipsis viginti dictionibus addendo]superaddendo L ‖

But know that after the name *ut* had been discovered, the discoverers placed the *ut* in certain of the other following expressions, following the manner that they thought appropriate. Accordingly, where originally C-*fa* had been said, they placed the name *ut* and the expression C-*faut* was composed; similarly, where earlier F-*fa* had been said, the name *ut* was placed and the expression F-*faut* was composed; similarly, where earlier G-*solre* had been said, the name *ut* was placed and the expression G-*solreut* was composed; similarly, where earlier C-*solfa* had been said, in high C, the name *ut* was placed and the expression C-*solfaut* was composed. In this manner, the discoverers of *ut* lengthened certain expressions, not by varying letters after the discovery of *ut* but simply by adding the name *ut*, following the manner seen.

Further, someone could wonder concerning the ordering of the six names named above several times, *ut, re, mi, fa, sol, la,* found in the twenty expressions written above, why it is that in certain of those twenty expressions only a single name is placed, but in certain others two are placed, and in certain others three, since it might appear that two alone, *la* and *ut*, could have sufficed in only three positions, low E, high C, and very high A, and thus mutation could have been made there alone; and that in other positions one single name could have sufficed, and consequently no mutation could have been made there. The twenty-one expressions in order might be: G-*ut*, A-*re*, B-*mi*, C-*fa*, D-*sol*, E-*laut*, F-*re*, G-*mi*, A-*fa*, B-*sol*, C-*laut*, D-*re*, E-*mi*, F-*fa*, G-*sol*, A-*laut*, B-*re*, C-*mi*, D-*fa*, E-*sol*, and F-*la* (adding this last F to the twenty expressions so that the order of the six syllables might be completed right up to the end). So, mutation could only be made from *la* to *ut*

sit fieri mutatio nisi de la in ut et de ut in la, ascendendo vel descendendo, et taliter omnes hee dictiones super manu ordinentur, ut hic,

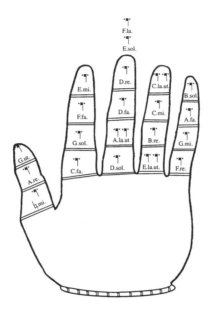

Item etiam est dubium quare in aliqua ipsarum dictionum ponuntur magis aliqua ipsorum nominum quam alia ab illis diversa, ut gratia exempli
5 quare in Gsolreut ponuntur potius solreut quam lafami, et sic de aliis.

Item est dubium quare posite sunt iste viginti dictiones potius super manu sinistra quam super manu dextra, et quare etiam sub tali modo quodammodo circulari, scilicet a summitate policis incipiendo et ad ipsius radicem descendendo, postea per omnes radices aliorum quatuor digitorum
10 progrediendo et ulterius super parvo digito ascendendo, et postea per omnes summitates quatuor digitorum procedendo, demum per nodos intermedios progrediendo, et cetera.
Pro declaratione primorum duorum dubiorum est sciendum quod in quibuslibet sex literis consequenter se habentibus in quibus sex nomina nota-
15 rum ordinate scripta reperiuntur ab ut incipiendo et ad la ordinate per

---

2 manu sinistra L | ut hic *om.* L ‖ 3 Item etiam est dubium]Aliud dubium est L ‖ 5 et sic de aliis *om.* L ‖ 6 Item est dubium]Et est etiam aliud dubium L ‖ 10 progrediendo]progeedi-endo *fort.* B ‖

and from *ut* to *la*, ascending or descending, and all these expressions would be set in such order on the hand, as here:

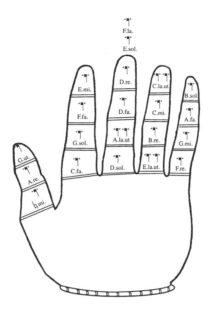

Again, there is also the problem why it is that in some of those expressions, some of those names are placed rather than others different from them: for example, why in G-*solreut* are *sol*, *re*, and *ut* placed rather than *la*, *fa*, and *mi*, and similarly for the other expressions?

Again there is the problem why these twenty expressions were placed on the left hand rather than on the right hand, and why in this somewhat circular manner, beginning from the tip of the thumb and descending to its base, then progressing through the bases of the other four fingers, later ascending up the little finger, then proceeding through the tips of all four fingers, then progressing through the intermediate joints, and so forth?

For the explanation of the first two problems, one must know that in any six adjacent letters in which are found the six names of notes written in order beginning with *ut* and progressing to *la* through the intermediate

nomina notarum intermedia progrediendo, vel e contra, debet hoc totaliter
ordinate scriptum reperiri, sic quod in prima litera debet ut reperiri, et in
secunda re, et in tercia mi, et in quarta fa, et in quinta sol, et in sexta la; et
ideo in prima litera manus repertum est hoc nomen note ut, scilicet in G
5 greco, quod sic scribitur, Γ, ut dictum est supra, et apud ipsos grecos gama
nominatur; in secunda vero, scilicet in A, repertum est hoc nomen re; in tercia vero, scilicet ♮, repertum est mi; in quarta vero, scilicet C, repertum est
fa; in quinta vero, scilicet D, repertum est sol; et in sexta, scilicet E, repertum est la. Sed quia ulterius propter nominum defectum absque mutatione
10 aliqua vocem gradatim elevare non poteramus, fuit neccessarium in ipso E
facere mutationem, et mutare illud la in mi et non in aliud nomen, ut dicere
valeremus in F sequenti hanc vocem fa, quam in ipso F neccessario dicere
debebamus propter fugere tritonum in musica valde dissonum et difficillime
elevationis et depositionis atque apud musicos omnino dimittendum, qui
15 tritonus causatus fuisset supra fa quod in C gravi reperitur si la in E gravi
repertum in aliud nomen quam in mi mutatum fuisset, ut patere potest cuilibet subtiliter inspicienti; quapropter fuit neccessarium associare mi cum la
in ipso E gravi, ut inde mutationes de uno in aliud fieri possent, et sic componere hanc dictionem Elami. Item ulterius fuisset neccessarium in D
20 immediate precedenti ponere re, et in C ut, et hoc ut voces quantum ad
descensum complerentur. Fuit etiam neccessarium in F immediate sequenti
ponere fa, et in G sol, in A acuto la, ut inde voces quantum ad elevationem
complerentur. Est autem tritonus duarum vocum combinatio tribus tonis
contexta. Item propter similes causas fuit neccessarium mutare la repertum
25 in A acuto in mi si ascendere volebamus ab F gravi ad b acutum, et sic
ulterius fuit neccessarium in G gravi immediate precedenti ponere re, et in F
ut, et hoc ut voces quantum ad descensum complerentur. Fuit etiam neccessarium in b acuto immediate sequenti ponere fa, et in C sol, et in D la, ut
inde voces quantum ad ascensum compleri possent. Item quia de litera in
30 literam sibi similem octava consonans formari debet, que ex quinque tonis et
duobus semitoniis constare dicitur, qua de causa accepte fuerunt solum septem litere, ut dictum est supra, et quia etiam in ponendo mi contra fa nunquam fieri potest octava consonans, ut alibi videri habet, eo quod tunc in

---

1 debet [primo] B ‖ 2 sic quod ... reperiri *in marg.* B ‖ 7 ♮]in ♮ L | C]in C L ‖ 8 D]in D L ‖
9 propter *om.* B ‖ 11 aliud]allud *ante corr.* B | ut]et hoc ut L ‖ 12 hanc]in hanc B ‖ 14 qui]q
B ‖ 18 in]i L ‖ 19 fuisset]fuit L ‖ 23 complerentur et sic hucusque habemus necessitatem
talis compositionis sex primarum dictionum gravium L ‖ 25 accutum sine tritono L ‖ 27
complerentur et sic habentur neccessaria compositionis istius dictionis Ffaut gravis L ‖ 29
ascensum]descensum L ‖ 31–32 septem litere]prime septem litere alphabeti L ‖

names of notes in order—or vice versa—the following ought to be found written completely in order. So, *ut* ought to be found on the first letter, *re* on the second, *mi* on the third, *fa* on the fourth, *sol* on the fifth, and *la* on the sixth. Thus was the note name *ut* found on the first letter of the hand, that is, on the Greek G, which is written thus, Γ (as was said above),[30] and among the Greeks is named *gamma*; the name *re* was found on the second letter, that is, on A; *mi* was found on the third, that is, ♮; *fa* was found on the fourth, that is, C; *sol* was found on the fifth, that is, D; and *la* was found on the sixth, that is, E. But because we were not able for lack of other names to elevate stepwise further without some mutation, it was necessary to make a mutation on that E, and to mutate that *la* to *mi*, and not to another name, so that we would have the ability to say the syllable *fa* on the following F. We were necessarily obliged to say *fa* on that F for the sake of evading the tritone, which in music is strongly dissonant and very difficult in elevation and deposition and among musicians is absolutely to be excluded. This tritone would have been caused above the *fa* that is found on low C if the *la* found on low E had been mutated to a name other than *mi*, as can be evident to anyone inspecting it carefully.[31] For this reason, it was necessary to associate *mi* with *la* on that low E so that mutations from one to the other could thus be made and so make up the expression E-*lami*. Again, it was further necessary to place *re* on the D immediately preceding and *ut* on C so that the syllables might be completed with respect to descent. It was also necessary to place *fa* on the F immediately following, *sol* on G, and *la* on high a so that the syllables might thus be completed with respect to elevation. The tritone is the interval of two pitches made up of three tones. Again, on similar bases, it was necessary to mutate the *la* found on high A to *mi* if we wanted to ascend from low F to to high b, and thus it was necessary, further, to place *re* on the low G immediately preceding and *ut* on F so that the syllables might be completed with respect to descent. It was also necessary to place *fa* on the high b immediately following, *sol* on C, and *la* on D so that the syllables could thus be completed with respect to ascent. Again, because the consonant octave, which is said to consist of five tones and two semitones, ought to be formed from one letter to a similar letter (on this basis, only seven letters were taken, as was said above)[32] and because a consonant octave can never be made by placing *mi* against *fa* (as must be seen else-

---

[30]*Plana musica* 1.3 (40–41).

[31]That is, any other mutation would have produced a whole tone above the E and thus a tritone above the C.

[32]*Plana musia* 1.6 (46–47).

74

ipsa octava reperirentur plura semitonia et pauciores toni aut plures toni et
pauciora semitonia quam esse deberent, ideo fuit neccessarium ponere in
ipso b acuto unum nomen note quod bonam octavam consonantem cum mi
reperto in B gravi causaret, sed quia non videbatur aliquod habilius ad hoc
5 quam nomen sibi simile, scilicet mi, ideo ipsum mi in ipso b acuto posuerunt, et ut melius ostenderent hoc mi in b acuto repertum fore simile alteri
mi quod in ♮ gravi reperitur, posuerunt immediate ante hoc mi in b acuto
repertum unum B simile ♮ gravi, scilicet ♮ quadrum, et inde formata fuit hec
dictio bfa♮mi, sic quod ♮ quadrum posuerunt inter fa et mi huius dictionis
10 bfa♮mi, ut apparet. Et ex hoc fuit postea neccessarium ut inde voces quantum ad descensum compleri possent in A accuto immediate precedenti
ponere re, et in G ut; et quantum ad ascensum in C acuto immediate
sequenti ponere fa, et in D sol, et in E la; item similiter propter fugere tritonum propter ipsius dissonantiam musice inimicum, et propter ad superiores
15 voces ascendere, fuit neccessarium la repertum in E acuto mutare in hoc
nomen mi et non in aliud, si ascendere volebamus a C acuto ad F acutum
tritonum dimittendo; et per consequens, ut inde voces quantum ad descensum complerentur, fuit neccessarium in D acuto immediate precedente
ponere re, et in C ut, et quantum ad ascensum ponere in F acuto immediate
20 sequenti fa, et in G sol, et in A superacuto la. Item propter eandem causam
fuit neccessarium mutare la repertum in A superacuto in mi si ab F acuto
ad b superacutum ascendere volebamus tritonum fugiendo; et per consequens, ut voces quantum ad ascensum et descensum complerentur, fuit neccessarium in G acuto immediate precedenti ponere re, et in F ut; item in b
25 superacuto immediate sequenti ponere fa, et in C sol, et in D la. Item propter sumere octavam consonantem ad mi repertum in b acuto fuit neccessarium ponere mi in b superacuto et eodem modo figurare bfa♮mi superacutum sicut figuratur bfa♮mi acutum, sic quod propter hoc fuit ulterius
neccessarium ut voces quantum ad ascensum et descensum complerentur
30 ponere in A superacuto immediate precedente re, et in G acuto ut; item in

3 b]B L ‖ 4 B]b B ‖ 5 ipsum]primum L | b]B L ‖ 7 ♮]B L | b]B L ‖ 8 ♮ (*pr.*)]B L | scilicet
unum L | inde postea L ‖ 12 ut quare habetur neccessitas compositionis istarum trium dic-
tionum, scilicet Gsolreut gravis et Alamire et bfa♮mi acutarum L | et (*sec.*)]demum L |
ascensum fuit neccessarium L ‖ 14 propter ipsius]ob sui L | et etiam L ‖ 16 aliud nomen L ‖
19 ut et inde habita est neccessitas compositionis istarum trium dictionum acutarum, scilicet
Csolfaut, Dlasolre, Elami L | et (*sec.*)]demum L | ascensum fuit neccessarium L ‖ 22 b]B L ‖
23 quantum]quam L | ascensum et *om.* L ‖ 24 ut sic habetur neccessitas compositionis huius
dictionis Ffaut acute L | item pro ascensu fuit neccessarium L ‖ 26 b]B L ‖ 27 mi sibi simile
L | b]B L ‖ 29 ad ascensum *in marg.* B ‖

where)[33]—because then there would be found more semitones and fewer tones or more tones and fewer semitones than there ought to have been—, it was therefore necessary to place on the high b the one name of a note that would cause a good consonant octave with the *mi* found on the low B. Because it did not seem that there was anything more suitable for this purpose than the name similar to the other, *mi*, they therefore placed *mi* on the high b. The better to show this *mi* found on high b to be similar to the other *mi* that is found on low ♮, they placed a B similar to low ♮, that is, square ♮, immediately before the *mi* found on the high b, and thus was formed the expression "b-*fa*-♮-*mi*." So, they placed the square ♮ between the *fa* and the *mi* of the expression "b-*fa*-♮-*mi*," as is evident. And because of this, it was later necessary—so that the syllables could be completed with respect to descent—to place *re* on the high A immediately preceding and *ut* on G, and with respect to ascent, to place *fa* on the high C immediately following, *sol* on D, and *la* on E. Again, similarly, in order to evade the tritone (inimical to music on account of its dissonance) and on account of ascending to higher syllables, it was necessary to mutate the *la* found on high E to the name *mi* and not to another if we wished to ascend from the high C to the high F while excluding the tritone. Consequently, so that the syllables might then be completed with respect to descent, it was necessary to place *re* on the high D immediately preceding and *ut* on C, and with respect to ascent, to place *fa* on the high F immediately following, *sol* on G, and *la* on very high A. Again, on the same basis, it was necessary to mutate the *la* found on very high A to *mi* if we wished to ascend from the high F to the very high b while evading the tritone. Consequently, so that the syllables might be completed with respect to ascent and descent, it was necessary to place *re* on the high G immediately preceding and *ut* on F, and again to place *fa* on the very high b immediately following, *sol* on C, and *la* on D. Again, to take an octave consonant with the *mi* found on the high b, it was necessary to place *mi* on the very high b and to draw the very high b-*fa*-♮-*mi* in the same manner as the high b-*fa*-♮-*mi* is drawn. So, on account of this, it was necessary further—so that the syllables could be completed with respect to ascent and descent—to place *re* on the very high A immediately preceding and *ut* on the high G; again, *fa* on the very high C, *sol* on D, and *la* on E. Thus you

---

[33]Prosdocimo, *Contrapunctus* 4.6 (ed. Herlinger, 62–65).

C superacuto fa, in D sol, et in E la. Habes igitur neccessitatem talis compositionis omnium viginti dictionum que in manu reperte sunt.

Sed causa quare predicte viginti dictiones potius posite sunt super manu sinistra quam super manu dextra, quod est tercium dubium in ordine quatuor
5 ultimorum dubiorum superius recitatorum, est hec, quia antiqui voluerunt ad maiorem comoditatem ponere has dictiones super manu a qua incipit modus noster scribendi, qui est a parte sinistra tendens versus partem dextram, qua de causa etiam inceperunt ipsas dictiones in parte sinistra ipsiusmet manus sinistre, scilicet in police. Causa autem quare sub tali modo circulari proces-
10 sit, quod est quartum dubium in ordine quatuor ultimorum dubiorum supratactorum, fuit hec, quoniam antiqui voluerunt in has viginti dictiones super manu sinistra ordinando similem modum observare quem observabant in reiteratione sex nominum notarum superius nominatorum, qui modus et circularis. Sed causa quare potius illam circuitionem ceperunt quam aliquam
15 aliam ab hac diversam fuit ut dictiones graves in loco infimo ponerentur, quod satis rationabile existit, cum etiam tales voces locum infimum obtinere videantur. A police autem inceperunt tanquam a primo manus digitorum.

---

9 *Huc pertinet emendatio quae in L invenitur:* ... scilicet in police. Et aliter potest dici quod hoc fecerunt ut comodius ostendere possemus quid super manu cantaremus; comodius nanque ostendimus cum manu dextra quam cum manu sinistra et ergo dictiones posuerunt super manu sinistra ut ipsas cum dextra ostendere possemus. Mos nanque erat antiquorum adhuc tentus apud grecos omnia cantare super manu et in manu dextra baculum tenebant per quem ostendebant loca manus sinistre secundum quod in ascensu et descensu loca variabant. Sed causa quare ...

16–17 *Huc pertinet emendatio quae in L inventiru:* ... locum infimum obtinere videantur. Et si diceres quod hac de causa debuissent ponere dictiones superacutas supra voces acutas, quod tamen non fecerunt, ut notum est, quoniam ipsas in medio, scilicet in iuncturis mediis digitorum posuerunt, excepta dictione Ela, dico quod hoc pro tanto fecerunt quoniam si sic fecissent circulationem processus non observassent. Aliter autem possemus

---

1 in (*pr.*)]et in L | la et sic habetur neccessitas compositionis harum dictionum, scilicet Gsolreut acuti, Alamire, bfa♮⟨mi⟩, Csolfa, Dlasol, et Ela superacutorum L | Habes igitur neccessitatem]Quare modo habes L | talis]totalis L ‖ 2 manu musicali L | sunt et per consequens primi et secundi dubii solutionem L ‖ 5 quia]quoniam L ‖ 8 manus]partis B ‖ 9–10 processit]ordo dictionum in manu musicali procedat L ‖ 10 quartum et ultimum L ‖ 11 quoniam]qui B ‖ 12 observabant]observant B ‖ 15 dictiones [g] B ‖

grasp the necessity of this composition of all twenty expressions that are found in the hand.

But the basis whereby the aforesaid twenty expressions are placed on the left hand rather than on the right—which is the third in order of the four last problems recited above—is this: because the ancients wished, for the sake of greater convenience, to place these expressions on that hand from which our manner of writing begins, which is from the left side proceeding toward the right. It was on this basis that they began those expressions on the left side of that left hand, on the thumb. The basis whereby the sequence progresses in circular fashion—which is the fourth in order of the last four problems touched on above—was this: inasmuch as the ancients wished, in setting in order these twenty expressions on the left hand to observe the same manner they had observed in reiterating the six names of notes named above, this manner is also circular. But the basis whereby they seized on that circuit rather than some other circuit different from it was so that they might place the low expressions in the lowest position, which is sufficiently reasonable, since these pitches do seem to occupy the lowest register. They began from the thumb as from the first of the digits of the hand.

---

9 ... on the thumb. And it can be said another way: they did this so that we could show more conveniently on the hand what we sing: for we show things more conveniently with the right hand than with the left hand, and therefore they placed the expressions on the left hand so we could show them with the right. Certainly it was the custom of the ancients—held up to the present among the Greeks—to sing everything on the hand; and they would hold a rod in the right hand with which they would show the positions on the left hand according to the change of positions in ascent and descent. The basis whereby ...

17–18 ... seem to occupy the lowest register. And if you should say that on this basis they ought to have placed the very high expressions above the high syllables—which, however, they did not do, as is known, inasmuch as (with the exception of the expression E-*la*) they placed them in the middle, that is, on the middle joints of the fingers—, I say that they did it this way inasmuch as if they had done it that way, they would not have observed the circulation in the progression. On the other hand, we could have said it

⟨12.⟩ Et hec pro totius manus musicalis declaratione pro nunc sufficiant, in qua manu musicali figurari possunt omnes cantus mundi, quapropter
fatue operantur multi moderni cantores, qui putantes quid magnum operari quosdam eorum cantus figurant manum musicalem ad infimum vel
5 supremum exeuntes, et male; cum hoc absque neccessitate operentur, quod
maximum vitium est in arte, cum ars insequatur naturam in quantum potest,
et natura non abundet in superfluis nec deficiat in neccessariis, ut asserit
Aristotiles secundo physicorum et tercio de anima.

---

dicere quod, ut facilius intelligamus, est sciendum quod tenoribus et contra-
tenoribus attribute sunt dictiones graves et de natura veri contratenoris est
non ascendere ultra tenorem sed bene plus quam tenor descendere potest.
Discantibus autem attribute sunt dictiones acute et de natura discantus est
plus tenore non posse descendere sed bene magis ascendere. Triplis autem
attribute sunt dictiones superacute et de natura tripli est plus discantu ascendere posse sed non plus descendere, quapropter posite fuerunt alique dictiones superacute infra quasdam acutas et alique pares cum quibusdam acutis et una supra acutas et ratio est quia tripli pro maiori parte stant mixti cum
discantibus nec supra discantum ascendunt comuniter plus una voce; sed
quia discantus pro maiori parte supra tenorem remanet, pro tanto voces
graves non miscuerunt cum acutis, sed ipsas per se in loco infimo manus
posuerunt, ut visum est. A police autem inceperunt ...

6–8 *Huc pertinet emendatio quae in L invenitur:* ... ars insequatur naturam
in quantum potest, per Aristotilem secundo physicorum, et natura non abundet in superfluis nec deficiat in neccessariis, ut asserit idem Aristotiles pluries tercio de anima.

---

1 totius [declaratione] B ‖ 5 operentur]aliqua operentur L ‖

12. Let these things suffice for now for the explanation of the entire musical hand, in which all chants whatsoever can be drawn. For this reason, many modern singers work foolishly who, thinking that they work something great, draw certain of their chants exceeding the musical hand at the lowest or highest limit. They do so improperly, since in this they work without necessity, which is the greatest vice in art, since art follows nature insofar as it can and nature neither abounds in superfluities nor lacks in necessities, as Aristotle states in the second book of the *Physics* and the third book *On the Soul*.[34]

---

another way, so that we might understand more easily: one must know that the low expressions were apportioned to tenors and contratenors and that by nature the true contratenor's lot is not to ascend beyond the tenor, though it may well descend more than the tenor; that the high expressions, on the other hand, were apportioned to discants and that by nature the discant's lot is not to be able to descend more than the tenor but to ascend more; that the very high expressions were apportioned to tripla and that by nature the triplum's lot is to be able to ascend more than the discant but not to descend more. For this reason, some very high expressions were placed below certain high ones, some at the same level as certain high ones, and one above the high expressions. The reason is because tripla are for the most part mixed with discants and do not commonly ascend more than one syllable above them; but because the discant stays above the tenor for the most part, they did not mix the low syllables with the high but placed them by themselves in the lowest position of the hand, as has been seen. They began from the thumb ...

6–9 ... art follows nature in so far as it can, according to Aristotle in the second book of the *Physics*, and nature neither abounds in superfluities nor lacks in necessities, as the same Aristotle states several times in the third book *On the Soul*.

---

[34]Aristotle *Physica* 2.1.9 (194a22) and *De anima* 3.2 (432b21–23).

80

⟨2⟩

⟨1.⟩ Declarata parte principali plane musice, que est manus musicalis explanatio, ad secundum intentum, quod est diversitatem tonorum declarare, accedamus, unde sciendum quod tonus quantum ad musicam spectat dupli-
5 citer sumi potest, primo pro eo quod contra semitonium distinguitur, qualiter sumebatur superius ubi diffiniebatur tonus et semitonium, et sic non sumitur in proposito; alio modo sumitur pro quodam totali processu cantus alicuius, antiphane, versus, responsorii, introitus, offertorii, psalmi, vel cantus alterius, et sic sumitur in proposito atque sic diffinitur: Tonus est quidam modus
10 notas sive figuras cantus alicuius ordinandi in toto processu cantus alicuius repertus, diversitatem unius cantus ab altero per principium, medium, et finem, necnon per elevationem et depositionem vocum nos agnoscere faci-ens. Et huiusmodi tonus antiquo more regula atque modus nominatur, eo quod cantum quemlibet taliter regulat et modificat quod unum ab altero cla-
15 rissime distinguitur. Tropus etiam, sive conversio, quod idem est, appelatur, eo quod in huiusmodi tonis, sive cantuum ordinibus, voces adinvicem taliter convertuntur, hoc est quando ab aliqua voce ascendendo vel descendendo recedimus et postea ad eandem vocem redimus, quod ex huiusmodi diversis conversionibus unus cantus ab altero maximam sumit diversitatem.

20 ⟨2.⟩ Et fuerunt huiusmodi toni primitus solum quatuor adinventi, istis quatuor diversis nominibus nominati, scilicet protus, deuterus, tritus, et tet-rardus, que quatuor nomina sonant primus, secundus, tercius, et quartus; et fuerunt toni solum quatuor inventi secundum quod solum quatuor erant, et sunt, voces in quas quilibet cantus in plana musica reperibilis, tam ascen-
25 dendo quam descendendo, finiri potest, atque poterat, propter quod est

---

2 parte]prima parte L ‖ 7 sumitur tonus L ‖ 8 antiphane Gradualis L | offertorii sequentie L | psami B ‖ 9 et]atque L ‖ 12 nos]vos L ‖ 13 antiquo more]antiquitus L | regula tropus L | nominabatur L ‖ 13–14 eo quod]et dicebatur regula et modus quoniam L ‖ 14 et]atque L ‖ 15 etiam]vero L | appelabatur L ‖ 16 eo quod]quoniam L ‖ 19 sumit]sumebat atque sumit L ‖ 20 Et]4 primitus modi *in marg. m. sec.* B ‖ 22 sonant tantum quantum hec quatuor, scilicet L ‖

2

1. The first part of *musica plana*—which is the exposition of the musical hand—having been explained, let us approach the second aim, which is to explain the difference between the tones. Accordingly, one must know that "tone," insofar as music is concerned, can be taken in two ways: first, as that which is distinguished from "semitone," as it was taken above where tone and semitone were defined,[1] and it is not so taken in this proposition. It is taken in another way, as a certain total progression of some chant—of an antiphon, verse, responsory, introit, offertory, psalm, or other chant—, and thus it is taken in this proposition and thus defined: a tone is a certain manner of setting in order notes or figures of some chant, found in the total progression of the chant, that makes us recognize the difference of one chant from another through its beginning, middle, and end, as well as through elevation and deposition of pitch. In the ancient custom, a tone of this sort is named "rule" and "mode" because it regulates and delimits any chant so that one is very clearly distinguished from another.[2] It is also called "trope"—or "conversion," which is the same thing—because in tones of this sort, or orders of chants, pitches are converted one to another thus: that is, when we depart from one pitch, ascending or descending, and afterward return to the same pitch, for one chant differs most from another on the basis of different conversions of this sort.[3]

2. Originally only four tones of this sort had been devised, named with these four different names, *protus, deuterus, tritus,* and *tetrardus*; these four names mean first, second, third, and fourth. Only four tones had been discovered as there were, and are, only four syllables on which any chant found in *musica plana* can, and could, be ended, ascending or descending.[4] On this

---

[1] *Plana musica* 1.7 (50–55).

[2] "Rule" [*regula*] because it regulates [*regulat*], "mode" [*modus*] because it delimits [*modificat*].

[3] Medieval theory frequently conjoins the terms *tonus, modus,* and *tropus.* See, for example, *Alia musica* (GS, 1:126); Guido, *Epistola de ignoto cantu* 266–68 (ed. Pesce, 502–3; cf. GS, 2:48); Regino, *Epistola de harmonica institutione* (GS, 1:232); Theoger, *Musica* (GS, 2:191); Marchetto, *Lucidarium* 11.1.2–8 (ed. Herlinger, 370–73); and Jacobus Leodiensis, *Speculum musice* 6.4 (ed. Bragard, 6:15). Still, I have found no text that is a match for Prosdocimo's particular formulation.

[4] Other theorists who report the division of four tones into eight include Guido, *Micrologus* 12 (ed. Smits van Waesberghe, 147–49; trans. Babb, 67–68); Aribo, *De musica* (*Aribonis De musica,* ed. Joseph Smits van Waesberghe, Corpus scriptorum de musica, vol. 2 [(Rome): American Institute of Musicology, 1951], 28–29); and Marchetto, *Lucidarium* 11.2 (ed. Herlinger, 372–77).

sciendum quod de sex vocibus superius nominatis, scilicet ut, re, mi, fa, sol, la, solum quatuor intermedie, scilicet re, mi, fa, sol, sunt, et erant, que alicuius cantus plane musice finales esse possunt, atque poterant, et hoc est quia solum ille voces sumi debent pro finalibus alicuius cantus plane
5 musice, que huiusmodi cantum, tam ascendendo quam descendendo, finire possunt, cuiusmodi non sunt due extreme voces, scilicet ut, la, quare pro finalibus alicuius cantus plane musice non assumpte sunt, sed bene solum quatuor intermedie, scilicet re, mi, fa, sol, ut dictum est, pro finalibus assumpte sunt, eo quod huiusmodi cantum, tam ascendendo quam descen-
10 dendo, bene finire possunt, et secundum diversitatem istarum quatuor vocum finalium assumpserunt antiqui quatuor tonos superius nominatos, et ipsos per eorum fines abinvicem distinxerunt, taliter quod voluerunt primum tonum hanc vocem re pro fine sibi sumere, secundum vero tonum in hanc vocem mi, tercium autem in hanc vocem fa, et quartum in hanc vocem sol
15 finiri debere. Habes ergo quomodo istarum quatuor vocum finalium diversitas fuit causa investigationis diversitatis quatuor tonorum superius nominatorum, quia sicut quatuor invente sunt voces finales abinvicem distincte, ita quatuor assumpti sunt toni abinvicem distincti, quorum quilibet suam habet finalem sibi propriam, ut dictum est.
20 ⟨3.⟩ Sciendum ulterius quod antiqui in istis suis quatuor tonis in cantu aliquo non descendebant sub fine ipsius cantus nisi tonum vel ad plus tonum cum semitonio; ascendebant autem supra finalem eius cantus ad plus usque ad vocem decimam, sic quod inter maiorem descensum et maiorem ascensum duodecimam comprehendebant; sed successores ulterius speculantes
25 alios quatuor invenerunt tonos cum quatuor primis in finalibus concordantes, ab ipsis tamen in vocum ascensu atque descensu, ipsarum finalium respectu, discrepantes, unde ubi primi quatuor descendere non poterant, neque possunt, ad plus nisi tonum cum semitonio, voluerunt isti successores hos quatuor tonos ultimo inventos quintam vocem ad plus descendere posse, semper
30 eorum finalium respectu; et ratio est quia, si bene consideras, primus istorum quatuor tonorum secundo inventorum, qui finiri habet in hanc vocem re, uti et primus quatuor primorum, finiri non potest in primo re, scilicet in Are, quia tunc a primo quatuor primorum per descensum non diversificaretur, eo quod tunc nisi tonum ad plus descendere posset, uti et primus quatuor pri-
35 morum, ut patere potest subtiliter intuenti; potest bene tamen in secundo re finiri, scilicet in Dsolre, et tunc descendendo usque ad gamaut inclusive

4 alicuius cantus]cantuum L ǁ 5 cantum]cantus L ǁ 6 ut et L ǁ 7 alicuius cantus]cantuum L ǁ 9 cantum]cantus L ǁ 11 assumpserunt]et sumpserunt L ǁ 12 distinxerunt abinvicem L ǁ 18 abinvicem]vel invicem B | quililibet B ǁ 22 eius]eiusdem L ǁ 33 diversicaretur *ante corr. in marg., fort. m. sec.* L ǁ 34 tonum]per tonum L ǁ

account, one must know that of the six syllables named above—*ut, re, mi, fa, sol, la*—it is, and was, only the four intermediate ones—*re, mi, fa, sol*—that can, and could, be finals of any chant in *musica plana*. This is because only those syllables ought to be taken as finals of any chant in *musica plana* that can end a chant of this sort, ascending or descending. The two extreme syllables—*ut, la*—are not of this sort, wherefore they were not taken up as finals of any chant of *musica plana*. Only the four intermediate ones—*re, mi, fa, sol*—were properly taken up as finals (as has been said) because they can properly end a chant of this sort, ascending or descending. The ancients took up the four tones named above according to the difference between these four final syllables and distinguished them one from another through their endings in such a way that they maintained that the first tone should take the syllable *re* as its ending, the second tone should end on the syllable *mi*, the third on the syllable *fa*, and the fourth on the syllable *sol*. Therefore, you grasp how the difference between these four final syllables was the basis for the investigation of the difference between the four tones named above: just as four final syllables had been discovered, distinct one from another, so were four tones taken up, distinct one from another, any one of which has its own final, as has been said.

3. One must know further that in any chant in these four tones of theirs, the ancients did not descend below the ending of the chant except by a tone or at most by a tone with semitone; they ascended above the final of the chant, on the other hand, to the tenth syllable at most. So, they encompassed a twelfth between the greatest descent and the greatest ascent. But their successors, speculating further, discovered another four tones agreeing with the first four in their finals while disagreeing from them in ascent and descent of pitch with respect to those finals. Accordingly, where the first four could not, nor cannot, descend except by a tone with semitone at most, these successors wished that these four tones last discovered could descend to the fifth syllable at most, always with respect to their finals. The reason is (if you consider it properly): the first of those four tones discovered secondly, which must end on the syllable *re* like the first of the first four, cannot be ended on the first *re*, that is, on A-*re*, because then it would not be differentiated in descent from the first of the first four in that it could descend only by a tone at most, like the first of the first four, as can be evident to one who contemplates it carefully. But it can be ended properly on the second *re*, that is, on D-*solre*, and then in descending to *gamma-ut*, it could descend prop-

bene quintam vocem et non ultra descendere poterit, ut cuilibet apparere potest; et ut omnes isti quatuor toni ultimo inventi equalem descensum haberent, voluerunt isti successores ipsos omnes tonos propter hoc quintam vocem ad plus descendere posse; sed ut postea inter maiorem descensum et
5 maiorem ascensum istorum quatuor tonorum ultimo inventorum duodecima clauderetur, uti et in quatuor primitus inventis, voluerunt isti successores predicti hos quatuor tonos ultimo inventos ad vocem octavam ad plus ascendere posse, semper ipsorum finalium respectu.

    Facti ergo in posterum sunt toni numero octo, taliter adinvicem ordinati
10 quod quilibet duo toni eundem finem habentes adinvicem colligati sunt, ut verbi gratia primus quatuor secundorum cum primo quatuor primorum, secundus cum secundo, tercius cum tercio, et quartus cum quarto, et sic insequutus est quilibet alteri colligatus immediate illum cui colligatus est in octo tonorum ordine, quare primus quatuor primorum primus omnium octo
15 factus est, et merito, quia primus quatuor primorum ascensum habentium, qui descensu nobilior reputatur, primus vero quatuor secundorum secundus in ordine est collocatus, ut insequatur immediate primum quatuor primorum cui colligatus est; in tercio vero loco secundus quatuor primorum repositus est, et in quarto secundus quatuor secundorum sibi colligatus; in quinto vero
20 loco tercius quatuor primorum aptatus est, et in sexto tercius quatuor secundorum sibi colligatus; septimus vero locus quarto quatuor primorum attributus est, et octavus quarto quatuor secundorum sibi colligato. Quatuor ergo loca imparia obtinent quatuor toni primitus inventi et quatuor loca paria quatuor ultimo reperti, ut apparet. Propter hoc ergo dividunt moderniores
25 hos octo tonos in duas partes equales, scilicet in quatuor primitus inventos et quatuor ultimo repertos, et vocant quatuor primitus inventos, qui sunt in ordine omnium octo primus, tercius, quintus, et septimus, autenticos, eo quod primitus et ab auctenticis auctoribus inventi sunt; quatuor vero ultimo inventos, qui in ordine omnium octo sunt secundus, quartus, sextus, et octa-
30 vus, nominant plagales, sive collaterales, quod idem est, eo quod collaterales quatuor primorum esse dicuntur, cum eosdem fines cum illis obtinebant, ut dictum est. Plagis nanque grece latine latus significat, unde plagalis tantum quantum lateralis sive collateralis importat. Secundum alios vero plagis

---

4 posse et hoc ut ars facilior redderetur, quoniam facilius est menti tenere quod omnes hii toni equaliter descendere debeant quam quod inequaliter L ‖ 7 hos]hoc *ante corr.* L ‖ 7–8 octavam … respectu]octavam supra finalem ad plus ascendere posse L ‖ 9 Facti ergo in posterum]Sic ergo in posterum facti L | numero *corr.* L ‖ 13 est insequutus L ‖ 14 quatuor]octo L ‖ 15 primus est L ‖ 31 obtineant L ‖ 32 significat]signat B significat *vel* signat L ‖ 32–33 tantum quantum]tanquam L ‖

erly to the fifth syllable and not further, as can be apparent to anyone. So that all these four tones last discovered might have an equal descent, these successors maintained that all these tones could descend to the fifth pitch at most. But so that a twelfth might then be enclosed between the greatest descent and the greatest ascent of these four tones last discovered, just as in the four originally discovered, the aforesaid successors wished that these four tones last discovered could ascend to the eighth syllable at most, always with respect to their finals.

Therefore, tones eight in number were fashioned for posterity, set in order with respect to each other in such a way that any two tones having the same ending were bound together, as for example the first of the second four with the first of the first four, the second with the second, the third with the third, and the fourth with the fourth. In the order of the entire eight tones, any one bound to another immediately followed the one to which it was bound. Wherefore, the first of the first four was made the first of the entire eight, and with good reason, because it is the first of the first four, having ascent, which is held to be nobler than descent;[5] the first of the second four, on the other hand, was assigned a position second in order so that it might directly follow the first of the first four, together with which it is bound; the second of the first four tones was placed in the third position, and the second of the second four tones, bound together with it, in the fourth position; the third tone of the first four was fitted to the fifth position, and the third of the second four, bound together with it, to the sixth; the seventh position, however, was apportioned to the fourth of the first four, and the eighth position to the fourth of the second four, bound together with it. Therefore, the four tones originally discovered occupy the four odd-numbered positions and the four found last the four even-numbered positions, as is apparent. For this reason, therefore, the more modern writers divide these eight tones into two equal parts, into the four originally discovered and the four found last. They call the four originally discovered (which are, of all eight in order, the first, third, fifth, and seventh) authentic because they were the ones originally discovered and were discovered by authoritative authors. The four devised last, however (which are, of all eight in order, the second, fourth, sixth, and eighth), they name plagals—or collaterals, which is the same thing— because they are said to be collaterals of the first four, since they occupied the same endings as those, as has been said. *Plagis* in Greek signifies *latus* in Latin; accordingly, "plagal" conveys as much as "lateral" or "collateral." But according to others, *plagis* in Greek signifies *sequutio* in Latin; accord-

---

[5]Prosdocimo raised the point of ascent being nobler than descent in *Plana musica* 1.9 (58–59) and will return to it in 2.4 (86–87).

grece latine sequutio, unde plagalis et sequax idem significant; et merito
dicuntur isti quatuor toni secundo inventi plagales, id est sequaces, quia
finales quatuor tonorum primitus inventorum insequuntur, quapropter omnes
octo toni talibus octo propriis nominibus abinvicem distinctis nominati sunt,
5 scilicet protus, plagalis proti, deuterus, plagalis deuteri, tritus, plagalis triti,
tetrardus, et plagalis tetrardi. Et scias quod quilibet modus cantandi, sive sit
in cantu plano sive in cantu mensurato, est alicuius octo modorum sive tonorum superius nominatorum.

⟨4.⟩ Alii autem dicunt hos octo tonos aliter inventos fuisse, unde dicunt
10 quod primorum quatuor tonorum superius nominatorum inventores in ipsis
suis quatuor tonis magnum ascensum atque descensum comprehendebant,
taliter quod in quolibet ipsorum tonorum supra ipsius finalem undecimam
ascendebant atque infra ipsam quintam descendebant, vocem quintam decimam humane voci comuni rationabilem inter maiorem ascensum et maiorem
15 descensum comprehendere volentes, sed moderniores, huiusmodi ascensum
atque descensum comuniter canentibus tediosum intuentes, quemlibet dictorum quatuor tonorum in duas diviserunt partes, uni quarum ascensum tribuerunt, alterique descensum; et inde postea octo procreati sunt toni, quatuor ascensum possidentes, quatuorque descensum; et ascensum habentibus,
20 qui descensu nobilior reputatur, ut dictum est, nomina prima tribuerunt, que
sunt hec, scilicet protus, deuterus, tritus, et tetrardus, atque ipsos autenticos
nominaverunt, eo quod nominibus ab autenticis auctoribus inventis nominati
erant, atque sunt, vel quia partem altam, sive maiorem scilicet ascensum,
sumere videntur, unde autenticus aliquando pro alto sive maiori sumitur, ut
25 hic. Alios vero quatuor tonos descensum habentes plagales, id est partiales,
nominaverunt, eo quod primorum partes dicuntur, ut dictum est. Plaga enim
aliquando idem quod pars significat, unde dicunt astrologi celum in quinque
plagas fore divisum, id est partes, similiterque terra; et ideo plagalis tantum
quantum partialis significat; vel plagales, id est subiugales, quia partem
30 subiugalem sive declinem, hoc est descensum, sumere videntur; plagis
nanque grece aliquando idem quod subiugalis videtur importare. Ordinati

1 significant]significant *vel* signant L ‖ 2 toni ⟦q⟧ B ‖ 4 distincte B ‖ 7 in cantu plano sive *in marg.* B ‖ 13 ipsam finalem L ‖ 20 prima tribuerunt *inc.* C (cf. 34.app3) ‖ 25 habentes ⟦ut⟧ C ‖ 27 significat]signat C significat *vel* signat L ‖ celum]et poete terram L ‖ 28 plagas … partes]partes fore divisum, id est plagas C ‖ 28 divisam L ‖ id est partes, similiterque terra *om.*L ‖ 29 significat]significat *vel* signat C ‖ 30 sive]id est L ‖ 31 idem quod aliquando C ‖

ingly, "plagal" and "follower" signify the same thing. These secondly discovered tones are with good reason called plagals—that is, followers—because they follow the finals of the four tones originally discovered. For this reason, all eight tones are named with their own names distinct from each other: protus, plagal of the protus, deuterus, plagal of the deuterus, tritus, plagal of the tritus, tetrardus, and plagal of the tetrardus. Know that any manner of singing, whether in plainchant or in measured song, is of some one of those eight manners or tones named above.[6]

4. Others, however, say that these eight tones were discovered in a different way:[7] they say that the discoverers of the first four tones named above encompassed a large ascent and descent in their four tones in such a way that in any of those tones, they ascended an eleventh above the final and descended a fifth below it, wishing to encompass a reasonable fifteenth syllable for the common human voice between the greatest ascent and the greatest descent. But the more modern writers, contemplating that an ascent and descent of this sort is wearisome for those who commonly sing, divided each of the said four tones into two parts, to one of which they apportioned ascent and to the other descent, and thus eight tones were then created, four possessing ascent and four descent. To those having ascent, which is held to be nobler than descent, as has been said,[8] they apportioned the first names, which are these: *protus, deuterus, tritus,* and *tetrardus*; and they named them authentic because they were named, and are named, with names devised by authoritative authors or because they seem to take the high part or the greater ascent. Accordingly, "authentic" is sometimes taken as "high" or "greater," as here. They named the other four tones having descent plagal, that is, "partial," because they are called parts of the first tones, as has been said. *Plaga*, you see, sometimes signifies the same as "part." Accordingly, astrologers say that the heavens are divided into five *plagae*, that is, parts, and likewise the earth. Thus, *plagalis* signifies as much as "partial." Or, they named them plagals, that is, "subjugals," because they seem to take the subjugal or declining part, that is, descent, for *plagis* in Greek seems sometimes to convey the same as subjugal. All eight tones, therefore, were then

---

[6]Prosdocimo's *Plana musica* is one of a very few medieval treatises in which polyphonic pieces (if that is what the term "measured song" implies) are said to belong to a tone. On this point, see the Introduction, 14.

[7]This account of the division of four tones into eight closely resembles Marchetto's in *Lucidarium* 11.2 (ed. Herlinger, 372–77). Marchetto agrees that each of the original four tones had the range of a fifteenth but differs in specifying that the fifteenth extends from a tenth above the final to a sixth below it.

[8]*Plana musica* 1.9; see also 2.3 (58–59 and 85–86).

ergo sunt postea omnes octo toni, ut dictum est, plagalem illi cuius plagalis esse dicitur immediate postponendo, nominatique etiam sunt modo supradicto.

⟨5.⟩ Sciendum ulterius quod istorum octo tonorum alius est perfectus,
5 alius imperfectus, alius plusquamperfectus, et alius mixtus sive commixtus. Perfectus tonus dicitur ille qui modum suum implet superius atque inferius. Implere autem modum suum in tonis autenticis est supra suum finem octavam ascendere et tonum infra ipsius finalem descendere, trito excepto, qui licentiam habet descendendi tonum cum semitonio, eo quod tonum descen-
10 dere non poterat sub sua finali per unam vocem descendendo, cum ipse tritus cum suo plagali fa finalem accipiat, ut dictum est; oportuit ergo terciam descendere vocem et inde descensum toni cum semitonio suscipere, si magis quam per semitonium, uti et alii autentici, descendere intendebat. Implere

---

2–3 *Huc pertinet emendatio quae in L invenitur:* ... modo supradicto. Debitus vero ascensus autenticorum ad plus fuit ad octavam supra suam finalem et debitus descensus fuit ad plus per tonum cum semitonio sub sua finali, sic quod inter maiorem ascensum et maiorem descensum decima comprehensa est, cantum planum canentibus comunissima. Debitus autem descensus plagalium ad plus fuit ad quintam sub sua finali, ratione superius dicta, et debitus ascensus ad plus fuit usque ad sextam supra suam finalem, et hoc ut inter maiorem ascensum et maiorem descensum etiam decima comprehenderetur sicut in autenticis.

7–8 *Huc pertinet emendatio quae in L invenitur:* ... supra suum finem debitum ascendere, scilicet octavam, ad plus et per tonum ad plus descendere sub sua finali, trito excepto ...

---

2 nominataque L ‖ 4 Sciendum ulterius]Preterea sciendum L ‖ 5 plusquamperfectus [a] C ‖ 9 descendendi ... semitonio]descendere per tonum cum semitonio sub sua finali L ‖ 10 vocem tamen L ‖ 11 pragali B | fa finalem]hanc vocem fa pro finali sibi L | accipiatur C | Oportuit [etiam] B ‖ 12 suscipe L ‖

set in order, as has been said, by placing the plagal immediately after that of which it is said to be plagal, and they are named, as well, in the aforesaid manner.

5. One must know further that of these eight tones, one is perfect, another imperfect, another pluperfect, and another mixed or intermixed.[9] The tone is called perfect that fills its measure above and below. To fill its measure in authentic tones is to ascend an octave above its ending and descend a tone below its final, the *tritus* excepted, which has the license of descending a tone with semitone because it was not able to descend a tone below its final by descending through one syllable, since the *tritus*, with its plagal, takes the final *fa*, as has been said; it therefore had to descend to the third syllable and thus to take the descent of a tone with semitone if it intended to descend by more than a semitone, like the other authentics.[10] To

---

2–3 … in the aforesaid manner. The requisite ascent of the authentics, however, was to the octave above their finals at most, and their requisite descent was a tone with semitone below their finals at most. So, between the greatest ascent and the greatest descent, a tenth was encompassed, most common for those singing plainchant. The requisite descent of the plagals, on the other hand, was to the fifth below their finals at most (for the reason stated above), and the requisite ascent was to the sixth above their finals at most. This was so that between the greatest ascent and the greatest descent a tenth might also be encompassed, as in the authentics.

7–8 … to ascend above its ending the requisite amount, that is, an octave at most, and to descend below its final a tone at most, the tritus excepted …

---

[9]This fivefold division of tones seems to have originated with Marchetto; cf. *Lucidarium* 11.2.20 (ed. Herlinger, 378–79), and the division had become widespread in Italy by the end of the fifteenth century; see Klaus Wolfgang Niemöller, "Zur Tonus-Lehre der italienischen Musiktheorie des ausgehenden Mittelalters," *Kirchenmusikalisches Jahrbuch* 40 (1956): 23–32, and Jan Herlinger, "Marchetto's Influence: The Manuscript Evidence," in *Music Theory and Its Sources: Antiquity and the Middle Ages*, ed. André Barbera, Notre Dame Conferences in Medieval Studies, vol. 1 (Notre Dame, IN: Notre Dame University Press, 1990), 235–58.

[10]Guido of Arezzo (*Micrologus* 13 [ed. Smits van Waesberghe, 155) stated that the fifth tone rarely descends below its final because of the semitone found there; Marchetto (*Lucidarium* 11.2.23, 11.4.168–72; ed. Herlinger, 378–79, 470–71) preceded Prosdocimo in allowing it to descend as far as the minor third below the final.

autem modum suum in tonis plagalibus est supra suum finem sextam vel septimam vocem ascendere et quintam sub ipso fine descendere. Secundum alios vero inpletio modi in autenticis tonis solum per ascensum cognoscitur, in plagalibus vero per descensum.

5   Tonus vero imperfectus dicitur ille qui modum suum non implet, sive hoc sit superius sive inferius.

1–6 *Huc pertinet emendatio quae in L invenitur:* ... supra suum finem debitum ascendere, scilicet ad sextam ad plus, et quintam ad plus sub suo descendere fine. Secundum vero alios impletio modi in autenticis tonis solum per debitum ascensum ad plus sibi traditum supra eorum finales superius habitum cognoscitur; in plagalibus vero solum per debitum descensum ad plus sibi traditum infra eorum finales superius habitum disernitur.

Tonus vero imperfectus dicitur ille qui modum suum non inplet, sive hoc sit superius sive inferius secundum primum modum. Secundum vero alium modum dicitur ille qui si sit in autenticis non implet suum modum superius solum; si vero sit in plagalibus, qui suum modum non implet inferius solum.

fill its measure in plagal tones is to ascend to the sixth or seventh syllable above its ending and to descend a fifth below that ending.[11] According to others, however, the filling of the measure is recognized in authentic tones only through ascent, in plagals only through descent.[12]

The tone is called imperfect that does not fill its measure, whether it be above or below.[13]

1–6 ... to ascend above its ending the requisite amount, that is, to the sixth at most,[14] and to descend below its ending a fifth at most. According to others, however, the filling of the measure in authentic tones is recognized only through the traditionally requisite maximum ascent above their finals (explained above); in the plagals, however, it is discerned only through the traditionally requisite maximum descent below their finals (explained above).

The tone is called imperfect that does not fill its measure, whether it be above or below, according to the first measure; according to another measure, however, it is said to be that which, if it is among the authentics, does not fill its measure only above its final; or, if it is among the plagals, that which does not fill its measure only below its final.[15]

---

[11]Cf. *Lucidarium* 11.2.25 (ed. Herlinger, 380–81), in which Marchetto defines the limits of the perfect plagal as a sixth above the final and a fourth below it.

[12]The *Compendium musicale* of Nicolaus de Capua (1415, roughly contemporaneous with Prosdocimo's *Plana musica*) recognizes the filling of the measure in this way (ed. La Fage, 312): "How are authentic tones made perfect? When authentic tones ascend to the octave above their final, they are perfect; if they ascend further, they are pluperfect; but if they ascend less, they are imperfect. How are plagals made perfect? When plagal tones descend four syllables below their finals, they are perfect; if they descend further, they are pluperfect; but if they descend less, they are imperfect [Quomodo toni authentici efficiuntur perfecti?—Quando toni authentici ascendunt ad octavam supra suam hanc finalem, tunc sunt perfecti; si vero plus ascendunt, plusquamperfecti sunt; si autem minus ascendunt, imperfecti sunt. Quomodo plagales efficiuntur perfecti?—Quando toni plagales descendunt ad quatuor voces sub suam hanc finalem, tunc sunt perfecti; si vero plus descendunt, plusquamperfecti sunt; si autem minus descendunt, imperfecti sunt]."

[13]Cf. *Lucidarium* 11.2.26 (ed. Herlinger 382–83), in which Marchetto defines the imperfect tones in the same way.

[14]Note that in the revision Prosdocimo has reduced the upper limit of plagals to the sixth above the final, which accords with Marchetto's teaching (n. 11 *supra*); the revision sets the total range of both authentics and plagals as a tenth.

[15]Cf. the passage in Nicolaus's *Compendium* quoted in n. 12.

Tonus vero plusquamperfectus dicitur ille qui, si autenticus est, plus quam octavam supra suum finem ascendit; si vero sit plagalis, dicitur ille qui plus quam quintam sub suo fine descendit.

Tonus vero mixtus sive commixtus, quod idem est, dicitur ille qui natu-
5 ram alterius toni suscipit, et naturam unam terciam ex sua et altera com-
ponit, ut verbi gratia si autenticus sit et plagalem suscipiat depositionem, vel si plagalis et autenticam sumat elevationem; vel si cantari debeat per ♮ quadrum et cantetur per b rotundum, vel e contra. Et scias quod talis tonus mixtus illius octo tonorum esse dicitur cuius naturam magis recipit, cum a
10 predominante fieri debeat denominatio.

1–6 *Huc pertinet emendatio quae in L invenitur:* ... qui suam perfectionem excedit, ut, si sit autenticus, plus quam octavam supra eius finem ascendit vel sub suo fine plus quam tonum cum semitonio descendit; si vero sit in plagalibus, dicitur ille qui plus quam quintam sub suo fine descendit vel supra eius finem plus quam sextam ascendit, et hoc est secundum primum modum. Secundum vero alium modum tonus plusquamperfectus in autenti-cis solum per ascensum cognoscitur, et est ille qui supra suum finem plus quam octavam ascendit; in plagalibus vero solum per descensum compre-henditur, et est ille qui plus quam per quintam sub suo fine descendit.

Tonus vero mixtus sive commixtus, quod idem est, dicitur ille qui natu-ram autenticam et plagalem insimul habet, ut verbi gratia si aliquis cantus autenticus sit et plagalem suscipiat depositionem ...

---

1 vero]autem C ‖ 1–2 si autenticus est ... dicitur ille qui *om.* (*saut du même au même*) C ‖ 2 supra *in marg.* B ‖ 4 ille *in marg.* B ‖

If it is authentic, the tone is called pluperfect that ascends more than an octave above its ending, or if it is plagal, that descends more than a fifth below its ending.[16]

The tone is called mixed—or intermixed, which is the same thing—that adopts the nature of another tone and composes a third nature from its own and the other's, as for instance if it were authentic and adopted the plagal deposition, if it were plagal and took the authentic elevation, or if it ought to be sung through square ♮ and were sung through round b or vice versa. Know that such a mixed tone is said to be of the one of the eight tones from which it most takes on a nature, since its denomination should be made from that which is predominant.[17]

1–7 ... that exceeds its perfection so that if it be authentic, it ascends more than an octave above its ending or descends more than a tone with semitone below its ending. If it be among the plagals, it is said to be that which descends more than a fifth below its ending or ascends more than a sixth above its ending, and this is according to the first measure. According to another measure, however, the pluperfect tone among the authentics is recognized only through ascent and is that which ascends more than an octave above its ending; but among the plagals, it is encompassed only through descent and is that which descends more than a fifth below its ending.[18]

The tone is called mixed—or intermixed, which is the same thing—that has authentic and plagal natures together, as for instance if some chant were authentic and adopted the plagal deposition ...

---

[16]Cf. *Lucidarium* 11.2.27–28 (ed. Herlinger, 384–85), in which Marchetto defines the pluperfect authentic as one that ascends past the diapason above its final "to the ninth or the tenth" and the pluperfect plagal as one that descends further than a fourth below it.

[17]In *Lucidarium* 11.2.31–35 (ed. Herlinger, 386–91), Marchetto differentiates the mixed (*mixti*) and intermixed (*commixti*) tones. The former are combinations of the tones of an authentic/plagal pair, the latter combinations of one tone with another not its plagal or authentic partner. He presents details of mixture and intermixture in *Lucidarium* 11.4 *passim*.

[18]Of the two sets of criteria for pluperfect tones given in the Lucca revision, only the second accords with the original version of *Plana musica* and Marchetto's doctrine (*Lucidarium* 11.2.29–30 [ed. Herlinger, 386–87]) that "every authentic mode is judged pluperfect only with regard to its upper part; every plagal mode is judged pluperfect only with regard to its lower part [omnis auctenticus tonus dicitur plusquamperfectus solum a parte supra; plagalis vero quilibet solum a parte infra]." The first set of criteria matches those given in a text La Fage published as part of the *Compendium musicale* of Nicolaus de Capua, where both authentics and plagals are pluperfect if they ascend *or* descend beyond

⟨6.⟩ Sed ad istorum octo tonorum maiorem noticiam, est sciendum quod novem sunt ea per que unusquisque octo tonorum ab altero distingui habet et que nos in noticiam ipsorum regulariter ducunt, et sunt ista, scilicet ascensus, descensus, corde, principia, fines, Seculorum amen differentie, species, 5 neume, et distinctiones, que omnia seriatim inferius declarabuntur.

⟨7.⟩ A primis ergo duobus, que sunt ascensus et descensus, incipiendo, dico quod autentici toni a plagalibus per ascensum et descensum sumunt differentiam, eo quod autentici sub suis finalibus solum tonum cum semitonio ad plus descendere possunt, plagalibus vero sub suis finalibus usque ad 10 quintam licitum est devenire; item plagales ultra septimam supra eorum finales ascendere non permittuntur, autentici vero supra eorum finales usque ad octavam ascendere possunt, quod totum etiam dictum est superius; ex quibus dictis sequitur quod per ascensum et descensum solum utrum tonus autenticus existat sive plagalis agnoscere possumus, nec hoc in totum 15 sufficit nisi tonus suam habeat perfectionem saltim in ascensu si sit autenticus vel saltim in descensu si sit plagalis.

1–2 *Huc pertinet emendatio quae in L invenitur:* ... quod septem sunt ea ...
4–5 *Huc pertinet emendatio quae in L invenitur:* ... Seculorum amen differentie, et combinationum species, que omnia ...
8–13 *Huc pertinet emendatio quae in L invenitur:* ... eo quod autentici sub suis finalibus solum tonum ad plus descendere possunt, trito excepto, qui licentiam habet descendendi tonum cum semitonio, ut dictum est, plagalibus vero sub suis finalibus usque ad quintam licitum est devenire; item plagales ultra sextam supra eorum finales ⟨ascendere non permituntur, autentici vero supra eorum finales⟩ usque ad octavam {descendere} ⟨ascendere⟩ possunt, quod totum dictum est superius in tonis perfectis; et ex his iam dictis sequitur ...

---

1 Sed]1. Ascensus, 2. Descensus, 3. Corde, 4. Principia, 5 Fines, 6. Seculorum amen differentie, 7. Species, 8. Neume, 9. Distinctiones *in marg. m. sec.* B | est ulterius L ‖ 3 ista]hec L ‖ 6 A]1, 2 *in marg. m. sec.* B | et descensus *om.* C | descensus insimul L ‖ 10 item quia BC ‖ 12 octavam]undecimam B ‖ 14–15 nec ... sufficit]quod in totum adhuc non sufficit L ‖ 16 saltim *om.* L ‖

6. But for a greater knowledge of these eight tones, one must know that there are nine things by means of which each of the eight tones must be distinguished from another and that lead us to the knowledge of them by means of rules. They are these: ascent, descent, chords, initials, endings, *differentiae* of the *Seculorum amen*, species, neumes, and distinctions, all of which will be explained below one by one.

7. Beginning, then, with the first two, which are ascent and descent, I say that authentic tones take a differentiation from plagals through ascent and descent because the authentics can descend below their finals only a tone with semitone at most, but it is licit for the plagals to attain the fifth below their finals. Again, the plagals are not permitted to ascend beyond a seventh above their finals, whereas the authentics can ascend to the octave above their finals (all of which has been said above).[19] From what has been said, it follows that we can recognize whether a tone is authentic or plagal only by means of ascent and descent—though this does not completely suffice unless the tone has its perfection at least in ascent if it is authentic or at least in descent if it is plagal.

1–2 ... that there are seven things ...

4–5 ... *differentiae* of the *Seculorum amen*, and species of intervals, all of which ...

9–14 ... because the authentics can descend below their finals only a tone at most, the *tritus* excepted, which has the license of descending a tone with semitone, as has been said,[20] but it is licit for the plagals to attain the fifth below their finals. Again, the plagals are not permitted to ascend beyond the sixth above their finals, whereas the authentics can ascend to the octave above their finals (all of which has been said above in the passage concerning perfect tones).[21] From what has already been said, it follows ...

---

the normal standard ("si autem plus ascendunt vel descendunt, plusquamperfecti sunt" [ed. La Fage, 318]). This passage contradicts that quoted in n. 12 *supra*; La Fage published both texts as part of a single work he had cobbled together from two Roman manuscripts that lay in fragments.

[19]**B** here has *supra eorum finales usque ad undecimam* (to the eleventh above their finals); the Lucca revision has *ad octavam*. I take *undecimam* as a scribe's error in assimilating the text here to that of *Plana musica* 2.4 (86–87), in which Prosdocimo had stated that the ranges of the four "original" tones (before they were divided into eight) extended to an eleventh above their finals, and I have corrected *undecimam* to *octavam* in accord with *Plana musica* 2.5 (88–89) and the Lucca version of the present passage.

[20]*Plana musica* 2.5 (88–89).

[21]*Plana musica* 2.5 (88–91).

⟨8.⟩ Si tamen cantus aliquis qui huiusmodi perfectione careat reperiatur, an sit plagalis vel autenticus per eius cordam iudicare possumus, que corda tercium in ordine declarandum existit; quapropter est sciendum quod quilibet tonus autenticus cum suo plagali suam habet cordam sibi propriam, unde
5 F grave primi et secundi toni corda esse dicitur, G vero grave tercio et quarto tono pro corda attribuitur, A vero acutum quinti et sexti toni pro corda reputatur, sed ♮ quadrum acutum septimi et octavi toni pro corda tenetur. Hoc scito in hunc modum quilibet tonus per eius cordam an sit plagalis vel autenticus est iudicandus, quoniam aspiciende sunt note supra et
10 infra eius cordam existentes, quia si plures sint note supra, autenticus est iudicandus; si vero infra, plagalis. Si vero tot supra quot infra, tunc tonus per cordam iudicari non potest, sed per species, de quibus inferius determinabitur, pro tunc est iudicandus. Puto tamen fore melius atque securius, antequam aliquis cantus cuius toni sit iudicetur, quod omnia novem superius
15 enumerata, scilicet ascensus, descensus, et cetera, considerentur, et inde postea tonus iudicetur; et hoc dico propter tonos mixtos, in quibus omnia hec novem sunt consideranda antequam sub aliquo octo tonorum reponantur. Item etiam hoc dico propter cantus prosaicos, qui sunt cantus ex longa serie verborum contexti, sicut sequentie, antiphane, et responsoria quedam,

---

7–8 *Huc pertinet emendatio quae in L invenitur:* ... septimi et octavi toni pro corda tenetur; et iste sunt quatuor corde tonorum principales; sed tamen reperiuntur alie quatuor corde tonorum secundarie et consecutive, quatuor principalibus correspondentes, scilicet C, D, F, G acuta. C pro primo et secundo tono, D pro tercio et quarto, F pro quinto et sexto, et G pro septimo et octavo. Hoc scito ...

14–15 *Huc pertinet emendatio quae in L invenitur:* ... omnia septem superius enumerata ...

16–17 *Huc pertinet emendatio quae in L invenitur:* ... omnia hec septem sunt consideranda ...

---

1 Si]3⁰, Corda F 1. et 2. Toni *in marg. m. sec.* B | Si tamen]Sed si L ‖ 4 propriam]appropriatam L ‖ 5 G]G Corda 3. et 4. Toni *in marg. m. sec.* B | grave (*sec.*) secundum L ‖ 6 attribuitur pro corda C | A]A Corda 5. et 6. Toni *in marg. m. sec.* B ‖ 7 sed]♮ 7. et 7. Toni *in marg. m. sec.* B | sed ♮ quadrum ... et in ca (126.7) *om.* C ‖ 18 prosaicos]Cantus prosaicos ex longa serie verborum contexti *in marg. m. sec.* B ‖ 19 sicut sunt L ‖

8. Nevertheless, if some chant should be found that lacks perfection of this sort, we can judge whether it is plagal or authentic by means of its chord, which is the third thing to be explained in order. On which account, one must know that any authentic tone with its plagal has its own chord. Accordingly, low F is said to be the chord of the first and second tones, low G is apportioned to the third and fourth tones as the chord, high A is held to be the chord of the fifth and sixth tones, and high square ♮ is held as the chord of the seventh and eighth tones. This known, any tone must be judged authentic or plagal through its chord in this way, inasmuch as the notes that are above and below its chord must be examined: if more notes are above the chord, the tone is to be judged authentic, but if more notes are below the chord, plagal. If, however, there are as many above as below, then the tone cannot be judged through the chord but is to be judged through species, which will be determined below. Nevertheless, I think it to be better and more reliable that before some chant is judged to be of a tone, all nine things enumerated above be considered—ascent, descent, etc.—and only then the tone be judged. I say this on account of the mixed tones, in which all nine things are to be considered before they are placed under some one of the eight tones. Again, I say this also on account of the prose chants, which are chants made up of a long series of words, like certain sequences, antiphons,

---

7–8 ... is held as the chord of the seventh and eighth tones. These are the four principal chords of the tones; four other secondary and consequent chords of the tones are found, however, corresponding to the four principal chords: high C, D, F, and G; C for the first and second tones, D for the third and fourth, F for the fifth and sixth, and G for the seventh and eighth.[23] This known, ...

15–16 ... all seven things enumerated above ...

17–18 ... all these seven things are to be considered ...

---

[22]In *Lucidarium* 12.1.21–27 (ed. Herlinger, 522–27), Marchetto describes the chord and judgment based on it in the same way Prosdocimo does here, but in *Lucidarium* 12.1.28–44 (ed. Herlinger, 526–33), he shows how melodies can be judged when judgment on the basis of the chord is equivocal. The doctrine of the chord seems to have originated with Marchetto; in the course of the fourteenth and fifteenth centuries, it became widely disseminated in music theory. Prosdocimo will discuss species in *Plana musica* 2.12 (110–17).

[23]I have found no other text that describes secondary chords, evidently analogous to the cofinals. Placing secondary chords on F for the fifth and sixth tones and on G for the seventh and eighth is problematic. As the cofinal of the fifth and sixth tones is C, E would seem to be their appropriate secondary chord; since melodies cannot be transposed from G to D without changing their intervallic structure, it is unclear which note could appropriately serve as the secondary chord for the seventh and eighth tones.

in quorum noticiam bene pervenire non possumus nisi omnia novem supradicta inspiciamus. Nullo ergo modo contentus existas in consideratione unius vel duorum vel trium vel quatuor vel et cetera novem superius nominatorum, sed omnia novem subtiliter inspicias atque intelligenter et a predomi-
5 nio sumas indicationem, et tunc tonum quemlibet recte iudicabis.

⟨9.⟩ Pro quarti vero in ordine declaratione, est sciendum quod quilibet octo tonorum, sive sit perfectus sive sit imperfectus sive plusquamperfectus sive mixtus, habet quasdam literas in quarum quamlibet suum habere potest exordium. Primi ergo toni octo sunt huiusmodi litere initiales, scilicet A, B,
10 C, D, E, F, et secundum G gravia, et A acutum. Secundi vero toni sunt iste septem, scilicet primum G grave, hoc est gama, et A, B, C, D, E, et F gravia. Tercii vero toni sunt iste quatuor, scilicet E, F, et secundum G gravia, et C acutum. Quarti vero toni sunt iste sex, scilicet C, D, E, F, et secundum G gravia, et A acutum. Quinti vero toni sunt iste quinque, scilicet D, F, et
15 secundum G gravia, et A et C acuta. Sexti vero toni sunt iste quinque, scilicet C, D, F, et secundum G gravia, et A acutum; sunt tamen aliqui qui

---

1–2 *Huc pertinet emendatio quae in L invenitur:* ... omnia septem supradicta ...

3–4 *Huc pertinet emendatio quae in L invenitur:* ... vel quatuor vel et cetera septem superius nominatorum, sed omnia septem subtiliter inspicias ...

---

6 Pro]4. Principia *in marg. m. sec.* B ‖ 7 sit (*sec.*) *om.* L ‖ 9 Primi]Principia 1. Toni *in marg. m. sec.* B ‖ 10 Secundi]2. Toni *in marg. m. sec.* B ‖ 12 Tercii]3. Toni *in marg. m. sec.* B | vero]autem L ‖ 13 Quarti]4. Toni *in marg. m. sec.* B | Quarti vero]Sed quarti L ‖ 14 Quinti]5. Toni *in marg. m. sec.* B | Quinti vero]Et quinti L ‖ 15 Sexti]6. Toni *in marg. m. sec.* B ‖

and responsories, of which we cannot properly come to a knowledge unless we consider all nine things stated above. Therefore, do not in any way be content with taking into account one, two, three, four, etc., of the nine things named above; rather, inspect all nine carefully and intelligently and take the designation from the predominant one. Then you will judge any tone rightly.

9. For the explanation of the fourth thing in order, one must know that any of the eight tones, whether it be perfect or whether it be imperfect or pluperfect or mixed, has certain letters on any of which it can begin. The initial letters of the first tone are eight, of this sort: low A, B, C, D, E, and F, the second low G, and high a.[24] Those of the second tone are these seven: the first low G, that is, *gamma*, and low A, B, C, D, E, and F.[25] Those of the third tone are these four: low E and F, the second low G, and high C.[26] Those of the fourth tone are these six: low C, D, E, and F, the second low G, and high A.[27] Those of the fifth tone are these five: low D and F, the second low G, and high A and C.[28] Those of the sixth tone are these five: low C, D, and F, the second low G, and high A. There are some who add a sixth letter,

---

2 ... all seven things stated above. Therefore, ...

3–4 ... or four, etc., of the seven things named above; rather, inspect all seven carefully ...

---

[24]For comparison, *Dialogus de musica* 11 (GS, 1:259) lists only low C, D, E, F, and G, and high A as initials for the first tone, and specifies that E is rarely used. In *Lucidarium* 11.4.50–84 (ed. Herlinger, 416–33), Marchetto lists the same letters as Prosdocimo, assigning low A and B to its mixed form and low E to its intermixed form, with the stipulation that it is rarely used; the others he calls proper.

[25]*Dialogus* 12 (GS, 1:260) lists the same notes as Prosdocimo plus the second low G, specifying that G, B, E and G are very rarely used. In *Lucidarium* 11.4.98–104 (ed. Herlinger, 436–39), Marchetto lists G, A, C, D, E, and F (B is included, exceptionally, in the version of the Chicago manuscript), assigning G to the pluperfect form of the tone and calling the others proper; G and E, he notes, are rarely used.

[26]*Dialogus* 13 (GS, 1:260) includes high A as well. Prosdocimo agrees with *Lucidarium* 11.4.114–19 (ed. Herlinger, 442–45).

[27]Prosdocimo agrees with both *Dialogus* 14 (GS, 1:261) and *Lucidarium* 11.4.129–35 (ed. Herlinger, 450–53).

[28]*Dialogus* 15 (GS, 1:261) omits D and states that G is rarely used. Prosdocimo agrees with *Lucidarium* 11.4.161–66 (ed. Herlinger, 466–69), though Marchetto specifies D as improper.

addunt literam sextam, scilicet b rotundum acutum, et, credo, male, quoniam nullus cantus supra initium sui Seculorum amen initiari debet, ut de omnibus aliis tonis patere potest. Declarabitur autem inferius loco suo quid sit hoc Seculorum amen. Septimi vero toni sunt iste sex, scilicet F et secundum G
5 gravia, et A, ♮ quadrum, C, et D acuta. Octavi vero toni sunt iste sex, scilicet C, D, F, et secundum G gravia, et A et C acuta.

⟨10.⟩ Item sciendum, et est declaratio quinti in ordine declarandi, quod sicut quilibet octo tonorum quasdam habet literas principales, ut dictum est, ita quilibet ipsorum, sive sit perfectus sive imperfectus sive plusquamper-
10 fectus sive mixtus, quasdam habet literas in quarum quamlibet suum potest habere finem. Primi ergo et secundi toni insimul sunt huiusmodi litere finales due, scilicet D grave et A acutum; tercii vero et quarti insimul sunt iste due, scilicet E grave et ♮ quadrum acutum; quinti vero et sexti insimul sunt iste due, scilicet F grave et C acutum; septimi vero et octavi insimul
15 sunt iste due, scilicet secundum G grave et D acutum. Scias tamen quod iste quatuor litere finales, scilicet D, E, F, et secundum G gravia, sunt octo tonorum propriissime finales; cetere vero finales litere, scilicet A, ♮ quadrum, C, et D acute, per reductionem ad finales proprias finales esse dicuntur. Reducitur nanque A acutum ad D grave, ♮ vero quadrum acutum
20 ad E grave, C vero acutum ad F grave, et D acutum ad secundum G grave. Quatuor ergo sunt octo tonorum finales proprie et quatuor per reductionem, ut visum est, et hee quatuor finales per reductionem quatuor finalium propri-

---

3 hoc [sed] B ‖ 4 Septimi]7. Toni *in marg. m. sec.* B | vero]autem L ‖ 5 Octavi]8. Toni *in marg. m. sec.* B | vero et ultimi L ‖ 6 et (*sec.*) *om.* L ‖ 7 Item]5. Finales *in marg. m. sec.* B | Item … declarandi]Preterea pro declaratione quinti in ordine declarandi est sciendum L ‖ 8 dictum]iam dictum L ‖ 11 Primi]1. 2. Toni *in marg. m. sec.* B | litere *om.* L ‖ 12 tercii]3. 4. Toni *in marg. m. sec.* B ‖ 13 quinti]5. et 6. Toni *in marg. m. sec.* B ‖ 14 septimi]7. et 8. Toni *in marg. m. sec.* B | septimi vero]sed septimi L ‖ 20 vero]autem L ‖ 22–102.1 propriarum finalium L ‖

high round b[29] and, I believe, improperly, inasmuch as no chant should begin above the initial of its *Seculorum amen*, as can be evident for all the other tones. What the *Seculorum amen* is will be explained below in its place.[30] The initials of the seventh tone are these six: low F, the second low G, and high A, square ♮, C, and D.[31] Those of the eighth tone are these six: low C, D, and F, the second low G, and high A and C.[32]

10. Again, one must know (and this is the explanation of the fifth thing to be explained in order) that just as any of the eight tones has certain principal letters (as has been said),[33] so does any of them, whether it be perfect or imperfect or pluperfect or mixed, have certain letters on any of which it can end. The final letters of the first and second tones together, then, are two of this sort, low D and high A; of the third and fourth together these two, low E and high square ♮; of the fifth and sixth together these two, low F and high C; of the seventh and eighth together these two, the second low G and high D. Nevertheless, know that these four final letters—low D, E, and F, and the second low G—are the most proper finals of the eight tones; the other final letters—high A, square ♮, C, and D, on the other hand—are said to be finals by relation[34] to the proper finals, for high A is related to low D, high square ♮ to low E, high C to low F, and high D to the second low G. Therefore, there are four proper finals of the eight tones and four by relation, as has been seen, and these four finals by relation are said to be cofinals of

---

[29]*Dialogus* 16 (GS, 1:262) lists low C, D, E, and F, and high A. In *Lucidarium* 11.4.178–82 (ed. Herlinger, 474–77), Marchetto lists the same notes as Prosdocimo, stating that the first three are customary (*usitata*) but the last three are "not in use in the melodies of Gregory."

[30]*Plana musica* 2.11 (102–9).

[31]Prosdocimo lists the same notes as both *Dialogus* 17 (GS, 1:262–63) and *Lucidarium* 11.4.189–95 (ed. Herlinger, 478–83); the *Dialogus* states that A is rarely used.

[32]Prosdocimo's lists of notes agrees with both *Dialogus* 18 (GS, 1:263) and *Lucidarium* 11.4.204–19 (ed. Herlinger, 484–89). Marchetto assigns low C to the pluperfect form of the tone.

[33]*Plana musica* 2.9 (99–101).

[34]*Reduco* is used in treatises on mensuration to refer to "the grouping of a perfection interrupted by intermediate notes" (C. Matthew Balensuela, ed. and trans., *Ars cantus mensurabilis mensurata per modos iuris*, Greek and Latin Music Theory, vol. 10 [Lincoln: University of Nebraska Press, 1994], 209, n. 108). Balensuela translates *reduco* and *reductio* as "reduce" and "reduction"; but "relate" and "relation" seem a better translation here and match the root meaning of *reduco* and *reductio*, "bring(ing) back."

arum confinales esse dicuntur. Alii autem aliter ponunt octo tonorum literas finales, licet non multum differenter a supradictis, unde dicunt primi et secundi toni esse has duas literas finales, scilicet D et A absolute, quia non curando utrum sint graves vel acute vel superacute; tercii vero et quarti
5 esse has duas, scilicet E et ♮ quadrum, etiam absolute; quinti vero et sexti esse has duas, scilicet F et C, etiam absolute; septimi vero et octavi unicam solam esse literam finalem, scilicet G etiam absolute. Voluntque etiam isti insimul cum aliis has quatuor literas, scilicet D, E, F, et secundum G gravia, propriissimas esse finales et reliquas per reductionem ad propriissimas pro
10 finalibus esse ponendas, atque confinales nominari debere.

⟨11.⟩ Pro declaratione vero sexti in ordine declarandi, est sciendum quod immediate post antiphanas comuniter reperiuntur Seculorum amen, que per hanc dictionem, Euouae, ut plurimum, importantur. Est nanque Euouae dic-

---

10 *Huc pertinet emendatio quae in L invenitur:* ... confinales nominari debere. Sunt et etiam nonnulli alii qui volunt absolute quod omnis litera in cuius dictione re vox reperitur primi et secundi toni finalis esse dicatur, et quod absolute omnis litera in cuius dictione mi vox reperitur tercii et quarti toni finalis esse dicatur, et quod absolute omnis litera in cuius dictione fa vox reperitur quinti et sexti toni finalis esse dicatur; et quod absolute omnis litera in cuius dictione sol vox reperitur septimi et octavi toni esse dicatur; de istis tamen tribus opinionibus prima comunior est et ab omnibus modernis comuniter obtenta.

12 *Huc pertinet emendatio quae in L invenitur:* ... Seculorum amen, id est cantus sub quibus pronuntiari debent ista, Seculorum amen ...

---

1 aliter *sup. lin.* B ‖ 3 has duas esse L ‖ 4 quarti toni L ‖ 5 scilicet *om.* L ‖ 6 octavi [esse] L ‖ 7 etiam (*sec.*) *om.* L ‖ 13 Euouae (*pr.*)]Seculorum Amen e u o u a e *in marg. m. sec.* B ‖

the four proper finals.[35] Others, however, place the final letters of the eight tones in another way, although not all that differently from what has been said above.[36] They say that there are two final letters of the first and second tones, D and A without qualification, not caring whether they are low or high or very high; that there are two of the third and fourth tones, E and square ♮, also without qualification; that there are two of the fifth and sixth tones, F and C, also without qualification; and that there is one single final letter of the seventh and eighth tones, G, also without qualification. Like the others, these also wish these four letters—low D, E, F, and the second low G—to be the most proper finals and the remaining ones to be placed as finals by reduction to the most proper ones—and the latter ought to be named cofinals.

11. For the explanation of the sixth thing to be explained in order, one must know that *Seculorum amen* are commonly found immediately after antiphons; they are most often conveyed through this expression, *Euouae*.

11–12 ... ought to be named cofinals. And there are also some others who maintain without qualification that every letter in the expression of which the syllable *re* is found be said to be a final of the first and second tones, without qualification that every letter in the expression of which the syllable *mi* is found be said to be a final of the third and fourth tones, without qualification that every letter in the expression of which the syllable *fa* is found be said to be a final of the fifth and sixth tones, and without qualification that every letter in the expression of which the syllable *sol* is found be said to be a final of the seventh and eighth tones.[37] Of these three opinions, the first is the most common and commonly held by all modern writers.

14 ... *Seculorum amen*, that is, chants under which this should be pronounced, *Seculorum amen* ...

---

[35] Among the many theorists who list D, E, F, and G as finals and a, ♮, c, and d as cofinals (or affinals) are Amerus, *Practica artis musice* (*Ameri Practica artis musice (1271)*, ed. Cesarino Ruini, Corpus scriptorum de musica, vol. 25 [(Rome): American Institute of Musicology, 1977], 94); Marchetto, *Lucidarium* 11.2.17–19 (ed. Herlinger, 376–77); and Gaffurio, *Practica musice* 1.8 (f. bvr).

[36] E.g., Guido, *Micrologus* 7 (ed. Smits van Waesberghe, 117–21); and Aribo, *De musica* (ed. Smits van Waesberghe, 2).

[37] E.g., Johannes de Muris, *Ars discantus* 3 (CS, 3:99); Jacobus Leodiensis, *Speculum musice* 6.75 (ed. Bragard, 217); *Quatuor principalia* 3.31 (CS, 4:233; and the text published as the *Compendium musicale* of Nicolaus de Capua (ed. La Fage, 329).

tio composita ex omnibus literis vocalibus in Seculorum amen repertis, si
bene consideras, sic quod Euouae est proprie Seculorum amen demptis
omnibus literis consonantibus; et hec dictio Euouae comuniter immediate
post quamlibet antiphanam reperitur et per ipsam in noticiam octo tonorum
5 taliter devenire possumus, quoniam aut cantus talis dictionis Euouae, sive
Seculorum amen, quod idem est, incipit in voce tercia supra finalem antiphane immediate precedentis aut in voce quarta aut in voce quinta aut in
voce sexta. Si in voce tercia, tunc antiphana immediate precedens secundi
vel sexti toni infallanter esse dicitur, et si in F gravi sumit exordium, sub
10 secundo reponitur tono; et si in A acuto, sexti toni esse vere reputatur. Si
vero incipit in voce quarta, tunc antiphana immediate precedens quarti vel
octavi toni esse dicitur, et si in A acuto sumit exordium, sub quarto reponitur tono; si vero in C acuto, octavi toni esse vere reputatur. Si vero incipit
in voce quinta, tunc antiphana immediate precedens primi vel quinti vel
15 septimi toni esse dicitur, et si in A acuto sumit exordium, sub primo tono
collocatur; si vero in C acuto, sub quinto tono reponitur; si vero in D
acuto, septimi toni vere esse reputatur. Si vero incipit in voce sexta, tunc
antiphana immediate precedens absque fallo tercii toni esse dicitur; ex quibus omnibus concludas quod per huiusmodi Seculorum amen devenire non
20 potest nisi in noticiam tonorum antiphanarum vel sibi equivalentium, cum
ipsa solis antiphanis sive sibi equivalentibus habeant famulari.

2–4 *Huc pertinet emendatio quae in L invenitur:* ... demptis omnibus literis
consonantibus, dato quod quandoque prima consonans litera dimittatur, et
componitur tunc hec dictio Seuouae, sed sive sic sive sic idem importatur; et
hec dictio Euouae, sive Seuouae, comuniter immediate ⟨post⟩ quamlibet
antiphonam reperitur, cum suis notulis, et per ipsam ...
5–6 *Huc pertinet emendatio quae in L invenitur:* ... Euouae, sive Seuouae,
sive Seculorum amen ...
9 *Huc pertinet emendatio quae in L invenitur:* ... in F grave vel in C acutum
sumit exordium ...
10 *Huc pertinet emendatio quae in L invenitur:* ... in A vel in E acuto ...
12 *Huc pertinet emendatio quae in L invenitur:* ... in A vel in E acuto ...
13 *Huc pertinet emendatio quae in L invenitur:* ... in C vel G acuto ...
15 *Huc pertinet emendatio quae in L invenitur:* ... in A vel in E acuto ...
16 *Huc pertinet emendatio quae in L invenitur:* ... in C vel G acuto ...
16–17 *Huc pertinet emendatio quae in L invenitur:* ... in D acuto vel A
superacuto ...

---

3 literis *sup. lin.* B ‖ 6 tercia]Euouae in voce 3. *in marg. m. sec.* B ‖ 7 quarta]in voce 4. *in marg. m. sec.* B | quinta]in voce 5. *in marg. m. sec.* B ‖ 8 sexta]in voce 6. *in marg. m. sec.* B ‖ 13 vere esse L ‖

Euouae, to be sure, is an expression composed of all the vowels found in *Seculorum amen* (if you consider it properly); so, *Euouae* is correctly *Seculorum amen* with all consonants purged. This expression *Euouae* is commonly found immediately after any antiphon. By means of it, in this way, we can attain a knowledge of the eight tones inasmuch as the melody of this expression *Euouae*—or *Seculorum amen*, which is the same thing—begins either on the third pitch above the final of the antiphon immediately preceding it or on the fourth pitch, the fifth pitch, or the sixth pitch. If it begins on the third pitch, then the antiphon immediately preceding is said to be of the second or the sixth tone without fail; if it begins on low F, it is placed under the second tone, and if on high A, it is truly held to be of the sixth tone. If it begins on the fourth pitch, then the antiphon immediately preceding is said to be of the fourth or the eighth tone; if it begins on high A, it is placed under the fourth tone, but if on high C, it is truly held to be of the eighth tone. If it begins on the fifth pitch, then the antiphon immediately preceding is said to be of the first, the fifth, or the seventh tone; if it begins on high A, it is assigned a position under the first tone, if on high C, it is placed under the fifth tone, but if on high D, it is truly held to be of the seventh tone. If, on the other hand, it begins on the sixth pitch, then the antiphon immediately preceding is said to be of the third tone without fail. From all these, draw the conclusion that by means of *Seculorum amen* of this sort you can attain a knowledge only of the tones of antiphons or their equivalents, since they must serve only antiphons or their equivalents.

3–4 ... with all consonants purged—granted that sometimes the first consonant is not excluded and the expression *Seuouae* is composed. But whether this way or that, the same thing is conveyed. This expression *Euouae*, or *Seuouae*, is commonly found immediately after any antiphon, with its notes. By means of it ...

6 ... *Euouae*, or *Seuouae*, or *Seculorum amen* ...

10 ... it begins on low F or on high C ...[38]

11 ... on high A or on high E ...

13 ... on high A or on high E ...

14 ... on high C or high G ...

17 ... on high A or on high E ...

17 ... on high C or high G ...

18 ... on high D or very high A ...

---

[38]In the revision, Prosdocimo has attempted to accommodate intonation formulas pitched a fifth higher than normal.

Per quasi similia vero etiam in noticiam tonorum omnium introituum devenire potes, unde omnis introitus desinens in D grave cuius versus sive psalmus in F grave sumit exordium primi toni esse dicitur; si vero eundem finem retinendo eius versus in D grave sumat exordium et postea in C grave

5   descendat, ad F grave postea ascendendo, secundi toni esse dicitur. Item omnis introitus desinens in E grave cuius versus sive psalmus in G grave secundum sumit exordium, ad C acutum inde sursum ascendendo, tercii toni esse dicitur; si vero eundem finem observando eius versus in A acutum sumat exordium, quarti toni esse dicitur. Item omnis introitus desinens in F

10 grave cuius versus sive psalmus in eodem F gravi sumat exordium et postea ad A acutum ascendat, ad C acutum ulterius ascendendo, quinti toni esse dicitur; si vero eundem finem observando eius versus in eundem finem, scilicet in F grave, sumat exordium et ad G grave secundum ascendat, iterum ad F grave descendendo, sexti toni esse dicitur. Item omnis introitus desin-

15 ens in G grave secundum cuius versus sive psalmus in eodem G gravi secundo sumit exordium et ad C acutum ascendat, usque ad F acutum in posterum deveniendo, septimi toni esse dicitur; si vero eundem finem observando in eundem finem eius versus sumat exordium ad C acutum ascendendo, non tamen ad F acutum deveniendo, octavi toni esse dicitur.

20 Item etiam simili modo in noticiam tonorum omnium responsorum devenire possumus, quoniam omne responsum desinens in D grave cuius versus in A acutum sumit exordium, vel in D grave et ascendit usque ad A acutum, primi toni esse dicitur; si vero eundem finem retinendo eius versus in C grave sumat exordium, vel in eodem D gravi et descendat in C grave,

25 usque in G grave secundum in posterum ascendendo, secundi toni esse dicitur. Item omne responsum desinens in E grave cuius versus in C acutum sumit exordium tercii toni esse dicitur; si vero eundem finem retinendo eius versus in A acutum sumat exordium, vel in E grave et ascendat usque ad A acutum, quarti toni esse dicitur. Item omne responsum desinens in F grave

30 cuius versus in C acutum sumit exordium quinti toni esse dicitur; si vero eundem finem observando eius versus in eundem finem, scilicet in F grave, sumat exordium et etiam ibidem finiatur, sexti toni esse dicitur. Item omne responsum desinens in G grave secundum cuius versus in D acutum sumat

---

19 *Huc pertinet emendatio quae in L invenitur:* ... octavi toni esse dicitur, et idem habere potes in confinalibus quod habuisti in finalibus, si bene consideras.

---

1 Per]Introitus *in marg. m. sec.* B ‖ 4 retinendo in secundam notam B retinendo in secunda nota L ‖ 11 descendat *ante corr.* L ‖ 20 Item]Responsor. *in marg. m. sec.* B ‖ 28 grave [vel] B ‖

But through more or less similar considerations, you can attain a knowledge of the tones of all introits as well.[39] Accordingly, every introit closing on low D of which the verse or psalm begins on low F is said to be of the first tone, but if, retaining that same ending, its verse begins on low D and then descends to low C, ascending then to low F, it is said to be of the second tone. Again, every introit closing on low E of which the verse or psalm begins on the second low G, ascending high up from there, to high C, is said to be of the third tone, but if, observing that same ending, its verse begins on high A, it is said to be of the fourth tone. Again, every introit closing on low F of which the verse or psalm begins on that same low F and then ascends to high A, further ascending to high C, is said to be of the fifth tone, but if, observing that same ending, its verse begins on that same ending, low F, and ascends to the second low G, again descending to the low F, it is said to be of the sixth tone. Again, every introit closing on the second low G of which the verse or psalm begins on that same second low G and ascends to high C, later attaining high F, is said to be of the seventh tone, but if, observing that same ending, its verse begins on that same ending, ascending to high C but not attaining high F, it is said to be of the eighth tone.

Again, in a similar way, we can attain a knowledge of the tones of all responsories inasmuch as every responsory closing on low D of which the verse begins on high A or low D and ascends to high A is said to be of the first tone, but if, retaining that same ending, its verse begins on low C or that same low D and descends to low C, ascending later to the second low G, it is said to be of the second tone. Again, every responsory closing on low E of which the verse begins on high C is said to be of the third tone, but if, retaining that same ending, its verse begins on high A or low E and ascends to high A, it is said to be of the fourth tone. Again, every responsory closing on low F of which the verse begins on high C is said to be of the fifth tone, but if, observing that same ending, its verse begins on that same ending, low F, and ends there, it is said to be of the sixth tone. Again, every responsory closing on the second low G of which the verse begins on high D, later

---

18 ... it is said to be of the eighth tone. You can grasp the same thing in cofinals that you have grasped in finals, if you consider it properly.

---

[39]Similar rules for both introits and responsories appear in section 22 of Biagio Rossetti, *Libellus de rudimentis musices*, ed. Albert Seay, Critical Texts, no. 12 (Colorado Springs: Colorado College Music Press, 1981), 60.

exordium ad F acutum in posterum ascendendo, septimi toni esse dicitur; si
vero eundem finem observando eius versus in C acutum sumat exordium,
vel in G grave secundum et ascendat usque ad C acutum, octavi toni esse
dicitur. Et quasi per hunc modum omnes cantus versum habentes cognos-
5 cuntur.

    Scias tamen quod ad bene cognoscendum modos sive tonos omnium
cantuum versus habentium oportet te fines illorum cantuum intuere et
ipsorum, et suorum versuum, elevationem et depositionem vocum supra ⟨et
infra⟩ finales illorum cantuum versus habentium inspicere, quoniam quilibet
10 cantus cum eius versu eundem modum intonandi, sive tonum, insequi debet.

---

10 *Huc pertinet emendatio quae in L invenitur:* ... eundem modum intonandi, sive tonum, insequi debet. Item scias quod per id quod dictum est in
his responsoriis cum suis versibus de finalibus principalibus, leviter intelligere poteris quid in his de confinalibus dicere habeas, si bene considerare
voles, quare in hoc non intendo tibi amplius prolongare sermonem.

---

6 quod *sup. lin.* B | modos]nodos B ‖ 8–9 *scripsi* ‖ 9 inspicere]bene inspicere L ‖

ascending to high F, is said to be of the seventh tone, but if, observing that same ending, its verse begins on high C or the second low G and ascends to high C, it is said to be of the eighth tone. And through this means, the tones of almost all chants having a verse are recognized.[40]

Nevertheless, know that in order to properly recognize the modes or tones of all chants having verses, you should contemplate the endings of those chants and their verses and inspect the elevation and deposition of pitches above and below the finals of those chants having verses inasmuch as any chant and its verse ought to follow the same manner of intonation— or the same tone.[41]

---

10 ... ought to follow the same manner of intonation—or the same tone. Again, know that through what has been said concerning the principal finals of these responsories with their verses, you will easily be able to understand what you have to say about them concerning their cofinals, if you will consider it properly. Wherefore, I do not intend to further prolong the discussion of this matter.

---

[40]Prosdocimo's rules correspond in substance to the tonal structure of responsories given in an unpublished version of the *Compendium musicale* of Nicolaus de Capua in Venice, Biblioteca Nazionale Marciana, lat. cl. VIII.82, f. 20r–v: "All responsories that end on low D of which the verses begin on high a are of the first tone; all responsories that end on low D of which the verses begin on C or on D are of the second tone; all responsories that end on low E of which the verses begin on high C are of the third tone, but if their verses begin on low E or on high A, they are of the fourth tone; all responsories that end on low F of which the verses begin on high C are of the fifth tone, and if their verses begin on low F or high A, they are of the sixth tone; all responsories that end on low G of which the verses begin on high D are of the seventh tone, but if their verses begin on low G or high E [*sic;* i.e., C], they are of the eighth tone [Omnia responsoria que finiunt in .d. grauj. et eorum versus incipiunt in .a. acuto sunt primj toni; omnia Responsoria que finiunt in d grauj et eorum versus incipiunt in c uel in d sunt secundi toni. Omnia Responsoria que finiunt in E grauj et eorum versus incipiunt in c acuto sunt tertij toni sed si eorum versus incipiunt in E grauj uel in a acuto sunt quartj tonj. Omnia Responsoria que finiunt in F. grauj et eorum versus incipiunt in c acuto sunt quintj tonj, et si eorum versus incipiunt in F graui uel in a acuto sunt sexti toni. Omnia responsoria que finiunt in g grauj et eorum uersus incipiunt in d acuto sunt septimj tonj. Sed si eorum versus incipiunt in g grauj uel in e acuto (i.e., C) sunt octauj]."

[41]This recalls Marchetto's injunction in *Lucidarium* 11.4.151–58 (ed. Herlinger, 462– 67) that the end of a verse and the repetend of its responsory should belong to the same melodic succession ("finis Versus cum principio repetende una et eadem consequentia esse debet"), though Marchetto was speaking specifically of the consistent use of b natural or b flat in such cases.

⟨12.⟩ Pro declaratione autem specierum, que in ordine septimum declarandum existunt, est sciendum quod species, quantum ad propositum spectat, est prepositionis, postpositionis, ac in medio positionis tonorum atque semitoniorum quedam diversitas in quibusdam vocum combinationibus
5 reperta, sicut gratia exempli in tercia, in quarta, in quinta, in sexta, in septima, in octava, et cetera; sed quia tales diversitates in quibusdam huiusmodi vocum combinationibus reperte proposito nostro utiles non existunt, ideo relinquende et de utilibus nostro proposito est determinandum, que solum due permanent, scilicet dyateseron et dyapente.
10 Est nanque dyateseron duarum vocum quedam combinatio que a modernis quarta minor, ex duobus tonis et uno semitonio contexta, nuncupatur; et dicitur dyateseron a dya grece, quod importat de latine, et teseron grece, quod latine dicitur quatuor, unde dyateseron nomen grecum est quod latine de quatuor importat, eo quod combinatio talis que dyateseron nuncupatur
15 quatuor in se continet voces, ex quibus duo toni et unum semitonium componuntur. Et hec dyateseron in se tres continet diversitates, que pro nunc species nuncupantur, secundum triplicem modum in ipsa dyateseron semitonium collocandi, unde in dyateseron quandoque semitonium in medio duorum tonorum collocatur, et tunc prima species dyateseron procreatur;
20 quandoque vero huiusmodi semitonium duobus tonis preponitur, et tunc secunda species dyateseron procreatur; quandoque vero huiusmodi semitonium duobus tonis postponitur, et tunc tercia species dyateseron procreatur.

1–2 *Huc pertinet emendatio quae in L invenitur:* ... que in ordine septimum et ultimum declarandum existunt ...

22 *Huc pertinet emendatio quae in L invenitur:* ... tercia species dyateseron procreatur. Et quia plures variationes collocandi semitonium in dyateseron quam tres non reperiuntur, pro tanto solum tres sunt species dyateseron abinvicem distincte iam supradicte.

---

8 et ... proposito]sunt et solum de proposito nostro utilibus L ‖ 10 combinatio quedam L ‖ 16 que diversitates L ‖ 17 nuncupantur tres dico L ‖ 19 procreatur]re mi fa sol *in marg. m. sec.* B ‖ 21 procreatur]2⁰ mi fa sol la *in marg. m. sec.* B procreatur [et quia plures variationes collocandi semitonium in dyateseron] L ‖ 22 procreatur]3⁰ ut re mi fa *in marg. m. sec.* B ‖

12. Now for the explanation of species, which are seventh in order of things to be explained, one must know that species, in respect to the proposition, is a certain difference of placing tones and semitones before, after, and between one another, found in certain intervals, as for example in the third, the fourth, the fifth, the sixth, the seventh, the octave, etc., but because the differences found in certain intervals of this sort are not useful for our proposition, they must be relinquished and what is useful for our proposition must be determined. Only two remain: the diatessaron and the diapente.

The diatessaron, then, which moderns call the minor fourth, is a certain interval of two pitches made up of two tones and one semitone. Diatessaron is derived from *dia* in Greek, which conveys *de* in Latin, and *tessaron* in Greek, which is called *quattuor* in Latin. Accordingly, diatessaron is a Greek noun that conveys *de quattuor* in Latin because the interval that is called diatessaron contains in itself four pitches, from which two tones and one semitone are composed.[42] This diatessaron contains in itself three differences, which for the present are called species, following the threefold manner of assigning the semitone a position within the diatessaron. Accordingly, in the diatessaron, the semitone is sometimes assigned a position between the two tones, and then the first species of the diatessaron is created; sometimes the semitone is placed before the two tones, and then the second species of the diatessaron is created; and sometimes the semitone is placed after the two tones, and then the third species of the diatessaron is created.[43]

1–2 ... which are seventh and last in order of things to be explained ...
22–23 ... the third species of the diatessaron is created. Because no more than three variations are found in assigning the semitone a position within the diatessaron, there are only the aforesaid three species of diatessaron distinct one from another.

---

[42]The same derivation appears in the Lucca revision of *Contrapunctus* 3.3 (ed. Herlinger, 40–41) and in *Musica speculativa* 1.8 (164–65). Similar derivations appear in many treatises, e.g., *Dialogus de musica* (GS, 1:268), Regino, *Harmonica* 16 (GS, 1:242); *Musica enchiriadis* 10 (Hans Schmid, ed., *Musica et scolica enchiriadis una cum aliquibus tractatulis adiunctis*, Bayerische Akademie der Wissenschaften, Veröffentlichungen der Musikhistorischen Kommission, Band 3 [München: Bayerische Akademie der Wissenschaften; C. H. Beck, 1981], 24; translated with introduction and notes by Raymond Erickson as *Musica enchiriadis and Scolica enchiriadis*, Music Theory Translation Series [New Haven, CT: Yale University Press, 1995], 13); Guido, *Epistola* 210–12 (ed. Pesce, 488–89; cf. GS, 2:46–47); and Marchetto, *Lucidarium* 3.1.6, 9.1.35–36 (ed. Herlinger, 168–71, 328–29).

[43]Marchetto, among others, constructs the species of the diatessaron identically in *Lucidarium* 9.1.38–41 (ed. Herlinger, 328–33).

Est autem dyapente duarum vocum quedam combinatio que a modernis quinta maior, ex tribus tonis et uno semitonio contexta, nuncupatur; et dicitur dyapente a dya grece, quod est de latine, et pente grece, quod latine dicitur quinque, unde dyapente nomen grecum est quod latine de quinque importare videtur, eo quod combinatio talis que dyapente dicitur quinque in se continet voces, ex quibus tres toni et unum semitonium componuntur. Et hec dyapente in se quatuor continet species, sicut in ipsa semitonium quadrupliciter collacare possumus. Si ergo supra primam speciem dyateseron tonum adiungamus, statim primam speciem dyapente componimus, que ex tono, semitonio, et duobus tonis constare dicitur; si vero supra secundam speciem dyateseron tonum adiungamus, statim secundam speciem dyapente componimus, que ex semitonio et tribus tonis constare dicitur; si autem supra terciam speciem ipsius dyateseron tonum adiungamus, non terciam speciem dyapente, sed quartam, componimus, que ex duobus tonis, semitonio, et tono constare dicitur. Tercia vero species dyapente ex nulla specie dyateseron sumit compositionem, sed ex se sola componitur, et ex tribus tonis et semitonio constare dicitur, et continet huiusmodi tercia species dyapente ita semitonium in fine, sicut et tercia species dyateseron.

Et scias quod huiusmodi species dyateseron et dyapente cognoscuntur per respectum note inferioris ad superiorem et non e contra, quoniam tunc descensus qui fit a la ad mi sub secunda specie dyateseron, sub qua vere dicitur esse, non collocaretur, sed sub tercia, quia in tali descensu ultimatur semitonium, uti debet ultimari in tercia specie; sed si nota inferior superiori comparetur, uti comparari debet, precedet semitonium tonos, ut in secunda

---

1 quedam *om.* B ‖ 2 maior *om.* B ‖ 7–8 species ... quadrupliciter]species, et non plures, sicut in ipsa dyapente quadrupliciter et non pluries semitonium L ‖ 20 superiorem]notam superiorem L ‖ 23 superiori]note superiori L ‖

The diapente, on the other hand, which moderns call the major fifth, is a certain interval of two pitches made up of three tones and one semitone. Diapente is derived from *dia* in Greek, which is *de* in Latin, and *pente* in Greek, which in Latin is called *quinque*. Accordingly, diapente is a Greek noun that seems to convey *de quinque* in Latin because the interval that is called diapente contains in itself five pitches, from which three tones and one semitone are composed.[44] The diapente contains in itself four species, as we can assign the semitone a position within it in four ways. Therefore, if we join a tone above the first species of the diatessaron, we compose the first species of the diapente forthwith, which is said to consist of a tone, a semitone, and two tones; if we join a tone above the second species of the diatessaron, we compose the second species of the diapente forthwith, which is said to consist of a semitone and three tones; but if we join a tone above the third species of the diatessaron, we compose not the third species of the diapente but the fourth, which is said to consist of two tones, a semitone, and a tone. The third species of the diapente, indeed, takes its composition from no species of diatessaron but is composed only of itself and is said to consist of three tones and a semitone. The third species of the diapente of this sort contains a semitone at the end, just like the third species of the diatessaron.[45]

And know that the species of the diatessaron and diapente of this sort are recognized as respecting the lowest note to the highest[46] and not vice versa, inasmuch as then the descent made from *la* to *mi* would not have been assigned a position under the second species of the diatessaron (under which it is truly said to be) but under the third because in such a descent, the semitone would be last (as it ought to be last in the third species). But if the lowest note were compared to the highest (as it ought to be compared), the semitone will precede the tones, as it ought to precede them in the second

---

[44]The same derivation appears in the Lucca revision of *Contrapunctus* 3.5 (ed. Herlinger, 44–45) and in *Musica speculativa* 1.9 (166–67). Similar derivations appear frequently, e.g., in *Dialogus de musica* (GS, 1:269); Regino, *Harmonica* 16 (GS, 1:242–43); *Musica enchiriadis* 10 (ed. Schmid, 25; trans. Erickson, 13–14); Guido, *Epistola* 212–14 (ed. Pesce, 488–89; cf. GS, 2:47); and Marchetto, *Lucidarium* 3.2.3 (ed. Herlinger, 170–73).

[45]Marchetto, among others, constructs the species of the diapente identically in *Lucidarium* 9.1.78–98 (ed. Herlinger, 342–55).

[46]That is, the sequences of tones and semitones are to be read from the bottom up.

specie dyateseron precedere debet, et sic secunda species dyateseron pro-
creabitur, et bene.

His ergo speciebus sic declaratis, per ipsas in noticiam tonorum taliter
pervenire possumus, quoniam quotienscunque super aliqua voce finali cantus
5 alicuius prima species dyapente reperitur et super voce dyapente supra finalem resonante prima species dyateseron invenitur, tunc talis cantus primi
toni esse dicitur; si vero supra finalem alicuius cantus prima species dyapente reperitur et infra eandem finalem prima species dyateseron invenitur,
tunc talis cantus secundi toni esse dicitur. Omnis vero cantus supra cuius
10 finalem secunda species dyapente reperitur et supra vocem dyapente supra
finalem resonantem secunda species dyateseron invenitur tercii toni esse
dicitur; si vero supra finalem alicuius cantus secunda species dyapente
reperitur et infra eandem finalem secunda species dyateseron invenitur,
quarti toni esse dicitur. Omnis vero cantus supra cuius finalem tercia species
15 dyapente reperitur et supra vocem dyapente supra finalem resonantem tercia
species dyateseron invenitur quinti toni esse dicitur; si vero supra alicuius
cantus finalem tercia species dyapente reperitur et infra ipsius finalem tercia
species dyateseron invenitur, sexti toni esse dicitur. Omnis vero cantus supra
cuius finalem quarta species dyapente reperitur et supra vocem dyapente
20 supra finalem resonantem prima species dyateseron invenitur septimi toni
esse dicitur; si vero supra alicuius cantus finalem quarta species dyapente
reperitur et infra ipsius finalem prima species dyateseron invenitur, octavi

---

2 *Huc pertinet emendatio quae in L invenitur:* ... et bene; et pariformiter de
speciebus dyapente. Sed ratio quare huiusmodi species potius cognosci
habeant per ascensum quam per descensum potest esse ista, quia ascensus
nobilior est descensu, eo quod inferiores voces sunt tanquam fundamentum
superiorum vocum, vel quia ad modum loquendi autorum in hac materia
voces inferiores precedunt voces superiores in ordine manus musicalis suarum scilicet viginti dictionum, et ideo in dyateseron que est a mi ad la vel e
contra dicimus mi precedere, cum sit inferior vox inter voces hanc dyateseron componentes, et sic secundam speciem dyateseron componere; et non
dicimus ipsum mi esse ultimam vocem illius dyateseron, et sic terciam speciem ipsius componere, quoniam inceptio fit ab inferiori et non a superiori,
uti in manu musicali apparet, prout dictum est.

---

4 quotienscunque]quandocunque L | super ... finali]supra aliquam notam finalem L || 5–6
super voce ... resonante]supra vocem ... resonantem L ||

species of the diatessaron, and thus the second species of the diatessaron will be created, and properly.

Therefore, these species having been thus explained, we can come to a knowledge of the tones as follows: whenever the first species of the diapente is found above the final pitch of some chant and the first species of the diatessaron is discovered above the pitch sounding the diapente above the final, that chant is said to be of the first tone; but if the first species of the diapente is found above the final of any chant and the first species of the diatessaron is discovered below that same final, that chant is said to be of the second tone. Every chant is said to be of the third tone above the final of which the second species of the diapente is found and the second species of the diatessaron is discovered above the pitch sounding the diapente above the final; but if the second species of the diapente is found above the final of any chant and the second species of the diatessaron is discovered below that same final, it is said to be of the fourth tone. Every chant is said to be of the fifth tone above the final of which the third species of the diapente is found and the third species of the diatessaron is discovered above the pitch sounding the diapente above the final; but if the third species of the diapente is found above the final of any chant and the third species of the diatessaron is discovered below its final, it is said to be of the sixth tone. Every chant is said to be of the seventh tone above the final of which the fourth species of the diapente is found and the first species of the diatessaron is discovered above the pitch sounding the diapente above the final; but if the fourth species of the diapente is found above the final of any chant and the first species of the diatessaron is discovered below its final, it is said to be of the eighth

---

2 ... and properly; and likewise for the species of the diapente. The reason why species of this sort must be recognized through ascent rather than through descent can be this: ascent is nobler than descent because lower pitches are, as it were, the fundamental of higher pitches; or in the manner of speaking of authors on this subject, the lower pitches precede the higher pitches in the order of the musical hand (that is, of its twenty expressions),[47] and thus in the diatessaron that is from *mi* to *la* or vice versa, we say that *mi* precedes, since it is the lowest pitch among the pitches that compose this diatessaron, and thus composes the second species of the diatessaron. We do not say that *mi* is the last pitch of that diatessaron and thus composes the third species, inasmuch as the inception is made from the lowest pitch, not the highest (as they appear in the musical hand), as has been said.[48]

---

[47]See *Plana musica* 1.3, 1.11 (38–39 amd 68–71).

[48]I.e., on pp. 112–13.

toni esse dicitur. Et si bene consideras, omnia hec ex his que de ascensu et descensu et literis finalibus tonorum dicta sunt inferri habent fundamentaliter.

Ad maiorem tamen noticiam cantuum qui modum suum non implent sursum nec deorsum, scire debes quod si aliquis sit cantus qui supra eius
5 finalem ultra sextam non ascendat nec sub eius finali sumat aliquem descensum, et qui pluries dyateseron sumat que est ab eius finali ad vocem quartam supra ipsam finalem, tunc, ut plurimum, talis cantus plagalis iudicatur, et tanto certius quanto pluries ipsam dyateseron in se resumit et huiusmodi plagalis quotum finem recipit totus in ordine iudicatur.
10 ⟨13.⟩ Pro declaratione autem octavi in ordine declarandi est sciendum quod neuma, secundum quod in proposito sumere volo, eo quod apud musicum multipliciter sumi solet, est coadunatio duarum vocum consonantiam

---

10 *Huc pertinet emendatio quae in L invenitur: cap. om.*

---

1 his]hic B ‖ 5 sit *om.* L ‖ 6 ab eius]a voce L | quartam vocem L ‖ 10 Pro]Neuma *in marg. m. sec.* B | autem *sup. lin.* B ‖

tone.[49] And if you consider it properly, all these things must be inferred fundamentally from the things that have been said concerning ascent and descent and the final letters of the tones.

But for a greater knowledge of chants that do not fill their measure above and below, you ought to know that if there is any chant that neither ascends beyond the sixth above its final nor descends below its final at all and that several times takes the diatessaron that is from its final to the fourth pitch above the final, then most often that chant is judged plagal, and the more certainly so the more times it takes that diatessaron; and in this manner, the whole chant in order is judged plagal, wherever it ends.[50]

13. For the explanation of the eighth thing to be explained in order, one must know that the neume (as I wish to take it in the proposition because it is customarily taken in many different ways by the musician) is a meeting of

---

11 Chapter omitted L

---

[49]Prosdocimo's rules for determining tone on the basis of pentachord and tetrachord species presuppose definitions of the tones as given most characteristically in Berno, *Musica* 7 (GS, 2:69–70), where the eight tones are defined in terms of species precisely as Prosdocimo's statements imply. Berno's definitions may be seen as a systematization of the earlier doctrine (e.g., in the *Dialogus de musica* 11–18 [GS, 1:259–63] and Guido, *Micrologus* 7 [ed. Smits van Waesberghe, 117–21]) that the eight tones were defined through the arrangement of tones and semitones, but they appear abstract in comparison to treatments that allow for the use of B-flat (e.g., the *Dialogus*). Prosdocimo's rules seem particularly abstract in comparison to Marchetto's system of defining tones, even though these are also defined through pentachord and tetrachord species; Marchetto's system takes into account the frequent occurrence of B-flat in modes 1, 2, 4, 5, and 6 (*Lucidarium* 11.4 [ed. Herlinger, 394–519 *passim*]). See the Introduction, 13–14.

[50]This recalls Marchetto's statement (*Lucidarium* 12.1.30–31 [ed. Herlinger, 526–27]) that melodies without overt characteristics of the authentic mode should be judged plagal because "any melody in an authentic mode [tends to] swell up to its perfection, or to a part of it; and if it cannot do this because of its brevity, there will always be some species, or segments of species, in it on the basis of which we can judge it authentic [quilibet auctenticus gliscit ad suam perfectionem, vel ad partem eius, ascendere, et si hoc facere nequit ob sui brevitatem, semper in eo sunt alique species, vel partes specierum, per quas ipsum possumus auctenticum iudicare]." Furthermore, according to the manuscript Brussels, Bibliothèque Royale Albert Ier, II 785, the *Lucidarium* (14.1.19 [ed. Herlinger, 522–23]) states that the frequent appearance of the *dyatessaron commune*, the span of pitches between the final and the note a fourth above it, shows that a melody belongs to the a plagal tone rather than its authentic counterpart. Though all other manuscripts read *dyapente commune* (the letters *tessaron* appear over an erasure in the Brussels manuscript), *dyatessaron commune* must be the correct reading, and it ought to have been signaled in my edition of the *Lucidarium*.

vel dissonantiam auribus reddentium, et licet tales neume plures existant, tamen solum tres sunt neume que nos ducunt in octo tonorum noticiam, scilicet dyateseron, dyapente, et dyapason. Quid autem sit dyateseron et dyapente dictum est superius. Dyapason vero est duarum vocum combinatio
5 quinque tonos et duo semitonia in se comprehendentium que apud modernos octava consonans nominatur; et dicitur dyapason a dya grece, quod est latine de, et pason, octo, unde dyapason nomen grecum est quod latine de octo importare videtur, eo quod talis dyapason in se octo comprehendit voces ex quibus quinque toni et duo semitonia componuntur. Per predictas ergo tres
10 neumas taliter in noticiam octo tonorum devenire possumus, quoniam quotienscunque videmus cantum aliquem supra eius finalem quintam sepissime ascendere et sub ipsa ad plus tonum descendere, tunc ipsum cantum autenticum habemus iudicare; et huiusmodi cantus totus in ordine autenticus iudicabitur quotum finem aut quotam speciem ipse resumet. Ipsum etiam
15 cantum autenticum iudicabimus si supra ipsius finalem dyapason sumere pernotabimus. Per neumam autem que dyateseron nominatur taliter in noticiam tonorum devenire possumus, quoniam quotienscunque est aliquis cantus qui multotiens frequenter dyateseron supra ipsius finalem ⟨ascendat⟩, tunc ipse statim plagalis est iudicandus. Item etiam si in aliquo cantu ab
20 ipsius litera finali ascensum ad quintam sine aliquo intervallo pernotabimus, statim ipsum autenticum iudicabimus; si vero ad quartam, ipsum tonum plagalem pernotabimus. Ex his ergo perpendere potes quantum huiusmodi tres neume iuvant ad octo tonorum differentias cognoscendum.

---

1 et]1. Neuma id est dyateseron, dyapente, et dyapason *in marg. m. sec.* B ‖ 18 *scripsi* ‖

two pitches rendering consonance or dissonance to the ears; and although there are several such neumes, there are only three that lead us to a knowledge of the eight tones: the diatessaron, the diapente, and the diapason. What the diatessaron and the diapente are has, indeed, been said above.[51] The diapason (which moderns name the consonant octave) is the interval of two pitches encompassing five tones and two semitones. Diapason is derived from *dia* in Greek, which is *de* in Latin, and *pason, octo*. Accordingly, diapason is a Greek noun that seems to convey *de octo* in Latin because this diapason encompasses in itself eight pitches, from which five tones and two semitones are composed.[52] Through the aforesaid three neumes, therefore, we can arrive at a knowledge of the eight tones as follows: whenever we see any chant very often ascend a fifth above its final and descend a tone at most below its final, we must judge that chant authentic; and in this manner, the whole chant in order will be judged authentic, whatever ending or whatever species it takes.[53] We shall also judge a chant authentic if we note that it takes the diapason above its final. Through the neume that is named diatessaron, we can attain a knowledge of the tones in this way: whenever there is any chant that frequently ascends a diatessaron above its final, it is to be judged plagal forthwith;[54] yet again, if in any chant we shall note an ascent to the fifth from its final letter without any intervening interval, we shall judge it authentic forthwith;[55] but if we shall note an ascent to the fourth, we shall note the tone as plagal.[56] From these things, you can assess how much the three neumes of this sort help in recognizing the differentiations among the eight tones.

---

[51] *Plana musica* 2.12 (110–17).

[52] The same derivation appears in the Lucca revision of *Contrapunctus* 3.5 (ed. Herlinger, 46–47) and in *Musica speculativa* 1.16 (170–71). Similar derivations are common in medieval music theory, e.g., in Regino, *Harmonica* 16 (GS, 1:243); *Musica enchiriadis* 10 (ed. Schmid, 26; trans. Erickson, 14–15); Guido, *Epistola* 218–20 (ed. Pesce, 490–91; cf. GS, 2:47); and Marchetto, *Lucidarium* 3.3.3 (ed. Herlinger, 174–75).

[53] The frequent ascent to the fifth above the final would be one of the overt characteristics of the authentic tone referred to in the passage quoted in n. 50 *supra*.

[54] See n. 50 *supra*.

[55] In the *Lucidarium*, Marchetto states that the skip of a fifth (by implication, between the final of a tone and the note a fifth above it) makes the melody authentic regardless of any other characteristics (*Lucidarium* 11.4.248–49 [ed. Herlinger, 516–17).

[56] Similarly, Marchetto assigned the D–G–a–G–D intermediation of the first species of the pentachord to the second tone in preference to the first (*Lucidarium* 11.4.238–39 [ed. Herlinger, 512–13]). Prosdocimo's statement represents an explicit extension of the principle to other plagal modes.

⟨14.⟩ Restat modo ultimum declarandum, quod distinctio nominatur. Est nanque distinctio locus in quo pausamus in cantu aliquo antequam ad finem eiusdem deveniamus. Et ut hoc melius intelligas, scire debes quod in quoli-bet cantu plano antequam ad ipsius finem deveniatur, quedam reperiuntur
5 linee lineas atque spatia eiusdem cantus occupantes, que pause dicuntur, sive distinctiones, et tales linee non debent omnes lineas atque spatia occu-pare sed solum aliquas et aliqua, ad finalium pausarum differentiam; de qui-bus distinctionibus, sive pausis, tres regule ab antiquis tradite sunt, quarum prima talis est, quod in quolibet cantu, cuiuscunque toni sit, tot debent esse
10 distinctiones quot principia. Secunda regula est hec, quod nulla distinctio cantus alicuius supra initium sui Seculorum finire debet. Tercia regula est hec, quod in quolibet cantu plura principia possidente reperiri debent plures distinctiones in finalem eiusdem cantus finientes. Dicuntur autem huiusmodi pause distinctiones, eo quod per ipsas unus modus sive tonus ab alio distin-
15 guitur atque cognoscitur, quoniam cognotis finalibus ipsarum distinctionum atque ipsarum numero, statim in noticiam tonorum pervenitur. Distinctiones etiam nominantur tales pause, eo quod per ipsas pausas species abinvicem distinguuntur, quod facillime per tales distinctiones specierum in noticiam tonorum pervenitur.
20 ⟨15.⟩ Declarata sunt ergo omnia novem ad cognitionem omnium octo tonorum neccessaria superius enumerata, que omnia subtiliter inspicias si aliquem tonum iudicare intendis, et in iudicando a predominantibus sume indicationem, et sic operando ad errorem tui iudicii nunquam pervenies.

⟨16.⟩ Sed quia quando aliquis supradictorum octo tonorum supra A
25 acutum multotiens ascendit est dubium an illum tonum per b rotundum cantare debeamus an per ♮ quadrum, est advertendum quod in omni modo cantandi evitanda est mutatio in quantum est possibile, eo quod in omni arte bene regulata iuxta possibilitatem est difficultas evitanda. Si ergo aliquando dubietas predicta cantandi per b rotundum vel per ♮ quadrum tibi occurat,
30 aspice ubi pauciores cadant mutationes, et illum modum assume in quo pau-ciores mutationes reperte sunt, sive talis cantandi modus b rotundum existat sive ♮ quadrum.

---

1 *Huc pertinet emendatio quae in L invenitur: cap. om.*
20 *Huc pertinet emendatio quae in L invenitur:* ... omnia septem ...

---

1 Est]Pause in cantu plano *in marg. m. sec.* B ‖ 5 linee]Linee *in marg. m. sec.* B ‖ 11 Ter-cia]Plures distinctiones conveniunt cum plurimis finalibus *in marg. m. sec.* B ‖ 20 Decla-rata]Declata B ‖ 27 in (*pr.*) *om.* B ‖ 30 pauciore B ‖ 31 modus cantandi L ‖

14. Only the last thing remains, which is named the distinction. A distinction, now, is a place in which we pause in a chant before we attain its ending. So that you might better understand this, you ought to know that in any plainchant, before we attain its ending, certain lines are found occupying the lines and spaces of that chant, and they are called rests or distinctions. To differentiate them from final rests, such lines ought not to occupy all lines and spaces but only some lines and some spaces. Concerning these distinctions, or rests, three rules have been handed down from the ancients, of which the first is this: in any chant, whatever its tone, there should be as many distinctions as there are beginnings. The second rule is this: no distinction of a chant should end higher than the first note of its *Seculorum*. The third rule is this: in any chant possessing several beginnings, many distinctions should be found ending on the final of that chant. Rests of this sort are called distinctions because through them, one manner or tone is distinguished from another and recognized inasmuch as when the finals of the distinctions and their number are recognized, we come to a knowledge of the tones forthwith. Such rests are named distinctions, too, because it is through these rests that the species are distinguished one from another and because we come to a knowledge of the tones most easily through them.

15. All nine things (enumerated above) necessary for the recognition of all eight tones, then, have been explained. Inspect all of them carefully if you intend to judge some tone, and in judging, take the designation from the predominant ones. Working in this way, you will never come to an error in your judgment.

16. Because when some one of the aforesaid eight tones ascends many times above high A there is the problem whether we should sing that tone through round b or through square ♮, one must attend to it that in every manner of singing, mutation is to be avoided insofar as possible because in every well-regulated art, difficulty is to be avoided to the extent possible. Therefore, if the aforesaid uncertainty ever strikes you whether to sing through round b or through square ♮, examine where the fewer mutations fall and take that manner in which the fewer mutations were found, whether that manner of singing involves round b or square ♮.[57]

---

1 Chapter omitted L
20 All seven things ...

---

[57]Prosdocimo's injunction to avoid mutation between F- and G-hexachords (so that B-flats and B-naturals are not mixed) must be understood in a long-standing tradition of theoretical discomfort with the two inflections of B, of which his rule is perhaps the most extreme statement; see the Introduction, 11–12.

122

⟨17.⟩ Expedito ergo modo cognoscendi tonos in quolibet cantu, psalmis exceptis, restat nunc declarare qualiter psalmi in ipsos intonando abinvicem per octo tonos diversificantur, qui modus per regulas aliquas non habetur, sed solum per exempla aliqua antiquitus usitata traditur, que comuniter
5 assignari solent in scripturis. Et quia talis modus psalmos intonandi duplex reperitur, scilicet modus in diebus solempnibus precipuis sive duplicibus retentus et modus in diebus ferialibus atque dominicis observatus, primo ponenda sunt exempla modorum psalmos intonandi in diebus solempnibus precipuis sive duplicibus cum differentiis suorum Seculorum amen; postque
10 absque medio ponentur exempla modorum psalmos intonandi in diebus ferialibus atque dominicis. Prima ergo exempla sunt hec primitus infrascripta.

Modus primi toni

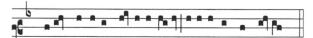

Dixit dominus domino meo. sede a dextris meis

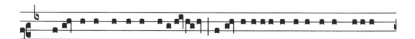

Benedictus dominus deus israel quia visitavit et fecit redemptionem

15

plebis sue

Magnificat   anima mea dominum

---

9 suorum]omnium suorum L | postque]postquam *ante corr.* B ‖ 11 infrascripta Amen L ‖ 12 Modus primi toni *in marg.* B *sup. exx. et rub. in marg.* L ‖

17. The manner of recognizing tones in any chant—the psalms excepted—having been expounded, it remains now to explain how the psalms are diversified one from another in intoning them according to the eight tones. The manner is not grasped through some rules but is handed down only through some examples anciently used, which are customarily assigned to written form.[58] Because this manner of intoning psalms is found to be twofold, the manner maintained on solemn, special, or duplex days and the manner observed on ferias and Sundays, examples of the manners of intoning psalms on solemn, special, or duplex days are to be placed first, with the *differentiae* of their *Seculorum amen*; directly afterwards, examples of the manners of intoning psalms on ferias and Sundays will be placed. The first examples, then, are these written first below.

Manner of the first tone

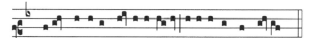

Dixit dominus domino meo. sede a dextris meis

Benedictus dominus deus israel quia visitavit et fecit redemptionem

plebis sue

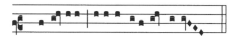

Magnificat anima mea dominum

---

[58]The text published by La Fage (329–32) as the *Compendium musicale* of Nicolaus de Capua, for instance, includes such a set of examples.

124

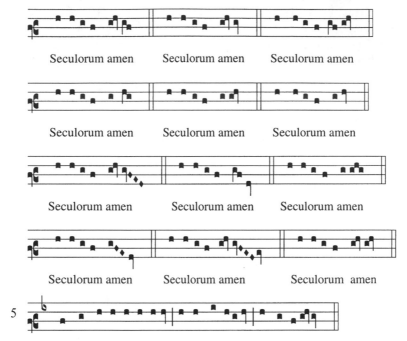

Seculorum amen   Seculorum amen   Seculorum amen

Seculorum amen   Seculorum amen   Seculorum amen

Seculorum amen   Seculorum amen   Seculorum amen

Seculorum amen   Seculorum amen   Seculorum amen

5

Primus tonus sic incipit et sic mediatur et sic finitur

1–4 *cum clave b rotundi* L || 1–5 *exx. num.* 1–13 *m. sec.* B | 1. Toni 1. 2. 3. 4. 5. 6. 7. 8. 9. 10. 11. 12. 13 *add. in marg. m. sec.* B || 5.6–8 a-g-a L | 5.17–20 ga-g B ||

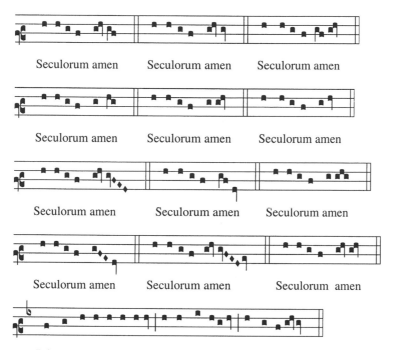

Seculorum amen   Seculorum amen   Seculorum amen

Seculorum amen   Seculorum amen   Seculorum amen

Seculorum amen   Seculorum amen   Seculorum amen

Seculorum amen   Seculorum amen   Seculorum amen

Primus tonus sic incipit   et sic mediatur   et sic finitur

Modus secundi toni

Dixit dominus domino meo. sede a dextris meis

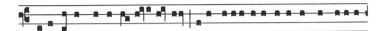

Benedictus dominus deus israel quia visitavit et fecit redemptionem

plebis sue

5

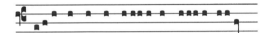

Magni ficat anima mea dominum

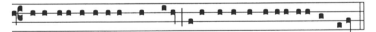

Beatus vir qui non abiit in consilio impiorum

et in via peccatorum non stetit. et in cathedra pestilentie non sedit

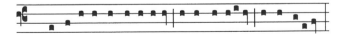

Seculorum amen

Secundus tonus sic incipit et sic mediatur et sic finitur

1 Modus secundi toni *in marg.* B *rub. in marg.* L ‖ 2.3–10 a-a-a-a-a-a-b-a B ‖ 7 [ca]thedra *resumit* C (cf. 96.7) ‖ 9.7–9 f-d-d L | 9.18–20 f-c-d L ‖

Manner of the second tone

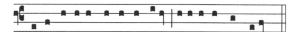

Dixit dominus domino meo. sede a dextris meis

Benedictus dominus deus israel quia visitavit et fecit redemptionem

plebis sue

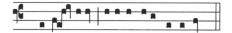

Magni ficat anima mea dominum

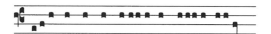

Beatus vir qui non abiit in consilio impiorum

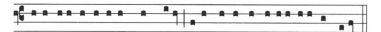

et in via peccatorum non stetit. et in cathedra pestilentie non sedit

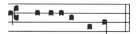

Seculorum amen

Secundus tonus sic incipit et sic mediatur et sic finitur

Modus tercii toni

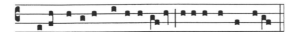

Dixit dominus domino meo. sede a dextris meis

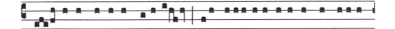

Benedictus dominus deus israel quia visitavit et fecit redemptionem

plebis sue

5

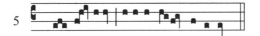

Magni ficat anima mea dominum

Seculorum amen   Seculorum amen   Seculorum amen

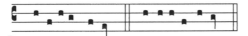

Seculorum amen   Seculorum amen

Tercius tonus sic incipit et sic mediatur   et sic finitur

---

1 Modus tercii toni *in marg.* BC *rub. in marg.* L ‖ 5.1–8 gagac-dc-c C ‖ 6–7 *exx. num.* 1–5 *m. sec.* B | Tertii toni 1. 2. 3. 4. 5. *add. in marg. m. sec.* B ‖ 8.1–3 g-ac-c L ‖

Manner of the third tone

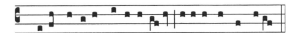

Dixit dominus domino meo. sede a dextris meis

Benedictus dominus deus israel quia visitavit et fecit redemptionem

plebis sue

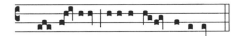

Magni ficat anima mea dominum

Seculorum amen   Seculorum amen   Seculorum amen

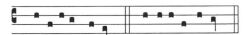

Seculorum amen   Seculorum amen

Tercius tonus sic incipit et sic mediatur et sic finitur

Modus quarti toni

Dixit dominus domino meo. sede a dextris meis

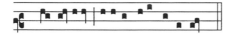

Magni ficat   anima mea dominum

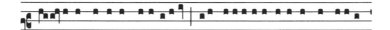

Benedictus dominus deus israel quia visitavit et fecit redemptionem

5

plebis sue

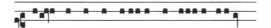

Beatus vir qui non abiit in consilio impiorum

et in via peccatorum non stetit. et in cathedra pestilentie non sedit

Seculorum amen   Seculorum amen   Seculorum amen

---

1 Modus quarti toni *in marg.* BC *rub. in marg.* L ‖ 3 *pausa post* Magnificat *om.* C ‖ 7.10–11
b-g C ‖ 8 *ex. num.* 1–3 *m. sec.* B | 4. toni 1. *add. in marg. m. sec.* B ‖

Manner of the fourth tone

Dixit dominus domino meo. sede a dextris meis

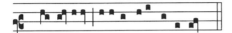

Magni ficat anima mea dominum

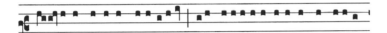

Benedictus dominus deus israel quia visitavit et fecit redemptionem

plebis sue

Beatus vir qui non abiit in consilio impiorum

et in via peccatorum non stetit. et in cathedra pestilentie non sedit

Seculorum amen   Seculorum amen   Seculorum amen

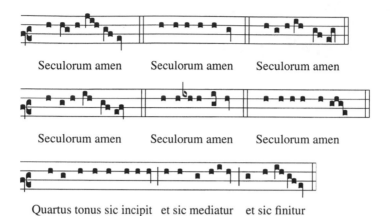

Seculorum amen   Seculorum amen   Seculorum amen

Seculorum amen   Seculorum amen   Seculorum amen

Quartus tonus sic incipit et sic mediatur   et sic finitur

1–2 *exx. num.* 4–9 *m. sec.* B ‖ 3.5 ♮-a C | 3.6–8 a-g-g L | 3.17–21 b-g-e L ‖

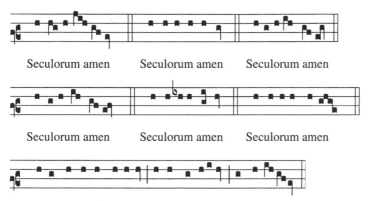

Seculorum amen   Seculorum amen   Seculorum amen

Seculorum amen   Seculorum amen   Seculorum amen

Quartus tonus sic incipit   et sic mediatur   et sic finitur

Modus quinti toni

Dixit dominus domino meo. sede a dextris meis

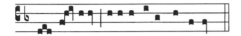

Magni ficat anima mea dominum

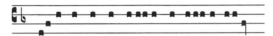

Beatus vir qui non abiit in consilio impiorum

5

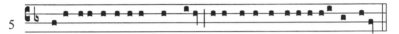

et in via peccatorum non stetit. et in cathedra pestilentie non sedit

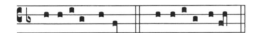

Seculorum amen   Seculorum amen

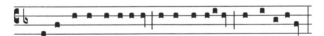

Quintus tonus sic incipit   et sic mediatur   et sic finitur

---

1 Modus quinti toni *in marg.* BC *rub. in marg.* L ‖ 3 *pausa post* Magnificat *om.* C ‖ 4.15–18
c-c-c-ca C ‖ 6–7 *ex. saeculorum amen (sec.) et Quintus tonus ... num.* 1–2 *m. sec.* B | 5. toni
1. 2. *add. in marg. m. sec.* B ‖ 7.6–8 c-a-a L ‖

Manner of the fifth tone

Dixit dominus domino meo. sede a dextris meis

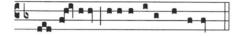

Magni ficat anima mea dominum

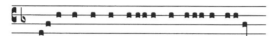

Beatus vir qui non abiit in consilio impiorum

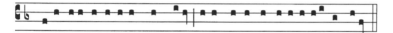

et in via peccatorum non stetit. et in cathedra pestilentie non sedit

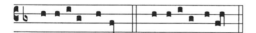

Seculorum amen   Seculorum amen

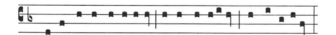

Quintus tonus sic incipit et sic mediatur   et sic finitur

136

Modus sexti toni

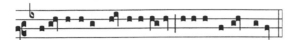

Dixit dominus domino meo. sede a dextris meis

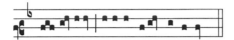

Magni ficat anima mea dominum

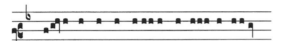

Beatus vir qui non abiit in consilio impiorum

5
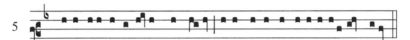

et in via peccatorum non stetit. et in cathedra pestilentie non sedit

Seculorum amen

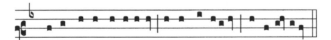

Sextus tonus sic incipit   et sic mediatur   et sic finitur

1 Modus sexti toni *in marg.* BC *rub. in marg.* L ‖ 3 *pausa post* Magnificat *om.* C ‖ 7.1–14 f-ga-a-a-a-a-g-g, a-g-a-♮-b-a-g-a L ‖

Manner of the sixth tone

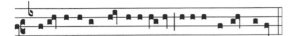

Dixit dominus domino meo. sede a dextris meis

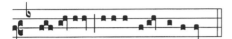

Magni ficat anima mea dominum

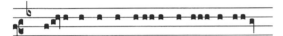

Beatus vir qui non abiit in consilio impiorum

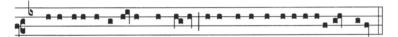

et in via peccatorum non stetit. et in cathedra pestilentie non sedit

Seculorum amen

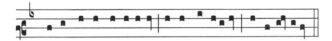

Sextus tonus sic incipit et sic mediatur et sic finitur

138

Modus septimi toni

Dixit dominus domino meo. sede a dextris meis

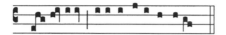

Magni ficat anima mea dominum

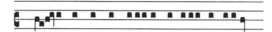

Beatus vir qui non abiit in consilio impiorum

5
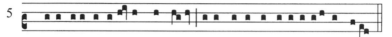

et in via peccatorum non stetit. et in cathedra pestilentie non sedit

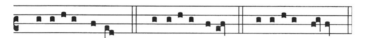

Seculorum amen   Seculorum amen   Seculorum amen

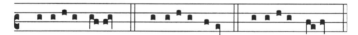

Seculorum amen   Seculorum amen   Seculorum amen

Seculorum amen

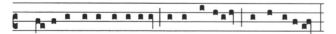

Septimus tonus sic incipit   et sic mediatur   et sic finitur

1 Modus septimi toni *in marg.* BC *rub. in marg.* L || 3 *pausa post* Magnificat *om.* C || 6–8
exx. num. 1–7 *m. sec.* B | 7. toni 1. 2. 3. 4. 5. 6. 7. *add. in marg. m. sec.* B || 9.8–10 d-c-c L |
9.19–22 d-c-ba L ||

Manner of the seventh tone

Dixit dominus domino meo. sede a dextris meis

Magni ficat anima mea dominum

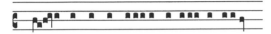

Beatus vir qui non abiit in consilio impiorum

et in via peccatorum non stetit. et in cathedra pestilentie non sedit

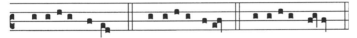

Seculorum amen   Seculorum amen   Seculorum amen

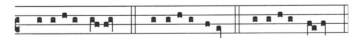

Seculorum amen   Seculorum amen   Seculorum amen

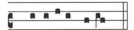

Seculorum amen

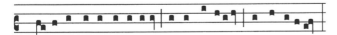

Septimus tonus sic incipit et sic mediatur   et sic finitur

140

Modus octavi toni

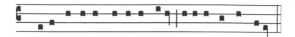

Dixit dominus domino meo. sede a dextris meis

Magni ficat anima mea dominum

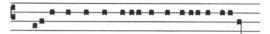

Beatus vir qui non abiit in consilio impiorum

5

et in via peccatorum non stetit. et in cathedra pestilentie non sedit

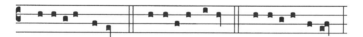

Seculorum amen   Seculorum amen   Seculorum amen

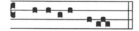

Seculorum amen

Octavus tonus sic incipit   et sic mediatur   et sic finitur

1 Modus octavi toni *in marg.* BC *rub. in marg.* L ‖ 3 *pausa post* Magnificat *om.* CL ‖ 6–7
exx. num. 1–4 *m. sec.* B | 8. toni 1. 2. 3. 4. *add. in marg. m. sec.* B ‖ 8.7–9 c-a-a L ‖

Manner of the eighth tone

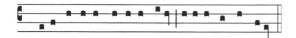

Dixit dominus domino meo. sede a dextris meis

Magni ficat anima mea dominum

Beatus vir qui non abiit in consilio impiorum

et in via peccatorum non stetit. et in cathedra pestilentie non sedit

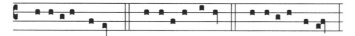

Seculorum amen   Seculorum amen   Seculorum amen

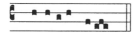

Seculorum amen

Octavus tonus sic incipit et sic mediatur et sic finitur

Alius modus novus octavi toni

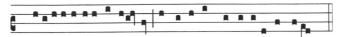

In exitu israel de egipto domus iacob de populo barbaro

Seculorum amen

Nova maneries sic incipit et sic mediatur et sic finitur

5   Propter hunc modum ultimum intonandi est sciendum quod hic ultimus intonandi modus a quibusdam sub octavo modo collocatur, a quibusdam vero aliis sub nullo octo tonorum reponitur, sed maneries per se et nona in ordine reputatur; unde ubi in exemplo superius posito scribitur nova mane-ries, scribitur ab aliis nona maneries, eo quod secundum ipsos nona mane-
10 ries existit in ordine. Sed quicquid sit, puto fore rationabilius ipsum modum ultimum ad aliquem octo modorum debere reduci quam propter ipsum solum nonum modum intonandi reperire, cum solum octo reperiantur toni, ut supradictum est; sed ad quem octo tonorum reduci habeat, dico, propter aliis non contradicere, quod ad octavum, licet magis sapiat naturam quarti,
15 ut michi videtur; unde dicunt multi qui ipsum tonum sub octavo reponunt

1 Alius … toni *in marg.* BC Alius novus modus intonandi *rub. in marg.* L ‖ 2 isdrael B |

In exitu israel de egipto domus iacob de populo barbaro   L ‖ 4   Nona maneries sic incipit et sic mediatur et sic finitur   L ‖

5 ultimum modum L | intonandi *in marg.* B ‖ 5–6 ultimus intonandi modus]modus ultimus intonandi L ‖ 6 sub octavo tono collocatur sive modo L ‖ 8–9 maneries [existit in ordine] C ‖ 9 secundum]per C ‖ 10 quicquid de hoc L ‖ 11 modorum sive tonorum L ‖ 12 solum nonum modum]modum sollum nonum C solum modum novum L ‖ 14 quod reducitur L ‖ 15 tonum iam dictum L ‖

Another, new, manner of the eighth tone

In exitu israel de egipto domus iacob de populo barbaro

Seculorum amen

Nova maneries sic incipit et sic mediatur et sic finitur

With regard to this last manner of intoning, one must know that this last manner of intoning is assigned a position under the eighth manner by certain writers; by certain others, it is put under none of the eight tones but held to be a mode *per se* and ninth in order. Accordingly, where *Nova maneries* is written in the example placed above, *Nona maneries* is written by others because according to them it is the ninth mode in order. But whatever it is, I think it more reasonable that this last manner ought to be related to some one of the eight manners than it is to find it alone as the ninth manner of intoning, since only eight tones are found, as has been said above.[59] But to which of the eight tones it must be related, I say, for the sake of not contradicting others, to the eighth, even though it smacks more of the nature of the fourth, as it seems to me. Accordingly, many who place this tone under the

---

[59]*Plana musica* 2.3 (84–87).

144

quod semel diabolus audiens duos monacos in coro existentes, atque inter se
supra hanc ultimam maneriem litigantes sub quo scilicet octo modorum
hanc ultimam maneriem reponere deberent, eos incepit deridere in hec verba
sub predicta ultima manerie suaviter sic prorumpens:

5   Duo monaci sunt in coro
       litigantes, ut in foro,
       octavum tonum nescientes
       ab aliis distinguere.
Et propter hoc dicunt isti hunc modum reponi debere sub octavo.

10   Nunc sequuntur exempla modorum psalmos intonandi in diebus ferialibus atque dominicis.

       Modus primi toni

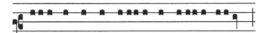

Beatus vir qui non abiit in consilio impiorum

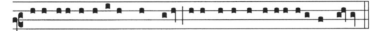

et in via peccatorum non stetit. et in cathedra pestilentie non sedit

15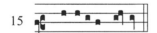

Seculorum amen

---

1 atque]ac C ‖ 1–2 atque … maneriem]circa hanc ultimam maneriem intonandi iam dictam
inter seque L ‖ 2 modorum supradictorum L ‖ 4 [supradicta] sub C | sub predicta]sub
supradicta BL subpredicta *ante corr.* C | sic suaviter L ‖ 5 Duo]No⟨ta⟩ *in marg.* L ‖ 7 mes-
cientes *ante corr.* C ‖ 9 isti autoritate diaboli L | octavo tono L ‖ 10 Nunc]Nunc [sequ] C
Nunc vero L ‖ 12 Modus primi toni *in marg.* B *om.* C ‖

eighth say that the devil, when once hearing two monks in the choir arguing between themselves over this last mode under which of the eight manners they should place this last mode, began to mock them, bursting out pleasantly in these words about the aforesaid last mode:

> Two monks are in the choir,
> arguing as if in the public square,
> ignorant of how to distinguish
> the eighth tone from the others.

On account of this, they say that this manner should be placed under the eighth tone.

Now there follow examples of the manners of intoning psalms on ferias and Sundays.

Manner of the first tone

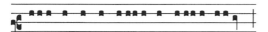

Beatus vir qui non abiit in consilio impiorum

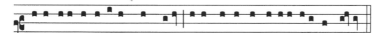

et in via peccatorum non stetit. et in cathedra pestilentie non sedit

Seculorum amen

146

Modus secundi toni

Beatus vir qui non abiit in consilio impiorum

et in via peccatorum non stetit. et in cathedra pestilentie non sedit

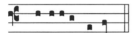

Seculorum amen

5   Modus tercii toni

Beatus vir qui non abiit in consilio impiorum

et in via peccatorum non stetit. et in cathedra pestilentie non sedit

Seculorum amen

---

1 Modus secundi toni *in marg.* BC *rub. in marg.* L ‖ 5 Modus tercii toni *in marg.* BC *rub. in marg.* L ‖

Manner of the second tone

Beatus vir qui non abiit in consilio impiorum

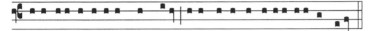

et in via peccatorum non stetit. et in cathedra pestilentie non sedit

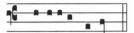

Seculorum amen

Manner of the third tone

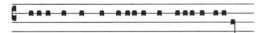

Beatus vir qui non abiit in consilio impiorum

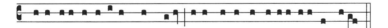

et in via peccatorum non stetit. et in cathedra pestilentie non sedit

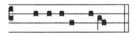

Seculorum amen

148

Modus quarti toni

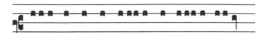

Beatus vir qui non abiit in consilio impiorum

et in via peccatorum non stetit. et in cathedra pestilentie non sedit

Seculorum amen

5   Modus quinti toni

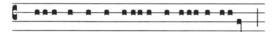

Beatus vir qui non abiit in consilio impiorum

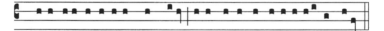

et in via peccatorum non stetit. et in cathedra pestilentie non sedit

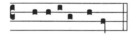

Seculorum amen

---

1 Modus quarti toni *in marg.* BC *rub. in marg.* L ‖ 5 Modus quinti toni *in marg.*BC *rub. in marg.* L ‖

Manner of the fourth tone

Beatus vir qui non abiit in consilio impiorum

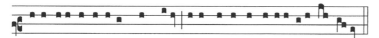

et in via peccatorum non stetit. et in cathedra pestilentie non sedit

Seculorum amen

Manner of the fifth tone

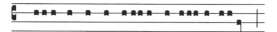

Beatus vir qui non abiit in consilio impiorum

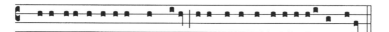

et in via peccatorum non stetit. et in cathedra pestilentie non sedit

Seculorum amen

150

Modus sexti toni

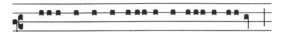

Beatus vir qui non abiit in consilio impiorum

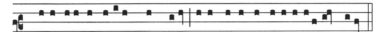

et in via peccatorum non stetit. et in cathedra pestilentie non sedit

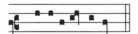

Seculorum amen

5   Modus septimi toni

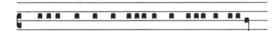

Beatus vir qui non abiit in consilio impiorum

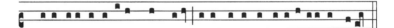

et in via peccatorum non stetit. et in cathedra pestilentie non sedit

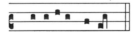

Seculorum amen

1 Modus sexti toni *in marg.* BC *rub. in marg.* L || 3.17–21 a-a-a-a-g B || 5 Modus septimi toni *in marg.* BC *rub. in marg.* L || 7.17–21 d-d-de-d-d C ||

Manner of the sixth tone

Beatus vir qui non abiit in consilio impiorum

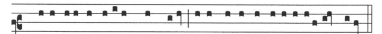

et in via peccatorum non stetit. et in cathedra pestilentie non sedit

Seculorum amen

Manner of the seventh tone

Beatus vir qui non abiit in consilio impiorum

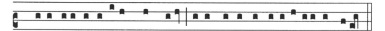

et in via peccatorum non stetit. et in cathedra pestilentie non sedit

Seculorum amen

Modus octavi toni

Beatus vir qui non abiit in consilio impiorum

et in via peccatorum non stetit. et in cathedra pestilentie non sedit

Seculorum amen

5   Propter omnia exempla superius posita est primo sciendum quod quilibet
modus psalmos intonandi, sexto excepto atque secundo, plures retinet in suo
fine diversitates, que in exemplis superius positis descripte sunt, et hee
diversitates, ut plurimum, in fine antiphanarum reperiuntur, que Seculorum
amen nominantur, et docent nos hee diversitates qualiter psalmum immedi-
10   ate ante antiphanam pronuntiandum finire debeamus.

⟨18.⟩ Item sciendum quod principia psalmos intonandi ultra exempla
superius posita per hos versus etiam habere possumus:
        Primus, cum sexto, fa sol la semper habeto;
        Tercius et octavus, ut re fa, sicque secundus;
15   La sol la, quartus; ut mi sol sit tibi quintus;
        Septimus, fa mi fa sol; sic omnes esse recordor.

8–9 *Huc pertinet emendatio quae in L invenitur:* ... que Seculorum amen
nominantur et, ut dictum est, per hanc dictionem Euouae sceu Seuouae
describuntur, et docent nos hee diversitates ...

---

1 Modus octavi toni *in marg.* BC *rub. in marg.* L ‖ 7–8 que ... diversitates *om.* (*saut du
même au même*) C ‖ 9 psalmum cuius est hec antiphona vel L ‖ 11 Item]Secundo L ‖

Manner of the eighth tone

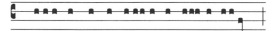

Beatus vir qui non abiit in consilio impiorum

et in via peccatorum non stetit. et in cathedra pestilentie non sedit

Seculorum amen

With regard to all the examples placed above, one must know, first, that any manner of intoning psalms, the sixth and the second excepted, includes several differences at its ending that have been written in the examples placed above, and these differences are most often found at the endings of antiphons. They are named *Seculorum amen*; and these differences teach us how we ought to end the psalm that is to be pronounced immediately before the antiphon.

18. Again, one must know, beyond the examples placed above, that we can grasp the beginnings for intoning psalms through these verses:

The first, with the sixth is always to be grasped *fa sol la*;
the third and the eighth, *ut re fa*, and the second as well;
la sol la, the fourth; *ut mi sol* is for you the fifth;
the seventh, *fa mi fa sol*; thus I call all to mind.[61]

---

9 ... They are named *Seculorum amen* and, as has been said, are written with the expression *Euouae* or *Seuouae*;[60] and these differences teach us ...

---

[60]*Plana musica* 2.11 (102–5).

[61]The verses are common in medieval music theory; they appear, e.g., in Ps.-Aristotle, *Tractatus de musica* (CS, 1:262); the Berkeley treatise 1.7 (*The Berkeley Manuscript: University of California Music Library, MS. 744 (olim Phillipps 4450): A New Critical Text and Translation*, ed. and trans. by Oliver B. Ellsworth, Greek and Latin Music Theory, vol. 2 (Lincoln: University of Nebraska Press, 1984), 82–83); *Anonymus ex codice vaticano lat. 5129*, ed. Albert Seay, Corpus scriptorum de musica, vol. 9 ([Rome]: American Institute of Musicology, 1964), 28; and Nicolaus de Capua, *Compendium musicale* (ed. La Fage, 329).

154

Item qualiter ipsi psalmi in ipsos intonando mediantur, etiam ultra
exempla superius posita, per hos versus habere possumus:
Septimus et primus et sextus fa mi re mi sibi tenet;
Quintus, sol la sol; fa sol fa dat octavus atque secundus;
5   Tercius, sol fa mi re fa; quartus ut re mi re sibi iungit.
Versus nanque huiusmodi de se clarissimi sunt, et ideo circa ipsos aliter
non insisto. Scias tamen quod psalmi taliter principiantur et mediantur
solum in diebus precipuis solempnibus sive duplicibus, ut per exempla
visum est superius.
10   Modi autem intonandi versus introituum et responsorum a quibusdam
poni solent, sed quia ipsi distincte per eorum figuras figurati immediate post
introitus et responsa reperiuntur, ipsos propter brevitatem dimisi.

⟨19.⟩ Istis ergo taliter ordinatis poterit quilibet boni ingenii prescripta
bene intelligens de se officium novum intonare. Si aliquod tale noviter into-
15 nandum sibi fuerit presentatum, et si cum hoc exemplariter in aliis officiis
inspexerit, nunquam ad errorem pervenire poterit, neque de hoc aliquam
admirationem sumere debes, cum et circa alias scientias laborantes in suis
operibus etiam alienis exemplis sepissime operentur, ut verbi gratia in arte
metrica operatores nanque huius artis in brevitatem vel longitudinem ali-
20 cuius sillabe cognoscendo, multotiens exemplo alterius operantur, ymo
quod plus est operari exemplariter est una de viis quibus metrorum compositores utuntur, in brevitatem vel longitudinem sillabarum cognoscendo,
et hoc quando carmina componere intendunt.

⟨20.⟩ Sit ergo finis huius parvi operis plane musice per Prosdocimum de
25 Beldemandis patavum, Montagnane, paduani districtus, anno 1412, taliter
ordinati. Deo gratias. Amen.
⟨21.⟩ Explicit tractatus plane musice a Prosdocimo de Beldemandis
patavo in castro Montagnane, paduani districtus, anno domini 1412, compilatus. Deo gratias. Amen.

---

7 [insixto] insisto C ‖ 8 precipuis [sive] C ‖ 10 responsorij *ante corr.* C ‖ 14 tale *om.* C ‖
18 etiam]ac etiam operationibus L | sepissime operentur]utuntur sepissime L ‖ 19 opera-
tores nanque huius artis]metrificatores nanque L | vel [alicuius] C ‖ 20 exemplo alterius
operentur]alieno utuntur exemplo L ‖ 21 operari exemplariter]hoc modo exemplariter ope-
rari L ‖ 22 longitudinem vel brevitatem L ‖ 23 carmina sua L ‖ 25 Beldemando L | Montag-
nane]in castro Montagnane L ‖ 26 Deo gratias]Ad laudem et gloriam omnipotentis Dei ac
totius curie supercelestis L ‖ 27 a Prosdocimo]per Prosdocimum C Prosdocimi L | Belde-
mando L ‖ 28 patavo]de Padua L ‖ 28–29 in castro … Amen *om.* L ‖

Again, we can grasp how the psalms are mediated in intoning them through these verses, as well as through the examples placed above:

The seventh, the first, and the sixth hold *fa mi re mi*;
the fifth, *sol la sol*; the eighth and the second give *fa sol fa*;
the third, *sol fa mi re fa*; the fourth joins *ut re mi re*.[62]

Verses of this sort, to be sure, are very clear in themselves, and for that reason I do not focus my attention on them. But know that psalms are thus begun and mediated only on special, solemn, or duplex days, as was seen above in the examples.

The manners of intoning the verses of introits and responsories are customarily given by certain writers, but because they are distinctly drawn by their figures immediately after the introits and responsories, for the sake of brevity I have excluded them.

<19>. These things having been thus set in order, anyone of good intellect who understands properly what has been written will be able to intone a new office on his own. If some such thing newly to be intoned will have been presented to him and he will have inspected it on the basis of examples in other offices, he will never be able to come to error. Nor ought you to take any admiration in this, since those laboring in other sciences, too, very often work with foreign examples in their own works, as for example workers in the art of metrics. In recognizing the shortness or length of some syllable in this art, they many times work with the example of another. More precisely, working on the basis of examples is one of the paths composers of metered lines use in recognizing the shortness or length of syllables when they intend to compose songs.

20. Let this, then, be the end of this little work on *musica plana* by the Paduan Prosdocimus de Beldemandis, thus set in order at Montagnana in the district of Padua in the year 1412. Thanks be to God. Amen.

21. Here ends the treatise on *musica plana* compiled by the Paduan Prosdocimus de Beldemandis in the fortified town of Montagnana, in the district of Padua, in the year of the Lord 1412. Thanks be to God. Amen.

---

[62]Ps.-Aristotle, *Tractatus de musica* (CS, 1:262); Jacobus Leodiensis, *Speculum musice* 6.83 (ed. Bragard, 6:233); and the Berkeley treatise (ed. Ellsworth, 82) give "sol fa mi fa" rather than "sol fa mi re fa" for the third tone.

⟨TRACTATUS MUSICE SPECULATIVE QUEM
PROSDOCIMUS DE BELDEMANDO PADUANUS
CONTRA MARCHETUM DE PADUA COMPILAVIT⟩

⟨Prefatio⟩

5   ⟨1.⟩ Dum quidam michi carus ac uti frater intimus Lucas, nomine, de castro Lendenarie, policinii rodigiensis oriundus sacerdosque honorandus, et
ego fraternalem caritatem a puerili etate insimul duxissemus, et multa vari-
aque volumina musicalia transcurrissemus, unum invenimus valde erroneum
atque veritati dissonum, Lucidarium nominatum, quem quidam Marchetus,
10   nomine, michi concivis paduanus, compilaverat. Et, ut rei veritas bene
detegatur et falsitas cognoscatur, libellus iste Ars pratice cantus plani ab
auctoremet intitulatur, cuius tamen anteriora quedam musice theoricalia sive

---

Tit.: ad finem tractatus ‖ 4 scripsi ‖ 6 Lendenarie]Lucas de castro Lendenarie in marg. m. sec.
B | redigiensis (rudiginensis ante corr.) L ‖ 7 et om. L ‖ 10 paduanus]Marchetus de Padua in
marg. m. sec. B ‖

TREATISE ON *MUSICA SPECULATIVA*, WHICH
THE PADUAN PROSDOCIMUS DE BELDEMANDIS
COMPILED AGAINST MARCHETUS OF PADUA

Preface

1. While a certain person dear to me and like a most intimate brother—Luca, by name, from the fortified town of Lendinara, a son of the Rovigo delta,[1] and a priest worthy of honor—and I had been leading a life of fraternal affection together from childhood and had been running through many and various volumes of music theory, we discovered one extremely erroneous and dissonant with the truth, named *Lucidarium*, which a certain person—Marchetus, by name, my fellow Paduan citizen—had compiled; and so that the truth of the matter might be properly disclosed and the falsehood recognized, that little book is titled *Ars practice cantus plani*[2] by the author himself. Its earlier parts treat certain theoretical or speculative aspects of

---

[1]Luca di Lendinara became Johannes Ciconia's successor as cantor at the cathedral of Padua on 13 July 1412 after the latter's death. Lendinara is some 25 km west of Rovigo. I thank Professor Kenneth Pennington of the Catholic University of America for informing me that *pollicinus*, or *polesinus*, is marsh land or unstable land such as very sandy soil, for providing the Italian cognate *polesine*, and for referring me to the Po delta. The *Dizionario Garzanti* in fact defines *polesine* as "zona pianeggiante compresa tra due bracci di un fiume, spec. nella zona del delta." In the Rovigo area, *Polesine* serves as a proper noun referring to the delta bounded by the Adige on the north and the Po on the south (http://www.polesine.com/pagine/polesine/geografia/a001.htm; accessed 17 April 2005) or even as a synonym for the province of Rovigo (http://www.consvipo.it/); so, *policinii rudigiensis oriundus* would seem to mean "born in (or, as here, "a son of") the Rovigo delta." A number of towns in the area, some of them even west of Rovigo, incorporate *Polesine* in their names; if Prosdocimo's *policinius* refers specifically to one of these as Luca's birthplace, Fratta Polesine, situated just 10 km southeast of Lendinara, is an attractive candidate.

[2]"The art of the plainchant practice." In the dedicatory letter, Marchetto refers to the work as "a *Lucidarium* on plainchant, or a work by means of which all musicians and singers might rationally understand what they sing in plainchant [Lucidarium plane musice … seu opus quo universi musici et cantores scirent rationabiliter in plana musica quid canta-

speculativa false pertractant; sed in posterum ad simplicem praticam cantus
plani se convertens, vere et solempniter scripsit atque egregie, adeo quod
hucusque de his que in hac materia legerim nichil solempnius viderim. Fuit
enim vir iste in scientia musice simplex praticus sed a theorica sive specula-
5   tiva omnino vacuus, quam tamen perfectissime intelligere deceptus se
putavit, et ideo agredi presumpsit que totaliter ignoravit. Concernens igitur
michi frater supradictus errores huius Marcheti per totam Ytaliam, et adhuc
extra, fore divulgatos, et verissimos a cantoribus, non tamen musicis, repu-
tatos, me rogavit ut sui amore contra hos errores opusculum componerem ut
10 mala atque falsa et in musica erronea que per unum patavum producta et
seminata fuerant, per alium patavum removerentur, et inde Ytalia a talibus
erroribus purgeretur. Et ego his rogationibus disentire non valens eis
aquievi. Sed quoniam, ut supra habitum est, tales errores solum circa partem
theoricalem sive speculativam huius artis versantur, ideo in hoc meo tracta-
15 tulo solum theoricalia sive speculativa agrediar musicalia, et etiam quia alias
circa partem quamlibet musice praticam opera compilavi; nec intendo in
hoc meo tractatulo omnia tangere que ab aliis in hac materia speculativa
tacta sunt, sed solum aliqua tangam que ad declarationem errorum supradicti
Marcheti neccessaria michi videbuntur, cum hoc tamen modum addendo
20 quo quilibet doctus in proportionibus et pratica arismetrice possit cuiuslibet
sonorum combinationis proportionem invenire atque cognoscere.

---

11 Ytalia inde L ||

music theory falsely,[3] but in the subsequent part, turning to the simple practice of plainchant, he wrote correctly, in an orthodox fashion,[4] and most
excellently, so much so that I have thus far seen nothing more orthodox in
what I have read on this subject. In the science of music, you see, this man
was a simple performer, totally lacking in its theoretical or speculative side,
which, mistakenly, he thought he understood most perfectly, and thus he
presumed to address that of which he was totally ignorant. Considering,
then, that the errors of this Marchetus had been circulated throughout Italy,
and beyond, and had been held as most true by singers (yet not by theorists),
my aforesaid brother entreated me, for his love, to compose a little work
against these errors so that the evils, lies, and mistakes concerning music
that had been brought forth and disseminated by one Paduan might be
removed by another, and thus Italy be purged of such errors. Powerless to
dissent from these entreaties, I agreed to them. But inasmuch as (as has been
explained above) these errors are pondered only in the theoretical or speculative part of this *Ars* (and also because I have elsewhere compiled works
pertaining to each practical part of music theory), in this little treatise of
mine, let me address only those aspects of music theory that are theoretical
or speculative; nor do I intend in this little treatise of mine to touch on all
aspects of this speculative subject that have been touched on by others; I
shall touch only on some things that seem to me necessary for the explanation of the errors of the aforesaid Marchetus, adding to these the methods by
which anyone learned in ratios and the practice of arithmetic might be able
to discover and recognize the ratio of any interval.

---

rent]"; in the colophon, it is called "*Lucidarium* on the art of plainchant [Lucidarium ... in
arte musice plane]." No extant manuscript gives *Ars practice cantus plani* as an alternative
title in either location. In *Pomerium* 14.2, 7; 17.19; and 19.8 (ed. Vecchi, 69, 70, 74, and
78), Marchetto refers to the *Lucidarium* simply as his *musica plana* or *opus musicae
planae*.

[3]For Prosdocimo, the terms "theoretical" and "speculative" seem to imply matters pertaining to tuning, i.e., matters explained in terms of numbers.

[4]*Solempniter* is translated as "in an orthodox fashion" following the definition of the
Oxford Latin Dictionary, s.v. *sollemnis*: "in accordance with the procedures of law, formal,
etc."

160

⟨1⟩

⟨1.⟩ Musica ergo de qua hic est sermo est de sono ad sonum relato; et quia talis relatio haberi non potest absque noticia proportionum et numerorum, ideo qui hanc cupit scientiam hec prius requirat neccessaria que tamen
5 hic dilatare propter operis brevitatem dimisi, et etiam quia circa has duas materias proprios tractatulos, unum scilicet de proportionibus et alium de pratica arismetrice, sive de pratica numerorum, compilavi. Sed quoniam ad ea que infra tractanda sunt neccessaria est noticia quorundam terminorum in pratica musice usitatorum, ideo prius premittattur talium terminorum decla-
10 ratio. Et ergo dato quod multe sint sonorum combinationes in manu musicali reperte, hic tamen solum 16 enumerabo principaliores, que tales sunt, scilicet unisonus, tonus, semitonium, diptonus, semidiptonus, tritonus, semitritonus, dyateseron cum tono, dyateseron cum semitonio, dyapente cum tono, dyapente cum semitonio, dyapente cum diptono, dyapente cum semidiptono,
15 dyapente cum tritono, dyapente cum dyateseron, et bisdyateseron cum semitonio. Sonorum enim combinatio est quorumcumque duorum sonorum insimul comparatorum adinvicem acceptio; et dixi sonorum et non vocum quoniam generalior est sonus quam vox.

⟨2.⟩ Unisonus est duorum sonorum equalium acceptio; et dicitur uniso-
20 nus quasi unus sonus, quoniam tales duo soni, ex quo sunt equales, videntur esse unus sonus et non duo, propter sui equalitatem.
⟨3.⟩ Tonus est duorum sonorum inequalium in duabus diversis et immediatis manus musicalis partibus existentium plene, perfecte, et complete tonantium acceptio; et dicitur tonus a tonando quoniam, ut habitum est, tales
25 duo soni immediati videntur perfecte, plene, et complete tonare, eo quod unus ipsorum alterius respectu perfecte, plene, et complete ascendit vel

---

2 ergo *sup. lin.* B ‖ 7 sive *sup. lin.* B ‖ 11–12 scilicet *sup. lin.* B ‖

1

1. The music theory, then, that is spoken of here is that of pitch related to pitch. Because this relationship cannot be grasped without knowledge of ratios and numbers,[1] let him who desires this science first inquire after the requisites that I have excluded enlarging upon here on account of the brevity of the work and also because I have compiled little treatises on these two subjects individually—that is, one on ratios and the other on the practice of arithmetic, or the practice of numbers.[2] But inasmuch as the knowledge of certain terms familiar in the practice of music is requisite for those things which must be treated below, let an explanation of those terms be set out in advance. Therefore, given that the intervals found in the musical hand are many, I shall here enumerate only the sixteen more basic ones, which are these: unison, tone, semitone, ditone, semiditone, tritone, semitritone, diatessaron with tone, diatessaron with semitone, diapente with tone, diapente with semitone, diapente with ditone, diapente with semiditone, diapente with tritone, diapente with diatessaron, and double diatessaron with semitone. An interval, to be sure, is the union of any two pitches taken in comparison to each other; and I said "of pitches" and not "of syllables" inasmuch as pitch is a more general term than syllable.[3]

2. The unison is the union of two equal pitches. It is called unison—"one pitch," as it were—inasmuch as two such pitches, because they are equal, seem to be one pitch and not two, on account of their equality.

3. The tone is the union of two unequal pitches existing in two different and adjacent parts of the musical hand, sounding full, perfect, and complete. Tone is derived from *tonando*,[4] inasmuch as—as has been explained[5]—two such adjacent pitches seem to sound perfect, full, and complete because one of them, with respect to the other, ascends or descends perfectly, fully, and

---

[1]Prosdocimo's opening recalls Johannes de Muris, *Tractatus de musica* (GS, 3:256): "Inasmuch as music concerns pitch related to numbers and vice versa, it is necessary for the musician to consider both things, that is, number and pitch [Quoniam musica est de sono relato ad numeros, et contra, ideo necessarium est musico, duo, scilicet numerum et sonum, considerare]."

[2]Prosdocimo, *Brevis summula ... Parvus tractatulus* (ed. Herlinger); previously edited in CS, 3:258–61. The treatise on arithmetic is the *Tractatus algorismi*; Peter Slemon is preparing an edition of the latter, which appears in several manuscripts and two prints (Padua: Matthaeus Cerdonis, 1483; Venice: Vulpinus, 1540).

[3]In *Contrapunctus* 3.1 (ed. Herlinger, 34–35), Prosdocimo had called intervals combinations of two syllables (*duarum vocum ... simul agregatio*).

[4]*Tonando*, "sounding."

[5]In *Plana musica* 1.7 (52–53).

descendit in comparatione ad alios duos sonos immediatos quandam sonorum combinationem semitonium nominatam producentes, de quo semitonio
statim erit sermo. Et huiusmodi tonus alio nomine secunda maior nominatur;
et dicitur secunda quoniam unus horum duorum sonorum huiusmodi tonum
5 producentium in secundo loco manus musicalis respectu alterius soni colo-
catur, ut est a primo G ad primum A; sed quare maior appeletur hic non
declaro, sed inferius immediate post declarationem omnium 16 combinationum sonorum superius nominatarum sub brevitate declarabitur quare
unaqueque combinatio sonorum maior, minor, vel etiam media nominetur,
10 et hoc feci ut opus brevius redderetur.

⟨4.⟩ Semitonium est duorum sonorum inequalium in duabus diversis
immediatis manus musicalis partibus existentium non plene sed imperfecte
et incomplete tonantium acceptio; et dicitur semitonium non a semi grece
quod est medium latine, sic quod semitonium dicatur quia medietas toni,
15 quoniam tonus musicus per medium dividi non potest, ut infra patebit; sed
dicitur semitonium a semi quod est imperfectum sive semum sive incompletum, ita quod semitonium tantum sonat quantum imperfectus sive semus
sive incompletus tonus, et hoc respectu toni musici de quo paulo ante habitus est sermo. Et vocatur etiam huiusmodi semitonium alio nomine secunda
20 minor; et nominatur secunda propter causam de tono immediate antedictam,
ut est a primo B ad primum C; sed quare minor appeletur suo loco predicto
declarabitur.

⟨5.⟩ Diptonus est duorum sonorum inequalium in duabus diversis et
mediatis manus musicalis partibus existentium tonosque duos amplectan-
25 tium acceptio; et dicitur diptonus quasi duorum tonorum, quoniam talis
diptonus in se duos continet tonos. Et alio nomine tercia maior nuncupatur;
tercia enim dicitur eo quod unus duorum sonorum talem diptonum producentium in tercio loco manus musicalis ab altero reperitur, ut est a primo G
ad primum B; sed quare dicatur maior suo loco patebit.

30 ⟨6.⟩ Semidiptonus est duorum sonorum inequalium in duabus diversis et
mediatis manus musicalis partibus existentium tonum et semitoniumque
amplectantium acceptio; et dicitur semidiptonus quasi semus sive imperfectus sive incompletus diptonus, quoniam ubi diptonus duos continet tonos,
ut habitum est, semidiptonus non continet nisi tonum cum semitonio, et sic

---

3 huiusmodi]huius B ‖ 11 diversis et L ‖ 13 acceptio]Semitonium dicitur a semis, sed non ut
dimidius tonus putetur, sicut nec semivocalis in literis pro medietate vocalis accipitur; ple-
num enim sonum non habet. Semidei semiviri dicuntur, ut scribit Priscianus, non quia
dimidiam partem deorum vel virorum habent, sed qui⟨a⟩ pleni dii vel viri non sunt. *in marg.*
fort. m. sec. L ‖ 33 ubi *bis* B ‖

completely in comparison to another two adjacent pitches producing a certain interval named the semitone, which will be spoken of directly. A tone of this sort is named with another name, major second. It is called a second inasmuch as one of the two pitches producing this tone is placed in the second position of the musical hand with respect to the other pitch, as from the first G to the first A. Why it is called major, however, I do not explain here; below, directly after the explanation of all sixteen intervals named above, I shall explain briefly why every interval is named major, minor, or medial.[6] I have done this so that the work might be rendered shorter.

4. The semitone is the union of two unequal pitches existing in two different and adjacent parts of the musical hand, sounding not full but imperfect and incomplete. Semitone is derived not from that *semi* in Greek which is *medium*[7] in Latin (so, semitone would be so derived because it would be half of the tone) inasmuch as the musical tone cannot be divided by a mean, as will become evident below.[8] Rather, semitone is derived from that *semi* which is "imperfect," "deficient," or "incomplete"; so, semitone means as much as "imperfect, deficient,[9] or incomplete tone,"[10] and this with respect to the musical tone that was spoken of a little earlier. A semitone of this sort is also called by another name, minor second. It is named a second for the reason just stated for the tone; it occurs as from the first B to the first C. Why it is called minor, however, will be explained in its stated place.

5. The ditone is the union of two unequal pitches existing in two different and nonadjacent parts of the musical hand and embracing two tones. It is called ditone—"of two tones," as it were—inasmuch as this ditone contains in itself two tones. It is called by another name, major third. It is called a third, to be sure, because one of the two pitches producing this ditone is found in the third position of the musical hand from the other, as from the first G to the first B. Why it is called major, however, will become evident in its place.

6. The semiditone is the union of two unequal pitches existing in different and nonadjacent parts of the musical hand and embracing a tone and a semitone. It is called semiditone—"deficient, imperfect, or incomplete ditone," as it were—inasmuch as where the ditone contains two tones, as has been explained, the semiditone contains only a tone with a semitone, and

---

[6]*Musica speculativa* 1.18 (172–73).

[7]*Medium*, "middle." Cf. *Plana musica* 1.7 (50–51)

[8]*Musica speculativa* 2.15 (194–201).

[9]"Deficient," *semus*. Cf. *Plana musica* 1.7 (50–51)

[10]Cf. *Plana musica* 1.7 (50–53). The statement is common in medieval theory.

semus, imperfectus, et incompletus est. Et alio nomine tercia minor appelatur; tercia enim dicitur propter causam de diptono immediate antedictam;
sed quare minor dicatur suo loco patebit, et huius exemplum est a primo A
ad primum C.

5 ⟨7.⟩ Tritonus est duorum sonorum inequalium in duabus diversis et
mediatis manus musicalis partibus existentium tresque tonos amplectantium
acceptio; et dicitur tritonus quasi trium tonorum, quoniam talis tritonus in se
tres continet tonos. Et alio nomine quarta maior nominatur; quarta enim
dicitur quoniam unus duorum sonorum talem tritonum producentium in
10 quarto loco manus musicalis ab altero reperitur, ut est ab ut primi F ad mi
secundi B; sed quare maior dicatur suo loco patebit.

⟨8.⟩ Semitritonus est duorum sonorum inequalium in duabus diversis et
mediatis manus musicalis partibus existentium tonos duos et semitoniumque
amplectantium acceptio; et dicitur semitritonus quasi semus sive imperfec-
15 tus sive incompletus tritonus, quoniam ubi tritonus tres continet tonos, ut
supra habitum est, semitritonus solum duos continet cum uno semitonio, et
sic semus, imperfectus, et incomplectus est. Et vocatur etiam alio nomine
quarta minor; quarta enim dicitur propter causam de tritono paulo ante dictam; sed quare minor dicatur suo loco patebit; et exemplum huius est a
20 primo G ad primum C.

Antiqui tamen hanc sonorum combinationem dyateseron appelarunt, et
inter consonantes combinationes collocarunt; unde dyateseron dicitur a dya,
quod est de latine, et teseron, quatuor, sic quod tantum sonat dyateseron
quantum de quatuor, quoniam ex quatuor sonis talis combinatio contexitur,
25 sive quia unus sonorum talem combinationem constituentium in quarto loco
manus musicalis ab altero reperitur; et licet tritonus, de quo paulo ante fuit
sermo, etiam dyateseron propter causam dictam appelari possit, antiqui
tamen propter sui dissonantiam ipsum dimittentes solum semitritonum
acceperunt, et ipsum hoc nomine dyateseron nominaverunt, quapropter
30 antiquos nostros in sequendo quandocunque in sequentibus fiet mentio de
dyateseron intelligendum est de semitritono et non de tritono.

---

2 antedicta L ‖ 7 acceptio *inter coll.* B ‖ 13 duo tonos L ‖ 14 semidritonus *ante corr.* B ‖ 20
primium *ante corr.* L ‖ 27 dictam]antedictam L ‖ 29 et ipsum … nominaverunt *in marg.* B ‖

thus it is deficient, imperfect, and incomplete. It is called by another name, minor third. It is called a third, to be sure, for the reason just stated for the ditone. Why it is called minor, however, will become evident in its place An example of it is from the first A to the first C.

7. The tritone is the union of two unequal pitches existing in two different and nonadjacent parts of the musical hand and embracing three tones. It is called tritone—"of three tones," as it were—inasmuch as this tritone contains in itself three tones. It is named with another name, major fourth.[11] It is called a fourth, to be sure, inasmuch as one of the two pitches producing this tritone is found in the fourth position of the musical hand from the other, as from *ut* of the first F to *mi* of the second B. Why it is called major, however, will become evident in its place.

8. The semitritone is the union of two unequal pitches existing in two different and nonadjacent parts of the musical hand and embracing two tones and a semitone. It is called semitritone—a "deficient" or "imperfect" or "incomplete tritone," as it were—inasmuch as where the tritone contains three tones, as has been explained above, the semitritone contains only two with one semitone, and thus it is deficient, imperfect, and incomplete. It is called by another name, minor fourth. It is called a fourth, to be sure, for the reason stated for the tritone a little earlier. Why it is called minor, however, will become evident in its place. An example of it is from the first G to the first C.

The ancients called this interval diatessaron, and placed it among the consonant intervals; whence diatessaron is derived from *dia*, which is *de* in Latin, and *tessaron, quatuor*.[12] So, diatessaron means as much as "of four" inasmuch as this interval is made up of four pitches, or because one of the pitches constituting this interval is found in the fourth position of the musical hand from the other. Although the tritone, which was spoken of a little before, could also be called a diatessaron for the reason stated, nevertheless the ancients, excluding it on account of its dissonance, took only the semitritone and named it with the name diatessaron. For this reason, following our ancients, whenever in the following mention will be made of the diatessaron, the semitritone must be understood and not the tritone.

---

[11]In this treatise, "major" and "minor" are to be taken in their literal meanings, "greater" and "lesser." Thus, Prosdocimo's "major" fourth is the one we call augmented and his "minor" fourth the one we call perfect, just as his "major" and "minor" fifths are our perfect and diminished fifths.

[12]The same derivation appears in the Lucca revision of *Contrapunctus* (ed. Herlinger), 40–41, and in *Plana musica* 2.12 (110–11), which see for citations of similar derivations.

Multo enim magis dissonat tritonus quam semitritonus, ymo semitritonus quodammodo medium tenet inter veram consonantiam et veram dissonantiam in tantum quod multotiens in musica non multum experti nec multum pratici in cantando semitritonum aure iudicant esse quintam maiorem, que conso-
5 nans est, et de qua statim post sermo fiet; et ideo ni mirum si antiqui ipsum semitritonum pro consonante acceptarunt.

⟨9.⟩ Dyateseron cum tono est duorum sonorum inequalium in duabus diversis et mediatis manus musicalis partibus existentium tres tonos et unum semitoniumque amplectantium acceptio; et dicitur dyateseron cum tono
10 quoniam talis combinatio ex dyateseron et tono contexitur. Et vocatur etiam alio nomine quinta maior: dicitur enim quinta eo quod unus sonorum talem combinationem producentium in quinto loco manus musicalis ab altero reperitur, ut est a primo G ad primum D; sed quare maior nuncupatur inferius suo loco declaribitur.
15 Et apud antiquos etiam hoc nomine dyapente nominabatur; unde dyapente dicitur a dya, quod est de, et pente, quinque, sic quod tantum sonat dyapente quantum de quinque, eo quod talis combinatio ex quinque sonis contexitur, sive quia unus sonorum talem combinationem constituentium in quinto loco manus musicalis ab altero reperitur.
20 ⟨10.⟩ Dyateseron cum semitonio est duorum sonorum inequalium in duabus diversis et mediatis manus musicalis partibus existentium duos tonos et duo semitoniaque amplectantium acceptio: et dicitur dyateseron cum semitonio quoniam talis combinatio ex dyateseron et semitonio contexitur. Et alio nomine quinta minor appelatur; dicitur enim quinta propter causam
25 paulo ante de dyateseron cum tono dictam; sed quare minor dicatur inferius suo loco patebit; et exemplum huius est a primo B ad primum F.

Et potest etiam appelari dyapente, uti dyateseron cum tono, propter causam de dyateseron cum tono dictam. Sed propter sui dissonantiam de ipsa ab antiquis auctoribus nulla mentio facta est, sed solum dyateseron cum
30 tono dyapente appelarunt, et ergo intentionem antiquorum in sequendo

---

8 tres *in ras.* L | unum *in ras.* L ‖ 9–14 et dicitur ... declaribitur]et dicitur dyateseron cum tono quia talis combinatio ex dyateseron et tono componitur. Et dicitur alio nomine quinta maior; dicitur enim quinta eo quod unus duorum sonorum talem combinationem producentium in quinto loco manus musicalis ab altero reperitur, ut est a primo G ad primum D; sed quare maior dicatur suo loco patebit *in marg. fort. m. sec.* L ‖ 15–19 Et apud antiquos ... reperitur]Antiqui tamen hanc sonorum combinationem dyapente appelarunt, unde dicitur dyapente a dya, quod est de, et pente, quinque, quasi de quinque, quoniam ex quinque sonis talis combinatio consistit, sive quia unus sonorum talem combinacionem constituencium in quinto loco manus musicalis ab altero erperitur *in marg. fort. m. sec.* L ‖ 20–22 Dyateseron ... acceptio *in marg. fort. m. sec.* L ‖ 21 existentibus *ante corr.* L ‖

The tritone, to be sure, dissonates much more than the semitritone; indeed, the semitritone in a certain way occupies a mean between true consonance and true dissonance insomuch that those not much experienced in music nor much practiced in singing many times judge the semitritone by ear to be the major fifth, which is consonant and which will be spoken of directly. No wonder, then, if the ancients took this semitritone as consonant.[13]

9. The diatessaron with tone is the union of two unequal pitches existing in two different and nonadjacent parts of the musical hand and embracing three tones and one semitone. It is called diatessaron with tone inasmuch as this interval is made up of a diatessaron and a tone. It is also called by another name, major fifth. It is called a fifth, to be sure, because one of the pitches producing this interval is found in the fifth position of the musical hand from the other, as from the first G to the first D. Why it is called major, however, will be explained below in its place.

Among the ancients, it also used to be named diapente; whence diapente is derived from *dia*, which is *de*, and *pente*, *quinque*.[14] So, diapente means as much as "of five" because this interval is made up of five pitches, or because one of the pitches constituting this interval is found in the fifth position of the musical hand from the other.

10. The diatessaron with semitone is the union of two unequal pitches existing in two different and nonadjacent parts of the musical hand and embracing two tones and two semitones. It is called diatessaron with semitone inasmuch as this interval is made up of a diatessaron and a semitone. It is called by another name, minor fifth. It is called a fifth, to be sure, for the reason stated for the diatessaron with tone a little earlier. Why it is called minor, however, will become evident below in its place. An example of it is from the first B to the first F.

It can also be called a diapente, like the diatessaron with tone, for the reason stated for the diatessaron with tone. But on account of its dissonance, no mention of it was made by ancient authorities (they called only the diatessaron with tone a diapente). Therefore, in following the intention of the

---

[13]Prosdocimo had made the same point in *Contrapunctus* 3.3 and elaborated on it in the Lucca revision (*Contrapunctus* [ed. Herlinger, 38–41]). See Margaret Bent, "Ciconia, Prosdocimus, and the Workings of Musical Grammar as Exemplified in *O felix templum* and *O Padua*," in *Johannes Ciconia: Musicien de la transition*, ed. Philippe Vendrix (Turnhout: Brepols, 2003), 75.

[14]The same derivation appears in the Lucca revision of *Contrapunctus* 3.5 (ed. Herlinger, 44–45), and in *Plana musica* 2.12 (112–13), which see for citations of similar derivations.

168

quandocunque fiet mentio de dyapente intelligendum est de dyateseron cum tono et non de dyateseron cum semitonio.

⟨11.⟩ Dyapente cum tono est duorum sonorum inequalium in duabus diversis et mediatis manus musicalis partibus existentium quatuor tonos et
5 unum semitoniumque amplectantium acceptio; et dicitur dyapente cum tono quoniam talis combinatio ex dyapente et tono componitur. Et alio nomine sexta maior appelatur; dicitur enim sexta eo quod unus duorum sonorum talem combinationem producentium in sexto loco manus musicalis ab altero reperitur, ut est a primo G ad primum E; sed quare maior dicatur suo loco
10 patebit.

⟨12.⟩ Dyapente cum semitonio est duorum sonorum inequalium in duabus diversis et mediatis manus musicalis partibus existentium tres tonos et duo semitoniaque amplectantium acceptio; et dicitur dyapente cum semitonio quoniam talis combinatio ex dyapente et semitonio componitur. Et alio
15 nomine sexta minor nuncupatur; dicitur enim sexta propter causam de dyapente cum tono dictam; sed quare dicatur minor inferius suo loco declarabitur; et exemplum huius est a primo B ad secundum G.

⟨13.⟩ Dyapente cum diptono est duorum sonorum inequalium in duabus diversis et mediatis manus musicalis partibus existentium quinque tonos et
20 unum semitoniumque amplectantium acceptio; et dicitur dyapente cum diptono quoniam talis combinatio ex dyapente et diptono componitur. Et alio nomine septima maior nominatur; dicitur enim septima quoniam unus duorum sonorum talem combinationem producentium in septimo loco manus musicalis ab altero reperitur, ut est a primo C ad mi secundi B; sed
25 quare maior nominetur suo loco patebit.

⟨14.⟩ Dyapente cum semidiptono est duorum sonorum inequalium in duabus diversis et mediatis manus musicalis partibus existentium quatuor tonos et duo semitoniaque amplectantium acceptio; et dicitur dyapente cum semidiptono quoniam talis combinatio ex dyapente et semidiptono componi-
30 tur. Et alio nomine septima minor nominatur; septima enim dicitur propter causam de dyapente cum diptono paulo ante dictam; sed quare minor dicatur suo loco patebit; et exemplum huius est a primo B ad secundum A.

⟨15.⟩ Dyapente cum tritono est duorum sonorum inequalium in duabus diversis et mediatis manus musicalis partibus existentium sex tonos et unum
35 semitoniumque amplectantium acceptio; et dicitur dyapente cum tritono quoniam talis combinatio ex dyapente et tritono componitur. Et denominatur

---

31 dicatur minor L ‖

ancients, whenever mention will be made of the diapente, the diatessaron with tone must be understood and not the diatessaron with semitone.

11. The diapente with tone is the union of two unequal pitches existing in two different and nonadjacent parts of the musical hand and embracing four tones and one semitone. It is called diapente with tone inasmuch as this interval is composed of a diapente and a tone. It is called by another name, major sixth. It is called a sixth, to be sure, because one of the two pitches producing this interval is found in the sixth position of the musical hand from the other, as from the first G to the first E. Why it is called major, however, will become evident in its place.

12. The diapente with semitone is the union of two unequal pitches existing in two different and nonadjacent parts of the musical hand and embracing three tones and two semitones. It is called diapente with semitone inasmuch as this interval is composed of a diapente and a semitone. It is called by another name, minor sixth. It is called a sixth, to be sure, for the reason stated for the diapente with tone. Why it is called minor, however, will be explained below in its place. An example of it is from the first B to the second G.

13. The diapente with ditone is the union of two unequal pitches existing in two different and nonadjacent parts of the musical hand and embracing five tones and one semitone. It is called diapente with ditone inasmuch as this interval is composed of a diapente and a ditone. It is named with another name, major seventh. It is called a seventh, to be sure, inasmuch as one of the two pitches producing this interval is found in the seventh position of the musical hand from the other, as from the first C to the *mi* of the second B. Why it is called major, however, will become evident in its place.

14. The diapente with semiditone is the union of two unequal pitches existing in two different and nonadjacent parts of the musical hand and embracing four tones and two semitones. It is called diapente with semiditone inasmuch as this interval is composed of a diapente and a semiditone. It is named with another name, minor seventh. It is called a seventh, to be sure, for the reason stated for the diapente with ditone a little earlier. Why it is called minor, however, will become evident in its place. An example of it is from the first B to the second A.

15. The diapente with tritone is the union of two unequal pitches existing in two different and nonadjacent parts of the musical hand and embracing six tones and one semitone. It is called diapente with tritone inasmuch as this interval is composed of a diapente and a tritone. It is also named the

etiam octava maior; octava enim nominatur quoniam unus duorum sonorum talem combinationem producentium in octavo loco manus musicalis ab altero reperitur, ut est a fa secundi B ad mi tercii B; sed quare maior dicatur suo loco patebit.

5 ⟨16.⟩ Dyapente cum dyateseron est duorum sonorum inequalium in duabus diversis et mediatis manus musicalis partibus existentium quinque tonos et duo semitoniaque amplectantium acceptio; et dicitur dyapente cum dyateseron quoniam talis combinatio ex dyapente et dyateseron componitur. Et appelatur etiam octava media; octava enim dicitur propter causam de

10 dyapente cum tritono paulo ante dictam; sed quare dicatur media suo loco patebit; et exemplum huius est a primo G ad secundum G.

Et ab antiquis hec combinatio appelabatur dyapason, unde dyapason dicitur a dya, quod est de, et pason, totum, ita quod dyapason tantum sonat quantum de toto; et merito hec combinatio vocatur de toto, quoniam in se

15 continet omnes sonorum combinationes quarum proportiones primitus invente fuerunt, que combinationes sunt hee quatuor, scilicet tonus, dyateseron, dyapente, et ipsamet dyapason.

⟨17.⟩ Bisdyateseron cum semitonio est duorum sonorum inequalium in duabus diversis et mediatis manus musicalis partibus existentium quatuor

20 tonos et tria semitoniaque amplectantium acceptio; et dicitur bisdyateseron cum semitonio quoniam talis combinatio ex duabus dyateseron et uno semitonio contexitur. Et alio nomine vocatur octava minor; octava enim dicitur propter causam de dyapente cum tritono dictam; sed quare minor dicatur statim post patebit; et exemplum huius est a primo B ad fa secundi B.

25 Et licet antiqui solum octavam mediam vocaverint hoc nomine dyapason, tamen octava maior potest etiam dyapason denominari, quoniam octava maior ita in se continet omnes sonorum combinationes quarum proportiones primitus invente fuerunt, sicut octava media ymo, et octava minor etiam

---

26 denominari]nominari L ‖

major octave.[15] It is called an octave, to be sure, inasmuch as one of the two pitches producing this interval is found in the eighth position of the musical hand from the other, as from *fa* of the second B to *mi* of the third B. Why it is called major, however, will become evident in its place.

16. The diapente with diatessaron is the union of two unequal pitches existing in two different and nonadjacent parts of the musical hand and embracing five tones and two semitones. It is called diapente with diatessaron inasmuch as this interval is composed of a diapente and a diatessaron. It is also called the medial octave. It is called an octave, to be sure, for the reason stated for the diapente with tritone a little earlier.[16] Why it is called medial, however, will become evident in its place. An example of it is from the first G to the second G.

This interval used to be called diapason by the ancients. Diapason is derived from *dia*, which is *de*, and *pason*, *totum*,[17] because diapason means as much as "of all." This interval is with good reason called "of all" inasmuch as it contains all the intervals whose ratios were discovered first. Those intervals are these four: the tone, the diatessaron, the diapente, and the diapason itself.[18]

17. The double diatessaron with semitone is the union of two unequal pitches existing in two different and nonadjacent parts of the musical hand and embracing four tones and three semitones. It is called the double diatessaron with semitone inasmuch as this interval is made up of two diatessarons and one semitone. It is called by another name, minor octave. It is called an octave, to be sure, for the reason stated for the diapente with tritone. Why it is called minor, however, will become evident directly. An example of it is from the first B to *fa* of the second B.

Although the ancients called only the medial octave by the name diapason, the major octave, nonetheless, can also be named diapason inasmuch as the major octave contains in itself all the intervals whose ratios were discovered first, as indeed does the medial octave. The minor octave also contains

---

[15]The intervals Prosdocimo calls *octaua minor, media,* and *maior* in *Musica speculativa* 1.15–17 (168–73) he had called *octava minor, maior,* and *maxima* in *Contrapunctus* 3.5 (ed. Herlinger, 46–49). Obviously, they are the octaves we call diminished, perfect, and augmented.

[16]*Musica speculativa* 1.15 (168–71).

[17]The same derivation appears in the Lucca revision of *Contrapunctus* 3.5 (ed. Herlinger, 46–47), and in *Plana musica* 2.13 (118–19), which see for citations of similar derivations.

[18]Prosdocimo will mention the discovery of these ratios by Pythagoras in *Musica speculativa* 2.1 (176–77).

omnes dictas combinationes continet una excepta, scilicet octava media, quare etiam a maiori parte denominando posset etiam ipsa dyapason denominari. Sed antiqui octavam maiorem et minorem propter earum dissonantias dimittentes solum octavam mediam dyapason nominarunt, quare
5 ipsos antiquos in sequendo ubicunque de dyapason aliqua fiet mentio semper intelligendum est de octava media et non de maiori neque de minori.

⟨18.⟩ Et quia in declaratione supradictarum sexdecim sonorum combinationum multotiens facta est mentio de maioritate et minoritate earum, est sciendum quod illa combinatio maior denominatur cuius soni ipsam consti-
10 tuentes magis a se invicem distant respectu alterius eiusdem nominis, et illa vocatur minor cuius soni ipsam constituentes minus a se invicem distant respectu alterius eiusdem nominis; ut verbi gratia quia duo soni constituentes tonum magis a se invicem distant quam duo soni constituentes semitonium, et tam tonus quam semitonium secunda denominatur, ut habitum
15 est supra, ideo tonus secunda maior et semitonium secunda minor denominantur; item quia duo soni constituentes diptonum magis a se invicem distant quam duo soni constituentes semidiptonum, et ipsorum uterque tercia denominatur, ideo diptonus tercia maior et semidiptonus tercia minor appelantur; et sic de aliis. Dyapason autem octava media denominatur, quoniam
20 medium tenet inter octavam maiorem et octavam minorem. Duo nanque soni constituentes dyapason minus a se invicem distant quam duo soni constituentes octavam maiorem et magis a se invicem distant quam duo soni constituentes octavam minorem, et ergo dyapason bene medium tenet inter octavam maiorem et octavam minorem, quare merito octava media nuncu-
25 pata est.

Plures preterea non declarantur hic sonorum combinationes, eo quod ex sexdecim habitis faciliter haberi potest noticia omnium aliarum sequentium quantum ad earum compositionem et ad numerum tonorum et semitoniorum in eis existentium et etiam quantum ad proportiones earum, ut inferius
30 patebit. Unde scito numero tonorum et semitoniorum in dyapason et aliis combinationibus supradictis existentium, scitur etiam numerus tonorum et semitoniorum in dyapason cum tono existentium, vel in dyapa-

---

2 etiam ipsa *in marg.* B ‖ 3 et minorem *inter coll.* B ‖ 4 mediam consonantem L ‖ 6 neque *vel* nec L ‖ 7 Et]Sed L ‖ 15–16 [appelantur] denominantur L ‖ 22–23 et magis … octavam minorem *in marg.* B ‖ 22 a]ad B ‖ 30 diapason [cum tono existentium] L ‖ 32 semitonorum *ante corr.* B ‖

all the stated intervals except one, the medial octave, wherefore it could also—from the denomination of its greater part—be denominated a diapason. But the ancients, excluding the major and the minor octave on account of their dissonance, named only the medial octave diapason. Wherefore, in following those ancients, wherever any mention will be made of the diapason, the medial octave must always be understood and not the major or the minor.

18. Because in the explanation of the aforesaid sixteen intervals, mention has frequently been made of their major and minor qualities, one must know that that interval is named major the constituent pitches of which lie more distant from one another with respect to those of the other interval of the same name, and that interval is called minor the constituent pitches of which lie less distant from one another with respect to those of the other interval of the same name.[19] For instance: because the two pitches constituting the tone lie more distant from one another than the two pitches constituting the semitone, and the tone as well as the semitone is named a second (as was explained above),[20] the tone is named the major second and the semitone the minor second; again, because the two pitches constituting the ditone lie more distant from one another than the two pitches constituting the semiditone, and either of them is named a third, the ditone is called the major third and the semiditone the minor third; and likewise for the others. Now the diapason is called the medial octave inasmuch as it occupies a mean between the major octave and the minor octave, for the two pitches constituting the diapason lie less distant from one another than the two pitches constituting the major octave and more distant from one another than the two pitches constituting the minor octave. Therefore, it is properly said that the diapason occupies a mean between the major octave and the minor octave, wherefore it is with good reason called the medial octave.

More concerning the intervals is not explained here, because from the sixteen that have been explained knowledge concerning all the others following can easily be had, as to their composition and the numbers of tones and semitones existing in them, and also as to their ratios, as will become evident below.[21] For which reason, when the number of tones and semitones existing in the diapason and the other aforesaid intervals are known, the number of tones and semitones is also known existing in the diapason with

[19]On the major and minor inflections of intervals, cf. *Contrapunctus* 3.5 (ed. Herlinger, 44–49).

[20]*Musica speculativa* 1.3, 4 (160–63).

[21]*Musica speculativa* 2 (176–219).

son cum semitonio, vel in dyapason cum diptono, vel in dyapason cum semidiptono, vel in dyapason cum tritono, vel in dyapason cum dyateseron, vel in dyapason cum dyapente, vel in dyapason cum dyapente et tono, vel in dyapason cum dyapente et semitonio, vel in dyapason cum dyapente et dip-
5 tono, vel in dyapason cum dyapente et semidiptono, vel in bisdyapason, et sic de aliis infinitis sonorum combinationibus sequentibus. Et similiter habitis proportionibus harum sexdecim sonorum combinationum et modis inveniendi ipsas proportiones, habebuntur etiam faciliter proportiones et modi inveniendi ipsas proportiones omnium aliarum sonorum combinationum
10 sequentium.

Multas etiam sonorum combinationes inter unisonum et octavam reperibiles pretermisi, eo quod licet fingendo reperibiles sint, in manu tamen musicali nullo modo reperiri possunt, et etiam quia habita plena noticia sexdecim sonorum combinationum principalium, de quibus habitus est sermo,
15 quantum scilicet ad earum compositiones et proportiones, faciliter etiam haberi poterit plena noticia harum combinationum sonorum in manu musicali non repertarum, quantum scilicet ad earum compositiones et proportiones. Et hee sonorum combinationes in manu musicali non reperibiles sunt sicut tercia duorum semitoniorum, quarta trium semitoniorum, quinta qua-
20 tuor semitoniorum, et sic de multis aliis.

3 vel in dyapason cum dyapente *om.* L | [et] et B ‖ 4 cum dyapente (*pr.*) *om.* B ‖ 6 de *sup. lin.* B ‖ 9 ipsas *vel* illas L ‖ 16 sonorum combinationum L ‖ 19 quarta trium semitoniorum *in marg.* B ‖

tone, the diapason with semitone, the diapason with ditone, the diapason with semiditone, the diapason with tritone, the diapason with diatessaron, the diapason with diapente, the diapason with diapente and tone, the diapason with diapente and semitone, the diapason with diapente and ditone, the diapason with diapente and semiditone, the double diapason, and likewise for the other intervals following infinitely.[22] Similarly, when the ratios of these sixteen intervals and the methods for discovering these ratios are grasped, the ratios and methods for discovering the ratios for all the other intervals following will easily be grasped as well.

I have excluded many intervals that can be found between the unison and the octave because although they can be found through artificial means, they cannot be found in the musical hand by any means; and also because when full knowledge of the sixteen basic intervals that have been spoken of has been grasped, as to their composition and their ratios, full knowledge will also be able to be easily grasped of the intervals not found in the musical hand, as to their composition and their ratios. These intervals that cannot be found in the musical hand are the third of two semitones, the fourth of three semitones, the fifth of four semitones, and many others.[23]

---

[22]After enumerating the intervals through the triple octave in *Contrapunctus* 3.2 (ed. Herlinger, 34–37), Prosdocimo had pointed out that intervals could be multiplied infinitely if the syllables or instruments could be extended to infinity.

[23]The third of two semitones (our diminished third), for example A♯-C; the fourth of three semitones (our doubly diminished fourth), for example A♯-D♭; the fifth of four semitones (our triply diminished fifth), for example, B♯-F♭. See Introduction, 16. Johannes Boen gave examples of the first two of these in his *Musica* 3.51–60 of 1357 (*Johannes Boens "Musica" und seine Konsonanzenlehre*, ed. Wolf Frobenius, Freiburger Schriften zur Musikwissenschaft, vol. 2 [Stuttgart: Musikwissenschaftliche Verlags-Gesellschaft, 1971], 55–56); part 3 of this work (pp. 51–64) develops the theory of such intervals. See Jan Herlinger, "Music Theory of the Fourteenth and Early Fifteenth Centuries," chapter 6 in *Music as Concept and Practice in the Late Middle Ages*, ed. Reinhard Strohm and Bonnie J. Blackburn, New Oxford History of Music, new ed., vol. 3/2 (Oxford: Oxford University Press, 2001), 254–55.

176

⟨2⟩

⟨1.⟩ His sexdecim sonorum combinationibus principalibus quantum ad earum compositiones sic declaratis, consequenter procedendum est ad suarum proportionum declarationem; et prius preponantur principia et funda-
5 menta cognitionis harum proportionum, que neque demonstrative nec persuasive sed solum experientia per Pitagoram ytalicum inventa sunt, ut vult Boetius primo sue Musice et Macrobius in De sompnio Scipionis et Johanes de Muris normandus in parte prima sue Musice speculative et multi alii. Ostendunt enim omnes hii in locis preallegatis quomodo Pitagoras ytalicus
10 principia et fundamenta cognitionis proportionum sonorum combinationum casu adinvenit et experientia, quem modum hic non recito ne opus prolungetur in vanum. Hec ergo principia et fundamenta sunt quatuor species proportionum quatuor sonorum combinationum, scilicet proportio toni, que est sexquioctava; proportio dyateseron, que est sexquitercia; proportio dya-
15 pente, que est sexquialtera; et proportio dyapason, que est dupla. Et hec, ut supra habitum est, non demonstrative nec persuasive sed solum casu et experientia per Pitagoram ytalicum inventa sunt.

---

5 neque]non L ‖ 6 ytalicum]Pitagoras *in marg. man. sec.* B ‖ 7 Boetius]Boetius *in marg. man. sec.* B | Macobrius B Macrobrius L ‖ 8 normandus]Ioannes de Muris Normandus *in marg. man. sec.* B ‖ 12–13 proportionum ⟦sunt⟧ B ‖

2

1. These sixteen principal intervals having been thus explained with respect to their composition, we must now proceed to the explanation of their ratios. Let principles and fundamentals of the recognition of these ratios be presented first, which were discovered neither through demonstration nor argument but only through observation by the Italian Pythagoras, as Boethius maintains in the first book of his *Musica*,[1] Macrobius in *De somnio Scipionis*,[2] the Norman Johannes de Muris in the first part of his *Musica speculativa*,[3] and many others. To be sure, all these show, in the passages cited, how the Italian Pythagoras discovered the principles and fundamentals of the recognition of the ratios of intervals by chance and through observation;[4] I do not relate the method here, lest the work be extended to no purpose. These principles and fundamentals, then, are the four species of ratios of four intervals, that is, the ratio of the tone, which is the sesquioctave; the ratio of the diatessaron, which is the sesquitertial; the ratio of the diapente, which is the sesquialter; and the ratio of the diapason, which is the duple.[5] And these, as has been explained above, were discovered by the Italian Pythagoras, not through demonstration or argument, but only by chance and through observation.

---

[1]Boethius *De institutione musica* 1.10, 11 (ed. Friedlein, 196–98; trans. Bower, 17–19). Pythagoras, though born on Samos, established a school at Croton, a Greek colony in southern Italy.

[2]Macrobius *In somnium Scipionis* 2.1.8–14 (*Opera*, vol. 2, *Commentarii in Somnium Scipionis, accedunt quatuor tabulae et Somnium Scipionis*, ed. James Willis [Leipzig: B. G. Teubner, 1963], 96–97; translated with introduction and notes by William Harris Stahl as *Commentary on the Dream of Scipio by Macrobius*, Records of Western Civilization [New York: Columbia University Press, 1952], 186–88).

[3]Johannes de Muris, *Musica (speculativa)* 1.1–3 (ed. Fast, 22–55).

[4]Prosdocimo will return to Pythagoras's discovery of these ratios in *Musica speculativa* 3.1 (220–21).

[5]The duple ratio is multiple, the other three mentioned here are superparticular. As Prosdocimo explains in *Brevis summula proportionum* 5, "Multiple ratio is said to occur when the greater quantity contains the lesser several times and nothing beyond. Superparticular ratio is said to occur when the greater quantity contains the lesser once and not several times, plus something beyond that is an aliquot part [i.e., a factor] of the lesser quantity [Proportio multiplex dicitur quando maior quantitas continet minorem pluries et nichil ultra. Proportio vero superparticularis dicitur quando maior quantitas continet minorem semel et

Et ex his principiis et fundamentis sequitur quod omnes toni inter se sunt equales, et similiter omnes dyateseron, et omnes dyapente, et omnes dyapason; nam omnes proportiones sexquioctave inter se sunt equales, et similiter omnes proportiones sexquitercie, et omnes proportiones sexquialtere, et
5 omnes proportiones duple. Sed omnis tonus consistit in proportione sexquioctava, et omnis dyateseron in proportione sexquitercia, et omnis dyapente in proportione sexquialtera, et omnis dyapason in proportione dupla, per principia et fundamenta supra habita; ergo omnes toni inter se sunt equales, et similiter omnes dyateseron, et omnes dyapente, et omnes dyapason. Una
10 enim sonorum combinatio non dicitur alteri equalis vel inequalis nisi secundum quod earum proportiones sibi invicem equales vel inequales reperiuntur. Et hoc posito, sequitur ultra quod omnia semitonia de quibus mentio facta est in sonorum combinationibus supradictis etiam inter se sunt equalia, nam ubi non equarentur (cum omne semitonium de supradictis si iungatur
15 cum duobus tonis, dyateseron producit; et cum tribus, dyapente; et cum quinque et uno semitonio de supradictis, dyapason, ut supra habitum est), sequeretur quod non omnes dyateseron essent equales inter se, nec similiter omnes dyapente, nec omnes dyapason, quod est contra iam supra demonstratum. Et sequitur demum ulterius quod omnes combinationes sonorum eius-
20 dem nominis ultimati inter se sunt equales, quod si non equarentur, sequeretur quod aut toni non equarentur inter se aut semitonia, quod est contra iam demonstratum.

⟨2.⟩ Istis principiis et tribus ex ipsis sequentibus sic declaratis, sequitur modo declarare proportiones reliquarum duodecim sonorum combinationum
25 principalium remanentium, et primo ab unisono principium faciamus, unde unisonus in proportione equalitatis consistit, nam ex quo unisonus est acceptio duorum sonorum equalium, ut supra habitum est, et inter quelibet duo equalia proportio equalitatis reperitur, sequitur unisonum in proportione equalitatis consistere, quod erat declarandum.

5–6 sexquiottava *ante corr.* B ‖ 8 supra]prius L ‖ 19 sonorum combinationes L ‖ 27 equalium]inter se equalium L ‖

From these principles and fundamentals, it follows that all tones are equal to each other; similarly all diatessarons, all diapentes, and all diapasons, for all sesquioctave ratios are equal to each other; and similarly all sesquitertial ratios, all sesquialter ratios, and all duple ratios. But every tone consists in the sesquioctave ratio, every diatessaron in the sesquitertial ratio, every diapente in the sesquialter ratio, and every diapason in the duple ratio by the principles and fundamentals explained above. Therefore, all tones are equal to each other, and similarly all diatessarons, all diapentes, and all diapasons. One interval is not said to be equal or unequal to another except according to whether their ratios are found to be equal or unequal to one another. This having been established, it follows, further, that all semitones of which mention has been made in the section on the aforesaid intervals[6] are also equal to each other, for if they were not equal (for every semitone of those aforesaid intervals, if it were joined with two tones, produces a diatessaron; with three, a diapente; and with five and one semitone of those aforesaid intervals, an octave, as has been explained above),[7] it would have followed that not all diatessarons were equal to each other nor, similarly, all diapentes nor all diapasons, which is contrary to what has been demonstrated above. In the end, it follows further that all intervals of the same specific name are equal to one another because, if they were not made equal, it would have followed that either tones or semitones were not made equal to each other, which is contrary to what has already been demonstrated.

2. These principles and three of their consequences having been thus explained, it follows only to explain the ratios of the remaining twelve principal intervals. First, let us begin with the unison. The unison consists in the ratio of equality: because the unison is the union of two equal pitches, as has been explained above,[8] and the ratio of equality is found between any two equal quantities,[9] it follows that the unison consists in the ratio of equality, which was to be explained.

---

non pluries et cum hoc aliquid ultra quod est pars aliquota quantitatis minoris]" (*Brevis summula ... Parvus tractatulus* [ed. Herlinger], 53). The sesquioctave ratio, 9:8 and its compounds; the sesquiterial, 4:3 and its compounds; the sesquialter, 3:2 and its compounds; the duple, 2:1 and its compounds.

[6]That is, in *Musica speculativa* 1 (160–76).

[7]*Musica speculativa* 1.8, 9, 16 (164–67, 170–71).

[8]*Musica speculativa* 1.2 (160–61).

[9]Cf. Prosdocimo, *Brevis summula proportionum* 4 (*Brevis summula ... Parvus tractatulus* [ed. Herlinger], 52–53).

⟨3.⟩ Semitonium, de quo pluries habitus est sermo in sonorum combinationibus supra habitis, in proportione super13partiente 243[as] consistit; nam ex quo dyateseron constat ex duobus tonis et uno semitonio, ut habitum est supra, si a dyateseron removeantur duo toni remanebit semitonium supra-

5 dictum; sed cum dyateseron consistat in proportione sexquitercia et tonus in proportione sexquioctava, ex fundamento supra habito, que sexquioctava minor est sexquitercia, cum species proportionis superparticularis semper tendant diminuendo per oppositum specierum proportionis multiplicis, que semper tendunt augmentando, sequitur pariformiter quod si a sexquitercia

10 subtrahantur due sexquioctave remanebit proportio semitonii supradicti; et ut hanc subtractionem facere scias, hanc nota regulam: si proportionem aliquam ab alia proportione a qua possit subtrahi subtrahere intendis, ipsas proportiones accipias in suis minimis numeris, et multiplica maiorem numerum uniuscuiusque ipsarum proportionum per minorem alterius et pro-

15 portio productorum ex his duabus multiplicationibus erit proportio remanens, tali subtractione facta. Capio ergo proportionem sexquiterciam in suis minimis numeris, qui sunt 4 et 3, et capio etiam proportionem sexquioctavam in suis minimis numeris, qui sunt 9 et 8, et multiplico primo maiorem

1 in]inde *vel* in de L ‖ 4 a *sup. lin.* B ‖ 5 sequitercia B ‖ 6 sexquioctava (*sec.*)]proportio sexquioctava L ‖ 7 sexquitercia]proportione sexquitercia L ‖ 7–8 semper tendant … specierum proportionis *om.* B ‖ 13 accipias]capias L ‖ 14 ipsarum duarum L ‖ 15 duabus [prope] L ‖

3. The semitone, which was spoken of several times in the section on intervals, which were explained above, consists in the ratio super13partient by 243rds:[10] because the diatessaron consists of two tones and one semitone, as has been explained above,[11] if two tones should be removed from the diatessaron, the aforesaid semitone will remain. But since the diatessaron consists in the sesquitertial ratio and the tone in the sesquioctave ratio (on the basis of the fundamental explained above)[12]—which sesquioctave is less than the sesquitertial, since the species of the superparticular ratio always tend toward decrease, contrary to the species of the multiple ratio, which always tend toward increase[13]—, it follows likewise that if two sesquioctaves are subtracted from the sesquitertial, the ratio of the aforesaid semitone will remain. So that you know how to make this subtraction, note this rule. If you intend to subtract some ratio from another ratio from which it can be subtracted, take those ratios in their least numbers, multiply the greater number of each of the ratios by the lesser of the other, and the ratio of the products of these two multiplications will be the ratio remaining when the subtraction has been made. I take, then, the sesquitertial ratio in its least numbers, which are 4 and 3, and I also take the sesquioctave ratio in its least numbers, which are 9 and 8. First, I multiply the greater number of the ses-

---

[10]I.e., 265:243. After explaining how to find the ratio of an interval that results from subtracting one interval from another, Prosdocimo will first find the ratio of the semiditone (minor third) by subtracting the tone (9:8) from the diatessaron (4:3), which is done by multiplying the smaller number of the one by the larger number of the other and vice versa, i.e., $(8 \times 4):(9 \times 3) = 32:27$; then, he will find the ratio of the minor semitone by subtracting the tone from the semiditone, which is done by multiplying the smaller number of the one by the larger number of the other and vice versa, i.e., $(8 \times 32):(9 \times 27) = 256:243$. The ratio 256:243 is superpartient. Prosdocimo, *Brevis summula proportionum* 5: "Superpartient ratio occurs when the greater quantity contains the lesser once and not several times, plus something beyond that is a non–aliquot part of the lesser quantity [i.e., not its factor] [Proportio vero superpartiens est quando maior quantitas continet minorem semel et non pluries et cum hoc aliquid ultra quod non est pars aliquota quantitatis minoris]" (*Brevis summula ... Parvus tractatulus* [ed. Herlinger], 55).

[11]*Musica speculativa* 1.8 (164–67).

[12]*Musica speculativa* 2.1 (176–79).

[13]Species of the multiple ratio "tend toward increase" in that the ratios of the two terms increase through the progression from one species to the next (2:1, 3:1, 4:1, ...); those of the superparticular ratio "tend toward decrease" in that the ratios of the two terms decrease through such a progression (3:2, 4:3, 5:4, ...). In *De institutione musica* 1.6 (ed. Friedlein, 193–94; trans. Bower, 14–15), Boethius associates multiplicity with the progressive increase of number (discrete quantity) toward infinity, superparticularity with the progressive decrease of continuous quantity toward the infinitesimal. Cf. *De institutione musica* 2.3 (ed. Friedlein, 228–29; trans. Bower, 53–54).

numerum proportionis sexquitercie, scilicet 4, per minorem numerum proportionis sexquioctave, scilicet per 8, et productum erit 32; secundo vero multiplico maiorem numerum proportionis sexquioctave, scilicet 9, per minorem numerum proportionis sexquitercie, scilicet per 3, et productum
5 erit 27; et ergo subtrahendo unam proportionem sexquioctavam ab una sexquitercia, remanet proportio que est inter 32 et 27, quorum differentia est 5, et ista est proportio super5partiens 27as, qua subtrahatur alia sexquioctava proportio, et ex quo stet in suis minimis numeris, multiplicabo primo maiorem numerum huius proportionis, scilicet 32, per minorem proportionis sex-
10 quioctave, scilicet per 8, et productum erit 256; secundo vero multiplicabo maiorem numerum proportionis sexquioctave, scilicet 9, per minorem numerum predicte proportionis, scilicet per 27, et productum erit 243; et ergo subtractis istis duabus sexquioctavis ab una sexquitercia ultimate, remanet proportio que est inter 256 et 243, quorum differentia est 13; et ista
15 est proportio super13partiens 243as, que erit proportio semitonii supradicti, quod erat declarandum.

Item alio modo declaratur hoc idem sic: iungantur enim insimul due sexquioctave et agregatum ex his subtrahatur ab una sexquitercia, et remanebit proportio semitonii supradicti; et ut modum addendi proportiones
20 adinvicem habeas, hanc nota regulam: si proportionem aliquam alteri proportioni addere intendis, ambas illas proportiones in suis minimis numeris capias, et multiplica maiorem numerum unius ipsarum per maiorem alterius et minorem per minorem, et proportio productorum ex his duabus multiplicationibus erit proportio agregati ex predictis duabus proportionibus. Quia
25 ergo in sexquioctava maior suorum minorum numerorum est 9 et minor est 8, multiplicetur primo 9 per 9 et productum erit 81; deinde multiplicetur 8 per 8 et productum erit 64. Proportio ergo 81 ad 64, quorum differentia est 17, que est proportio super17partiens 64as, erit proportio agregati ex duabus sexquioctavis, et per consequens ex duobus tonis; et cum sit in suis minimis
30 numeris si subtrahatur ab una sexquitercia per modum supradictum remanebit proportio semitonii supradicti, scilicet proportio super13partiens 243as.

5–6 sexquitercia]proportione sexquitercia L || 6 remanent B || 8 stet]ipsa est L || 9 minorem numerum [numerum] L || 13 duabus proportionibus L || 21 numeris *sup. lin.* B || 26 multiplicetur (*sec.*)]multiplicentur B || 28 17]7 B | super17partiens]super7partiens B ||

quitertial ratio, 4, by the lesser number of the sesquioctave ratio, 8, and the product will be 32. Second, I multiply the greater number of the sesquioctave ratio, 9, by the lesser number of the sesquitertial ratio, 3, and the product will be 27. Therefore, subtracting one sesquioctave ratio from one sesquitertial, the ratio remains that is between 32 and 27, of which the difference is 5. This is the ratio super5partient by 27ths. From this, let another sesquioctave ratio be subtracted. Because it already stands in its least numbers, I shall first multiply the greater number of this ratio, 32, by the lesser number of the sesquioctave ratio, 8, and the product will be 256. Second, I shall multiply the greater number of the sesquioctave ratio, 9, by the lesser number of the aforesaid ratio, 27, and the product will be 243. Therefore, when these two sesquioctaves have been subtracted specifically from the one sesquitertial, the ratio remains that is between 256 and 243, of which the difference is 13. This is the ratio super13partient by 243rds, which will be the ratio of the aforesaid semitone, which was to be explained.

Again, this same thing is explained in another way, thus.[14] Let two sesquioctaves be joined, let their aggregate be subtracted from one sesquitertial, and the ratio of the aforesaid semitone will remain. So that you grasp the method of adding ratios to each other, note this rule: if you intend to add some ratio to another ratio, take both those ratios in their least numbers and multiply the greater number of one of them by the greater of the other and the lesser by the lesser, and the ratio of the products of these two multiplications will be the ratio of the aggregate of the two aforesaid ratios. Because in the sesquioctave, then, the greater of its numbers is 9 (in their least form) and the lesser is 8, first let 9 be multiplied by 9 and the product will be 81. Then, let 8 be multiplied by 8 and the product will be 64. Therefore, the ratio of 81 to 64, of which the difference is 17—which is the ratio super17partient by 64ths—will be the ratio of the aggregate of two sesquioctaves and consequently of two tones. Since it is in its least numbers, if it is subtracted from one sesquitertial by the aforesaid method, the ratio of the aforesaid semitone will remain, that is, the ratio super13partient by 243rds.

---

[14]After explaining how to find the ratio of an interval that results from adding two intervals together, Prosdocimo will find the ratio of the minor semitone by first adding one whole tone (9:8) to another to obtain the ditone, which is done by multiplying the larger numbers and the smaller numbers of the two 9:8 ratios, i.e., $(9 \times 9):(8 \times 8) = 81:64$; then, he will find the ratio of the minor semitone by subtracting the ditone (81:64) from the diatessaron (4:3), which is done by multiplying the larger number of the one by the smaller number of the other and vice versa, i.e., $(64 \times 4):(81 \times 3) = 256:243$.

184

Item aliter declaratur hoc idem sic: inveniatur unus numerus super quem absque fractionibus intendi possint duo toni continui sive due sexquioctave continue, qui numerus per hanc talem regulam inveniri potest: quot proportiones sexquioctavas continuas absque fractionibus habere intendis, tot pro-
5 portiones octuplas continuas ab unitate accipias et numerus ultimus octuplarum erit numerus quesitus. Quia ergo invenire intendimus unum numerum supra quem absque fractionibus possint intendi precise due sexquioctave continue, inveniam duas octuplas continuas ab unitate sic, nam primo supra unitatem invenio unum numerum octuplum, scilicet 8, deinde
10 supra 8 alium invenio numerum octuplum, scilicet 64. Hic ergo numerus ultimus, scilicet 64, est numerus quesitus, nam supra ipsum absque fractionibus possunt precise intendi due sexquioctave: ut si supra 64 addas suam octavam partem, scilicet 8, habebis 72, cui si addas suam octavam partem, scilicet 9, habebis 81, cuius non est integris octava pars. Ordinentur ergo sic
15 isti tres numeri, scilicet 64, 72, 81, qui erunt adinvicem proportionati proportionalitate continua sexquioctava duas sexquioctavas continuas et per consequens duos tonos continuos producentes. Hoc facto supra 64 intendatur dyateseron sive una proportio sexquitercia, et quoniam hoc fieri non potest absque fractionibus, eo quod 64 dividi non potest equaliter per 3, pro
20 tanto ne per fractiones procedamus, quemlibet trium numerorum paulo ante in una linea ordinatorum multiplicemus per 3, et producta dividi poterunt per tria, et remanebunt in eadem proportione in qua prius fuerunt multiplicata scilicet sexquioctava et producent duas sexquioctavas continuas, ut prius per regulam talem: si aliqui numeri per unum et eundem numerum
25 multiplicentur, producta eandem proportionem servabunt que reperiebatur inter numeros multiplicatos. Multiplica ergo 64 per 3 et habebis 192; deinde multiplica 72 per 3 et habebis 216; deinde multiplica 81 per 3 et habebis 243; qui tres numeri sic producti taliter in una linea ordinentur, 192, 216, 243; quo facto supra 192 addatur sua tercia pars, scilicet 64, et habebis 256.
30 Postea vero taliter ordinentur hii quatuor numeri, scilicet 192, 216, 243, 256, in quo ordine apparet quomodo proportio primi numeri, scilicet 192, ad ultimum, scilicet ad 256, est proportio dyateseron, que componitur ex duo-

2 duo]precise duo L | sexquioctave]proportiones sexquioctave L || 4 habere]precise habere L || 7 precise]precipue B || 10 Hic]Iste L || 12 precise]precipue B || 14 integris non est L || 21–22 dividi poterunt per tria, et *om.* B || 23 scilicet in L || 26 multiplicatos que regula est 18ᵃ conclusio 7ⁱ Ellementorum Euclidis L || 30 hii]isti L || 31 scilicet [scilicet] L || 32 ultimum numerum L ||

Again, this same thing is explained otherwise, thus.[15] Let one number be discovered above which two consecutive tones or two consecutive sesquioctaves could be erected without fractions. That number can be discovered through this rule: however many consecutive sesquioctave ratios you intend to have without fractions, take that many consecutive octuple ratios starting from unity, and the last number of the octuples will be the number sought. Because, then, we intend to discover one number above which precisely two consecutive sesquioctaves could be erected without fractions, I shall discover two consecutive octuples from unity, thus. First, I discover one octuple number above unity, that is, 8. Then, above 8 I discover a second octuple number, that is, 64. This last number, 64, then, is the number sought, for above it precisely two sesquioctaves can be erected without fractions. If above 64 you add its eighth part, 8, you will have 72; and if to this you add its eighth part, 9, you will have 81, of which there is no whole eighth part. Let these three numbers, 64, 72, 81, be set in order; set in proportion to each other in a consecutive sesquioctave proportionality, they will be the numbers producing two consecutive sesquioctaves and consequently two consecutive tones. This having been done, let a diatessaron, or one sesquitertial ratio, be erected above 64. Inasmuch as this cannot be done without fractions—because 64 cannot be divided evenly by 3—, so that we might proceed without fractions, let us multiply by 3 each of those three numbers that were set in a series a little earlier. The products will be divisible by 3; will remain in the same ratio into which they had first been multiplied, the sesquioctave; and will produce two consecutive sesquioctaves, as earlier stated by this rule. If some numbers are multiplied by one and the same number, the products will preserve the same ratio that was found between the numbers that had been multiplied. So, then, multiply 64 by 3 and you will have 192. Then, multiply 72 by 3 and you will have 216. Then, multiply 81 by 3 and you will have 243. Let the three numbers thus produced be set in one series, 192, 216, 243. After this is done, let there be added above 192 its third part, 64, and you will have 256. Then, let these four numbers be set in order, 192, 216, 243, 256. In this order, it is apparent that the ratio of the first number, 192, to the last, 256, is the ratio of the diatessaron, which is composed of

[15]Prosdocimo now finds the ratio of the minor semitone through a third procedure that he explains step by step.

bus tonis et uno semitonio propter prehabita; et ista est proportio sexquitercia; et apparet etiam quomodo proportio primi numeri ad secundum est proportio toni, scilicet sexquioctava, et quomodo proportio secundi numeri ad
tercium est etiam proportio toni, quare sequitur quod proportio tercii numeri
5   ad quartum erit proportio semitonii, de quo pluries sermo, et cum hec sit proportio super13partiens 243as, sequitur quod semitonium de quo pluries sermo
consistit in proportione super13partiente 243as, quod fuit declarandum.

⟨4.⟩ Diptonus in proportione super17partiente 64as consistit; nam si due
sexquioctave, que sunt due proportiones duorum tonorum in uno diptono
10 contentorum, insimul agregentur per regulam datam proveniet proportio que
est inter 81 et 64, quorum differentia est 17; et ista est proportio diptoni
supradicta.
Item probatur hoc idem aliter sic: supra 64, qui est terminus secunde
octuple, intendantur due sexquioctave continue, quarum prima erit ad 72 et
15 secunda ad 81, et taliter ordinentur isti tres numeri, scilicet 64, 72, 81, et
patet quod numeri extremi, scilicet 64 et 81, continent diptonum et eius
proportionem iam dictam.
⟨5.⟩ Semidiptonus in proportione super5partiente 27as consistit; nam si
proportio toni a proportione dyateseron subtrahatur per regulam datam,
20 remanebit proportio que est inter 32 et 27, quorum differentia est 5; et ista
est proportio semidiptoni supradicta.
⟨6.⟩ Tritonus in proportione super217partiente 512as consistit; nam si tres
sexquioctave, que sunt proportiones trium tonorum in uno tritono contentorum, insimul agregentur per regulam datam taliter quod primo agregentur
25 due sexquioctave adinvicem, deinde huic agregato agregetur tercia sexquioctava, proveniet proportio que est inter 729 et 512, quorum differentia est
217; et ista est proportio tritoni supradicta.

---

1 prehabita]habita L ‖ 5 sermo factus est L ‖ 6 sermo habitus est L ‖ 16 et (*pr.*) *om.* L ‖ 25
tercia *in marg.* L ‖

two tones and one semitone on account of what has already been explained, and this is the sesquitertial ratio. It is also apparent that the ratio of the first number to the second is the ratio of the tone, the sesquioctave, and that the ratio of the second number to the third is also the ratio of the tone. Wherefore, it follows that the ratio of the third number to the fourth will be the ratio of the semitone, which has been spoken of several times. Since this is the ratio super13partient by 243rds, it follows that the semitone, which has been spoken of several times, consists in the ratio super13partient by 243rds, which was to be explained.

4. The ditone consists in the ratio super17partient by 64ths,[16] for if two sesquioctaves, which are the two ratios of the two tones contained in one ditone, are aggregated by the rule given, the ratio will result that is between 81 and 64, of which the difference is 17. This is the ratio of the aforesaid ditone.

Again, this same thing is proven otherwise, thus. Above 64, which is the term of the second octuple, let two consecutive sesquioctaves be erected, of which the first will be to 72 and the second to 81, and let these three numbers be set in order thus, 64, 72, 81. It is evident that the outer numbers, 64 and 81, contain the ditone and its ratio already stated.

5. The semiditone consists in the ratio super5partient by 27ths,[17] for if the ratio of the tone is subtracted from the ratio of the diatessaron by the rule given, the ratio will remain that is between 32 and 27, of which the difference is 5. This is the aforesaid ratio of the semiditone.

6. The tritone consists in the ratio super217partient by 512ths,[18] for if three sesquioctaves, which are the ratios of the three tones contained in one tritone, are aggregated by the rule given so that first the two sesquioctaves are aggregated and then with this aggregate is aggregated the third sesquioctave, the ratio will result that is between 729 and 512, of which the difference is 217. This is the aforesaid ratio of the tritone.

---

[16]I.e., 81:64. Prosdocimo finds the ratio of the ditone by combining two tones in the ratio 9:8, which is done by multiplying together the larger numbers of each and the smaller numbers of each, i.e., $(9 \times 9):(8 \times 8) = 81:64$.

[17]I.e., 32:27. Prosdocimo finds the ratio of the semiditone by subtracting the tone (9:8) from the diatessaron (4:3), which is done by multiplying together the smaller number of the one and the larger number of the other and vice versa, i.e., $(8 \times 4):(9 \times 3) = 32:27$.

[18]I.e., 729:512. Prosdocimo finds the ratio of the tritone by first combining two tones in the ratio 9:8, which is done by multiplying together the larger numbers of each and the smaller numbers of each, i.e., $(9 \times 9):(8 \times 8) = 81:64$; then, he combines the major third thus obtained with another tone, which is done by multiplying together the larger numbers and the smaller numbers of their ratios, i.e., $(81 \times 9):(64 \times 8) = 729:512$.

Item probatur hoc idem aliter sic: supra 512, qui est terminus tercie octuple, intendantur tres sexquioctave continue, quarum prima erit ad 576 et secunda ad 648 et tercia ad 729, et sic ordinentur isti quatuor numeri, scilicet 512, 576, 648, 729; et patet quod numeri extremi huius ordinis, scilicet 512 5 et 729, continent tritonum et eius proportionem iam dictam.

⟨7.⟩ Dyateseron cum semitonio in proportione super295partiente 729as consistit; nam si proportio semitonii supra habita cum proportione dyateseron adiungatur per regulam datam, proveniet proportio que est inter 1024 et 729, quorum differentia est 295; et ista est proportio dyateseron cum semi-
10 tonio supradicta.

⟨8.⟩ Dyapente cum tono in proportione super11partiente 16as consistit; nam si proportio dyapente cum proportione toni per regulam datam adiungatur, proveniet proportio que est inter 27 et 16, quorum differentia est 11; et ista est proportio dyapente cum tono supradicta.

15 ⟨9.⟩ Dyapente cum semitonio in proportione super47partiente 81as consistit; nam si proportio dyateseron et proportio semidiptoni, que simul iuncta faciunt dyapente cum semitonio, insimul iungantur, producent proportionem que est inter 128 et 81, quorum differentia est 47; et ista est proportio dyapente cum semitonio supradicta.

20 ⟨10.⟩ Dyapente cum diptono in proportione super115partiente 128as consistit; nam si proportio dyapente et proportio diptoni insimul iungantur, producent proportionem que est inter 243 et 128, quorum differentia est 115; et ista est proportio dyapente cum diptono supradicta.

1–2 tercia octupla B ‖

Again, this same thing is proven otherwise, thus.[19] Above 512, which is the term of the third octuple, let three consecutive sesquioctaves be erected, of which the first will be to 576, the second to 648, and the third to 729. Let these four numbers be set in order thus: 512, 576, 648, 729. It is evident that the extreme numbers of this order, 512 and 729, contain the tritone and its ratio already stated.

7. The diatessaron with semitone consists in the ratio super295partient by 729ths,[20] for if the ratio of the semitone made known above is joined with the ratio of the diatessaron by the rule given, the ratio will result that is between 1024 and 729, of which the difference is 295. This is the aforesaid ratio of the diatessaron with semitone.

8. The diapente with tone consists in the ratio super11partient by 16ths,[21] for if the ratio of the diapente is joined to the ratio of the tone by the rule given, the ratio will result that is between 27 and 16, of which the difference is 11. This is the aforesaid ratio of the diapente with tone.

9. The diapente with semitone consists in the ratio super47partient by 81sts;[22] for if the ratio of the diatessaron and the ratio of the semiditone (which joined together make up the diapente with semitone) are joined together, they will produce the ratio that is between 128 and 81, of which the difference is 47. This is the aforesaid ratio of the diapente with semitone.

10. The diapente with ditone consists in the ratio super115partient by 128ths,[23] for if the ratio of the diapente and the ratio of the ditone are joined together, they will produce the ratio that is between 243 and 128, of which the difference is 115. This is the aforesaid ratio of the diapente with ditone.

[19]Prosdocimo now finds the same ratio by constructing three consecutive sesquioctave ratios.

[20]I.e., 1024:729. Prosdocimo finds the ratio of the diatessaron with semitone (our diminished fifth) by combining the diatessaron (4:3) and the semitone (256:243), which is done by multiplying together the larger numbers and the smaller numbers of their ratios, i.e., $(4 \times 256):(3 \times 243) = 1024:729$.

[21]I.e., 27:16. Prosdocimo finds the ratio of the diapente with tone (the major sixth) by combining the diapente (3:2) and the tone (9:8), which is done by multiplying together the larger numbers and the smaller numbers of their ratios, i.e., $(3 \times 9):(2 \times 8) = 27:16$.

[22]I.e., 128:81. Prosdocimo finds the ratio of the diapente with semitone (the minor sixth) by combining the diatessaron (4:3) and the semiditone (32:27), which is done by multiplying together the larger numbers and the smaller numbers of their ratios, i.e., $(4 \times 32):(3 \times 27) = 128:81$.

[23]I.e., 243:128. Prosdocimo finds the ratio of the diapente with ditone (the major seventh) by combining the diapente (3:2) and the ditone (81:64), which is done by multiplying together the larger numbers and the smaller numbers of their ratios, i.e., $(3 \times 81):(2 \times 64) = 243:128$.

Item probatur hoc idem aliter sic: supra 64, terminum secunde octuple, intendantur due sexquioctave continue ad 72 et ad 81; et quoniam supra 81 non potest in integris intendi dyapente, cum sit indivisibilis in duas medietates, augeantur isti tres numeri ad duplum, scilicet 64, 72, 81 et provenient
5   128, 144, 162, qui tres numeri poterunt per duo equalia dividi et in eadem proportione se habebunt in qua tres priores sic duplati per regulam supra habitam, modo supra ultimum terminum trium numerorum ex duplatione productorum, scilicet supra 162, addatur sua medietas, scilicet 81, et proveniet 243; et tunc sic ordinentur isti quatuor numeri, scilicet 128, 144, 162,
10   243; et patet quod numeri extremi continent diptonum cum dyapente sive dyapente cum diptono, quod idem est, et eius proportionem iam dictam.

⟨11.⟩ Dyapente cum semidiptono in proportione super7partiente 9[as] consistit; nam si due proportiones duarum dyateseron, scilicet due sexquitercie, que due dyateseron simul iuncte faciunt dyapente cum semidiptono,
15   insimul iungantur, producent proportionem que est inter 16 et 9, quorum differentia est 7; et ista est proportio dyapente cum semidiptono supradicta.

⟨12.⟩ Dyapente cum tritono in proportione dupla super139partiente 1024[as] consistit; nam si proportio tritoni et proportio dyapente insimul iungantur, producent proportionem que est inter 2187 et 1024, quorum diffe-
20   rentia est 1163; et ista est proportio dyapente cum tritono supradicta.

---

5 poterunt ... dividi et *om.*B ‖ 20 1163]116 B ‖

Again, this same thing is proven otherwise, thus.[24] Above 64, the term of the second octuple, let two consecutive sesquioctaves be erected, to 72 and to 81. Inasmuch as a diapente cannot be erected above 81 with whole numbers since it is indivisible into two halves, let these three numbers 64, 72, 81 be doubled, and the numbers 128, 144, 162 will result. These three numbers can be divided evenly by 2 and will stand in the same ratios to each other as the three earlier numbers thus doubled, by the rule made known above.[25] But above the last term of the three numbers produced by the doubling—that is, above 162—, let its half, 81, be added, and 243 will result. Then, let these four numbers be set in order thus, 128, 144, 162, 243. It is evident that the extreme numbers contain the ditone with diapente or the diapente with ditone (which is the same thing) and its aforesaid ratio.

11. The diapente with semiditone consists in the ratio super7partient by ninths,[26] for if the two ratios of two diatessarons, that is, the two sesquitertials (which two diatessarons joined together make up the diapente with semiditone) are joined together, they will produce the ratio that is between 16 and 9, of which the difference is 7. This is the aforesaid ratio of the diapente with semiditone.

12. The diapente with tritone consists in the ratio duple super139partient by 1024ths,[27] for if the ratio of the tritone and the ratio of the diapente are joined together, they will produce the ratio that is between 2187 and 1024, of which the difference is 1163. This is the aforesaid ratio of the diapente with tritone.

---

[24]Prosdocimo now finds the same ratio by constructing two consecutive sesquioctave ratios (representing two consecutive whole tones) followed by a sesquialter (representing the diapente).

[25]In *Musica speculativa* 2.3 (184–85)

[26]I.e., 16:9. Prosdocimo finds the ratio of the diapente with semiditone (the minor seventh) by combining two diatessarons in the ratio 4:3, which is done by multiplying together the larger numbers and the smaller numbers of their ratios, i.e., $(4 \times 4):(3 \times 3) = 16:9$.

[27]I.e., 2187:1024. Prosdocimo finds the ratio of the diapente with tritone (our augmented octave) by combining the tritone (729:512) and the diapente (3:2), which is done by multiplying together the larger numbers and the smaller numbers of their ratios, i.e., $(729 \times 3):(512 \times 2) = 2187:1024$. Because the ratio is *duple* superpartient, 1024 must then be subtracted from 2187 twice to yield the remainder. The ratio 2187:1024 belongs to the class of multiple superpartient ratios. Prosdocimo, *Brevis summula proportionum* 5: "Multiple superpartient ratio occurs when the greater quantity contains the lesser several times plus something beyond that is a non-aliquot part of the lesser quantity [Proportio autem multiplex superpartiens est quando maior quantitas continet minorem pluries et cum hoc aliquid ultra quod non est pars aliquota quantitatis minoris]" (*Brevis summula ... Parvus tractatulus* [ed. Herlinger], 55).

Item probatur aliter hoc idem sic, nam captis duobus minimis numeris in quibus consistit proportio tritoni, scilicet 512 et 729, si supra maiorem intendatur dyapente, producetur inter primum et tercium proportio dyapente cum tritono predicta; sed quoniam maior dictorum duorum numerorum, sci-
5 licet 729, dividi non potest per medium, propter quod haberi non potest in his numeris proportio dyapente cum tritono absque fractionibus; ne per fractiones, sed per integra, procedamus, duplentur ambo numeri, et remanebit eadem proportio in productis que erat in multiplicatis per regulam supra habitam; duplato ergo 512 producetur 1024 et duplato 729 producetur
10 1458, cui si addatur eius medietas, scilicet 729, producetur 2187, et tunc sic ordinentur isti tres numeri, scilicet 1024, 1458, 2187, et patet quod numeri extremi continent dyapente cum tritono et eius proportionem iam dictam.

⟨13.⟩ Bisdyateseron cum semitonio in proportione super1909partiente 2187as consistit; nam si due proportiones duarum dyateseron et proportio
15 semitonii insimul iungantur, producent proportionem que est inter 4096 et 2187, quorum differentia est 1909; et ista est proportio bisdyateseron cum semitonio supradicta.

⟨14.⟩ Nec mireris si ad declarationem proportionum quarundam sonorum combinationum plures adduxerim probationes et ad aliquas solum unam,
20 nam licet ille que unica demonstratione declarate sunt pluribus etiam demonstrationibus declarari possent, hoc tamen fieri non posset in minimis terminis illius proportionis, et ideo alias demonstrationes dimisi intelligentibus. Omnes enim proportiones supradictarum sonorum combinationum in suis minimis numeris declarate sunt, ne intellectus in his magis confundetur, licet
25 pluribus et pluribus demonstrationibus etiam declarari potuissent, sed non in earum minimis numeris; propter hoc ergo alie demonstrationes ingeniosis relinquantur, qui intellectis regulis supra habitis de se faciliter multas alias demonstrationes inveniri poterunt.

---

1 hoc idem aliter L ‖ 3 intendantur B | producetur ... dyapente *om.* B ‖

Again, this same thing is proven otherwise, thus. When the two least numbers have been taken in which the ratio of the tritone consists, 512 and 729, if above the greater a diapente is erected, the aforesaid ratio of the diapente with tritone will be produced between the first and the third. Inasmuch as the larger of the two said numbers, 729, cannot be divided by a mean—on account of which the ratio of the diapente with tritone cannot be had in these numbers without fractions—, so that we might proceed not through fractions but through whole numbers, let both numbers be doubled, and the same ratio will remain between the products that was between the numbers multiplied, by the rule made known above. When 512 is doubled, then, 1024 will be produced, and when 729 is doubled, 1458 will be produced. If to this its own half, 729, is added, 2187 will be produced. Then, let these three numbers be set in order thus, 1024, 1458, 2187. It is evident that the extreme numbers contain the diapente with tritone and its aforesaid ratio.

13. The double diatessaron with semitone consists in the ratio super1909partient by 2187ths,[28] for if the two ratios of the two diatessarons and the ratio of the semitone are joined together, they will produce the ratio that is between 4096 and 2187, of which the difference is 1909. This is the aforesaid ratio of the double diatessaron with semitone.

14. Do not wonder if I have introduced several proofs for the explanation of the ratios of certain intervals and for some only one, for although those that were explained with one demonstration could also have been explained with several demonstrations, this could not have been done with the ratios in their least terms. Thus, I excluded the other demonstrations for those who understand them. That is to say, all the ratios of the aforesaid intervals have been explained in their least numbers lest the understanding be the more confused in these matters, even though they also could have been explained with several demonstrations (though not in their least numbers). For this reason, then, let the other demonstrations be relinquished to the clever, who, when they have understood the rules made known above, will easily be able to discover many other demonstrations for themselves.

---

[28]I.e., 4096:2187. Prosdocimo finds the ratio of the double diatessaron with semitone (our diminished octave) by first combining two diatessarons in ratio 4:3, which is done by multiplying together the larger numbers and the smaller numbers of their ratios, i.e., $(4 \times 4):(3 \times 3) = 16:9$; and then combining this double diatessaron with the semitone (256:243), which is done by multiplying together the larger numbers and the smaller numbers of their ratios, i.e., $(16 \times 256):(9 \times 243) = 4096:2187$.

194

⟨15.⟩ Tonus, de quo prius sermo, nullo modo divisibilis est in partes equales, quoniam nec in duas medietates, nec in tres tercias, nec in quatuor quartas, nec in quinque quintas, nec in sex sextas, et sic ultra; nam nulla proportio superparticularis divisibilis est in partes equales, quare nec pro-
5 portio sexquioctava, et per consequens nec tonus, qui consistit in ipsa proportione sexquioctava, per supra habita. Et quod nulla proportio superparticularis divisibilis sit in partes equales multipliciter declaratur, et primo sic, nam si aliqua proportio superparticularis divisibilis sit in partes equales, cum non sit maior ratio de una quam de alia, sit ergo ista proportio taliter divisa
10 proportio sexquioctava circa quam magis insistimus, et arguitur sic, proportio sexquioctava divisa est in partes equales, ergo per medium vel per media continue proportionabilia duas vel plures proportiones similes producentia, cum proportio non dividatur nisi in proportiones, et si in partes equales, in proportiones equales, ex quinto Elementorum Euclidis propositionibus
15 decima et undecima. De illis que preponuntur coniunctionibus tunc ultra arguitur sic, Proportio sexquioctava divisa est in partes equales per medium vel per media continue proportionabilia, sed cum si inter quoscunque duos terminos certam proportionem producentes unum vel plura media continue proportionabilia reperiantur inter quoscunque duos alios similis proportionis
20 tot etiam media continue proportionabilia reperiri debent ex octava, octavi Elementorum Euclidis; sequitur quod si proportio sexquioctava divisa sit in partes equales, per medium vel per media continue proportionabilia, quod tunc inter quoslibet duos terminos inter quos similis proportio reperietur, tot media continue proportionabilia etiam reperientur. Hoc autem est falsissi-
25 mum, quoniam in omni specie proportionis superparticularis reperibiles sunt termini inter quos nullum medium reperitur, ut patet discurrendo per singulas species proportionis superparticularis, ut verbi gratia inter 3 et 2, inter 4 et 3, inter 5 et 4, inter 6 et 5, inter 7 et 6, inter 8 et 7, inter 9 et 8, et sic ultra, inter quos cadunt iste proportiones specie distincte, scilicet sexquialtera, sexqui-
30 tercia, sexquiquarta, sexquiquinta, sexquisexta, sexquiseptima, et sexquioc-

1 sermo factus est L ‖ 4 divisibilis]in discretis divisibilis L | nec nec L ‖ 5 tonus qui est de genere discretorum et L ‖ 7 divisibilis]in discretis divisibilis L ‖ 8 divisibilis]in discretis divisibilis L ‖ 10–11 circa quam … proportio sexquioctava]in discretis L ‖ 12 proportionabilia]proportionalia B ‖ 14 propositionibus]proportionibus B ‖ 15 ultra et B ‖ 16 divisa]in discretis divisa L ‖ 19 alios]aliquos B ‖ 21 divisa]in discretis divisa L ‖

15. The tone, of which mention was made earlier, is not divisible into equal parts in any way, inasmuch as it is not divisible into two halves, nor into three thirds, four fourths, five fifths, six sixths, and so forth; for no superparticular ratio is divisible into equal parts. Wherefore, neither is the sesquioctave ratio, nor, consequently, the tone, which consists in this sesquioctave ratio, on the basis of what has been explained above.[29] That no superparticular ratio is divisible into equal parts is explained in many different ways, and first in this way: if some superparticular ratio were divisible into equal parts, since the ratio of one would not be greater than that of another, let the ratio so divided be the sesquioctave ratio (on which we focus our attention more sharply), and it is argued, thus. The sesquioctave ratio has been divided into equal parts, therefore producing by a mean or by consecutive proportionable means two or more similar ratios (since a ratio is divided only into ratios, and if into equal parts, into equal ratios, on the basis of the tenth and eleventh propositions of the fifth book of Euclid's *Elements*).[30] From those compound propositions set out above, it is then argued further, thus. The sesquioctave ratio has been divided into equal parts by a mean or by consecutive proportionable means. If between any two terms producing a certain ratio, one or more consecutive proportionable means are found, the same number of consecutive proportionable means ought to be found between any two others of a similar ratio, on the basis of the eighth proposition of the eighth book of Euclid's *Elements*.[31] It follows that if the sesquioctave ratio has been divided into equal parts by a mean or by consecutive proportionable means, then, between any two terms between which a similar ratio will be found, the same number of consecutive proportionable means will be found. But this is utterly false, inasmuch as in every species of the superparticular ratio, one finds terms between which no mean is found, as is evident in running through the species of superparticular ratio one by one, for example, between 3 and 2, between 4 and 3, between 5 and 4, between 6 and 5, between 7 and 6, between 8 and 7, between 9 and 8, and so forth. Between these paired numbers fall these ratios of distinct species, to wit: the sesquialter, the sesquitertia, the sesquiquarta, the sesquiquinta,

---

[29]*Musica speculativa* 2.1 (176–77).

[30]Euclid *Elementa* 5.10, 11. The tenth proposition states that if the ratio of quantity a to quantity c is greater than the ratio of quantity b to quantity c, a is greater than b; the eleventh that ratios equal to the same ratio are equal to each other. See H. L. L. Busard, ed., *The Latin Translation of the Arabic Version of Euclid's "Elements" Commonly Ascribed to Gerard of Cremona*, Asfar: Publikaties van het Documentatiebureau Islam-Christendom van de Rijksuniversiteit te Leiden, vol. 2 (Leiden: Brill, 1984), coll. 125–26.

[31]*The Latin Translation of the Arabic Version of Euclid's "Elements,"* 189–210.

196

tava, que est proportio toni, ut supra habitum est; et tamen, ut patet, inter
nullos duos predictorum terminorum aliquam supradictarum proportionum
producentium est aliquod medium, cum sint immediati, et sic patet propositum, scilicet quod nulla proportio superparticularis divisibilis sit in partes
5 equales.

Et quoniam pluries supra facta est mentio de numeris adinvicem proportionabilibus, et adhuc in sequentibus fiet mentio, est sciendum quod quando
sic invenies, semper intelliges de proportionabilibus adinvicem proportiona-
tis proportionalitate geometrica et non arismetrica nec armonica.

10 Item et secundo probatur aliter quod nulla proportio superparticularis sit
divisibilis in partes equales; nam discurrendo per singulas species proportionis superparticularis nunquam reperietur medium nec media continue
proportionabilia inter duos terminos proportionem aliquam superparticularem producentes, modo ad hoc, ut aliqua proportio in partes equales divida-
15 tur, requiritur quod inter duos terminos suos medium vel media continue
proportionabilia reperiantur, ut vult Euclides quinto suorum Elementorum;
ergo sequitur quod nulla proportio superparticularis est divisibilis in partes
equales.

Item et tercio probatur aliter quod nulla proportio superparticularis
20 divisibilis sit in partes equales; nam cum hoc fieri non possit absque medio
vel mediis interpositis, si hoc medium vel media ponantur inter duos terminos proportionem aliquam superparticularem reddentes, proportiones medii
vel mediorum et extremorum nomine variebuntur, et per consequens etiam
re, cum in proportionibus ad variationem nominis sequatur etiam variatio
25 proportionis, ergo ille proportiones intermedie non erunt equales, quare
sequitur quod proportio extremorum, que est superparticularis, non dividetur
in partes equales, quare et cetera.

4 divisibilis in discretis L | sit]est L || 6 Et quoniam]Sed quia L || 8–9 proportionatis *om.* B ||
10 superparticularis in discretis L | sit]sic B || 14 proportio in discretis L || 17 superparticu-
laris in discretis L || 20 divisibilis]in discretis divisibilis L || 24 proportionibus superparti-
cularibus B || 25 proportiones ille L | non *sup. lin.* B ||

the sesquisexta, the sesquiseptima, and the sesquioctave. This last is the ratio of the tone, as has been explained above. Nonetheless, as is evident, there is no mean between any two of the aforesaid terms producing any of the ratios named above, since they are adjacent. Thus, the proposition is evident that no superparticular ratio is divisible into equal parts.

Inasmuch as mention has been made several times above of numbers proportionable to each other (and mention will yet be made in what follows), you must know that when you discover it thus stated, you must always understand that these proportionable numbers are taken in the geometric proportionality to each other and not in the arithmetic or the harmonic.[32]

Again, and secondly, it is proven otherwise that no superparticular ratio is divisible into equal parts, for in running through the individual species of the superparticular ratio, there will never be found a mean or consecutive proportionable means between two terms producing any superparticular ratio. As to this, for some ratio to be divided into equal parts, it is necessary that a mean or consecutive proportionable means be found between its two terms, as Euclid maintains in the fifth book of his *Elements*.[33] Therefore, it follows that no superparticular ratio is divisible into equal parts.

Again, and thirdly, it is proven otherwise that no superparticular ratio is divisible into equal parts. Since this could not be done without a mean or means interposed, if this mean or means were placed between two terms rendering some superparticular ratio, the ratios of the mean or of the means with the extremes would be different in name and consequently also in nature, since in ratios, a variation of ratio follows a variation of name. Therefore, those intermediate ratios will not be equal, wherefore it follows that the ratio of the outer terms, which is superparticular, will not be divided into equal parts; wherefore, et cetera.

---

[32]A proportionality a:b:c is geometric if the ratio of a and b equals the ratio of b and c, arithmetic if the difference of a and b equals the difference of b and c, harmonic if the ratio of a and c equals the ratio of the difference between a and b and the difference between b and c:

geometric $a{:}b = b{:}c$, e.g., 4:2:1
arithmetic $a - b = b - c$, e.g., 3:2:1
harmonic $a{:}c = (a - b){:}(b - c)$, e.g., 6:4:3.

See, for example, Boethius *De institutione musica* 2.12 (ed. Friedlein, 241–42; trans. Bower, 65–66).

[33]*The Latin Translation of the Arabic Version of Euclid's "Elements,"* 117–36.

198

Item et quarto arguitur aliter quod nulla proportio superparticularis sit divisibilis in partes equales; nam ubi sic esset divisibilis, cum proportio non dividatur nisi in proportiones, tunc proportio superparticularis esset divisibilis in proportiones equales que simul sumpte constituerent illam proportio-
5 nem superparticularem sic divisam, quod falsissimum est, quoniam capta una proportione superparticulari, quecunque sit illa, cum sit maior ratio de una quam de alia, ut sit gratia exempli una sexquioctava circa quam magis insistimus que per adversarium dividatur in partes equales per unicum medium interpositum, ut in his tribus numeris, 16, 17, 18, inter quorum
10 extremos cadit proportio sexquioctava, cum unico medio, ut patet, manifeste apparebit quod due proportiones ab illis tribus numeris producte non sunt adinvicem equales, eo quod nomine, et per consequens re, variantur, et pariformiter si in plures partes per plura media dividentur, ut in his quatuor numeris, 24, 25, 26, 27, quorum quatuor numerorum extremi sunt in sexqui-
15 octava proportione et similiter in multis aliis exemplis, quare et cetera.

Et sic patet his quatuor rationibus quomodo nulla proportio superparticularis, et per consequens nulla sexquioctava, est divisibilis in partes equales, quare nec tonus, qui in proportione sexquioctava consistit, quod erat declarandum.
20 Secundo vero principaliter probatur quod tonus nullo modo sit divisibilis in partes equales sic; nam ubi sic divisibilis esset, etiam sua proportio, scilicet sexquioctava, sic divisibilis esset, et quoniam talis divisio fieri non potest absque medio vel mediis, et inter 9 et 8, qui sunt primi et minimi termini proportionis sexquioctave, nullum reperitur medium, quare in ipsis fieri non
25 potest talis divisio, multiplicentur dicti numeri, scilicet 9 et 8, per unum et eundem numerum, et producetur in productis eadem proportio que est inter 9 et 8 per regulam supra habitam. Multiplicentur ergo primo 9 et 8 per 2 et producentur 18 et 16, inter quos cadit unicum medium, scilicet 17; sed 17 non est medium continue proportionale inter 18 et 16, quod tamen requirere-
30 tur si proportio extremorum per ipsum dividi deberet per equalia, ut patet; ergo illud medium non dividit proportionem extremorum, que est sexquioctava, in partes equales. Item multiplicentur 9 et 8 per 3 et producentur 27 et 24, inter quos sunt duo media, scilicet 25 et 26, sed non inter se et cum extremis continue proportionabilia, ut notum est; ergo non dividunt propor-

---

1 superparticularis in discretis L ‖ 3 superparticularis in discretis L ‖ 6 cum non sit BL ‖ 7 ut]et B ‖ 11–12 quod … variantur]quod si due proportiones ab illis tribus numeris producte simul iungantur per regulam supra habitam, producent proportionem a sexquioctava distinctam B ‖ 13 divideretur L ‖ 17 sexquioctava in discretis L ‖ 21 esset cum tonus sit de genere discretorum L ‖ 22 sexquioctava in discretis L ‖ 26 producentur B ‖ 33 sed]si B | [et cum] et B ‖

Again, and fourthly, it is argued otherwise that no superparticular ratio is divisible into equal parts. Were it so divisible, since a ratio is divided only into ratios, then the superparticular ratio would be divisible into equal ratios that, taken together, would constitute that superparticular ratio thus divided. This is utterly false, inasmuch as when a superparticular ratio is taken, whatever it be, the ratio of one part is greater than that of the other. For example, let there be a sesquioctave (on which we focus our attention more sharply), and, to play devil's advocate,[34] let it be divided into equal parts through a single interposed mean, as in these three numbers, 16, 17, 18, between the extreme terms of which falls the sesquioctave ratio with a single mean, as is evident. It will appear clearly that the two ratios produced by those three numbers are not equal to each other because they differ in name and consequently in nature. Likewise, if it were divided into a greater number of parts by a greater number of means, as in these four numbers, 24, 25, 26, 27, the extremes of these four numbers are in the sesquioctave ratio; and similarly in many other examples; wherefore, et cetera.

So it is evident, for these four reasons, that no superparticular ratio, and consequently no sesquioctave, is divisible into equal parts. Wherefore, neither is the tone, which consists in the sesquioctave ratio, which was to be explained.

But second, principally, it is proven in this way that the tone is in no way divisible into equal parts. If it were divisible in this way, its ratio, the sesquioctave, would also be divisible in this way. Inasmuch as no such a division can be made without a mean or means, between 9 and 8, which are the primary and least terms of the sesquioctave ratio, no mean is found; wherefore, the division cannot be made in these terms. Let the said numbers, 9 and 8, be multiplied by one and the same number, and the same ratio will be produced in the products as lies between 9 and 8, by the rule made known above.[35] Let 9 and 8, then, first be multiplied by 2, and 18 and 16 will be produced, between which there falls a single mean, 17. But 17 is not a consecutive proportional mean between 18 and 16, which, nonetheless, would be required if the ratio of the extremes ought to be divided equally by it, as is evident. Therefore, that mean does not divide the ratio of the extremes (which is the sesquioctave) into equal parts. Again, let 9 and 8 be multiplied by 3, and 27 and 24 will be produced, between which there are two means, 25 and 26; but they are not consecutive proportionables with each other or with the extremes, as is known. Therefore, they do not divide the ratio of the

---

[34]*Adversarius*, "the devil." J. F. Niermeyer, ed., *Mediae latinitatis lexicon minus* (Leiden: Brill, 1997), 24.

[35]*Musica speculativa* 2.3 (184–85).

tionem extremorum in partes equales. Item multiplicentur 9 et 8 per 4 et producentur 36 et 32, inter quos sunt tria media, scilicet 33, 34, et 35, sed non continue proportionabilia, ut de se notum est; ergo non dividunt proportionem extremorum in partes equales. Item multiplicentur 9 et 8 per 5 et
5 producentur 45 et 40, inter quos sunt quatuor media, scilicet 41, 42, 43, et 44, sed non continue proportionabilia, ut clare patet; ergo non dividunt proportionem extremorum in partes equales; et sic ultra in infinitum procedendo. Ergo nullo modo dicendum est proportionem sexquioctavam fore divisibilem in partes equales, et per consequens nec tonum, cuius proportio
10 est ipsa sexquioctava, ut habitum est supra, quod erat principaliter declarandum, ex quo sequitur quod si tonus in duas dividatur partes, ille neccessario erunt inequales, et quia universaliter tonus apud musicos in duas dividitur partes, neccessario ille erunt inequales, propter quod dixerunt antiqui, et bene, maiorem harum duarum partium semitonium maius appelari et mino-
15 rem minus semitonium nuncupari, non tamen a semi quod est medium, cum hoc inveniri sit impossibile, ut est demonstratum, sed a semi quod est imperfectum, semum, vel incompletum, ut supra habitum est. Et scias quod differentia que inter maius et minus semitonium reperitur apud musicos coma nominatur.

20   ⟨16.⟩ Semitonium de quo supra in de sonorum combinationibus pluries sermo habitus est semitonium minus existit, nam si dupletur huiusmodi semitonium, sive ad se ipsum addatur, quod idem est, id est eius proportio, non perficit tonum sive eius proportionem; ergo est minor pars vera medietate toni, sive semitonium minus. Si enim perficeret tonum sive eius propor-
25 tionem vera toni medietas existeret, quam inveniri est impossibile per prius habita. Et si tonum transcenderet plus toni vera medietate et semitonium maius existeret. Et quod ex duplatione semitonii supradicti, sive eius proportionis, producatur proportio minor sexquioctava, que est proportio toni, sic declaratur; nam per regulam supra habitam addantur insimul duo huius-
30 modi semitonia, sive eorum proportiones, et producetur proportio que est

extremes into equal parts. Again, let 9 and 8 be multiplied by 4, and 36 and 32 will be produced, between which there are three means, 33, 34, and 35; but they are not consecutive proportionables, as is self evident. Therefore, they do not divide the ratio of the extremes into equal parts. Again, let 9 and 8 be multiplied by 5, and 45 and 40 will be produced, between which there are four means, 41, 42, 43, and 44; but they are not consecutive proportionables, as is clearly evident. Therefore, they do not divide the ratio of the extremes into equal parts. And so on, proceeding to infinity. Therefore, in no way is it to be said that the sesquioctave ratio is divisible into equal parts, and consequently neither the tone, the ratio of which is the sesquioctave, as has been explained above, which was principally to be explained. From this, it follows that if the tone is divided into two parts, they will necessarily be unequal; and because universally among musicians the tone is divided into two parts, they will necessarily be unequal. For this reason, the ancients said, and properly, that the greater of these two parts was called the major semitone and the lesser was called the minor semitone, not from that *semi* which is a mean, since it would be impossible to discover this, as has been demonstrated, but from that *semi* which is imperfect, deficient, or incomplete, as has been explained above.[36] And know that the difference that is found between the major semitone and the minor is named the comma among musicians.

16. The semitone of which mention has been made several times in the discussion of intervals is the minor semitone. If this semitone—that is, its ratio—were doubled or added to itself (which is the same thing), it does not make up a complete tone or its ratio; therefore, it is the part smaller than the true half of the tone—or the minor semitone. To be sure, if it did make up a complete tone or its ratio, it would be the true half of the tone, which it is impossible to discover, on the basis of what has been explained earlier;[37] and if it did exceed the tone, it would be more than the true half of the tone—and it would be the major semitone. And that from the doubling of the aforesaid semitone or its ratio, a ratio would be produced that is smaller than the sesquioctave (which is the ratio of the tone) is explained thus. By the rule made known above,[38] let two such semitones or their ratios be added

---

[36]*Musica speculativa* 1.8. Among the "ancients," see for instance Boethius *De institutione musica* 1.16 (ed. Friedlein, 203; trans. Bower, 26).

[37]*Musica speculativa* 2.15 (194–201).

[38]*Musica speculativa* 2.3 (182–83).

inter 65536 et 59049, quorum differentia est 6487; et ista est proportio super6487partiens 59049ᵃˢ, que est minor una sexquioctava, quare et cetera.

Et quod talis proportio duorum semitoniorum insimul iunctorum sit minor una sexquioctava sic declaratur, et primo notetur hec regula: si sint
5 due proportiones specie distincte, et velis scire que ipsarum sit maior, capias ipsas in suis minimis terminis et multiplica maiorem unius per minorem alterius, ut facis in subtractione unius proportionis ab alia, et illa duarum proportionum ex cuius maioris termini multiplicatione cum minore alterius producitur maior numerus dicitur maior proportio. Verbi gratia, captis
10 minimis terminis unius sexquialtere et unius sexquitercie, qui sunt 3 2 et 4 3, ex quo multiplicando 3, qui est maior duorum minorum terminorum unius sexquialtere, per 3, qui est minor duorum terminorum minorum unius sex-quitercie producitur 9, maior numerus quam sit numerus productus ex mul-tiplicatione 4, qui est maior terminus duorum minimorum terminorum unius
15 sexquitercie, per 2, qui est minor terminus duorum minorum terminorum unius sexquialtere, scilicet 8, hinc est quod dicimus sexquialteram propor-tionem maiorem esse sexquitercia. Et quoniam multotiens proposita aliqua proportione in terminis dubium est an illi termini sint minimi illius propor-tionis, ut hoc cognosci possit, notanda est hec regula: si proponatur tibi aliqua
20 proportio in terminis et scire velis an illi sint termini minimi illius propor-tionis dividas maiorem illorum duorum terminorum per minorem, et si ali-quid restat post divisionem per illud dividas divisorem, et si adhuc aliquid restat ex tali divisione per illud dividas secundum divisorem, et sic ultra de tercio et quarto et aliis divisoribus, si provenerint, quousque tibi remaneat
25 aut unitas ante nichil aut nichil ante unitatem. Si unitas ante nichil, dicen-dum est illos terminos fuisse minimos illius proportionis et si nichil ante unitatem dicendum est illos terminos non fuisse minimos illius proportionis. Queras ergo suos minimos terminos verbi gratia de proportione que est inter 9 et 5, volo videre si tales sint minimi termini huius proportionis, et divido
30 primo 9 per 5 et restat 4; deinde divido 5, qui fuit divisor, per 4, residuum, et restat unitas antequam nichil, quare dico supradictam proportionem fuisse in suis minimis terminis. Item de proportione que est inter 15 et 9 volo scire si hii sunt eius minimi termini, et divido primo 15 per 9 et restat 6; deinde divido 9, divisorem, per 6, residuum, et restat 3; deinde divido 6, secundum

5 scire velis L ‖ 12 minorum terminorum L ‖ 14–15 unius sexquitercie … minorum termi-norum *om.* (*saut du même au même*) B ‖ 20 minimi termini L ‖ 21 maiorum L ‖ 31 ante-quam *corr. in marg.* L ‖

together, and the ratio will be produced that is between 65536 and 59049, the difference of which is 6487.[39] This is the ratio super6487partient by 59049ths, which is less than one sesquioctave; wherefore, et cetera.

And that this ratio of two semitones joined together is less than one ses-quioctave is explained thus. First note this rule: if there should be two ratios of distinct species and you should wish to know which of them is greater, take them in their least terms; multiply the greater term of one by the lesser term of the other, as you do in the subtraction of one ratio from another; and that one of the two ratios from which the greater number is produced by multiplication of its greater term by the lesser term of the other is said to be the greater ratio. For instance, when a sesquialter and a sesquitertial are taken in their least terms, which are 3, 2 and 4, 3, we say that the sesquialter ratio is larger than the sesquitertial because by multiplying 3, which is the greater of the two least terms of a single sesquialter, by 3, which is the lesser of the two least terms of a single sesquitertial, 9 is produced, a greater num-ber than the number produced by the multiplication of 4, which is the greater of the two least terms of a single sesquitertial, by 2, which is the lesser of the two least terms of a single sesquialter, namely 8. Inasmuch as when some ratio is given in terms, there is often doubt whether these are the least terms of the ratio, note this rule so that this can be recognized. If some ratio is given to you in terms and you should wish to know whether these are the least terms of the ratio, divide the greater of the two terms by the lesser, and if anything is left over after that division, divide the divisor by that, and if then anything is left over from that division, divide the second divisor by that, and so forth for the third and fourth and other divisors, if they appear, until the remainder is either 1 before it is 0 or 0 before it is 1. If the remain-der is 1 before it is 0, it is said that those terms are the least terms of the ratio; if the remainder is 0 before it is 1, it is said that those terms are not the least terms of the ratio.[40] Seek then, for example, the least terms of the ratio 9:5. I wish to see if these are the least terms of this ratio, and first I divide 9 by 5, and 4 is left over; then I divide 5, which was the divisor, by 4, the remainder, and 1 is left over before 0. Wherefore, I say that the aforesaid ratio was in its least terms. Again, I wish to know of the ratio 15:9 if these are its least terms, and first I divide 15 by 9 and 6 is left over; then I divide 9, the divisor, by 6, the remainder, and 3 is left over; then I divide 6, the

[39]Prosdocimo finds the ratio of this interval by combining two semitones in the ratio 256:243, which is done by multiplying together the larger numbers and the smaller numbers of their ratios, i.e., $(256 \times 256):(243 \times 243) = 65536:59049$.

[40]That is, follow the procedure described until the remainder is either 1 or 0. If it is 1, the ratio was in least terms; if 0, it was not.

divisorem, per 3, secundum residuum, et restat nichil priusquam unitas, quare dico supradictam proportionem non fuisse in suis minimis terminis.

Sed minimi termini per hanc regulam inveniuntur; nam facta ultima divisione ex qua tibi nichil remansit, capias divisorem huius ultime divi-
5 sionis et per ipsum dividas quemlibet terminorum producentium proportionem quam invenisti non esse in suis minimis terminis, et quotientia erunt minimi termini illius proportionis, verbi gratia quia visum est proportionem que est inter 15 et 9 non esse in suis minimis terminis, et factis divisionibus 3, ⟨qui⟩ fuit divisor ultime divisionis, per ipsum 3 dividam 15 et quotiens erit
10 5; postea per ipsum 3 dividam 9 et quotiens erit 3; et tunc dicam quod 5 et 3 sunt minimi termini proportionis que erat inter 15 et 9.

Istis regulis sic positis sumatur proportio duorum supradictorum semitoniorum insimul iunctorum in suis minimis terminis, qui sunt 65536 et 59049; sumaturque etiam proportio toni in suis minimis terminis, qui sunt 9
15 et 8, et multiplicetur maior terminus unius proportionis per minorem alterius, ut dictum est, et reperietur quod productum ex multiplicatione maioris termini proportionis toni, scilicet sexquioctave, per minorem terminum proportionis duorum supradictorum semitoniorum insimul iunctorum est maius quam productum ex multiplicatione maioris termini proportionis duorum
20 supradictorum semitoniorum simul iunctorum per minorem terminum proportionis toni, scilicet sexquioctave, quare concluditur ex regula prehabita quod proportio toni, scilicet sexquioctava, maior est quam proportio duorum semitoniorum supradictorum insimul iunctorum, et per consequens proportio duorum supradictorum semitoniorum insimul iunctorum est minor una
25 sexquioctava, quod erat declarandum.

⟨17.⟩ Semitonium maius, quod cum minori tonum constituit, in proportione super139partiente 2048[as] consistit, nam si a proportione toni proportio semitonii minoris subtrahatur remanebit proportio que est inter 2187 et 2048, quarum differentia est 139, et ista est proportio semitonii maioris
30 supradicta.

1 restat 3 deinde divido 3, divisorem tercium, per 3, residuum tercium, et restat L ‖ 4 nichil tibi *in marg. fort. m. sec.* L ‖ 7 visum]usum *fort.* L ‖ ‖ 9 *scripsi* ‖ 20 simul]insimul L ‖ 21 scilicet *sup. lin.* B ‖ 22 scilicet *om.* B ‖ 23 supradictorum semitoniorum L ‖

second divisor, by 3, the second remainder, and 0 is left over before 1. Wherefore, I say that the aforesaid ratio was not in its least terms.

The least terms, now, are discovered by this rule. When the last division has been made, from which 0 was left over, take the divisor of this last division, divide by it each of the numbers producing the ratio that you discovered not to be in its least terms, and the quotients will be the least terms of the ratio. For instance, because it has been seen that the ratio 15:9 is not in its least terms, when divisions have been made by 3, which was the divisor of the last division, I shall divide 15 by that 3 and the quotient will be 5; then, I shall divide 9 by that 3 and the quotient will be 3; and then, I shall say that 5 and 3 are the least terms of the ratio 15:9.

These rules having been given, let the ratio of the two aforesaid semitones joined together be taken in its least terms, which are 65536 and 59049, and let the ratio of the tone also be taken in its least terms, which are 9 and 8. Let the greater term of one ratio be multiplied by the lesser of the other (as has been said), and it will be found that the product of the multiplication of the greater term of the ratio of the tone (of the sesquioctave) by the lesser term of the ratio of the two aforesaid semitones joined together is greater than the product of the multiplication of the greater term of the ratio of the two aforesaid semitones joined together by the lesser term of the ratio of the tone (that is, of the sesquioctave).[41] Wherefore, we conclude from the rule that has been explained that the ratio of the tone, the sesquioctave, is greater than the ratio of the two aforesaid semitones joined together, and consequently that the ratio of the two aforesaid semitones joined together is less than one sesquioctave, which was to be explained.

17. The major semitone, which with the minor semitone constitutes a tone, consists in the ratio super139partient by 2048ths.[42] If the ratio of the minor semitone is subtracted from the ratio of the tone, the ratio will remain that is between 2187 and 2048, of which the difference is 139. This is the ratio of the aforesaid major semitone.

---

[41]That is, 9 × 59049 (= 531331) is greater than 65536 × 8 (= 524288).

[42]I.e., 2187:2048. Prosdocimo finds the ratio of the major semitone by subtracting the minor semitone (256:243) from the tone (9:8), which is done by multiplying together the smaller number of the one and the larger number of the other and vice versa, i.e., (9 × 243):(8 × 256) = 2187:2048.

Item probatur hoc idem aliter sic: a proportione tritoni subtrahatur dyatesaron et remanebit proportio dicta, cum enim tritonus consistat ex tribus tonis et dyateseron ex duobus cum uno semitonio minori, ut constat ex precedentibus, superabit tritonus dyateseron per unum semitonium maius.

5 ⟨18.⟩ Coma in proportione super7153partiente 524288as consistit, nam si a proportione semitonii maioris proportio semitonii minoris subtrahatur restabit proportio que est inter 531441 et 524288, quorum differentia est 7153; et ista est proportio comatis predicta.

⟨19.⟩ Omnia semitonia maiora inter se sunt equalia, nam ex quo omnia
10 semitonia minora inter se sunt equalia, et per simile omnes toni, ut supra declaratum est, et tonus non differt a semitonio minori nisi per semitonium maius, ut patet ex supradictis, neccessario erunt omnia semitonia maiora inter se equalia.

Item probatur hoc idem aliter sic: nam ubi non equarentur, sequeretur
15 quod non omnes sonorum combinationes eiusdem ultimate denominationis essent adinvicem equales, ut patet, quod est contra superius demonstratum.

⟨20.⟩ Omnia comata inter se sunt equalia; nam ex quo omnia minora semitonia inter se sunt equalia, et per simile omnia maiora semitonia, et maius non differt a minori nisi per unum coma, ut habitum est, neccessario
20 erunt omnia comata inter se equalia.

Item probatur aliter hoc idem sic: nam ubi non equarentur, sequeretur quod non omnes sonorum combinationes eiusdem denominationis ultimate essent adinvicem equales, ut patet, quod est contra unum supra demonstratum.

---

21 hoc idem aliter L ‖

Again, this same thing is proven otherwise, thus.[43] Let the ratio of the diatessaron be subtracted from the ratio of the tritone, and the said ratio will remain. Since the tritone consists of three tones and the diatessaron of two with one minor semitone (as is established from the preceding),[44] the tritone will exceed the diatessaron by one major semitone.

18. The comma consists in the ratio super7153partient by 524288ths.[45] If the ratio of the minor semitone is subtracted from the ratio of the major semitone, the ratio will be left over that is between 531441 and 524288, of which the difference is 7153. This is the ratio of the aforesaid comma.

19. All major semitones are equal to each other. Because all minor semitones are equal to each other, and likewise all tones, as has been explained above,[46] and the tone differs from the minor semitone only by the major semitone, as is evident from what has been said above,[47] all major semitones will necessarily be equal to each other.

Again, this same thing is proven in another way, thus. If they were not equal, it would follow that not all intervals of the same specific denomination would be equal to each other, as is evident, which is contrary to what has been demonstrated above.[48]

20. All commas are equal to each other. Because all minor semitones are equal to each other, and likewise all major semitones, and the major semitone differs from the minor only by one comma, as has been explained,[49] all commas will necessarily be equal to each other.

Again, this same thing is proven in another way, thus. If they were not equal, it would follow that not all intervals of the same specific denomination would be equal to each other, as is evident, which is contrary to one thing demonstrated above.[50]

---

[43]Here Prosdocimo finds the same ratio by subtracting the perfect fourth (4:3) from the tritone (729:512), which is done by multiplying together the smaller number of the one and the larger number of the other and vice versa, i.e., $(729 \times 3):(512 \times 4) = 2187:2048$.

[44]*Musica speculativa* 1.7, 8 (164–67).

[45]I.e., 531441:524288. Prosdocimo finds the ratio of the comma by subtracting the minor semitone (256:243) from the major semitone (2187:2048), which is done by multiplying together the smaller number of the one and the larger number of the other and vice versa, i.e., $(2187 \times 243):(2048 \times 256) = 531441:524288$.

[46]*Musica speculativa* 2.1 (178–79).

[47]*Musica speculativa* 2.17 (204–5).

[48]*Musica speculativa* 2.1 (178–79).

[49]*Musica speculativa* 2.18 (206–7).

[50]*Musica speculativa* 2.1 (178–79).

⟨21.⟩ Duo semitonia minora cum uno comate tonum comprehendunt; nam ex quo semitonium minus cum semitonio maiori tonum constituit et semitonium minus exceditur a maiori per unum coma, sequitur quod ista tria, scilicet duo minora semitonia et unum coma, quod additum ad semito-
5 nium minus semitonium maius constituit, tonum facit completum, quod erat ostendendum.

⟨22.⟩ Omnis sonorum combinatio minor a semetipsa maiori solum per unum semitonium maius exceditur, octava excepta et qualibet sibi equiva-lenti, uti duplex octava, triplex octava, et sic ultra, que maior minorem
10 excedit per duo semitonia maiora, sed maior mediam et media minorem solum per unum semitonium maius excedit; nam quelibet sonorum combi-natio maior, octava excepta et qualibet sibi simili vel equivalenti, differt a se ipsa minori solum in numero tonorum, ut si maior duos continet tonos, minor unum solum continet et loco alterius ponitur unum semitonium
15 minus; et si maior tres continet tonos minor solum duos continet et loco alterius minus ponitur semitonium; et sic ultra; quare manifeste apparet quod minor combinatio, octava et qualibet sibi equivalenti excepta, minuit a se ipsa maiori solum semitonium maius, cum tonus in duo solum semitonia, maius scilicet et minus, dividatur, et non in plura, ut habitum est supra; et
20 per simile etiam octava maior et quelibet sibi equivalens differt a se ipsa media, et media a se ipsa minori, solum in numero tonorum, sic quod loco unius toni ponitur unum semitonium minus, ut in aliis sonorum combinatio-nibus, quare etiam sequitur quod octava media et quelibet sibi equivalens minuit a se ipsa maiori, et minor a se ipsa media, solum semitonium maius;
25 et finaliter sequitur quod octava minor et quelibet sibi equivalens minuit a se ipsa maiori duo semitonia maiora, quare patet propositum. Et ex his sequitur quod habita aliqua combinatione minori que non sit octava nec sibi equiva-lens, si reduci debeat ad maioritatem, hoc fieri habet per additionem semito-nii maioris ad ipsam, et si habita aliqua combinatione maiori que non sit
30 octava nec sibi equivalens, si reduci debeat ad minoritatem, hoc fieri habet per subtractionem semitonii maioris ab ipsa; et si habita octava maiori vel sibi equivalenti quam reducere velles ad mediam, vel habita media quam

9 uti est L ‖ 12 simili vel *om.* L ‖ 18 maiori]minori B ‖ 24 minor]*fort.* minori B ‖ 26 maiori in B ‖

21. Two minor semitones with one comma encompass a tone. Because the minor semitone constitutes the tone with the major semitone and the minor semitone is exceeded by the major by one comma, it follows that these three intervals, two minor semitones and one comma (which, added to the minor semitone, constitutes a major semitone) complete the tone, which was to be shown.

22. Every minor interval is exceeded by the corresponding major interval by one major semitone only,[51] except for the octave and anything equivalent to it (such as the double octave, the triple octave, and so forth), among which the major interval exceeds the minor by two major semitones, whereas the major interval exceeds the medial and the medial the minor by one major semitone only. Any major interval, except for the octave and anything similar or equivalent to it, differs from the corresponding minor interval only in the number of tones: so, if the major interval contains two tones, the minor contains only one, and a minor semitone is set in place of the other; if the major interval contains three tones the minor contains only two, and a minor semitone is set in place of the other; and so forth. Wherefore, it manifestly appears that a minor interval, except for the octave and anything equivalent to it, deducts from the corresponding major interval nothing but a major semitone, since the tone is divided into two semitones only, a major one and a minor one, and not into more, as has been explained above.[52] Similarly, the major octave and anything equivalent to it differs from the corresponding medial interval, and the medial from the corresponding minor interval, only in the number of tones: so, one minor semitone is set in place of one tone, as in the other intervals. Wherefore, it also follows that the medial octave and anything equivalent to it deducts from the corresponding major interval, and the minor interval from the corresponding medial interval, only a major semitone. Finally, it follows that the minor octave and anything equivalent to it deducts from the corresponding major interval two major semitones. Wherefore, what has been proposed is evident. From these considerations, it follows that given some minor interval that is neither an octave nor equivalent to it, if it is supposed to be changed to the major inflection, this must be done through the addition to it of a major semitone; given some major interval that is neither an octave nor equivalent to it, if it is supposed to be changed to the minor inflection, this must done through the subtraction from it of a major semitone; given a major octave or its equivalent that you should wish to change to the medial,

---

[51]Cf. *Contrapunctus* 3.8 (ed. Herlinger, 54–55).

[52]*Musica speculativa* 2.17 (204–5).

reducere velles ad minorem, hoc per simile fieri habet per subtractionem
semitonii maioris ab ipsa; et si habita octava minori vel sibi equivalenti
quam reducere velles ad mediam, vel habita media quam reducere velles ad
maioritatem, hoc per simile fieri habet per additionem semitonii maioris ad
5   ipsam; et si habita octava maiori vel sibi equivalenti quam reducere velles
ad minoritatem, hoc fieri habet per subtractionem duorum semitoniorum
maiorum ab ipsa, et si habita octava minori vel sibi equivalenti quam reducere velles ad maioritatem, hoc fieri habet per additionem duorum semitoniorum maiorum ad ipsam, ex quo cum precedentibus sequitur quod semitonio
10 minori solum utimur in cantando quando scilicet fit ascensus a mi ad fa vel e
contra descensus a fa ad mi, et semitonio maiori solum utimur in addendo
vel diminuendo in variatione combinationum, scilicet quando facimus de
maiori combinatione minorem vel de minori maiorem, vel de maiori mediam,
vel de media minorem, vel de minori mediam, vel de media maiorem.

15   Et ex hoc manifeste apparet veritas antiquorum a modernis cantoribus
non intellecta, qui antiqui in coloratione consonantiarum per veram vel
fictam musicam solum duo posuerunt signa, scilicet duo B distincta, unum
scilicet cum corpore quadro, ut hic, ♮, et aliud cum corpore rotundo, ut hic,
b, volentes quod ubicunque reperiebatur corpus ♮ quadri, sive hoc esset in
20 linea sive in spatio, proferre deberemus hanc vocem mi, et ubicunque
reperiebatur corpus b rotundi, sive hoc esset in linea sive in spatio, proferre
deberemus hanc vocem fa, que omnia cum ratione posuerunt quam hic narrare propter brevitatem dimitto, et etiam quia hec pertinent ad praticam et
declarata sunt partim in quodam tractatu de cantu plano et partim in quodam
25 tractatu de contrapuncto per me compilatis, ita quod illuc recurre si horum
rationes desideras. Ista ergo duo signa supraposita sufficiunt ad reducendum combinationem maiorem ad minorem vel minorem ad maiorem, vel
maiorem ad mediam, vel mediam ad minorem, vel minorem ad mediam, vel
mediam ad maiorem, secundum quod oportet. Et ut hoc melius intelligas

---

2–5 et si habita octava minori ... per additionem semitonii maioris ad ipsam *om.* L ‖ 12
combinationum]sonorum combinationum L ‖ 14 vel de media maiorem, vel de media minorem, vel de minori mediam L ‖ 28–29 vel mediam ad maiorem, vel mediam ad minorem,
vel minorem ad mediam L ‖

or given a medial that you should wish to change to the minor, this, likewise, must be done through the subtraction from it of a major semitone; given a minor octave or its equivalent that you should wish to change to the medial, or given a medial that you should wish to change to the major inflection, this likewise must be done through the addition to it of a major semitone; given a major octave or its equivalent that you should wish to change to the minor inflection, this must be done through the subtraction from it of two major semitones; and given a minor octave or its equivalent that you should wish to change to the major inflection, this must be done through the addition to it of two major semitones. From this, along with the preceding, it follows that we use the minor semitone in singing only when an ascent is made from *mi* to *fa* or, vice versa, a descent from *fa* to *mi*, and we use the major semitone only in augmenting or diminishing in the variation of intervals—that is, when we make a minor interval of a major one, a major interval of a minor one, a medial interval of a major one, a minor interval of a medial one, a medial interval of a minor one, or a major interval of a medial one.

From this, the truth of the ancients, not understood by modern singers, manifestly appears; these ancients, in the coloration of consonances through *musica vera* or *musica ficta*, placed only two signs, that is, two distinct Bs, one with a square body, like this, ♮, and the other with a round body, like this, b, maintaining that wherever the body of the square ♮ was found, whether on a line or in a space, we ought to deliver the syllable *mi*, and wherever the body of the round b was found, whether on a line or in a space, we ought to deliver the syllable *fa*—all of which they posited with a reasoning that I exclude recounting here for the sake of brevity and also because these matters pertain to practice and have been explained partly in a certain treatise on plainchant and partly in a certain treatise on counterpoint compiled by myself; hasten to them should you desire reasons for these matters.[53] These two signs set down above, then, suffice to change a major interval to a minor one, a minor interval to a major one, a major interval to a medial one, a medial interval to a minor one, a minor interval to a medial one, or a medial interval to a major one, as appropriate. So that you might

---

[53]Prosdocimo, *Plana musica* 1.3 (40–43); *Contrapunctus* 5.3 (ed. Herlinger, 74–77). It is a commonplace in medieval theory that round b indicates *fa* and square ♮ *mi*. Cf. Anonymous II, *Tractatus de discantu*, ed. Albert Seay, Critical Texts with Translation, vol. 1 (Colorado Springs: Colorado College Music Press, 1978), 32, corresponding to CS, 1:312; Marchetto, *Lucidarium* 8.1.8–10 (ed. Herlinger, 274–75), where the rule is attributed to one Richardus Normandus; Philippe de Vitry, *Ars contrapunctus* (CS, 3:26); and Ugolino, *Declaratio* 2.34.29–30 (ed. Seay, 2:46).

dabo tibi duo exempla que tibi sufficient, et primum exemplum sit hoc: sit
enim tenor descendens a mi E gravis ad re D gravis et cantus superior sit
ascendens a fa C acuti ad sol D acuti, et manifestum est quod a mi E gravis
ad fa C acuti est una sexta minor que in hoc loco maior esse deberet, ut
5 videri habet in materia de contrapuncto. Antiqui ergo in volendo reducere
hanc sextam minorem ad sui maioritatem ponebant ante dictum fa unum ♮
quadrum, cuius corpus erat in linea ipsius fa, volentes quod in loco de fa
proferre ficte deberemus mi, ut paulo ante dictum est, et bene, quoniam per
talem mutationem nominis et vocis perducitur talis sexta minor ad suam
10 maioritatem, quod sic declaratur, nam ascendendo a fa ad sol in cantu
superiori ascendimus tonum, sed si loco de fa fingamus mi, ut nobis osten-
ditur per signum antepositum, tunc ordinate ascendendo loco de sol
fingemus fa voce non mutata, et sic ascendemus semitonium minus, cum a
mi ad fa semper sit semitonium minus, ut habitum est supra, quare elevabi-
15 mus vocem supra verum fa per unum semitonium maius quod est a vero fa
ad fictum mi, quoniam si a vero fa ad sol sit tonus et a ficto mi ad fictum fa
sit semitonium minus, neccessario a vero fa ad fictum mi erit semitonium
maius, et sic addetur illud semitonium maius ad illam sextam minorem,
quare per hanc additionem maior efficietur, ut esse debet cum maior mino-
20 rem non excedat nisi per semitonium maius, ut habitum est supra. Moderni
tamen factum non intelligentes, sed ad libitum et absque ratione agentes,
loco ♮ quadri ponunt talem crucem ✳, et aliqui moderniores tale signum, ♭,
etiam ad libitum et absque ratione operantes, et horum plurimi et maxime
ytalici, falsam doctrinam Marcheti paduani insequentes.

---

21 factum]hoc L | agentes]operantes L ‖

better understand this, I shall give you two examples that will suffice, and the first example is this. Let there be a tenor descending from the *mi* of low E to the *re* of low D and let there be an upper voice ascending from the *fa* of high C to the *sol* of high D. It is manifest that from the *mi* of low E to the *fa* of high C there is a minor sixth, which in this case ought to be major, as must be seen in the material on counterpoint.[54] The ancients, then, in wishing to change this minor sixth to its major inflection, set down a square ♮ before the said *fa*, the body of which was on the line of that *fa*, wishing that in place of *fa* we ought to deliver *mi* through *musica ficta* (as has been said just before)—and properly, inasmuch as through this mutation of name and pitch, this minor sixth is changed to major, which is explained thus. In ascending from *fa* to *sol* in the upper voice, we ascend a tone, but if in place of *fa* we feign *mi*, as is shown to us by the sign placed before, then, ascending in order, in place of *sol*, we shall feign *fa* with the pitch unmutated, and thus we shall ascend a minor semitone, since from *mi* to *fa* is always a minor semitone, as has been explained above. Wherefore, we shall raise the pitch above the true *fa* by one major semitone, which is from the true *fa* to the feigned *mi* (inasmuch as if from the true *fa* to *sol* is a tone and from the feigned *mi* to the feigned *fa* is a minor semitone, there will necessarily be a major semitone from the true *fa* to the feigned *mi*), and thus that major semitone will be added to that minor sixth. Wherefore, it will be made major through this addition—as it ought to be, since the major interval exceeds the minor by a major semitone only, as has been explained above. The moderns, however, not understanding this fact, but acting arbitrarily and without reason, set down in place of square ♮ a cross like this, ✖, and some of the more modern ones a sign like this, ♭, also proceeding arbitrarily and without reason—the greater part of these, and especially the Italians, following the false teaching of the Paduan Marchetus.[55]

---

[54]The sixth must be made major so that it lies as close as possible to the octave to which it progresses. See Prosdocimo, *Contrapunctus* 5.6 (ed. Herlinger, 78–95).

[55]Marchetto, *Lucidarium* 8.1.4–20 (ed. Herlinger, 272–81), esp. 8.1.17, where Marchetto criticizes those who do not distinguish what Prosdocimo calls the cross from the conventional square ♮. Marchetto describes the form of the square ♮ in *Lucidarium* 8.1.14–18 and the "cross" (not his terminology; see p. 217, n. 60 *infra*) in *Pomerium* 17 (ed. Vecchi, 71–74). Guido frater, active probably not too long after Marchetto, distinguishes between the two signs in *Ars musice mensurate* 6 (F. Alberto Gallo, ed., *Mensurabilis musicae tractatuli*, Antiquae musicae italicae scriptores, vol. 1 [Bologna: Università degli Studi di Bologna, Istituto di Studi Musicali e Teatrali - Sez. Musicologia, 1966], 28); on the dating of this treatise, see Herlinger, Introduction to *Lucidarium*, 6–7, n. 7. In the Lucca revision of *Contrapunctus* 5.6 as well (ed. Herlinger, 86–93), Prosdocimo criticizes the "moderns" for introducing the new sign.

Et alii nominant hec duo signa hoc nomine, dyesis, ignorantes quid apud musicos hoc nomen dyesis importet, nam dyesis apud musicos est medietas semitonii minoris, teste Boetio primo sue Musice in fine capituli de additione cordarum et earum nominibus, et teste etiam Johane de Muris nor-
5   mando conclusione quinta secunde partis sue Theorice musice. Dicit tamen Boetius libro secundo sue Musice capitulo de semitoniis in quibus minimis numeris constent, ad principium capituli, quod antiqui qui fuerunt multum ante ipsum quodlibet semitonium dyesim sive lima appelarunt. Dicitque ulterius maior pars horum modernorum, et maxime ytalicorum, ex falsa
10   doctrina sui Marcheti paduani, quod pro tanto ista signa vocantur hoc nomine dyesis, quoniam per illa signa in ascensu fit additio unius dyesis, que dyesis apud suum Marchetum et suos sequaces, est quinta pars toni, et in descensu fit subtractio ipsius dyesis, et hoc pro mutatione alicuius combinationis de sui maioritate ad sui minoritatem vel de sui minoritate ad sui
15   maioritatem, que omnia falsa sunt, eo quod tonus nullo modo divisibilis est in quinque quintas, sive in quinque partes equales, ut supra demonstratum est; et ubi adhuc per possibile tonus foret divisibilis in quinque partes equales, per talem tamen additionem vel subtractionem talis quinte partis, que apud ipsos modernos dyesis appelatur, ad aliquam combinationem vel ab aliqua com-
20   binatione non reduceretur talis combinatio de maioritate ad minoritatem vel e contra, cum sibi non adderetur vel ab ipsa subtraheretur debitum, scilicet unum semitonium maius quod apud ipsos modernos ex tribus vel quatuor de istis suis dyesibus copulatur. Aliqui etiam alii moderni duo supradicta signa

1 alii]multi etiam alii L || 5 sue Musice speculative sive theorice L || 8 sive]et etiam L || 14 sui *sup. lin.* B || 21 contra et cetera L ||

Others, too, name these two signs with the name diesis,[56] ignorant of what the name diesis means among musicians. Among musicians, the diesis is half the minor semitone, by witness of Boethius in the first book of his *Musica*, at the end of the chapter on the addition of strings and their names, and by witness also of the Norman Johannes de Muris in the fifth conclusion of the second part of his *Theorica musice*.[57] Nevertheless, Boethius says in the second book of his *Musica*, in the chapter on the least numbers of which the semitones consist, at the beginning of the chapter, that the ancients who lived long before him called any semitone diesis or limma.[58] The greater part of these moderns, and especially the Italians, state further (on the basis of the false teaching of their Paduan Marchetus) that these signs are called by the name diesis inasmuch as through these signs is made the addition of one diesis in ascent (a diesis that for their Marchetus and his followers is a fifth of the tone) and the subtraction of that diesis in descent and that this is done for the sake of the mutation of some interval from its major to its minor inflection or from its minor to its major inflection. All of these statements are false because the tone is in no way divisible into five fifths, or into five equal parts, as has been demonstrated above.[59] Even if it were granted as possible that the tone were divisible into five equal parts, an interval would not be changed from its minor inflection to its major inflection, or vice versa, by the addition or subtraction of this fifth part, which those moderns call a diesis, since the requisite quantity—one major semitone, which according to those moderns is a coupling of three or four of those dieses of theirs—would not have been added to it or subtracted from it. Some other

---

[56]Cf. *Contrapunctus* 5.6 (ed. Herlinger, 86–89).

[57]Boethius *De institutione musica* 1.21 (ed. Friedlein , 213; trans., Bower, 40); see also *De institutione musica* 4.6 (ed. Friedlein, 318–22, trans., Bower, 131–34). The former chapter's title is "Concerning the Genera of Song [De generibus cantilenae]"; it is the preceding chapter that is titled "Concerning the Addition of Strings and Their Names [De additionibus chordarum earumque nominibus]," at least in Friedlein's edition and Bower's translation. Cf. Muris, *Musica* ⟨*speculativa*⟩ 2.5.30 (ed. Fast, 286).

[58]Boethius *De institutione musica* 2.28 (ed. Friedlein, 260; trans., Bower, 82). Here Boethius treats *diesis*, *limma*, and *semitonium* as synonyms; in *De institutione musica* 3.8, he indicates that the diesis is the difference by which the sesquitertial ratio (that of the perfect fourth) exceeds two tones; so, it is the one Prosdocimo (and most medieval theorists) would have called the minor semitone. Both senses of *diesis* (as the minor semitone and as half the minor semitone) retained currency during the Middle Ages and the Renaissance. See Prosdocimo, *Monacordum* 4.1 (*Brevis summula ... Parvus tractatulus* [ed. Herlinger], 87, n. 29).

[59]*Musica speculativa* 2.15 (194–201).

falsam sive fictam musicam nominant, et minus male primis, quoniam ubi primi in totum male, hii secundi non in totum bene nec in totum male, eo quod talia signa non semper denotant fictionem aliquam musice, sed quandoque sic et quandoque non, ut clare patere potest cuilibet bene conside-
5 ranti.

Secundum exemplum sit hoc: ascendat enim tenor ab ut secundi G gravis ad re A acuti et cantus superior descendat a mi B acuti ad re A acuti, et manifestum est quod ut et mi predicta faciunt unam terciam maiorem, que in hoc loco minor esse deberet, ut ex contrapuncto videri habet; unde anti-
10 qui, et etiam moderni, in volendo reducere hanc maioritatem ad minoritatem quandoque apponunt ante predictum mi unum B rotundum, cuius corpus in spatio de mi collocatur, volentes innuere quod per tale b rotundum mutetur nomen de mi in fa per regulam contrapuncti supra habitam, ut postea in A acuto dicatur mi, ex cuius nominis mutatione mutatur postea talis tercia
15 maior in minorem, sic quod fit ab ipsa tercia maiori per illud b rotundum subtractio unius semitonii maioris, prout oportet, nam si a re A acuti ad mi B acuti sit tonus et a mi A acuti ad fa B acuti sit semitonium minus, neccessario a fa B acuti ad mi eiusdem B acuti erit semitonium maius, quod subtrahitur ab illa tercia maiori ut minor efficiatur.

20 Discrepant tamen antiqui a modernis circa b rotundum in hoc, quoniam antiqui volunt quod illud quod addit vel diminuit b rotundum sit unum semitonium maius, quod verum est et superius declaratum; sed moderni, et

---

12 talem B ‖ 16 mi]fa B ‖ 17 A *in marg.* L | minus]maius B ‖

moderns also name the aforesaid signs *musica falsa* or *ficta*,[60] and this less improperly than the first moderns, inasmuch as where the first moderns proceed totally improperly, these second moderns proceed neither totally properly nor totally improperly because these signs do not always denote *musica ficta* but sometimes do and sometimes do not, as can be clearly evident to whoever considers it properly.[61]

Let this be the second example. Let a tenor ascend from the *ut* of the second low G to the *re* of high A and let an upper voice descend from the *mi* of high B to the *re* of high A. It is manifest that the aforesaid *ut* and *mi* make a major third, which in this case ought to be minor, as is to be seen from the *Contrapunctus*.[62] For this reason, the ancients—and also the moderns—, wishing to change the major inflection to the minor, sometimes place before the aforesaid *mi* a round b, the body of which is placed in the space of the *mi*, wishing to signal that through this round b, the name should be mutated from *mi* to *fa* by the rule of counterpoint made known above so that afterwards *mi* might be sung on high A. Through this mutation of name, this major third is mutated to minor. So, a subtraction of one major semitone from the major third is made through that round b, as is appropriate, for if from the *re* of high A to the *mi* of high B there is a tone and from the *mi* of high A to the *fa* of high B there is a minor semitone, from the *fa* of high B to the *mi* of the same high B there will necessarily be a major semitone, which is subtracted from that major third so that it is made minor.

Nevertheless, as concerns round b, the ancients disagree with the moderns about this: inasmuch as the ancients wish that what round b adds or subtracts should be one major semitone, which is true and has been

---

[60]Marchetto reported that the sign that divides the tone into a chromatic semitone and a diesis, or divides the enharmonic semitone in half, is commonly called *falsa musica*. See *Lucidarium* 8.1 (ed. Herlinger, 270–81); *Pomerium* 2.4, 13.1 (ed. Vecchi, 40, 68). Cf. *Musica speculativa* 3.12 (240–41).

[61]In *Contrapunctus* 5.1 (ed. Herlinger, 70–71), Prosdocimo defines *musica ficta* as "the feigning of syllables or the placement of syllables in a location where they do not seem to be—to apply mi where there is no mi and fa where there is no fa, and so forth" [vocum fictio sive vocum positio in loco ubi esse non videntur, sicut ponere mi ubi non est mi, et fa ubi non est fa, et sic ultra]"; in the Lucca revision, Prosdocimo replaced the phrase "in a location where they do not seem to be" with the more strongly worded "in any location on the musical hand where they are in no way to be found [in aliquo loco manus musicalis ubi nullo modo reperiuntur]." Accordingly, the square ♮ does not indicate *musica ficta* when placed before an E, a B, or an A, and the round b does not indicate *musica ficta* when placed before an F, a C, or the Bs in the upper two registers.

62Again, Prosdocimo, *Contrapunctus* 5.6 (ed. Herlinger, 78–95). The third must be made minor so that it lies as close as possible to the unison to which it progresses.

maxime Marchetum supradictum insequentes, volunt quod illud quod addit vel diminuit b rotundum sit una de suis dyesibus, sive una de quinque partibus equalibus toni, quod falsissimum est, cum talis quinta pars non sit dabilis, ut supra demonstratum est; item quia data tali quinta parte per possibile, adhuc non perficeretur intentum per additionem vel subtractionem ipsius quinte partis ad aliquam combinationem vel ab aliqua combinatione, ut supra declaratum est. Dimittamus ergo istos modernos cum suo Marcheto, qui talia impossibilia et in musica erronea seminaverunt, et adheremus antiquis nostris, qui veram musice scientiam habuerunt, et sic ipsam veram musice scientiam acquirere poterimus.

---

8 seminarunt L ||

explained above, the moderns, especially those following the aforesaid Marchetus, wish that what round b adds or subtracts should be one of those dieses of theirs, or one of the five equal parts of the tone. This is most egregiously false, since this fifth part of the tone is unobtainable, as has been demonstrated above.[63] Again, even granted this fifth part were possible, the addition or subtraction of this fifth part to or from some interval would not fulfill their claim, as has been explained above. Let us exclude these moderns, then, along with their Marchetus, who disseminated such impossible and erroneous things in music. We stick with our ancients, who knew the true science of music, and so we shall be able to acquire that true science of music.

---

[63]*Musica speculativa* 2.15 (194–201).

220

⟨3⟩

⟨1.⟩ Restat nunc narrare ea falsa et erronea que Marchetus paduanus supradictus in suo Lucidario collegit.

⟨2.⟩ Dicit enim primo supradictus Marchetus in suo Lucidario, tractatu
5 primo et capitulo primo, auctoritate Macrobii in De sompnio Scipionis, quod Pitagoras ytalicus fuit primus inventor musice, quod falsum est, quoniam musica inventa fuit ante diluvium per Iubalchaim, qui fuit de stirpe Chaim filii Adde, et Pitagoras ytalicus fuit post diluvium per magnum tempus; nec etiam verum est quod Macrobius loco preallegato hoc asserat, sed ibi scribit
10 quomodo Pitagoras ytalicus pervenit in noticiam proportionum combinationum sonorum, sic quod Pitagoras ytalicus non fuit primus inventor musice, licet bene fuerit primus inventor proportionum combinationum sonorum, ut dictum est. Ymo antequam Pitagoras ytalicus ⟨hanc⟩ invenisset musicam, habebat praticam, non tamen speculativam, et hoc etiam asserit
15 ipsemet Marchetus in fine predicti capituli, auctoritate Tulii in Questionibus tusculanis.

⟨3.⟩ Item capitulo cuius rubrica talis est, De genere generalissimo et specie specialissima in musica, dicit in fine capituli quod ista tria nomina, scilicet enarmonicum, dyatonicum, et cromaticum, sunt nomina trium semitoni-

---

5 Macobrii *ante corr.* L ‖ 9 Macobrius *ante corr.* L ‖ 12 bene *sup. lin.* B ‖ 13 hanc]hoc BL ‖ 17 talis rubrica L ‖

3

1. It is now left to relate the false and erroneous things that the aforesaid Paduan Marchetus collected in his *Lucidarium*.

2. First, the aforesaid Marchetus says, in his *Lucidarium*, in the first treatise and the first chapter, on the authority of Macrobius in *De somnio Scipionis*,[1] that the Italian Pythagoras was the first discoverer of music. This is false, inasmuch as music was discovered before the flood by Jubal-Cain, who was of the branch of Cain the son of Adam, and the Italian Pythagoras lived a long time after the flood.[2] Nor is it even true that Macrobius asserted this in the passage adduced; rather, he wrote there how the Italian Pythagoras came to the knowledge of the ratios of intervals. So, the Italian Pythagoras was not the first discoverer of music, although he was properly the first discoverer of the ratios of intervals, as has been said. On the contrary, before the Italian Pythagoras had discovered this music, he grasped its practice but not its theory,[3] and Marchetus himself even asserts this at the end of the aforesaid chapter, on the authority of Cicero in the *Questiones tusculane*.[4]

3. Again, in the chapter of which the rubric is *De genere generalissimo et specie specialissima in musica*,[5] he says at the end of the chapter that these three names, enharmonic, diatonic, and chromatic, are the names of

---

[1]*Commentarii in Somnium Scipionis* 2.1.8–14 (ed. Willis, 96–97; trans. Stahl, 186–88); Marchetto, *Lucidarium* 1.1.1–8 (ed. Herlinger, 72–75); actually, when Marchetto wrote that Pythagoras discovered music (*adinvenit musicam*), he may well have taken the noun as meaning "music theory."

[2]Isidore *Etymologiae* 3.15.1 (*The* Etymologies *of Isidore of Seville*, trans. Stephen A. Barney, W. J. Lewis, J. A. Beach, and Oliver Berghof, with the collaboration of Muriel Hall [Cambridge: Cambridge University Press, 2006], 95), reporting the conflicting biblical (Gen. 4:21) and Greek accounts of the discovery of music, placed Jubal (whom he called Tubal) "before the flood." Jacques de Liège, *Speculum musicae* 1.6 (ed. Bragard, 1:25–26) anticipated Prosdocimo in stating that Pythagoras had not discovered the consonances but had found their ratios. On the Jubal-Pythagoras controversy, see James McKinnon, "Jubal vel Pythagoras, Quis Sit Inventor Musicae?" *Musical Quarterly* 64 (1978): 1–28; reprinted in his *The Temple, the Church Fathers, and Early Western Chant*, Variorum Collected Studies (Aldershot: Ashgate, 1998).

[3]I.e., the theory of interval ratios.

[4]Marchetto, *Lucidarium* 1.1.9 (ed. Herlinger, 74–77): "Doubtless Pythagoras did make use of [string instruments] and melody [Verum ipse fidibus et cantu usus est]." Cf. Cicero *Tusculanae Disputationes* 4.2 (*Cicero in Twenty-Eight Volumes*, vol. 18, *Tusculan Disputations*, ed. and trans. J. E. King, Loeb Classical Library [Cambridge: Harvard University Press, 1966], 328–31).

[5]"On the Broadest Genus and the Irreducible Species in Music"; Marchetto, *Lucidarium* 1.16.5 (ed. Herlinger, 104–7).

orum specie distinctorum, quod falsum est, quoniam ista tria nomina non
sunt nomina semitoniorum sed sunt nomina trium diversorum tetracordorum, teste Boetio, libro primo sui Musice, capitulo cuius rubrica talis est,
De generibus cantilene, et etiam teste Johane de Muris normando, conclu-
5 sione quinta secunde partis sue Musice speculative; et ista fuit una de principalioribus falsitatibus quas dictus Marchetus per totam Ytaliam seminavit.
Et est in presenti hec falsitas apud cantores in tanto valore, quod qui eam
habet solempnissimus inter cantores reputatur. Et ut melius que dicta sunt de
tribus nominibus habitis intelligantur, sciendum est quod antiqui ymagina-
10 bantur dyateseron in quatuor cordis tripliciter variari posse, nam capiebant
quatuor cordas, quarum prima ad ultimam semper dyateseron sonabat, et
primo hanc dyateseron in his quatuor cordis taliter ordinabant quod prima
corda ad secundam semitonium minus sonabat, et secunda ad terciam
tonum, et per simile tercia ad quartam, et talis modus dividendi dyateseron
15 apud ipsos dyatonicus vocabatur, sic quod talis dyateseron, sive tale tetracordum, dicebatur dyatonicum, quasi sub modo dyatonico divisum. Et idem
fuisset si illud minus semitonium ita positum fuisset in medio cordarum vel
in fine sicut positum est in principio. Tetracordum enim dicitur a tetra, quod
est quatuor, et corda; unde tetracordum quasi instrumentum quatuor cor-
20 darum. Secundo vero dictam dyateseron in quatuor cordis taliter ordinabant, ut prima corda ad secundam semitonium minus sonaret, et per simile
secunda ad terciam, sed tercia ad quartam tonum cum semitonio maiori
resonabat; et talis modus apud ipsos cromaticus nominabatur, sic quod tale
tetracordum dicebatur cromaticum, quasi sub modo cromatico divisum. Et
25 idem fuisset si ille tonus cum semitonio maiori ita positus fuisset in principio vel in medio sicut positus est in fine. Tercio autem dictam dyateseron in
quatuor cordis taliter ordinabant, ut prima corda ad secundam dyesim sonaret, que dyesis est medietas semitonii minoris, et per simile secunda ad terciam, sed tercia ad quartam diptonum sonabat; et talis modus apud ipsos
30 enarmonicus appelabatur, sic quod tale tetracordum enarmonicum dicebatur,
quasi sub modo enarmonico divisum. Et idem fuisset si diptonus ita positus
fuisset in principio vel in medio sicut positus est in fine. De istis tamen

---

4 normando]Ioannes de Muris normandus *in marg. man. sec.* B ‖ 5–6 principalioribus falsitatibus *in ras.* B ‖

three semitones distinct in species. This is false, inasmuch as these three names are not names of semitones but names of the three different tetrachords, by witness of Boethius, in the first book of his *Musica*, in the chapter of which the rubric is *De generibus cantilene*;[6] and also by witness of the Norman Johannes de Muris, in the fifth conclusion of the second part of his *Musica speculativa*.[7] This was one of the more principal falsehoods that the said Marchetus disseminated throughout Italy. Indeed, at the present time, this falsehood has so much dignity among singers that one who holds it is considered the most orthodox[8] among singers. So that what has been said concerning the three names that have been explained might be better understood, one must know that the ancients imagined the diatessaron in four strings as able to be varied in three ways. They took the four strings, of which the first always sounded the diatessaron with the last, and first they set them in order in such a way that the first string sounded a minor semitone to the second, the second a tone to the third, and likewise the third a tone to the fourth. This manner of dividing the diatessaron was called the diatonic by them; so, such a diatessaron, or such a tetrachord, was called diatonic—divided in the diatonic manner, as it were. It would have been the same if that minor semitone had been placed in the middle of the strings or at the end as it was when placed at the beginning. Tetrachord, in fact, is derived from *tetra*, which is four, and *chorda*; whence the tetrachord is, as it were, an instrument of four strings. Second, they set in order the said diatessaron in four strings in such a way that the first string sounded a minor semitone to the second, and likewise the second a minor semitone to the third, but the third to the fourth sounded a tone with major semitone. This manner was named the chromatic by them; so, such a tetrachord was called chromatic—divided in the chromatic manner, as it were. It would have been the same if that tone with major semitone had been placed at the beginning or in the middle as it was when placed at the end. Third, they set in order the said diatessaron in four strings in such a way that the first string sounded a diesis to the second—which diesis is half the minor semitone[9]—and likewise the second a diesis to the third, but the third to the fourth sounded a ditone. This manner was called the enharmonic by them; so, such a tetrachord was called enharmonic—divided in the enharmonic manner, as it were. It would have been the same if the ditone had been placed at the beginning or in the middle

---

[6]"Concerning the Genera of Song"; Boethius *De institutione musica* 1.21 (ed. Friedlein, 212–13; trans. Bower, 39–41).

[7]Johannes de Muris, *Musica (speculativa)* 2.5.31–32 (ed. Fast, 286–91).

[8]On the translation of *solempnissimus*, see p. 159, n. 4 *supra*.

[9]Cf. *Musica speculativa* 2.22 (214–15 and n. 57).

modis dividendi tetracordum duo ultimi, scilicet cromaticus et enarmonicus,
tanquam extranei dimissi sunt, primo retento, scilicet modo dyatonico. Patet
ergo ex his que dicta sunt quomodo illa tria nomina non sunt nomina trium
semitoniorum sed trium tetracordorum, quare sequitur Marchetum nostrum
5 supradictum auctores huius artis in tali passu non intellexisse, ymo nunquam
visum est musicos dividisse tonum nisi in duo semitonia, nec unquam
appellasse hec duo semitonia aliquo trium nominum supradictorum, sed bene
maius et minus, vel lima vel dyesis apud valde antiquos.

⟨4.⟩ Item capitulo cuius rubrica talis est, In quibus numeris constituatur
10 tonus, dicit se velle demonstrare quare tonus consistat in proportione numeri
novenarii ad octenarium, quod ne dum demonstrari sed nec persuadi potest, et
ubi adhuc hoc demonstrari vel persuadi posset errat hoc velle facere in quantum musicus, cum hoc sit in musica principium, ut supra habitum est. Modo
artifex sua principia probare non debet, sed presupponere, ut vult Aristotiles
15 Posteriorum primo.

⟨5.⟩ Dicitque ulterius eodem capitulo quod ad demonstrandum quare tonus
consistat in proportione numeri novenarii ad octenarium tria facere intendit,
et primo intendit ostendere quare tonus consistat in numero novenario et non
in maiori nec in minori, quod impossibile est ostendere, cum tonus consistat
20 in proportione et non in numero, licet bene in numeris adinvicem relatis.

⟨6.⟩ Dicitque ulterius quod secundo intendit ostendere quomodo tonus se
habeat ad octenarium numerum, quod etiam fieri est impossibile, quoniam ex
quo tonus consistit in proportione vellet ostendere quomodo se haberet una

---

1 et enarmonicus *om.* L || 3 tetracordorum specie distinctorum L || 6 musicos veros L || 19 in
minori, quod *om.* L || 21 ostendere intendit L ||

as it was when placed at the end. Nevertheless, of these manners of dividing the tetrachord, the last two, the chromatic and the enharmonic, were excluded as extraneous, with the first, the diatonic manner, retained. From what has been said, it is evident, then, that those three names are not the names of three semitones but of the three tetrachords. Wherefore, it follows that our aforesaid Marchetus did not understand the authorities of this art in a passage like this. On the contrary, it has never come to light that musicians had divided the tone in any other way than into two semitones or that they had ever called these two semitones by any of the three aforesaid names; rather, they called them (and properly) the major semitone and the minor— or, among the very ancient, either limma or diesis.[10]

4. Again, in the chapter of which the rubric is *In quibus numeris constituatur tonus*,[11] he says that he wishes to demonstrate why the tone consists in the ratio of the novenary number to the octonary, which can neither be demonstrated nor convincingly argued. Still, were this capable of being demonstrated or convincingly argued, it would be an error to wish to do this—insofar as one is a music theorist—since this is a principle in music, as has been explained above.[12] The practicioner ought not to prove its principles but presuppose them, as Aristotle maintains in the first book of the *Analytica Posteriora*.[13]

5. He says further in the same chapter that to demonstrate why the tone consists in the ratio of the novenary number to the octonary, he intends to do three things. First, he intends to show why the tone consists in the novenary number and not in a larger or a smaller one.[14] This is impossible to show, since the tone consists in a ratio and not in a number (although properly in numbers related to each other).[15]

6. He says further that, second, he intends to show how the tone is related to the octonary number.[16] This is also impossible to do, inasmuch as—because the tone consists in a ratio—he wishes to show how one ratio is

---

[10]Cf. *Musica speculativa* 2.22 (214–15 and n. 57).

[11]"The Numbers in Which the Whole Tone is Constituted"; Marchetto, *Lucidarium* 2.4.2–4 (ed. Herlinger, 110–13).

[12]*Musica speculativa* 2.1 (176–77).

[13]Aristotle *Analytica posteriora* 1.10 (76a31–36).

[14]Marchetto, *Lucidarium* 2.4.5 (ed. Herlinger, 112–13).

[15]In *De institutione musica* 2.3 (ed. Friedlein, 229; trans. Bower, 53–54), Boethius distinguished between two sorts of numbers, those "discrete in themselves" (3, 4, etc.) and those "discrete in relation to something" (duple, triple, etc.). Prosdocimo is saying that Marchetto confuses the two sorts of numbers.

[16]Marchetto, *Lucidarium* 2.4.6 (ed. Herlinger, 112–13).

proportio ad unum numerum, que nullo modo sunt adinvicem comparabilia, cum sint diversorum generum propinquorum.

⟨7.⟩ Dicitque adhuc ulterius quod tercio intendit concludere quod natura toni consistit in proportione numeri novenarii ad octenarium et non in pro-
5 portionibus aliorum numerorum, sic quod duo videtur asserere, primum quod natura toni consistit in proportione numeri novenarii ad octenarium, quod verum est; secundum quod natura toni non consistit in aliis numeris quam in istis duobus, et hoc falsum est, quoniam natura toni consistit in omnibus duobus numeris inter quos cadit proportio sexquioctava, et isti sunt
10 infiniti, ut bene consideranti manifestum est, nisi vellet intelligere quod natura toni non consistit in proportionibus aliorum numerorum, id est in proportionibus numerorum sexquioctavam proportionem non producentium, et tunc verum diceret.

⟨8.⟩ Et ut bene intelligatur modus quo intendit suum primum probare
15 intentum, sciendum est quod divisionum alicuius continui quedam est redu-cibilis et quedam non reducibilis; et illa vocatur reducibilis cuius denomi-nator ex numeris agregatur, ut verbi gratia quia denominator divisionis con-tinui quaternarie, id est in quatuor partes, est numerus quaternarius, qui componitur ex duobus binariis, pro tanto dicimus talem divisionem quater-
20 nariam esse reducibilem, quia reduci potest ad binariam; item etiam quia denominator divisionis quinarie, scilicet numerus quinarius, componitur ex tribus et duobus, pro tanto dicimus ipsam divisionem quinariam esse redu-cibilem, quia ad binariam et ternariam; et sic de multis aliis. Illa vero divisio continui dicitur non reducibilis cuius denominator ex numeris non agregatur,

10 manifestum est bene consideranti L ‖ 16–17 nominator *ante corr. sup. lin.* B ‖ 17–18 quaternarie continui L ‖ 20 binariam]duas divisiones binarias L ‖ 23 binariam]divisionem binariam L | ternariam]divisionem ternariam L ‖

related to one number, which are in no way comparable to each other, since they are of different proximate genera.[17]

7. And, yet further, he says that, third, he intends to conclude that the nature of the tone consists in the ratio of the novenary number to the octonary and not in ratios of other numbers.[18] So, he seems to assert two things: first, that the nature of the tone consists in the ratio of the novenary number to the octonary, which is true; second, that the nature of the tone does not consist in numbers other than these two. This is false, inasmuch as the nature of the tone consists in all pairs of numbers between which the sesquioctave ratio falls, and these are infinite, as is manifest to one who considers it properly[19]—unless he meant that the nature of the tone does not consist in the ratios of other numbers, that is, in the ratios of numbers that do not produce the sesquioctave ratio; then, he would have been speaking the truth.

8. So that the method by which he intends to prove his first claim be properly understood, one must know that of the divisions of a continuum, certain ones are reducible and certain ones not reducible, and that a division is called reducible in which the denominator is aggregated of numbers.[20] For example, because the denominator of the quaternary division of a continuum (that is, the division into four parts) is the quaternary number and it is composed of two binary numbers, for that reason we say that such a quaternary division is reducible because it can be reduced to the binary. Yet again, because the denominator of the quinary division, that is, the quinary number, is composed of 3 and 2, for that reason we say that this quinary division is reducible because it can be reduced to the binary and the ternary; and thus for many others. A division of a continuum is said to be not reducible, on the other hand, in which the denominator is not aggregated of numbers.

---

[17]In *Brevis summula proportionum* 2, Prosdocimo had pointed out that "ratio as properly so called is the mutual relationship of several quantities of the same proximate genus [proportio proprie dicta est plurium quantitatum eiusdem generis propinqui adinvicem habitudo]" and in the following section that "ratio that is rational is the mutual relationship of several commensurable quantities [proportio rationalis est plurium quantitatum commensurabilium adinvicem habitudo]," i.e., those "among which is found a common measure capable of measuring any of those quantities [quibus reperitur una comunis mensura quamlibet illarum quantitatum commensurare potens]" (*Brevis summula ... Parvus tractatulus* [ed. Herlinger], 48–52 [see also the introduction, 3]). A ratio and a number do not belong to the same proximate genus and have no such common measure.

[18]Marchetto, *Lucidarium* 2.4.7 (ed. Herlinger, 112–13).

[19]By definition, the sesquioctave ratio falls between any two numbers of which one is equal to $1\frac{1}{8}$ of the other: 9:8, 18:16, 27:24, 36:32, and so forth to infinity.

[20]*Denominator* here refers not to the lower number of a fraction but to an entity that denominates—gives its name to—something else.

et iste sunt solum due, scilicet divisio binaria et divisio ternaria; et divisio
ternaria maior est divisione binaria, eo quod in plures partes totum dividit,
nam licet binarius numerus, qui est denominator divisionis binarie, ex duabus unitatibus agregetur, non tamen agregatur ex numeris, quoniam unitas
5   non est numerus sed principium numeri; item licet ternarius numerus, qui est
denominator divisionis ternarie, agregetur ex binario et unitate, non tamen
agregatur ex numeris sed ex numero et principio numeri, ut notum est.

Hoc premisso, capit Marchetus noster supradictus unum continuum,
quod primo dividit in tres partes, demum quamlibet harum trium partium
10   dividit in tres partes, sic quod totum remanet postea divisum in novem
partes; quamlibet autem harum novem partium dividit adhuc in tres partes,
et tunc fit totum divisum in 27 partes, et sic ultra ad libitum. Hoc ymaginato
dicit consequenter Marchetus supradictus quod cum per hanc divisionem
maiorem non reducibilem pervenerimus ad divisionem novenariam continui,
15   non est ulterius procedendum nec infra ipsam standum, eo quod nulla
divisio infra novenariam nec supra est perfecta, sed ipsa sola perfecta dicitur. Sed certe hoc dictum est valde extraneum, quoniam videre nescio quare
non sit procedendum ultra divisionem novenariam continui et quare etiam
non sit standum infra ipsam, et quare sola divisio novenaria continui sit per-
20   fecta et alie imperfecte; nunquam enim visum est aliquem auctorem
posuisse perfectionem et imperfectionem in divisione continui, quare con-
cludo michi hoc dictum fore mere voluntarium et sine ratione positum, sed
tamen suum videamus intellectum. Primo enim dividit totum in tres partes et
quamlibet partium in tres partes, que postea novem numero efficiuntur;
25   deinde capit quamlibet trium partium principalium totius pro uno toto diviso
in tres partes, et tunc iterum dividendo quamlibet suarum trium partium in
tres partes habebimus adhuc novem partes, et si iterum quelibet novem partium principalium totius pro uno toto acciperetur, et quelibet suarum trium
partium in tres partes divideretur, iterum haberemus novem partes, et sic in
30   infinitum procedendo, et partes pro toto accipiendo; et sic semper procede-

2 in plures partes totum dividit]per ipsam totum in plures partes partitur L ‖ 4 unitati-
bus]mutationibus *ante corr.* B ‖ 16 nec supra *om.* L ‖ 18 divisionem]dictam B ‖ 28 toto in
tres partes diviso L ‖ 30 toto in tres partes diviso L ‖

There are only two of these, the binary division and the ternary division; the ternary division is greater than the binary division because it divides the whole into a greater number of parts. Though the binary number, which is the denominator of the binary division, is aggregated of two unities, it is nevertheless not aggregated of numbers, inasmuch as unity is not a number but the principle of number.[21] Again, though the ternary number, which is the denominator of the ternary division, is aggregated of the binary and unity, it is nevertheless not aggregated of numbers but of a number and of the principle of number, as is known.

This having been stated as a premise, our aforesaid Marchetus takes a continuum, which he first divides into three parts; then, he divides each of these three parts into three parts. So, the whole is then left divided into nine parts.[22] Indeed, he divides each of these nine parts into yet another three parts, and then the whole has been divided into twenty-seven parts, and so on as far as he pleases. Having imagined this much, the aforesaid Marchetus says as a consequence that since through this "greater" nonreducible division we will have come to the novenary division of the continuum, it is impossible to proceed further or to stop short of it because no division below the novenary or above it is perfect, but it alone is called perfect. But certainly this statement is completely extraneous, inasmuch as I do not see why it should be impossible to proceed further than the novenary division of the continuum, why it should be impossible to stop short of it, and why the novenary division of the continuum alone should be perfect and the others imperfect. It has never come to light that some authority had placed perfection and imperfection in the division of a continuum. Wherefore, I conclude that the statement is really arbitrary and without reason. But nevertheless, let us see his understanding of it. First, then, he divides the whole into three parts and each of the parts into three parts, and these are thereupon made nine in number; then, he takes each of the three principal parts of the whole as one whole divided into three parts; and then, again dividing each of its three parts into three parts, we will have yet another nine parts. If again each of the nine principal parts of the whole were taken as one whole, and each of its three parts were divided into three parts, we would again have nine parts, and so on, proceeding to infinity and taking parts as wholes. So, we would

---

[21]The concept of unity being not a number but the source, origin, or principle of number is common in medieval arithmetic theories. See for instance Macrobius *In Somnium Scipionis* 1.6.7 (ed. Willis, 19; trans. Stahl, 100); Isidore *Etymologiae* 3.3.1 (trans. Barney et al., 89); Remigius, *Commentum in Martianum Capellam*, 2 vols., ed. Cora E. Lutz (Leiden: Brill, 1962–65), 285.14.

[22]The procedure described in this section is expounded in *Lucidarium* 2.4.8–24 (ed. Herlinger, 112–23).

remus de una divisione novenaria ad aliam divisionem novenariam ad suum intellectum, sed tamen propter hoc non sequeretur quod divisio novenaria sit perfecta divisio, quoniam etiam sic in infinitum procedere possemus per divisionem ternariam, et per alias infinitas divisiones maiores novenaria.

5   Ulterius vero capit unam diffinitionem, quam ponit Hencheridion Ubaldi de tono, que talis est: Tonus est legiptimum spatium de sono in sonum, et per hanc diffinitionem cum quodam alio falso fundamento vult probare quod natura toni consistit in numero novenario et non in maiori nec in minori, quod erat primum declarandum, et arguit sic: Tonus est legiptimum spatium
10 de sono in sonum, sed hic transitus, sive spatium, de sono in sonum fit transeundo de novenario in novenarium, ergo in novenario numero et non in plus nec in minus consistit natura toni. Huius autem rationis maior est diffinitio toni iam paulo antedata et minor, que ut fundamentum sue probationis existit, veritatem non continet, quoniam talis transitus de sono in
15 sonum, qui tonus appelatur, non fit solum transeundo de novenario in novenarium, sed fit transeundo de quocunque numero, quicunque sit ille, in alium sibi sexquioctavum vel subsexquioctavum. Et si diceres Marchetum intelligere fieri transitum de novenario in novenarium, id est de uno sono invento per unam divisionem novenariam continui in alium sonum inventum
20 per aliam divisionem novenariam continui, hoc etiam non semper verum est, ut quando fit transitus a fa ad sol, qui est tonus, quoniam fa sonus non est inventus per divisionem novenariam continui in ascensu, ut notum est, et etiam quando fit transitus a mi ad re, qui tonus est, quoniam mi sonus etiam non est inventus per divisionem novenariam continui in descensu, ut etiam
25 notum est; et ergo ratio Marcheti nichil concludit per quam volebat probare naturam toni consistere in numero novenario et non in plus nec in minus. Si

---

2 sequitur L ǁ 5 Heucheridion B ǁ 10 sed hic ... in sonum *in marg.* B ǁ 15 solum *om.* B ǁ

always proceed from one novenary division to another novenary division—according to his understanding. But still it would not have followed on this account that the novenary division would be the perfect division, inasmuch as we could have proceeded to infinity in this way through the ternary division and through an infinite number of other divisions greater than the novenary.

He further takes up a definition that the *Enchiridion* of Hucbald posits of the tone, which is this: the tone is the regular distance from one pitch to another pitch.[23] On the basis of this definition, along with a certain other false fundamental, he claims to prove that the nature of the tone consists in the novenary number and not in a greater one nor in a lesser (which was the first thing to be understood), and he argues thus.[24] The tone is the regular distance from one pitch to another pitch; but this passage, or distance, from one pitch to another pitch is made in passing from one novenary to another novenary; therefore, the nature of the tone consists in the novenary number and not in a greater one nor in a lesser. Now the major premise of this reasoning is the definition of the tone given shortly before, and its minor premise (which is, as it were, the fundamental of his proof) does not contain truth inasmuch as the passage from one pitch to another pitch that is called the tone is made not only in passing from one novenary to another novenary; rather, it is made in passing from whichever number, whatever it be, to another number that is its sesquioctave or its subsesquioctave.[25] If you were to say that Marchetus understood the passage to be made from one novenary to another novenary, that is, from one pitch discovered through a novenary division of the continuum to another pitch discovered through another novenary division of the continuum, this too is not always true, as when a passage is made from *fa* to *sol* (which is a tone) inasmuch as the pitch *fa* is not discovered through the novenary division of a continuum in ascent, as is known;[26] and also when a passage is made from *mi* to *re* (which is a tone) inasmuch as neither is the pitch *mi* discovered through the novenary division of a continuum in descent, as is known.[27] Therefore, Marchetus's reasoning (by which he claimed to prove that the nature of the tone consists in the novenary number and not in a greater or a lesser one) reaches no conclusion.

---

[23]The source is *Musica enchiriadis* 9 (ed. Schmid, 21; trans. Erickson, 12); Marchetto recalls it first in *Lucidarium* 2.1.3 (ed. Herlinger, 106–7).

[24]*Lucidarium* 2.4.25–29 (ed. Herlinger, 122–25).

[25]That is, the numbers related to it as 9:8 or 8:9—18:16 or 16:18, 27:24 or 24:27, etc.

[26]That is, however *fa* might have been found, it would not have been through a sesquioctave relation with a note a whole-tone below.

[27]That is, however *mi* might have been found, it would not have been through a sesquioctave relation with a note a whole-tone above.

tamen per naturam toni consistere in numero novenario intelligere vellet
tonum reperiri in continuo per divisionem novenariam continui, conclusio
sua haberet veritatem. Sed quando bene lego eius textum, quandoque videtur
hunc habere intellectum et quandoque ab hoc vero intellectu variare et ad
5   falsum tendere, sic quod intricat semetipsum, et non propter aliud nisi quod
ea que scripsit non intellexit. Et adhuc supposito illo vero intellectu non
tamen propter hoc demonstraret nec persuaderet suam conclusionem, ut si ad
intellectum verum datum sic argueret: tonus est legiptimum spatium de sono
in sonum, sed illud legiptimum spatium in continuo reperitur per divisionem
10   novenariam continui, ergo tonus invenitur in continuo per divisionem novenariam continui, ratio bona esset. Sed minor huius rationis demonstrari vel
persuadi deberet si conclusio sua deberet esse demonstrata vel persuasa. Dico
tamen quod maior, minor, et conclusio huius argumentationis habent veritatem per experientiam habitam et non per aliquam demonstrationem nec per-
15   suasionem, sicut credidit Marchetus, qui putavit totum demonstrasse et nichil
demonstravit nec persuasit. False etiam loquutus est Marchetus dum dixit
tonum reperiri non posse in continuo per divisionem continui maiorem
novenaria, quoniam etiam reperiri potest per quamlibet divisionem continui
maiorem novenaria reducibilem tamen ad novenariam, ut per 18, per 27, et
20   per 36, et sic ultra; sed facilius per novenariam.

⟨9.⟩ Pro declaratione vero secundi et tercii insimul capit unum continuum, quod primo dividit divisione prima et minori non reducibili, scilicet in
duas partes; postea quamlibet harum duarum partium dividit etiam in duas
partes, et iterum quamlibet harum ultimarum partium dividit in duas partes,
25   et sic ultra sine fine; et tunc patet quod, ad suum intellectum, talis divisio
semper fit de quaternario in quaternarium, quamlibet partem pro uno toto
semper accipiendo et ipsam bina divisione dividendo, prout divisum fuit
totum. Hoc posito, subdit quod ex quo talis divisio fit de quaternario in quaternarium, ad suum intellectum, hinc est quod per quaternarium debemus

7 conclusionem suam L ‖ 10 tonus [tonus] B ‖ 15 nichil tamen L ‖ 19 et *om.* L ‖ 20 ultra de
aliis infinitis divisionibus, ut notum est L ‖ 23 etiam *sup. lin.* B ‖

If, on the other hand, by the nature of the tone consisting in the novenary number he wished to understand that the tone is found in a continuum through the novenary division of the continuum, his conclusion would have had truth.[28] But when I read his text properly, it seems sometimes that this is what he understands and sometimes that he departs from this understanding and tends toward the false. So, he tangles himself up, and for no other reason than that he did not understand what he wrote. Even supposing that his understanding was the one that is true, he would not on this account have demonstrated or argued his conclusion convincingly. Had he argued the true meaning thus, "The tone is the regular distance from one pitch to another pitch; but this regular distance is found in a continuum through the novenary division of the continuum; therefore, the tone is discovered in a continuum through the novenary division of the continuum," the reasoning would have been good. But the minor premise of the reasoning ought to have been demonstrated or argued convincingly for his conclusion to have been demonstrated or argued convincingly. Nevertheless, I say that the major premise, the minor premise, and the conclusion of this argument have truth that is obtained through observation and not through any demonstration or convincing argument, as Marchetus believed, who thought that he had demonstrated everything and neither demonstrated nor argued anything convincingly. Marchetus also spoke falsely when he said that the tone cannot be found in a continuum through the division of the continuum by a division greater than the novenary inasmuch as it can be found through any division of the continuum greater than the novenary and reducible to the novenary, as through 18, 27, 36, and so forth—though more easily through the novenary.

9. But for the explanation of the second and third points together,[29] he takes a continuum, which first he divides by the first and lesser nonreducible division, that into two parts. Next, he also divides each of these two parts into two parts, and again each of these last parts he divides into two parts, and so forth without end. Then, it is evident—to his understanding—that such a division is always made from one quaternary to another quaternary, always taking any part as a whole and dividing it through the binary division, just as the whole had been divided. This having been stated, he adds that because this division is made from one quaternary to another quaternary—to his understanding—, it is through the quaternary that we ought to

---

[28] In monochord divisions the whole-tone is often found by dividing a string or string segment into ninths and finding the point that marks eight of the ninths. On monochord divisions, see Jan Herlinger, "Medieval Canonics," chapter 6 in *The Cambridge History of Western Music Theory*, ed. Thomas Christensen (Cambridge: Cambridge University Press, 2002), 168–92.

[29]*Lucidarium* 2.4.30–42 (ed. Herlinger, 124–31).

234

reducere omnes proportiones musicales que duplicari possunt; sed hic dupliciter errat Marchetus. Primo enim errat quia ratio eius nichil concludit, nam
non valet hec argumentatio: Divisio continui que fit per minorem divisionem
non reducibilem semper fit de quaternario in quaternarium, ad suum intel-
5 lectum, ergo omnes proportiones musicales que duplicari possunt debent
reduci per quaternarium. Secundo errat quia videtur velle aliquas proportiones musicales duplicari posse et aliquas non, quod falsissimum est, cum
omnis proportio duplicabilis sit. Sed videamus, amore Dei, quomodo iste
bonus homo reducit proportiones musicales ad quaternarium, nam capit
10 unam proportionem duplam in suis minimis terminis, scilicet 2, 1, que proportio dupla facit consonantiam dyapason, unde quia sicut est dyapason, 2
ad 1, ita est etiam dyapason 1 ad 2, et quoniam etiam in tali conversione sunt
quatuor termini, scilicet due unitates et duo binarii, hinc est quod dicitur
hanc proportionem duplam reductam esse ad quaternarium, secundum eius
15 intellectum, et si iterum reduceretur aliqua alia proportio musicalis modo
simili ad quatuor terminos, haberemus in istis duabus proportionibus quaternarium numerum duplicatum, scilicet octenarium. Hoc declarato videamus
quomodo suum arguit intentum. Arguit ergo sic: Tonus consistit in numero
novenario, quod sub falso intellectu credidit demonstrasse, et novenarius
20 numerus continet octenarium numerum et unitatem, qui octenarius continet
proportiones duplicatas, id est duas proportiones que ad suum intellectum
continent 8 terminos; ergo tonus continet proportiones duplicatas et unitatem, et per consequens habetur quomodo se habeat tonus ad octenarium
numerum, quia scilicet continet ipsum et unitatem, vel proportiones duplica-
25 tas et unitatem, quod fuit suum secundum declarandum. Et ex istis duobus
suo modo sic declaratis infert postea tercium, ut sic per ipsum arguatur:
Tonus consistit in numero novenario, quod fuit suum primum, quod credidit
demonstrasse; et tonus habet respectum ad octenarium, quod fuit suum
secundum, quod etiam credidit demonstrasse, et tamen nec demonstravit nec
30 persuasit; ergo natura toni consistit in proportione numeri novenarii ad
octenarium, quod fuit tercium suum concludendum. Sed ratio hec non plus
valet quam valeat ista: Homo est asinus et capra est leo, ergo Deus est; cuius
consequens est neccessarium, quod materialiter ad quodlibet sequi potest, et
utraque premissarum impossibilis, uti in eius ratione, quare sequitur quod
35 nec demonstrat nec persuadet quod demonstrare intendebat; sed videas, amore
Dei, quales falsitates et trufulas adducit iste bonus homo cum suis divisionibus novenariis et cum suis quaternariis duplicatis et cum suo fundamento

---

8 duplicalis B ‖ 11 diapason facit consonantiam L ‖ 20 numerum *om.* B ‖ 21–22 id est …
proportiones duplicatas *om.* (*saut du même au même*) L ‖ 26 sic suo modo L ‖ 32 ista sibi
similis L ‖ 33 quolibet B ‖ 33–34 et utraque … in eius ratione *om.* B ‖ 37 novenariis et quaternariis L ‖

reduce all musical ratios that can be doubled. But here Marchetus errs two-fold. He errs first, indeed, because his reasoning reaches no conclusion, for this argument is not valid: the division of the continuum that is made through the lesser nonreducible division is always made from one quater-nary to another quaternary—to his understanding—; therefore, all musical ratios that can be doubled ought to be reduced through the quaternary. Sec-ond, he errs because he seems to claim that some musical ratios can be dou-bled and others cannot. This is utterly false, since every ratio is capable of being doubled. But let us see, for the love of God, how this good man reduces musical ratios to the quaternary: he takes one duple ratio in its least terms, that is, 2:1, and this duple ratio makes the consonance of the diapa-son; whence, because just as the diapason is 2:1, so is the diapason also 1:2. Inasmuch as in this conversion there are four terms, two unities and two binaries, this duple ratio is said to have been reduced to the quaternary—according to his understanding—; and if again any other musical ratio were reduced to four terms in a similar manner, we would have in these two ratios the quaternary number doubled, that is, the octonary. This having been explained, let us see how he argues his claim; he argues, then, thus: The tone consists in the novenary number—which, under a false understanding, he believes to have demonstrated—and the novenary number contains the octonary number and unity; this octonary contains doubled ratios, that is, two ratios that—to his understanding—contain eight terms; therefore, the tone contains doubled ratios and unity. Consequently, we know how the tone relates to the octonary number: because, namely, it contains that octo-nary and unity, or the doubled ratios and unity, which was his second point to be explained. On the basis of these two points explained thus in his way, he next infers a third point so that it is argued by him as follows: the tone consists in the novenary number (this was his first point, which he believed he had demonstrated); the tone has a relationship to the octonary (this was his second point, which he also believed he had demonstrated, and never-theless neither demonstrated it nor argued convincingly); therefore, the nature of the tone consists in the ratio of the novenary number to the octo-nary (this was his third conclusion to be reached). But this reasoning is no more valid than this would be: a man is an ass and a goat is a lion; therefore, God exists. The conclusion of this syllogism, which could potentially follow anything, is necessary, and both of its premises are impossible, just as in his reasoning, wherefore it follows that he neither demonstrates nor argues con-vincingly what he intended to demonstrate. But see, for the love of God, what sorts of falsehoods and deceptions this good man adduces with his novenary divisions, his doubled quaternaries, and his utterly false funda-

falsissimo de consistentia toni in numero novenario ad demonstrandum suum intentum; item videas falsam loquutionem dum dicit tonum continere proportiones duplicatas et unitatem, quoniam ubi sic esset, tonus tunc componeretur ex proportionibus duplicatis et unitate, quod falsissimum est, eo
5 quod tonus, cum sit quedam proportio sive consistat in quadam proportione, non componitur ex numeris nec ex principiis numeri sed ex proportionibus, et per consequens non ex unitate sibi addita. Preterea si notabis modos suarum deductionum improprie et false loquitur et nichil veri concludit. Melius enim fuisset huic viro ab ignorantibus commendato non scripsisse quam
10 talia falsa et erronea seminasse. Doleo enim de sua prosumptuositate, quia michi concivis.

⟨10.⟩ Item in capitulo cuius rubrica talis est, Demonstratio partium toni, multas scribit falsitates, et prima earum est quia dicit tonum habere quinque partes et non plures neque pauciores, nam eius proportio habet quinque
15 partes et pauciores et plures ymo infinitas, cum hoc simile habeat quelibet proportio, ut notum est; ergo tonus etiam habebit quinque partes et pauciores et plures ymo infinitas. Secunda falsitas est quia dicit tonum consistere in proportione novenarii numeri, ut credidit probasse, que tamen proportio nunquam audita nec reperta est in rerum natura. Tercia falsitas est quia dicit
20 novenarium numerum non posse dividi in partes equales, quod falsissimum est, cum in novem unitates dividi possit. Quarta falsitas est quia dicit

mental concerning the tone's consisting in the novenary number to demonstrate his claim. Again, see the false locution when he states that the tone contains doubled ratios and unity, inasmuch as were this so, the tone would have been composed of doubled ratios and unity. This is utterly false, because the tone, since it is a certain ratio, or consists in a certain ratio, is not composed of numbers or of the principles of number but of ratios and consequently not of a unity added to them. Moreover, if you will take note of the methods of his deductions, he speaks incorrectly and falsely and reaches no conclusion of truth. In fact, it would have been better for this man, esteemed by the ignorant, not to have written than to have disseminated such false and erroneous things. I am truly grieved at his presumption, because he was a fellow citizen of mine.

10. Again, in the chapter of which the rubric is *Demonstratio partium toni*,[30] he writes many falsehoods, and the first of them is that he says the tone has five parts and neither more nor fewer,[31] for its ratio has five parts, and fewer, and more—or rather, an infinite number of parts, since any ratio has the same as these, as is known.[32] Therefore, the tone also will have five parts, and fewer, and more—or rather, an infinite number. The second falsehood is that he says the tone consists in the ratio of the novenary number[33]— as he believed he had proven—but this ratio has never been heard of or found in the nature of things. The third falsehood is that he says that the novenary number cannot be divided into equal parts.[34] This is utterly false, since it can be divided into nine unities. The fourth falsehood is that he says

---

[30]"Demonstration of the Parts of the Tone"; *Lucidarium* 2.5 (ed. Herlinger, 130–41).

[31]*Lucidarium* 2.5.15 (ed. Herlinger, 136–37): "the whole tone can have only five parts, neither more nor [fewer] [tonus non potest habere nisi quinque partes, neque plures, neque pauciores]."

[32]As demonstrated for the sesquioctave ratio in *Musica speculativa* 2.15 (194–201).

[33]*Lucidarium* 2.5.8 (ed. Herlinger, 132–33): "the whole tone consists in the *perfection* of the number 9 [tonum consistere in perfectione numeri novenarii]." The Catania and Venice manuscripts (Catania, Biblioteche Riunite Civica e Antonio Ursino-Recupero, Ursino-Recupero D.39; Venice, Biblioteca Nazionale Marciana, lat. cl. VIII.85), however, have *in proportione* (in the ratio) in place of *in perfectione*, and the Washington manuscript (Washington, Library of Congress, ML171.J6) has *in proportione id est in perfectione* (in the ratio, that is, in the perfection).

[34]*Lucidarium* 2.5.9 (ed. Herlinger, 132–33): "the number 9 can never be divided into equal parts [novenarius numerus nunquam potest dividi in partes equales]." I have argued that Marchetto, building on Macrobius and Remigius, equated the tone with the number 9 and that the cryptic statement quoted here is linked to the tradition of the tone's not being divisible into two equal parts. See the *Lucidarium* 2.5.10 (ed. Herlinger, 133–35, n. e) and "Marchetto's Division of the Whole Tone," *Journal of the American Musicological Society* 34 (1981): 193–216.

numerum novenarium solum dividi posse in quinque partes, quod falsissimum est, cum possit dividi in 2, in 3, in 4, in 5, in 6, in 7, in 8, et in 9 partes
ad plus, ut notum est. Et ex istis tribus ultimis falsitatibus concludit primam,
scilicet quod tonus non habeat plures neque pauciores quinque partibus, ut
5 sic per ipsum arguatur: Numerus novenarius non habet plures neque pauciores quinque partibus, sed in numero novenario consistit natura et ratio
toni, ut credit probasse; ergo tonus non habet plures neque pauciores quinque
partibus. Sed istius rationis maior et minor false sunt, et ideo non est miran-
dum si sua conclusio etiam habeat falsitatem.

10 ⟨11.⟩ Item consequenter in predicto capitulo subdit adhuc alias quam-
plures falsitates, quarum prima est hec, quia dicit tonum esse divisibilem in
quinque partes equales, quod est impossibile, ut supra demonstratum est, et
hec etiam est una de principalibus falsitatibus ab ipso per totam Ytaliam
seminatis. Secunda falsitas est quia dicit quamlibet illarum quinque partium
15 equalium nominari debere hoc nomine dyesis, ignorans quid apud auctores
musice hoc nomen dyesis importet, cum sit semitonium vel medietas semitonii minoris, ut habitum est supra; modo semitonium vel medietas semitonii
minoris non est quinta pars toni, quoniam si esset quinta pars toni, tunc
tonus fuisset divisibilis in quinque partes equales, cuius oppositum demon-
20 stratum est supra, et ista secunda falsitas est etiam una de principalibus falsitatibus per Ytaliam ab ipso seminatis. Tercia vero falsitas etiam de principalibus per Ytaliam ab ipso seminatis est quia dicit quod si quinque dyeses
de suis insimul iungantur tonum producunt completum, et si pauciores
quinque insimul agregentur tonum completum non producunt sed semito-
25 nium, et quoniam de istis suis dyesibus possunt insimul agregari due, tres, et
quatuor, facient, secundum ipsum, tria semitonia distinctarum specierum,
quorum unum in se duas continebit de istis suis dyesibus et aliud tres et
aliud quatuor; et subdit quod semitonium continens duas dyeses enarmonicum appelatur et illud quod continet tres dyatonicum nominatur et illud

---

1 quod etiam L ‖ 13 principalioribus L ‖ 17 ⟦vel⟧ vel L ‖ 20 ista ⟦est⟧ B | una *om.* B | prin-
cipalioribus L ‖ 20–21 falsitatibus *om.* B ‖ 21–22 principalioribus L ‖

the novenary number can be divided into five parts only.[35] This is utterly false, since it can be divided into two, three, four, five, six, seven, eight, and nine parts at most, as is known. From these last three falsehoods, he draws the first conclusion, that the tone has neither more nor fewer than five parts, as is argued by him thus: the novenary number has neither more nor fewer than five parts, but the nature and ratio of the tone consist in the novenary number (as he believes he has proven); therefore, the tone has neither more nor fewer than five parts. But the major and minor premises of this reasoning are false, and on that account, it is no wonder if his conclusion should also have falsehood.

11. Again, subsequently in the aforesaid chapter, he adds many other falsehoods besides, of which the first is that he says the tone is divisible into five equal parts,[36] which is impossible, as was demonstrated above.[37] This is also one of the principal falsehoods disseminated by him throughout all Italy. The second falsehood is that he says any of those five equal parts ought to be named with the name diesis,[38] ignoring what among the authorities of music the name diesis means, since it is the semitone or half the minor semitone, as has been explained above.[39] But the semitone or half the minor semitone is not a fifth part of the tone inasmuch as if it were a fifth part of the tone, then the tone would have been divisible into five equal parts, the opposite of which was demonstrated above.[40] This second falsehood is also one of the principal falsehoods disseminated by him throughout Italy. The third falsehood (also one of the principal ones disseminated by him throughout Italy) is that he says that if five of those dieses of his were joined together, they produce a complete tone, and if fewer than five are aggregated together, they do not produce a complete tone but a semitone. Inasmuch as two, three, or four of those dieses of his can be aggregated together, they will make—according to him—three semitones of distinct species, of which one will contain in itself two of those dieses of his, another three, and another four. He adds that the semitone containing two dieses is called enharmonic, and that which contains three is named diatonic,

---

[35]*Lucidarium* 2.5.15 (ed. Herlinger, 136–37). See p. 237, n. 31 *supra*.

[36]Actually, Marchetto never states explicitly that the the five parts of the tone are equal, but he speaks as if they are and several times speaks of the parts as fifths of tones.

[37]*Musica speculativa* 2.15 (194–201).

[38]*Lucidarium* 2.5.23 (ed. Herlinger, 138–39): "Any one of these fifth parts is called a diesis—the last reduction or division, as it were [Quarum quelibet quinta pars voctur dyesis, quasi decisio seu divisio summa]."

[39]*Musica speculativa* 2.22 (214–15).

[40]*Musica speculativa* 2.15 (194–201).

quod continet quatuor cromaticum nuncupatur, sic quod apud ipsum tria
erunt semitonia specie distincta, scilicet enarmonicum, dyatonicum, et cromaticum, et hec omnia falsissima sunt, cum hec tria nomina sint nomina
trium specierum tetracordi et non semitoniorum, ut supra declaratum est.
5 Semitonia enim apud musice auctores solum duo inventa sunt et non tria,
maius scilicet et minus nuncupata, et non aliter.

⟨12.⟩ Preterea in capitulo De dyesi nominato dicit quod quando, gratia
exempli, ascendimus ab una tercia ad unam quintam per unam vocem, ut a
fa ad sol supra re ut, et illa tercia reperiatur minor, que maior esse deberet,
10 ut ex Contrapuncto haberi potest, si ad fa anteponatur tale signum, ※, quod
apud Marchetum et suos sequaces dyesis nominatur, tunc per tale signum fit
divisio toni qui est a fa ad sol, et subdit quod prima pars talis divisionis est
illud de suis semitoniis quod cromaticum appellabat et secunda pars est
quinta pars toni sive una de suis dyesibus; sed in hoc suo dicto multipliciter
15 errat, et primo errat quia ponit signum non neccessarium, quoniam ibidem
poni deberet ♮ quadrum ad reducendum illam terciam minorem ad suam
maioritatem, ut aliquantulum supra declaratum est, et illud ♮ quadrum bene
dividit tonum qui est a fa ad sol. Secundo errat quia dicit illud signum nominari debere hoc nomine dyesis, quod falsum est, eo quod nulla sonorum
20 combinatio est per aliquod signum signabilis, et per consequens nec dyesis,
que etiam est quedam sonorum combinatio, licet in manu musicali non
reperibilis. Tercio errat quia dicit quod prima pars divisionis toni qui est a fa
ad sol in casu posito est suum semitonium cromaticum et secunda pars est
quinta pars toni sive una sua dyesis, que ambo falsa sunt per supra habita,
25 nam ex quo divisio toni in quinque partes equales est impossibilis, ut supra

---

2 erunt]sunt L ‖ 13 crematicum B ‖ 15 ibi L ‖ 21 combinatio [huius] L ‖

and that which contains four is called chromatic. So, according to him, there will be three semitones distinct in species, the enharmonic, the diatonic, and the chromatic.[41] All these things are utterly false, since these three names are the names of three species of tetrachord and not of semitones, as was explained above.[42] Among the authorities of music, indeed, only two semitones have been discovered, called the major and the minor, and not three; it is not otherwise.

12. Moreover in the chapter named *De diesi*,[43] he says that when (for example) we ascend from a third to a fifth through one syllable, as from *fa* to *sol* above *re ut*, and that third is found to be minor which ought to have been major (as can be known from the *Contrapunctus*),[44] if the sign ※, which Marchetus and his followers name the diesis, is placed before the *fa*, a division of the tone from *fa* to *sol* is effected by the sign. He adds that the first part of such division is that of his semitones which he called chromatic and the second part is a fifth tone or one of his dieses. But in this statement, he errs in many different ways. First, he errs because he sets down an unnecessary sign, inasmuch as in that place, a square ♮ ought to have been set down to change that minor third to its major, as has been explained a bit earlier,[45] and that square ♮ properly divides the tone that is from *fa* to *sol*. Second, he errs because he says that sign ought to be named with the name diesis. This is false, because no interval is capable of being indicated by a sign, and consequently not the diesis, which is a certain interval, though it is not to be found in the musical hand. Third, he errs because he says that the first part of the division of the tone that is from *fa* to *sol* in the given case is his chromatic semitone and the second part is a fifth tone or one diesis of his, both of which statements are false on the basis of what has been explained above. Because the division of the tone into five equal parts is

---

[41]*Lucidarium* 2.5.24–27 (ed. Herlinger, 138–41). The various semitones are described further in 2.6–8 (140–57).

[42]*Musica speculativa* 3.3 (220–25).

[43]"On the Diesis"; *Lucidarium* 2.6 (ed. Herlinger, 140–43). The upper voices of these progressions show chromatic ascents, a chromatic semitone followed by a diesis. The middle notes of these upper voices are preceded in most manuscripts by a sign that resembles the modern sharp. Nowhere does Marchetto call such a sign diesis, though he does call it *falsa musica* in *Lucidarium* 8.1 (ed. Herlinger, 270–81) and in *Pomerium* 2.4, 13.1 (ed. Vecchi, 40, 68). Cf. *Musica speculativa* 2.22 (214–15).

[44]In *Contrapunctus* 5.6 (ed. Herlinger, 78–95), Prosdocimo had explained the rules of *musica ficta*, including the rule pertinent here: imperfect consonances should if necessary be altered in size through the application of accidental signs, so that they lie as close as possible to the perfect consonances to which they progress.

[45]*Musica speculativa* 2.22 (212–13).

demonstratum est, positio suorum semitoniorum et suarum dyesium etiam
impossibilis erit, quare non erit verum quod divisio toni per illud suum signum sit in suum semitonium cromaticum et suam dyesim iam quod ista in
rerum natura non sunt reperibilia, sed divisio toni per ♮ quadrum anteposi-
5 tum ad fa est in semitonium maius et semitonium minus, ut esse debet. Breviter, ergo, ubicunque invenies Marchetum vel aliquem suum sequacem
aliquid loqui de istis suis semitoniis et de istis suis dyesibus, non auscultes
ipsum, quoniam isti tantum de hoc sciverunt quantum boves. Putavit enim
Marchetus quod in collocando semitonia in monacordo tonus dividi deberet
10 in quinque partes equales et quod ad secundam vel terciam partem poni
deberet semitonium, sed confidens de se graviter erravit. Penitus enim ignoravit modum collocandi semitonia in monacordo, quem modum hic dilatare
dimitto propter operis brevitatem, et etiam quia de divisione monacordi pro-
prium tractatum compilavi, in quo reprobantur duo modi comuniter usitati
15 tanquam imperfecti et ultimo additur tercius modus qui omnem continet perfectionem possibilem. Erravit etiam Marchetus quia ex suo modo collocandi
semitonia in monacordo supradicto expresse sequitur quod divisio toni que
fit per suum tale signum, ※, suprapositum, quod apud ipsum dyesis nominatur, est in semitonium maius et minus vel in minus et maius, que apud ipsum
20 enarmonicum et dyatonicum appelantur, et non in suum cromaticum et suam
dyesim, quod est contra eius opinionem superius recitatam; et hoc evidenter
apparere potest cuilibet subtiliter advertenti.

---

2 suum *sup. lin.*B ‖ 6 Marchetum supradictum L ‖ 7 abscultes B ‖ 9 Marchetus]dictus Marchetus L ‖ 16 Marchetus]dictus Marchetus L ‖ 17 expresso B ‖ 20 dyatonicum et enarmonicum B ‖

impossible, as was demonstrated above,[46] the placing of his semitones and of his dieses will also be impossible. Wherefore, it will not be true that the division of the tone effected by that sign of his is a division into his chromatic semitone and his diesis, because they are not to be found in the nature of things. Rather, the division of the tone by a square ♮ placed before the *fa* is a division into the major semitone and the minor semitone, as it ought to be. Briefly, then, wherever you discover Marchetus or any follower of his saying anything about those semitones of his and those dieses of his, do not heed him, inasmuch as in this matter they wrote like oxen. Marchetus, to be sure, thought that in locating semitones in the monochord, the tone ought to be divided into five equal parts and that a semitone ought to be placed at the second or third part;[47] though self-confident, he erred seriously. Indeed, he was thoroughly ignorant of the method of locating semitones in the monochord, a method I exclude reporting on account of the brevity of the work, and also because I have compiled a treatise devoted to the division of the monochord, in which the two methods commonly used are shown to be— shall I say—defective, and, finally, a third method is added that contains every perfection possible.[48] Marchetus also erred because from his aforesaid method of locating semitones in the monochord, it follows explicitly that the division of the tone that is effected by ⚹, that sign of his presented above (which he named the diesis), is a division into the major semitone and the minor or into the minor and the major, which he calls enharmonic and diatonic, and not into his chromatic semitone and his diesis, which is contrary to his own opinion reported above. This can appear clearly to whoever attends to it carefully.

---

[46]*Musica speculativa* 2.15 (194–201).

[47]*Lucidarium* 2.5.22–27 (ed. Herlinger, 138–41).

[48]*Parvus tractatulus de modo monacordum dividendi*; section 3 (ed. Herlinger, 72–82) describes the construction of *musica vera*; sections 5–6 and 7–8 (90–111) describe two methods of constructing *musica ficta* (one with flats, the other with sharps) and their deficiences; finally section 9 (112–18) describes the third method, a conflation of those two methods, neither sufficient in itself.

244

⟨13.⟩ Dicitque in capitulo De numeris musicalibus et de consonantiis in generali alias multas et varias falsitates, quarum prima est hec, quod species consonantiarum sunt tantum sex, quod falsum est, cum sint numero infinite, ut supra habitum est. Secunda falsitas est quia dicit quod quaternarius
5 numerus vocatur epitritus, eo quod est supra ternarium, nam epitritus dicitur ab epi, quod est supra, et tritos, tres, quasi numerus supra ternarium, et ille est quaternarius; et falsitas huius secundi dicti est quia epitritum est nomen proportionis et non numeri. Proportio nanque epitrita est proportio sexquitercia, et bene verum est quod epitritum dicitur ab epi, quod est supra, et
10 tritos, tres, quoniam in omni proportione sexquitercia maior quantitas minorem excedit per terciam partem minoris, et non quia numerus supra ternarium, ut dicit Marchetus, quoniam tunc non solum quaternarius sed quilibet maior epitritus vocaretur, cum quilibet numerus maior quaternario sit supra ternarium. Tercia falsitas est quia dicit quod numerus ternarius dicitur emio-
15 lius, quod falsum est, cum emiolium sit nomen proportionis et non numeri.

2 alias]aliquas B ‖ 15 emilium *ante corr.* L ‖

13. In the chapter *De numeris musicalibus et de consonantiis in generali*,[49] he says many and various other falsehoods, of which the first is this, that there are only six species of consonances.[50] This is false, since they are infinite in number, as has been explained above.[51] The second falsehood is that he says that the quaternary number is called epitrite, because it is above the ternary, for epitrite is derived from *epi*, which is above, and *tritos*, three; "the number above the ternary," as it were, and that is the quaternary.[52] The falsehood of this second statement is that epitrite is the name of a ratio and not of a number. The epitrite ratio is, to be sure, the sesquitertial ratio, and it is properly true that epitrite is derived from *epi*, which is above, and *tritos*, three, inasmuch as in every sesquitertial ratio the greater quantity exceeds the lesser by one-third the lesser. This is not because the number is above the ternary, as Marchetus says, inasmuch as then not only the quaternary but any greater number would have been called epitrite, since any number greater than the quaternary is above the ternary. The third falsehood is that he states that the ternary number is called the hemiolic.[53] This is false, since

---

[49]"On Musical Numbers and on the Consonances in General"; *Lucidarium* 3.1 (ed. Herlinger, 168–71). The title of the chapter is actually *De numeris musicalibus et de consonantiis in speciali*; no extant manuscript shows the reading *in generali*.

[50]*Lucidarium* 3.1.2 (ed. Herlinger, 168–69). The statement that there are six consonances and that they are the diatessaron, diapente, diapason, diapason diatessaron, diapason diapente, and bisdiapason goes back at least to Cassiodorus *Institutiones* 2.5.7 (*Cassiodori Senatoris Institutiones*, ed. R. A. B. Mynors [Oxford: Clarendon Press, 1937], 144–45; translated with introduction and notes by Leslie Webber Jones as *An Introduction to Divine and Human Readings by Cassiodorus Senator*, Records of Western Civilization [New York: Columbia University Press, 1946], 191–92; new translation by James W. Halporn as *Institutions of Divine and Secular Learning and On the Soul*, introduction by Mark Vessey, Translated Texts for Historians, vol. 42 [Liverpool: Liverpool University Press, 2004], 218–19).

[51]In *Musica speculativa* 1.18 (174–75), Prosdocimo showed that intervals can be increased infinitely by extending them through octave equivalents; if the number of intervals is infinite, the number of consonances must accordingly be infinite.

[52]*Lucidarium* 3.1.7–8 (ed. Herlinger, 170–71): "In numbers, this consonance is called 'epitrite,' because it is constituted in the epitrite number. Epitrite numbers are four in comparison to three and the like [Hec enim consonantia in numeris epitrita nuncupatur, eo quod sit in epitrito numero constituta, nam epitritus numerus est quaternarius ternario comparatus et hiis similes]."

[53]*Lucidarium* 3.2.4–5 (ed. Herlinger, 172–73): "In numbers, this consonance is called 'hemiolia,' because it is constituted in the hemiolic number. Hemiolic numbers are three in comparison to two and the like [Hec igitur consonantia in numeris emiolia vocatur, eo quod sit in emiolio numero constituta. Estque emiolius numerus ternarius binario comparatus et

246

Proportio enim emiolia est proportio sexquialtera, et dicitur emiolium ab emi, quod est dimidium, et olon, totum, eo quod in omni proportione sex- quialtera maior quantitas minorem continet totam et ipsius minoris medie- tatem. Et, breviter, in omnibus suarum sex consonantiarum proportionibus,
5 que sex sue consonantie sunt dyapente, dyateseron, dyapason, dyapason cum dyateseron, dyapason cum dyapente, et bisdyapason, nomina propor- tionum attribuit numeris, unde proportionem sexquiterciam appelat numerum epitritum, et proportionem sexquialteram appelat numerum emiolium, et proportionem duplam appelat numerum duplum, et proportionem duplam
10 superbipartientem appelat numerum duplum superbipartientem, et propor- tionem triplam appelat numerum triplum, et proportionem quadruplum appelat numerum quadruplum, et etiam proportionem sexquioctavam appe- lat numerum sexquioctavum; et describit omnia ista ac si describeret pro- portiones, sic quod cepit numeros pro proportionibus, et male, eo quod
15 numerus et proportio specie abinvicem distinguntur. Dico tamen quod pro- prie loquendo unus numerus bene dici potest epitritus ad alium, et emiolius ad alium, et duplus ad alium, et duplus superbipartiens ad alium, et triplus ad alium, et quadruplus ad alium, et sexquioctavus ad alium, sed non in se, ut cepit Marchetus, quare improprie et false loquutus est. Quarta falsitas est
20 quia dicit proportiones in quibus consonantie consistunt fore solummodo sex, quod falsum est, eo quod sunt numero infinite, uti consonantie.

2 [supra] dimidium L || 9 duplam [appelat] B || 16–18 alium]aliam *septies* B || 20 dicit quod L ||

hemiolic is the name of a ratio and not of a number. The hemiolic ratio, indeed, is the sesquialter ratio, and hemiolic is derived from *hemi*, which is half, and *olon*, whole, because in every sesquialter ratio the greater quantity contains all the lesser plus half of the lesser. Indeed, to put it briefly, in all the ratios of his six consonances (and his six consonances are the diapente, the diatessaron, the diapason, the diapason with diatessaron, the diapason with diapente, and the double diapason), he attributes the names of ratios to numbers, whence he calls the sesquitertial ratio the epitrite number, the sesquialter ratio the hemiolic number, the duple ratio the duple number, the duple superbipartient ratio the duple superbipartient number, the triple ratio the triple number, the quadruple ratio the quadruple number, and the sesquioctave ratio the sesquioctave number.[54] He describes all these as if he were describing ratios. So, he took numbers as ratios, and he did this improperly, because number and ratio are distinguished in species from each other. Nevertheless, I say that, speaking correctly, one number can properly be called epitrite *to another*, hemiolic *to another*, duple *to another*, duple superbipartient *to another*, triple *to another*, quadruple *to another*, and sesquioctave *to another*[55]—but not in themselves, as Marchetus took them. Wherefore, he spoke incorrectly and falsely. The fourth falsehood is that he says that there are only six ratios in which consonances consist. This is false, because they are infinite in number, like the consonances.[56]

hiis similes]." Prosdocimo will soon concede (246–47) that "one number can properly be called epitrite *to another*, hemiolic *to another*"; this is in fact very close to what Marchetto writes.

[54]*Lucidarium* 3.1–6 *passim* (ed. Herlinger, 168–81).

[55]Compare Cassiodorus *Institutiones* 2.4.5 (ed. Mynors, 135–36); Isidore *Etymologiae* 3.6.2 (*Isidori Hispalensis Episcopi Etymologiarum sive originum libri XX*, ed. W. M. Lindsay, 2 vols. [Oxford: Clarendon, 1911]): "Per se numerus est, qui sine relatione aliqua dicitur, ut III. IV. V. VI, et ceteri similes. Ad aliquid numerus est, qui relative ad alios conparatur; ut verbi gratia IV ad II dum conparatus fuerit, duplex dicitur [et multiplex], VI ad III, VIII ad IV, X ad V; et iterum III ad unum triplex, VI ad II, IX ad III et ceteri." See p. 245, nn. 52–53 *supra*.

[56]*Lucidarium* 3.1.2 (ed. Herlinger, 168–69).

248

⟨14.⟩ Item dicit ibidem quod proportiones membrorum consonantiarum sunt tantum tres, quod falsum est, cum sunt numero infinite, ut clare patet bene advertenti, nam ex quo consonantie sunt infinite, ut supra habitum est, erunt etiam eorum membra infinita, et per consequens proportiones conso-
5   nantiarum et suorum membrorum erunt etiam numero infinite.

⟨15.⟩ Preterea extraneo modo probat numerum ternarium esse numerum perfectum, qui tamen perfectus non est, sed numerus senarius est primus numerorum perfectorum. Arguit nanque sic: Si tria et bis tria insimul comperentur, producunt proportionem duplam; et si bis tria et ter tria insimul
10   comperentur, producunt proportionem sexquialteram, et si tria et ter tria insimul comperentur, producunt proportionem triplam; et si ter tria et quater

---

1–2 *Huc pertinet emendatio quae in L invenitur:* ... proportiones membrorum consonantiarum sunt tantum tres, scilicet proportio toni et due proportiones duorum semitoniorum, maioris scilicet et minoris, quas dicit esse proportionem sexquioctavam, proportionem sexquisextam decimam, et proportionem sexquiseptimam decimam, et proportionem sexquioctavam esse proportionem toni, et proportionem sexquisextam decimam esse proportionem semitonii maioris, et proportionem sexquiseptimam decimam esse proportionem semitonii minoris; sed in hoc dupliciter errat, primo quia dicit proportiones membrorum consonantiarum esse tantum tres; hoc enim falsum est, eo quod sunt numero infinite ...
5 *Huc pertinet emendatio quae in L invenitur:* ... erunt numero infinite. Secundo errat quia dicit proportionem sexquisextam decimam esse proportionem semitonii maioris et proportionem sexquiseptimam decimam esse proportionem semitonii minoris, nam hoc falsum est, ut patet ex supra habitis.

8–9 [com] comperentur B ‖ 9 [bis] L ‖ 10–11 producunt ... comperentur *om.* (*saut du même au même*) L ‖

14. Again he says in that same place[57] that there are only three ratios of members of consonances. This is false, since they are infinite in number, as is clearly evident to one who attends to it properly. Because the consonances are infinite, as has been explained above,[58] their members will also be infinite, and consequently the ratios of consonances and of their members will also be infinite in number.

15. Moreover he proves, extraneously, that the ternary number is a perfect number,[59] yet it is not perfect; rather, the senary number is the first of the perfect numbers. He argues thus: if 3 and 2×3 are compared to each other, they produce the duple ratio; if 2×3 and 3×3 are compared to each other, they produce the sesquialter ratio; if 3 and 3×3 are compared to each other, they produce the triple ratio; and if 3×3 and 4×3 are compared to

---

1–2 … there are only three ratios of members of consonances, the ratio of the tone and the two ratios of the two semitones, the major and the minor, which he says are the sesquioctave ratio, the sesquisextadecimal ratio, and the sesquiseptimadecimal ratio. He says the sesquioctave ratio is the ratio of the tone, the sesquisextadecimal ratio is the ratio of the major semitone, and the sesquiseptimadecimal ratio is the ratio of the minor semitone. But in this he errs twofold: first, because he states that there are only three ratios of the members of consonances. This, indeed, is false, because they are infinite in number …

6 … will be infinite in number. Second, he errs because he says that the sesquisextadecimal ratio is the ratio of the major semitone and the sesquiseptimadecimal ratio is the ratio of the minor semitone. This is false, as is evident from what has been explained above.[60]

---

[57]*Lucidarium* 4.2.3 (ed. Herlinger, 184–85): "The [ratios] in which members of consonances consist are three, the sesquioctave, the sesquisextadecimal, and the sesquiseptimadecimal. [Proportiones vero in quibus membra consonantiarum consistunt sunt tres, scilicet sesquioctava, sesquisexta decima, et sesquidecima septima]." These "members of consonances" are the tone and the major and minor semitones, which, in addition to calling 3/5 and 2/5 tone, Marchetto defines in *Lucidarium* 2.10, 11.2–4 (ed. Herlinger, 192–93), contradictorily, as 17:16 and 18:17. In *Lucidarium* 9.1.6 (ed. Herlinger, 310–11), Marchetto will add two intervals to the list of members of consonance: "Syllables in music are the whole tone, the semitone, the ditone, and the semiditone; they are properly called members of consonant intervals. [Sillaba in musica est tonus, semitonium, ditonus, et semiditonus, que consonantiarum membra proprie nuncupantur]."

[58]*Musica speculativa* 1.18 (172–75).

[59]*Lucidarium* 6.3.5–9 (ed. Herlinger, 232–35).

[60]*Musica speculativa* 2.3, 17 (180–87, 204–7).

tria insimul comperentur, producunt proportionem sexquiterciam; ergo numerus ternarius est numerus perfectus; nam hec ratio non plus valet quam valeat hec: Deus est, et homo est animal; ergo capra est leo. Ignoravit enim iste bonus homo quid esset numerus perfectus, qui numerus perfectus ab
5 Euclide in principio noni suorum Elementorum sic describitur: Numerus perfectus est qui omnibus suis partibus quibus numeratur est equalis.

⟨16.⟩ Item in capitulo in quo intendit probare quod dyapason cum dyateseron non sit consonantia dicit quod inter duplam et triplam non reperitur aliqua proportio, quod falsum est, nam inter ipsas reperitur proportio dupla
10 sexquialtera, dupla sexquitercia, dupla sexquiquarta, et sic ultra in infinitum; item dupla superbipartiens, dupla supertripartiens, dupla superquadripartiens, et sic ultra in infinitum; quarum quelibet maior est dupla et minor tripla.

3–4 *Huc pertinet emendatio quae in L invenitur:* ... ergo capra est leo, cuius rationis utraque premissarum est vera, sive eius antecedens et conclusio falsa, sicut in eius ratione ignoravit enim iste bonus homo ...

---

5 noni suorum]noni libri suo L ‖

each other, they produce the sesquitertial ratio; therefore, the ternary number is a perfect number. This reasoning is no more valid than this would be: God exists, and man is an animal; therefore the goat is a lion. This good man was ignorant of what a perfect number was; the perfect number was described thus by Euclid at the beginning of the ninth book of his *Elementa*: the perfect number is that which is equal to all of its parts by which it is factored.[61]

16. Again, in the chapter in which he intends to prove that the diapason with diatessaron is not a consonance, he says that no ratio is found between the duple and the triple.[62] This is false, for between them are found the duple sesquialter ratio, the duple sesquitertial, the duple sesquiquartal, and so forth to infinity; again, the duple superbipartient, the duple supertripartient, the duple superquadripartient, and so forth to infinity—any of which is greater than the duple and less than the triple.

3–4 ... therefore the goat is a lion. Both premises of this reasoning are true, but the antecedent and conclusion are false, as in his reasoning this good man was ignorant ...

---

[61]*Elementa* 9.38; *The Latin Translation of the Arabic Version of Euclid's "Elements,"* 232. An alternative tradition defines 3 and 9 also as "perfect" numbers: 3 because it has "beginning, middle, and end"; 9 because it is the last of the "first order" of numbers. This is supported by Remigius, *Commentum in Martianum Capellam* 44.5 (ed. Lutz, 1:148); Martianus's text is given in uppercase, Remigius's commentary in lowercase: NAM ET ILLE id est ternarius numerus, PERFECTO id est certe, PERFECTUS EST, QUOD id est eo quod, RATIO DISPENSAT id est ordinat et disponit, PRINCIPIUM et MEDIUM et FINEM. Ideo, inquit, ternarius datur rationi quia ratio in hominibus INITIUM rei et MEDIUM et FINEM considerat. See also *Commentum in Martianum Capellam* 44.12 (ed. Lutz, 1:149): IDEM NUMERUS id est ternarius, SEMINARIUM id est origo, est PERFECTORUM numerorum SEXTI ATQUE NONI id est senarii et novenarii. Senarius perfectus dicitur quia suis partibus impletur, nam medietas eius tres, tertia eius duo, sexta unus; unus, duo, tres, sex restituunt. Novenarius autem idcirco perfectus dicitur quia finis est primi versus vel ordinis numerorum. Quod autem dicit ALTERNA DIVERSITATE, IUNCTURAE significat quia uterque numerus, id est senarius et novenarius, a ternario nascuntur, sed diversa procreatione. Namque bis terni sex, ter autem terni, novem faciunt. Hoc est quod dicit ALTERNA id est varia et dissimili, DIVERSITATE IUNCTURAE id est coniunctionis. In senario enim ternarius et binarius iungitur, in novenario vero ternarius per se ipsum multiplicatur.

[62]*Lucidarium* 6.5.5–7 (ed. Herlinger, 248–51).

⟨17.⟩ Item in capitulo De coniunctionibus vocum dicit quod diptonus et semidiptonus non consistunt in proportione aliqua, quod falsum est, eo quod omnis sonorum combinatio in aliqua proportione consistit, ut clare patet ex supradictis. Multasque etiam alias falsitates scripsit supradictus Marchetus
5 quas scribere dimisi propter brevitatem et etiam quia intellectis que supra habita sunt, poterit quilibet omnes eius cognoscere falsitates.

⟨18.⟩ Et sic sit finis huius tractatus per Prosdocimum de Beldemando patavum anno domini nostri Yesu Xristi 1425 Padue compilati ad laudem, gloriam, et honorem omnipotentis Dei. Amen.
10   ⟨19.⟩ Explicit tractatus Musice speculative quem Prosdocimus de Beldemando paduanus contra Marchetum de Padua compilavit. Deo gratias. Amen.

---

1 in *om.* L ‖ 2 non *sup. lin.* B ‖ 4 supradictis]suprahabitis L ‖ 4–12 falsitates … Amen *om.* B ‖

17. Again, in the chapter *De coniunctionibus vocum*,[63] he says that the ditone and the semiditone do not consist in any ratio. This is false, because every interval consists in some ratio, as is clearly evident from what has been said above.[64] The aforesaid Marchetus wrote many other falsehoods that I have excluded writing down for the sake of brevity and also because when one understands what has been explained, anyone will be able to recognize all his falsehoods.

18. Let this be the end of this treatise compiled by the Paduan Prosdocimus de Beldemando in the year of our Lord Jesus Christ 1425 at Padua for the praise, glory, and honor of the omnipotent God. Amen.

19. Here ends the treatise of speculative music that the Paduan Prosdocimus de Beldemando compiled against Marchetus of Padua. Thanks be to God. Amen.

---

[63]"On Intervals: How They Are Defined and How Many They Are [De coniunctionibus vocum: quod sint et quot]"; *Lucidarium* 6.3.5–9 (ed. Herlinger, 232–35).

[64]Prosdocimo probably refers to *Musica speculativa* 2 in its entirety. In actuality, of course, tempered intervals do not consist in ratios of whole numbers; but such intervals lie outside Prosdocimo's frame of reference.

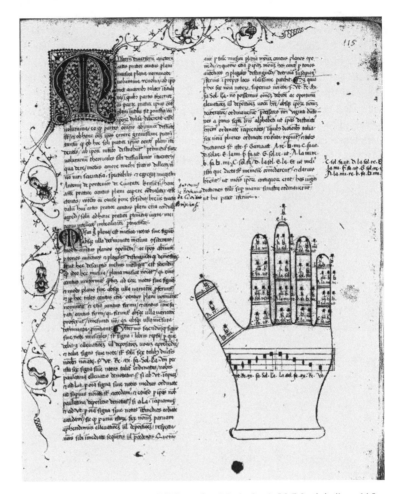

Plate 1: Bologna, Civico Museo Bibliografico Musicale, A.56 (Martini, 4), p. 115.

By permission of the Museo internazionale e biblioteca della musica di Bologna.

Plate 2: Lucca, Biblioteca Statale, 359, f. 49r.

Plate 3: Bologna, Civico Museo Bibliografico Musicale, A.56 (Martini, 4), p. 248.

By permission of the Museo internazionale e biblioteca della musica di Bologna.

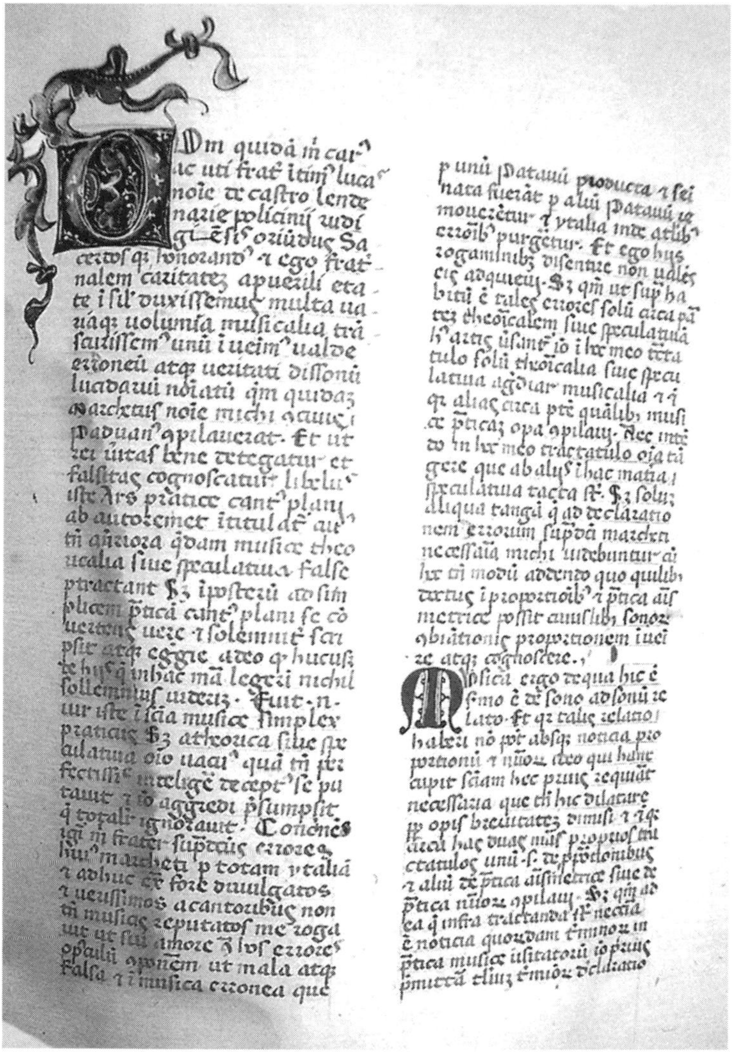

Plate 4: Lucca, Biblioteca Statale, 359, f. 79r.

WORKS CITED

Manuscripts

Bergamo, Biblioteca Civica "Angelo Mai," Manoscritti antichi bergamaschi, 21 (*olim* Σ.IV.37).

Bologna, Civico Museo Bibliografico Musicale, A.56 (Martini, 4).

Brussels, Bibliothèque Royale Albert Ier, II 785.

Catania, Biblioteche Riunite Civica e Antonio Ursino-Recupero, Ursino-Recupero D.39.

Cremona, Biblioteca Governativa, 252.

Einsiedeln, Benediktinerkloster, 689.

Florence, Biblioteca Medicea-Laurenziana, Ashburnham 206.

Lucca, Biblioteca Statale, 359.

Milan, Biblioteca Ambrosiana, I.20.inf.

Venice, Biblioteca Nazionale Marciana, lat. cl. VIII.82.

Venice, Biblioteca Nazionale Marciana, lat. cl. VIII.85.

Washington, Library of Congress, ML 171.J6.

Collections of Frequently Cited Treatises

Coussemaker, Edmond de, ed. *Scriptorum de musica medii aevi nova series a Gerbertina altera*. 4 vols. Paris: Durand, 1864–1976; reprint, Hildesheim: Olms, 1963; hereafter CS.

Gerbert, Martin, ed. *Scriptores ecclesiastici de musica sacra potissimum*. 3 vols. St. Blaise: Typis San-Blasianis, 1784; reprint, Hildesheim: Olms, 1963; hereafter GS.

Treatises

Amerus. *Practica artis musice*. Ed. Cesarino Ruini. Corpus scriptorum de musica, vol. 25. [Rome]: American Institute of Musicology, 1977.

Anonymous. "Alia musica." In GS, 1:125–52.

259

—————. *Ars cantus mensurabilis mensurata per modos iuris*. Ed. and trans. C. Matthew Balensuela. Greek and Latin Music Theory, vol. 10. Lincoln: University of Nebraska Press, 1994.

—————. *The Berkeley Manuscript: University of California Music Library, MS. 744 (*olim *Phillipps 4450): A New Critical Text and Translation*. Ed. and trans. Oliver B. Ellsworth. Greek and Latin Music Theory, vol. 2. Lincoln: University of Nebraska Press, 1984.

—————. "Cum notum sit." In CS, 3.60–62.

—————. "Dialogus de musica." In GS, 1:252–64.

—————. *Quaestiones et* solutiones. Ed. Albert Seay. Critical Texts, no. 2. Colorado Springs: Colorado College Music Press, 1977.

—————. "Quattuor principalia." In CS, 4:200–298.

—————. "Ratio contrapuncti est ista." Milan, Biblioteca Ambrosiana, I.20.inf., ff. 27v–28r.

Anonymous II. *Tractatus de discantu*. Ed. Albert Seay. Critical Texts with Translation, vol. 1. Colorado Springs: Colorado College Music Press, 1978.

Anonymus ex codice vaticano lat. 5129. Ed. Albert Seay. Corpus scriptorum de musica, vol. 9. [Rome]: American Institute of Musicology, 1964.

Aribo. *De musica*. Ed. Joseph Smits van Waesberghe. Corpus scriptorum de musica, vol. 2. [Rome]: American Institute of Musicology, 1951.

Aristotle. *Analytica posteriora*.

—————. *De anima*.

—————. *Physica*.

Berno. "Musica." In GS, 2:62–79.

Boen, Johannes. "Musica." In *Johannes Boens "Musica" und seine Konso-nanzenlehre*, ed. Wolf Frobenius, 32–78. Freiburger Schriften zur Musikwissenschaft, vol. 2. Stuttgart: Musikwissenschaftliche Verlags-Gesellschaft, 1971.

Boethius, A. M. S. "De institutione musica." In *De institutione arithmetica libri duo, De institutione musica libri quinque*, ed. Godofredus Friedlein, 177–371. Leipzig: B. G. Teubner, 1867.

—————. *Fundamentals of Music*. Trans. with introduction and annotations by Calvin Bower. Music Theory Translation Series. New Haven, CT: Yale University Press, 1989.

Burzio, Nicola. *Florum libellus* (=*Musices opusculum*). Ed. Giuseppe Massera. "Historiae Musicae Cultores" Biblioteca, vol. 28. Florence: Olschki, 1975.

——. *Musices opusculum*. Trans. Clement A. Miller. Musicological Studies and Documents, no. 37. Neuhausen-Stuttgart: Hänssler-Verlag for the American Institute of Musicology, 1983.

Busard, H. L. L., ed. *The Latin Translation of the Arabic Version of Euclid's "Elements" Commonly Ascribed to Gerard of Cremona*. Asfar: Publikaties van het Documentatiebureau Islam-Christendom van de Rijksuniversiteit te Leiden, vol. 2. Leiden: Brill, 1984.

Cassiodorus Senator. *Cassiodori Senatoris Institutiones*. Ed. R. A. B. Mynors. Oxford: Clarendon Press, 1937.

——. *An Introduction to Divine and Human Readings by Cassiodorus Senator*. Trans. with introduction and notes by Leslie Webber Jones. Records of Western Civilization. New York: Columbia University Press, 1946.

——. *Institutions of Divine and Secular Learning and On the Soul*. New trans. James W. Halporn with introduction by Mark Vessey. Translated Texts for Historians, vol. 42. Liverpool: Liverpool University Press, 2004.

Cicero. *Cicero in Twenty-Eight Volumes*. Vol. 18, *Tusculan Disputations*. Ed. and trans J. E. King. Loeb Classical Library. Cambridge: Harvard University Press, 1966.

Ciconia, Johannes. *Nova musica and De proportionibus: New Critical Texts and Translations*. Ed. and trans. Oliver B. Ellsworth. Greek and Latin Music Theory, vol. 9. Lincoln: University of Nebraska Press, 1993.

Franco of Cologne. *Ars cantus mensurabilis*. Ed. Gilbert Reaney and André Gilles. Corpus scriptorum de musica, vol. 18. [Rome]: American Institute of Musicology, 1974.

Gaffurio, Franchino. *Practica musice*. Milan: Ioannes Petrus de Lomatio, 1496; reprint, Farnborough: Gregg, 1967.

Guido d'Arezzo. "Epistola de ignoto cantu." In GS, 2:43–50.

——. *Guido d'Arezzo's Regule rithmice, Prologus in antiphonarium, and Epistola ad Michahelem: A Critical Text and Translation*. Ed. Dolores Pesce. Musicological Studies, vol. 73. Ottawa: Institute of Mediæval Music, 1999.

————. *Micrologus*. Ed. Joseph Smits van Waesberghe. Corpus scriptorum de musica, vol. 4. [Rome]: American Institute of Musicology, 1955.

————. "Micrologus." In *Hucbald, Guido, and John on Music: Three Medieval Treatises*, trans. Warrren Babb, ed. with introductions by Claude V. Palisca, 57–83. Music Theory Translation Series. New Haven, CT: Yale University Press, 1978.

————. "Prologus in antiphonarium." In GS, 2:34–41.

————. "Regule rithmice." In GS, 2:25–34.

Guido frater. "Ars musice mensurate." In *Mensurabilis musicae tractatuli*, ed. F. Alberto Gallo, 19–39. Antiquae musicae italicae scriptores, vol. 1. Bologna: Università degli Studi di Bologna, Istituto di Studi Musicali e Teatrali – Sez. Musicologia, 1996.

Isidore of Seville. *Etymologiae*. Ed. W. M. Lindsay. 2 vols. Oxford: Clarendon Press, 1911.

————. *The* Etymologies *of Isidore of Seville*. Trans. Stephen A. Barney, W. J. Lewis, J. A. Beach, and Oliver Berghof, with the collaboration of Muriel Hall. Cambridge: Cambridge University Press, 2006.

Jacques de Liège. *Speculum musice*. Ed. Roger Bragard. 7 vols. Corpus scriptorum de musica, vol. 3. N.p.: American Institute of Musicology, 1955–73.

Johannes de Garlandia. "Introductio musicae planae secundum magistrum Johannem de Garlandia." In *Musica plana Johannis de Garlandia*, ed. with Introduction and Commentary by Christian Meyer, 63–97. Collection d'études musicologiques, no. 91. Baden-Baden: Éditions Valentin Koerner, 1998.

————. "Introductio musice secundum magistrum de Garlandia." In CS, 1:157–75.

Johannes de Muris, "Ars discantus." In CS, 3:68–113.

————. *Musica ⟨speculativa⟩*. Ed. Susan Fast. Musicological Studies, vol. 61. Ottawa: Institute of Mediæval Music, 1994.

————. "Tractatus de musica." In GS, 3:256–83.

Johannes Gallicus. *Ritus canendi*. Ed. Albert Seay. 2 vols. Critical Texts, nos. 13–14. Colorado Springs: Colorado College Music Press, 1981.

————. "Ritus canendi." In CS, 4:346–396.

Macrobius. *Opera*. Vol. 2, *Commentarii in Somnium Scipionis, accedunt quatuor tabulae et Somnium Scipionis*. Ed. James Willis. Leipzig: B. G. Teubner, 1963.

————. *Commentary on the Dream of Scipio by Macrobius.* Trans. with introduction and notes by William Harris Stahl. Records of Western Civilization. New York: Columbia University Press, 1952.

Marchetto of Padua. *The Lucidarium of Marchetto of Padua: A Critical Edition, Translation, and Commentary.* Ed. Jan W. Herlinger. Chicago: University of Chicago Press, 1985.

————. *Pomerium.* Ed. Ioseph Vecchi, Corpus scriptorum de musica, vol. 6. [Rome]: American Institute of Musicology, 1961.

Musica et scolica enchiriadis. Ed. Hans Schmid. Bayerischen Akademie der Wissenschaften. Veröffentlichungen der Musikhistorischen Kommission, Band 3. Munich: Bayerische Akademie der Wissenschaften; C. H. Beck, 1981.

Musica enchiriadis and Scolica enchiriadis. Trans. with notes and introduction by Raymond Erickson. Music Theory Translation Series. New Haven, CT: Yale University Press, 1995.

Nicolaus of Capua. "Compendium musicale." In *Essais de dipthérographie musicale*, ed. Adrien de La Fage, 308–38. Paris: Legouix, 1864; reprint ed., Amsterdam: Knuf, 1964.

Odington, Walter. *De speculatione musice.* Ed. Frederick F. Hammond. Corpus scriptorum de musica, vol. 14. [Rome]: American Institute of Musicology, 1970.

Peter of Abano. *Conciliator differentiarum philosophorum et praecipue medicorum.* Ed. Franciscus Argilagnes. Pavia: Gabriel de Grassis, 1490.

Philippe de Vitry. "Ars contrapunctus." In CS, 3:23–27.

————. *Ars nova.* Ed. Gilbert Reaney, André Gilles, and Jean Maillard. Corpus scriptorum de musica, vol. 8. [Rome]: American Institute of Musicology, 1964.

Prosdocimo de' Beldomandi. *Brevis summula proportionum quantum ad musicam pertinet and Parvus tractatulus de modo monacordum dividendi: A New Critical Text and Translation.* Ed. and trans. Jan Herlinger. Greek and Latin Music Theory, vol. 4. Lincoln: University of Nebraska Press, 1987.

————. "Brevis summula proportionum quantum ad musicam pertinet." In CS, 3:258–61.

————. *Contrapunctus: A New Critical Text and Translation.* Ed. and trans. Jan Herlinger. Greek and Latin Music Theory, vol. 1. Lincoln: University of Nebraska Press, 1984.

———. "Contrapunctus." In CS, 3:193–99.

———. *Expositiones tractatus pratice cantus mensurabilis magistri Johannis de Muris.* Ed. F. Alberto Gallo. Antiqui musicae italicae scriptores, no. 3: Prosdocimi de Beldemandis opera, vol. 1. Bologna: Antiquae Musicae Italicae Studiosi, 1966.

———. "Parvus tractatulus de modo monacordum dividendi." In CS, 3:248–58.

———. "Tractatus practice cantus mensurabilis." In CS, 3:200–228.

———. "Tractatus musice speculative." In D. Raffaello Baralli and Luigi Torri, "Il *Trattato* di Prosdocimo de' Beldomandi contro il *Lucidario* di Marchetto da Padova per la prima volta trascritto e illustrato." *Rivista musicale italiana* 20 (1913): 731–62.

———. "Tractatus pratice cantus mensurabilis ad modum Ytalicorum." In Claudio Sartori, *La notazione italiana del Trecento in una redazione inedita del "Tractatus practice cantus mensurabilis ad modum ytalicorum" di Prosdocimo de Beldemandis*, 35–71. Florence: Olschki, 1938.

———. "Tractatus pratice cantus mensurabilis ad modum Ytalicorum." In CS, 3:228–48.

———. *A Treatise on the Practice of Mensural Music in the Italian Manner.* Trans. Jay A. Huff. Musicological Studies and Documents, no. 29. [Rome]: American Institute of Musicology, 1972.

Ps.-Aristotle. "Tractatus de musica." In CS, 1:251–81.

Regino. "Epistola de harmonica institutione." GS, 1:230–47.

Remigius. *Commentum in Martianum Capellam.* 2 vols. Ed. Cora E. Lutz. Leiden: Brill, 1962–65.

Rossetti, Biagio. *Libellus de rudimentis musices.* Ed. Albert Seay. Critical Texts, no. 12. Colorado Springs: Colorado College Music Press, 1981.

Theoger of Metz. "Musica." In GS, 2:182–96.

Tinctoris, Johannes. *Dictionary of Musical Terms.* Ed. Carl Parrish. Glencoe: Free Press, 1963.

———. "Expositio manus." In *Johannis Tinctoris Opera theoretica*, ed. Albert Seay, 2:31–57. 3 vols. in 2. Corpus scriptorum de musica, vol. 22. [Rome]: American Institute of Musicology, 1975–78.

Ugolino di Orvieto. *Declaratio musicae disciplinae*. Ed. Albert Seay. 3 vols. Corpus scriptorum de musica, vol. 7. [Rome]: American Institute of Musicology, 1959–62.

Secondary Sources

Acta graduum academicorum gymnasii patavini ab anno 1400 ad annum 1450. 2d ed. Ed. Gasparo Zonta and Giovanni Brotto. 3 vols. Padua: Antenore, 1970.

Bartal, Antal, ed. *Glossarium mediae et infimae latinitatis Regni Hungariae*. Leipzig: B. G. Teubner, 1901; reprint Hildeshem: Olms, 1970.

Bent, Margaret. "Ciconia, Prosdocimus, and the Workings of Musical Grammar as Exemplified in *O felix templum* and *O Padua*." In *Johannes Ciconia: musicien de la transition*, ed. Philippe Vendrix, 65–106. Collection «Épitome musical», no. 16. Turnhout: Brepols, 2003.

———. *Counterpoint, Composition, and* Musica Ficta. Criticism and Analysis of Early Music. New York: Routledge, 2002.

———. "Diatonic Ficta," *Early Music History* 4 (1984): 1–48.

———. "Musica Recta and Musica Ficta." *Musica disciplina* 26 (1972): 73–100.

Berger, Karol. "The Hand and the Art of Memory." *Musica disciplina* 35 (1981): 87–120.

Blackburn, Bonnie, and Leofranc Holford-Strevens. *The Oxford Companion to the Year*. Oxford: Oxford University Press, 1999.

Crocker, Richard L. "Pythagorean Mathematics and Music." *Journal of Aesthetics and Art Criticism* 22 (1964): 189–98, 325–35.
    Reprinted in his *Studies in Medieval Music Theory and the Early Sequence*. Variorum Collected Studies. Aldershot: Variorum, 1997.

Dictionary of Scientific Biography. 16 vols. New York: Scribner, 1970–80.

Favaro, Antonio. "Appendice agli studi intorno alla vita ed alle opere di Prosdocimo de' Beldomandi, matematico padovano del secolo XV." *Bullettino di bibliografia e di storia delle scienze matematiche e fisiche* 18 (1885): 405–23.

———. "Intorno alla vita ed alle opere di Prosdocimo de' Beldomandi, matematico padovano del secolo XV." *Bullettino di bibliografia e di storia delle scienze matematiche e fisiche* 12 (1879): 1–74, 115–251.

Gallo, F. Alberto. "La tradizione dei trattati musicali di Prosdocimo de Beldemandis." *Quadrivium* 6 (1964): 57–84.

Glare, P. G. W., ed. *Oxford Latin Dictionary*. Oxford: Clarendon Press, 1982.

Herlinger, Jan. "Marchetto's Division of the Whole Tone." *Journal of the American Musicological Society* 34 (1981): 193–216.

———. "Marchetto's Influence: The Manuscript Evidence." In *Music Theory and Its Sources: Antiquity and the Middle Ages*, ed. André Barbera, 235–58. Notre Dame Conferences in Medieval Studies, vol. 1. Notre Dame, IN: Notre Dame University Press, 1990.

———. "Medieval Canonics." In *The Cambridge History of Western Music Theory*, ed. Thomas Christensen, chapter 6. Cambridge: Cambridge University Press, 2002.

———. "Music Theory of the Fourteenth and Early Fifteenth Centuries." In *Music as Concept and Practice in the Late Middle Ages*, ed. Reinhard Strohm and Bonnie J. Blackburn, chapter 6. New Oxford History of Music, new ed., vol. 3/2. Oxford: Oxford University Press, 2001.

———. "Singing Exercises from a Bergamo Convent." Paper read at the 41st International Congress on Medieval Studies, Western Michigan University, 4–7 May 2006, and in revised versions at the Medieval and Renaissance Music Conference, Cambridge, 17–20 July 2006, and the Annual Meeting of the American Musicological Society, Los Angeles, 2–5 November 2006.

Lindley, Mark. "Pythagorean Intonation and the Rise of the Triad." *Royal Musical Association Research Chronicle* 16 (1980): 4–61.

McKinnon, James. "Jubal vel Pythagoras, Quis Sit Inventor Musicae?" *Musical Quarterly* 64 (1978): 1–28.
     Reprinted in his *The Temple, the Church Fathers, and Early Western Chant*. Variorum Collected Studies. Aldershot: Ashgate, 1998.

Niemöller, Klaus Wolfgang. "Zur Tonus-Lehre der italienischen Musiktheorie des ausgehenden Mittelalters." *Kirchenmusikalisches Jahrbuch* 40 (1956): 23–32.

Niermeyer, J. F., ed. *Mediae latinitatis lexicon minus*. Leiden: Brill, 1993.

Il nuovo dizionario italiano Garzanti. Milan: Garzanti, 1984.

Pacioli, Luca. *Summa de arithmetica, geometria, proportioni, et proportionalita*. Venice: Paganinus de Paganinis, 1494.

Page, Christopher. "Around the Performance of a 13th-Century Motet." *Early Music* 28 (2000): 343–57.

————. "Polyphony before 1400." In *Performance Practice: Music before 1600*, ed. Stanley Sadie and Howard Mayer Brown, chapter 5. New York: Norton, 1990.

Rashdall, Hastings. *The Universities of Europe in the Middle Ages*. 3 vols. New ed. by F. M. Powicke and A. B. Emden. Oxford: Clarendon Press, 1936.

Sachs, Klaus-Jürgen. *Der Contrapunctus im 14. und 15. Jahrhundert: Untersuchungen zum Terminus, zur Lehre und zu den Quellen*. Beihefte zum *Archiv für Musikwissenschaft*, vol. 13. Wiesbaden: Steiner, 1974.

Siraisi, Nancy G. *Arts and Sciences at Padua: The Studium of Padua before 1350*. Studies and Texts, no. 25. Toronto: Pontifical Institute of Mediaeval Studies, 1973.

Strayer, Joseph R., ed. *Dictionary of the Middle Ages*. 13 vols. New York: Charles Scribner's Sons, 1982–89.

Strohm, Reinhard. "Modal Sounds as a Stylistic Tendency of the Mid-Fifteenth Century: E-, A-, and C-Finals in Polyphonic Song." In *Modality in the Music of the Fourteenth and Fifteenth Centuries*, ed. Ursula Günther, Ludwig Finscher, and Jeffrey Dean, 149–75. Musicological Studies and Documents, no. 49. Neuhausen-Stuttgart: Hänssler Verlag for the American Institute of Musicology, 1996.

Tomasin, Giacomo Filippo. *Bibliothecae patavinae manuscriptae publicae et privatae quibus diversi scriptores hactenus incogniti recensentur ac illustrantur*. Udine, 1639.

Wiering, Frans. *The Language of the Modes: Studies in the History of Polyphonic Modality*. Criticism and Analysis of Early Music. New York: Routledge, 2001.

Websites

Consorzio per lo Sviluppo del Polesine. http://www.consvipo.it.html (accessed 17 April 2005).

http://www.polesine.com/pagine/polesine/geografia/a001.html (accessed 17 April 2005).

INDEX VERBORUM

appelare, 164.21; 214.8; 224.7; 240.13; 246.7, 8, 9, 10, 11, 12, 12–13; appelari, 80.15; 162.6, 21; 164.1–2, 27; 166.24, 27, 30; 168.7; 170.9, 12; 172.18–19; 200.14; 214.19; 222.30; 230.15; 238.29; 242.20
apperiri, 64.4, 5
applicare, 64.27
apponere, 66.17, 32; 68.1, 3; 216.11; apponi, 64.24; 68.5, 6, 8
apprehendere, 36.13–14; 38.6
aptari, 84.20
aquiescere, 158.13
arguere, 230.9; 232.8; 234.18 (bis); 248.8; argui, 194.10, 16; 198.1; 234.26; 238.5
argumentatio, 232.13; 234.3
arismetrica, 64.26–27, 27–28; v. pratica arismetrice, proportionalitas arismetrica
arismetricalis, v. cifra arismetricalis
Aristotiles, 78.9; 224.14
armonicus, v. proportionalitas armonica
ars, 34.3, 12, 13; 46.7; 52.6; 56.7; 60.25; 62.1; 64.25; 78.6 (bis); 120.27; 154.19; 158.14; 224.5; ars metrica, 154.18–19; Ars pratice cantus plani, 156.11
artifex, 224.14
ascendere, 64.9; 72.25; 74.15, 16, 22; 82.22; 84.7–8; 86.13; 88.8; 90.2; 92.2; 94.11, 12; 106.11, 13, 16, 22, 28; 108.3; 116.5; 118.12, 18; 120.25; 160.26; 212.11, 13; 216.6; 240.8; ascendens, 212.3; ascendi, 42.18; 70.1, 10; 80.17, 24–25; 82.5, 9; 106.5, 7, 11, 18–19, 25; 108.1; 212.10, 12
ascensus, 72.29; 74.12, 19, 23, 29; 82.23–24, 26; 84.5, 15; 86.11, 14, 15, 17, 19 (bis), 23; 90.3; 94.3–4, 6, 7, 13, 15; 96.15; 116.1; 118.20; 214.11; 230.22; ascensus a mi ad fa, 210.10
asinus, 234.32
asperitas, 58.11
aspere (adv.), 58.7
aspicere, 120.30; aspici, 96.9
asserere, 58.11; 78.7; 220.9, 14; 226.5
assignari, 54.19; 58.20; 122.5
assimilari, 64.11
associare, 66.15; 72.17
assuescere, 54.20, 22
assumere, 82.11; 120.30; assumi, 56.24; 82.7, 9, 18
astrologi, 86.27
attribuere, 246.7; attribui, 84.21–22; 96.6
auctor, 34.3, 4; 224.5; 228.20; auctormet, 156.12; auctores antiqui, 54.9; 56.14; 166.29; auctores autentici, 84.28, 86.22; auctores musice, 46.16, 238.15–16; 240.5
auctoritas, 220.5, 15
audiens, 144.1; auderi, 236.19
augeri, 190.4
augmentari, 180.9

aures, 118.1

aureus, *v.* numerus aureus

auris, *v.* iudicare aure

auscultare, 242.7

autenticus, 36.4; 38.10, 84.27; 86.21, 24; 88.13; 92.1, 6; 94.8, 11, 14, 15–16; 96.2, 9, 10; 118.12–13, 13, 15, 21; *v.* auctores autentici, elevatio autentica, tonus autenticus

B, 40.21; 42.4; 46.17, 18, 20; 56.18, 20, 21; 58.2; 62.17; 74.8; b, 40.25; 60.22, 30; 210.19; b acutum, 72.25, 28; 74.3, 5, 6, 7, 26: bfa♮mi, 38.19, 20; 40.15, 21; 48.11, 15 (bis); 56.17, 20, 23, 24, 27, 30; 74.9, 10; bfa♮mi acutum, 54.3, 5, 7, 14; 60.10; 62.21; 74.28; bfa♮mi superacutum, 54.3, 14; 60.10; 62.17; 74.27–28; bmi, 68.20; Bre, 68.21; Bsol, 68.20; B acutum, 216.7, 17 (bis), 18 (bis); B duo distincta, 210.17; B grave, 74.4; 98.9–10, 11; b molle, 58.3, 6, 22; b primum, 40.24, 42.5; 58.4, 9; 162.21, 29; 166.26; 168.17, 32; 170.24; b rotundum, 40.26;; 56.21, 22, 23, 26, 30, 31, 31–32; 58.2, 4; 60.20, 21 (bis), 22, 23, 35; 62.15, 16–17, 17, 20, 21, 25; 92.8; 120. 25, 29, 31; 216.11, 12, 15, 20, 21; 218.2; b rotundum sive molle, 58.19, 28, 30; b rotundum acutum, 100.1; b secundum, 40.26; 164.11; 168.24; 170.3, 224; b superacutum, 74.22, 24–25, 27; b tercium, 170.3; ♮, 42.3; 72.7; 210.18; ♮mi, 38.18; 46.3; 48.8; 60.8; ♮ durum, 58.3, 8; ♮ grave, 62.18; 74.7, 8; ♮ quadrum, 42.3; 56.21–22, 23, 24, 29, 32, 33, 34; 58.2, 58.6–7, 23; 60.20, 25, 32 (bis); 74.8, 9; 92.7–8; 100.19; 102.5; 120.26, 29, 32; 212.6–7, 22; 240.16, 17; 242.4; ♮ quadrum sive durum, 58.19–20; 60.2, 4, 6–7, 11–12; ♮ quadrum acutum, 96.7; 100.5, 13, 17–18, 19; ♮ secundum, 58.6, 10; *v.* corpus b rotundi, corpus ♮ quadri, signum b rotundi, signum ♮ quadri, clavis b rotundi sive mollis, clavis ♮ quadri sive duri

bene, *v.* bonus

binarius, 46.5; 226.19, 20, 23; 228.6; 234.13; *v.* divisio binaria, numerus binarius

binus, 40.21; 56.20; 58.2; 232.27

bis, 248.8, 9

bisdyapason, 174.5; 246.6

bisdyateseron cum semitonio, 160.15–16; 170.18, 20–21; 192.13

bisillabus, 40.19

Boetius, 176.7; 214.3, 6; 222.3

bonus, 74.3; 232.11; bene, 40.4, 17, 20; 42.14; 60.24; 62.1, 9, 1; 64.10, 26; 66.3; 82.7, 10, 30, 35; 84.1; 98.1; 104.2; 108.6; 114.2; 116.1; 120.28; 154.14; 156.10; 172.23; 200.14; 212.8; 216.2, 4; 220.12; 224.7, 20; 226.10, 14; 232.3; 240.17; 244.9; 246.16; 248.3; melius (adv.), 36.5; 38.20; 40.13; 44.9; 74.6; 96.13; 120.3; 210.29; 222.8; 236.8; *v.* homo bonus, ingenium bonum

bos, 242.8

brevis, 34.13; brevior, 162.10; breviter, 242.5–6; 246.4

brevitas, 154.12, 19, 22; 160.4; 162.8; 210.23; 242.13; 252.5

breviter, *v.* brevis

Brixiensis, 34.12

demonstrare, 224.10; 232.7, 15, 16; 234.19, 28, 29 (bis), 35 (bis); demonstrans, 36.4; demonstrari, 200.16; 214.16; 218.4, 224.11, 12, 16; 232.11,
12; 236.1; 238.12, 19–20; 242.1; demonstratus, 178.18–19, 22; 206.16,
23
demonstrative (adv.), 176.5, 16
demonstratio, 192.20, 20–21, 22, 25, 26, 28; 232.13; 236.12; Demonstratio
partium toni, 236.12
demptus, 104.2
denominari, 168.36; 170.26; 172.2, 3, 9, 14, 15–16, 18, 19
denominatio, 92.10; denominatio ultimata, 206.15, 22
denominator, 226.16–17, 17, 21, 24; 228.3, 6
denotare, 216.3; denotans, 64.27, 28–29; denotari, 38.2, 4
Deo gratias, 154.26, 29; 252.11
deorsum, 116.4
depictus, 44.13
depositio, 38.4, 7; 52.9, 13, 14; 72.14; depositio plagalis, 92.6; depositio vocis
(–cum), 52.9; 108.8; v. elevatio vel depositio, elevatio vel depositio vocum
depressio, 46.14
deprimi, 46.15
deridere, 144.3
descendere, 82.21, 27, 29, 34; 84.1, 4; 86.13; 88.8, 9–10, 12, 13; 92.2, 3;
94.9; 106.5, 24; 118.12; 162.1; 216.7; descendens, 212.2; descendi, 70.1,
9; 80.17, 25; 82.5, 9–10, 36; 88.9, 10; 106.14
descensus, 72.21, 27; 74.11, 17–18, 23, 29; 82.23, 26, 33; 84.2, 4, 16; 86.11,
15, 16, 18, 19, 20, 25, 30; 88.12; 90.4; 94.4, 6, 7, 13, 16; 96.15; 112.21,
22; 116.2, 5–6; 214.13; 230.24; descensus a fa ad mi, 210.11
describere, 246.13 (bis)
describi, 46.12; 152.7; 250.5
descriptio, 36.5; 46.15; 48.17; 52.11, 14
desiderare, 210.26
desinens, 106.2, 6, 9, 14–15, 21, 26, 29, 33
destrutor musice, 64.13
detegari, 156.11
determinari, 96.12–13; 110.8; determinatus, 36.2–3, 10–11
Deus, 234.32; 250.3; 252.9; v. amore Dei
deuterus, 80.21; 86.5, 21; v. plagalis deuteri
devenire, 94.10; 104.5, 19; 106.2, 21; 118.10, 17; 120.3; deveniri, 106.17, 19;
120.4
dexter, v. manus dextra, pars dextra
diabolus, 144.1
dicere, 40.15, 17 (bis), 26; 42.3; 48.15; 56.10, 25, 28; 58.12; 60.29; 62.12;
64.1, 7, 17; 68.3; 72.11, 12; 86.9 (bis), 27; 94.7; 96.16, 18; 102.2; 142.13;
142.15; 144.9; 160.17; 200.13; 200.16; 202.31; 204.2, 10; 214.5, 8;
220.4, 18; 224.10, 16, 21; 226.3, 13, 19, 22; 228.13; 230.17; 232.12, 16;
236.2, 13, 17, 19, 21; 238.11, 14, 22; 240.7, 18, 22; 244.1, 4, 12, 14;
246.15, 20; 248.1; 250.8; 252.1; dici, 38.20; 42.12; 40.17; 46.4, 6; 50.10;
54.2, 4, 8, 13, 18, 22; 56.6, 11, 20, 22, 23, 31, 32, 33, 34; 58.11; 60.6,

168.11, 13–14; 188.15, 17; dyapente cum tono, 160.13; 168.3, 5, 15–16; 188.11; dyapente cum tritono, 160.15; 168.33, 35; 170.10, 23; 190.17; 192.12; dyapente prima species, 112.9; 114.5, 7–8; dyapente secuna species, 112.11; 114.10, 12; dyapente tercia species, 112.13–14, 15, 17–18; 114.14–15, 17; dyapente quarta species, 112.14, 19, 21; *v.* dyapason cum dyapente, dyapason cum dyapente et diptono, dyapason cum dyapente et semidiptono, dyapason cum dyapente et semitonio, dyapason cum dyapente et tono, proportio dyapente, vox dyapente supra finalem

dyateseron, 110.9, 10, 12, 13, 14, 16, 17, 18; 112.16, 19; 116.6, 8; 118.3 (bis), 16, 18; 164.21, 22, 23, 27, 29, 31; 166.10, 23; 170.8, 16–17, 21; 178.2, 6, 9, 15, 17; 180.3, 4, 5; 184.18; 190.13, 14; 206.1–2, 3, 4; 222.10, 11, 12, 14, 15, 20, 26; 246.5; dyateseron cum semitonio, 160.13; 166.20, 22–23; 168.2; 188.6; dyateseron cum tono, 160.13; 166.7, 9, 25, 27, 28, 29–30; 168.1–2; dyateseron prima species, 110.19; 112.8; 114.6, 8, 20, 22; dyateseron secunda species, 110.21; 112.10–11, 21, 24–114.1, 114.1, 11, 13; dyateseron tercia species, 110.22; 112.13, 18, 21–22; 114.15–16, 17–18; *v.* dyapason cum dyateseron, dyapente cum dyateseron, proportio dyateseron

dyatonicus, 220.19; 222.15, 16; 238.29; 240.2; 242.20; *v.* modus dyatonicus

dyesis, 214.1, 2 (bis), 8, 12, 19, 23; 218.2; 222.27, 28; 224.8; 238.15, 16, 22, 25, 27, 28; 240.7, 11, 14, 19, 20, 24; 242.1, 3, 7, 18, 21; *v.* additio unius dyesis, subtractio dyesis

E, 46.17; 72.8, 10; 74.13; 76.1; 102.5; Ela, 38.20; 40.12; Elami, 38.18, 19; 40.7, 10; 46.5; 48.8; 72.19; Elaut, 68.20; Emi, 68.20; Esol, 68.21; E acutum, 74.15; E grave, 68.16; 72.15, 18; 98.10, 11, 12, 13–14; 100.13, 16, 20; 102.8; 106.6, 26, 28; 212.2, 3; E primum, 168.9; e contra, 50.7; 58.15; 72.1 92.8; 112.20; 210.10–11, 214.21; e converso, 38.4; 42.7; 48.12, 13, 20, 21, 22, 23; 50:1, 2

effici, 212.19; 216.19; 228.24

egregius, 34.11; egregie (adv.), 158.2

Elementa, 196.16; 250.5; Elementa Euclidis, 194.14, 21

elevare, 72.10; 212.14–15; elevari, 42.15, 44.8; 46.15; 58.4, 5, 7

elevatio, 38.2, 7; 46.14; 52.7; 72.14, 22; elevatio autentica, 92.7; elevatio vel depositio, 52.12–13, 15–54.1; elevatio vel depositio vocis (–cum), 36.13; 38.13–14; 44.10; 50.4–5, 5–6, 6, 8; 52.11–12, 14–15; 64.28; 80.12; elevatio vocum, 108.8

emi, 246.2

emiolium (n.), 244.15; 246.1

emiolius, 244.14–15; 246.16; *v.* numerus emiolius, proportio emiolia

enarmonicus, 220.19, 30 (bis); 224.1; 238.28–29; 240.2; 242.20; *v.* modus enarmonicus

enumerare, 160.11; enumeratum, 96.15; 120.21

epata, 40.3

epi, 244.6, 9

epitritum (n.), 244.7, 9

epitritus, 244.5 (bis), 13; 246.16; *v.* numerus epitritus, proportio epitrita

8, 12, 15, 22, 28; 74.9, 13, 20, 25; 76.1; 82.1, 2, 8, 14; 88.11; 152.13, 14, 16 (bis); 154.3, 4 (bis), 5 (bis); 170.3, 24; 210.22; 212.3, 4, 6, 7 (bis), 10, 11, 13, 14; 216.12, 17, 18; 230.21 (bis); 240.9, 10, 12, 18, 22; 242.5; fa fictum, 212.16; fa verum, 212.15 (bis), 16, 17; *v.* ascensus a mi ad fa, descensus a fa ad mi, mi contra fa

facere, 64.18; 72.11; 162.10; 178.25; 180.11; 188.17; 190.14; 202.7; 208.5; 210.12; 216.8; 224.11, 17; 234.11; 238.26; faciens, 80.12–13

facilis, 46.10; facilior, 56.1, 4; 60.26 (bis); 62.1; facillimum, 64.20; faciliter, 174.8, 15; 192.27; facilius (adv.), 232.20; facillime, 120.18

factum (n.), 212.21

fallum (n.), 104.18

false (adv.), *v.* falsus

falsitas, 156.11; 222.7; 234.36; 236.13, 17, 19, 21; 238.3, 9, 11, 14, 20, 21; 244.2, 4, 7, 14; 246.19; 252.4, 6; falsitas principalis, 238.13, 20–21; falsitas principalior, 222.5–6

falsus, 158.10; 214.15; 220.2, 6; 222.1; 226.8; 230.7; 232.5; 236.2, 10; 238.8; 240.19, 24; 244.3, 15; 246.21; 248.2; 250.9; 252.2; falsissimus, 194.24–25; 198.5; 218.3; 234.7; 236.4, 20; 238.1–2; 240.3; false (adv.), 158.1; 232.16; 236.8; 246.19; *v.* doctrina falsa, fundamentum falsissimum, intellectus falsus, musica falsa

famulari, 40.23, 24; 42.1, 5; 56.32, 34; 60.22, 32, 33; 104.21

fatue (adv.), 78.3

ferialis, v. dies feriales atque dominice

fictio musice, 216.3

fieri, 34.5; 42.7; 46.10; 48.7, 11, 16, 18, 20 (bis), 21 (bis), 22, 23 (bis); 50:1 (bis), 2 (bis), 7; 54.4, 6, 18; 56.5, 10, 15, 19; 60.5, 10; 68.18, 19; 70.1; 72.18, 33; 84.9, 15; 92.10; 164.30; 166.5, 29; 168.1; 172.5, 8; 178.13; 184.18; 192.21; 196.6, 7, 20; 198.22, 24; 208.28, 30; 210.1, 4, 6, 8, 10; 216.15; 224.22; 230.10, 15, 16, 18, 21, 23; 232.26; 234.3, 4; 240.11; 242.18; factus, 180.16; 184.17, 29; 204.3, 8

figura, 36.2, 7, 12; 80.10; 154.11

figurare, 62.23; 64.14; 74.27; 78.4; figurari, 62.26; 74.28, 78.2; figuratus, 56.21; 154.11

figuratio, 64.24

filius, 220.8

finalis, 82.3, 4, 7, 8, 11, 22, 25, 26, 30; 84.8; 86.3, 12; 88.8, 10, 11; 94.8, 9, 11 (bis); 100.18; 102.10; 104.6; 108.9; 114.7, 8, 10, 12, 13, 14, 17 (bis), 19, 21, 22; 116.5 (bis), 6; 118.11, 15, 18; 120.7, 13, 15; finalis per reductionem, 100.21, 22; 102.9; finalis propria, 82.19; 100.18, 21, 22–102.1; finalis propriissima, 100.17; 102.9; finaliter, 208.25; v. litera finalis, vox dyapente supra finalem, vox finalis

fingere, 212.11, 13; fingi, 174.12; ficte (adv.), 212.8; *v.* fa fictum, mi fictum, musica ficta

finire, 82.5, 10; 120.11; 152.10; finiens, 120.13; finiri, 80.25; 82.15, 31, 32, 36; 106.32

finis, 42.16, 17; 80.12; 82.12, 13, 21; 84.10, 31; 88.7; 90.1, 2; 92.2, 3; 94.4; 100.11; 106.4, 8, 12 (bis), 17, 18, 23, 27, 31 (bis); 108.2, 7; 112.18;

116.9; 118.14; 120.2, 4; 152.7, 8; 154.24; 214.3; 220.15, 18; 222.18, 26, 32; 232.25; 252.7

firmus, v. cantus firmus; firmiter, 36.9

forma, 40.25; 42.2, 5, 6; 58.9, 10, 13; 62.19

formari, 72.30; 74.8

forum, 144.6

fractio, 184.2, 4, 7, 11–12, 19, 20; 192.5, 7

frater, 34.10; 156.5; 158.7

fraternalis, 156.7

frequenter, 118.18

fugere, 72.13; 74.13; fugi, 74.22

fundamentum, 180.6; 230.7, 13; fundamentum falsissimum, 234.37–236.1; v. principia et fundamenta

fundamentaliter, 116.2

G, 40.16 (bis); 46.17; 58.23; 60.1, 13; 66.4, 8, 24, 26 (bis), 29; 72.22; 74.12, 20; 102.7; Gmi, 68.20; Gsol, 68.21; Gsolre, 68.6; Gsolreut, 38.18–19, 19; 40.9, 12; 48.22–23; 56.28; 60.3; 68.7; 70.5; Gsolreut acutum, 58.28; Gsolreut grave, 58.28; Gut, 40.17; 66.28; 68.20; G acutum, 74.24, 30; G grave, 72.26; 96.5; 106.15, 15–16; G grave primum, 98.11; G grave secundum, 98.10, 12, 13–14, 15, 16; 100.4–5, 6, 15, 16, 20; 102.8; 106.6–7, 13, 25, 33; 108.3; 216.6–7; G grecum, 40.19; 66.31–32; 72.4–5; G primum, 162.6, 28; 164.20; 166.13; 168.9; 170.11; G secundum, 168.17; 170.11

Γ, 40.20; 66.32; 72.5; Γut, 40.21

gama, 40.15, 16, 19; 66.32; 72.5; 98.11; gamaut, 38.18; 40.7, 15 (bis), 17; 42.10, 16; 46.2; 48.8; 60.2, 4, 12; 66.28; 88.36

generalis, 244.2; generalior, 160.18; v. genus generalissimum

genus cantilene, 222.4; genus generalissimum, 220.17; genus propinquum, 226.2

geometricus, v. proportionalitas geometrica

gloria, 252.9

gradata, 50:4; 52.7, 8–9; gradatim, 42.14–15, 18; 64.8; 72.9

gramatica, 66.30 (bis)

gratia, v. Deo gratias

gravis, 42.9, 13, 21, 22; 44.2; 46.5; 56.26, 28, 29; 60.3; 62.14; 76.15; 102.4; graviter, 242.11; gravissime (adv.), 34.7; v. B grave, b grave, C grave, E grave, F grave, G grave, G grave primum, G grave secundum

gravitare, 42.19

grecus, 66.30, 34; 72.5; grece (adv.), 40.16; 50.10, 11; 84.32; 86.1, 31; 110.12 (bis); 112.3 (bis); 118.6; 162.13; v. G grecum, nomen grecum

gubernari, 56.13

habere, 38.14, 16; 40.23, 25; 42.2, 3, 5 (bis); 44.15; 52.2, 6; 54.21; 56.12; 58.18, 24, 25, 26, 27, 28, 29, 30; 60.2 (bis), 6, 11, 23, 27–28, 29, 34; 62.12–13, 19, 25; 64.7, 8, 16, 17; 66.22; 72.33; 76.1; 82.15, 18, 31; 84.2–3; 88.9; 94.2, 15; 96.4; 98.8; 100.8, 10, 11; 104.21; 116.2; 118.13; 142.13; 152.12, 13; 154.2; 184.4, 13, 14, 26, 27 (bis), 29; 190.6; 208.28, 30; 210.1, 4, 6, 8; 212.5; 216.9; 220.14; 224.22, 23; 228.27, 29; 232.3, 4, 13; 234.16, 23, 28; 236.13, 15, 16; 238.4, 7, 9; habens, 48.14; 50:3; 70.14; 84.10, 15; 86.19, 25; 108.4, 7, 9; haberi, 38.21; 122.3; 158.13;

160.3, 24; 162.18–19, 34; 164.16; 172.14–15, 27; 174.8, 14, 16; 176.16;
178.16, 27; 180.1, 3; 182.20; 192.5; 196.1; 200.10, 12, 21; 206.19;
208.19; 212.14, 20; 218.9; 224.13; 234.23; 238.17; 240.10; 244.4; 248.3;
252.6; habitus, 172.27; 174.6–7, 13; 178.8; 180.2, 6; 188.7; 190.7; 192.9,
27; 194.6; 198.27; 200.26, 29; 208.27, 29, 31, 32; 210.2, 3, 5, 7; 216.13;
222.9; 232.14; 240.24
habilius, 74.4
Henchiridion Ubaldi, 230.5
homo, 44.8; 234.32; 250.3; homo bonus, 234.9, 36; 250.4
honor, 66.22; 252.9
honorari, 156.6
hostia, 64.4
humana, 44.6; 56.1; *v.* vox humana
ignorare, 158.6; 242.11–12; 250.3; ignorans, 62.19; 214.1; 236.9; 238.15
imbecilitas, 34.15
immediatus, 160.22–23, 25; 162.1, 12; 196.3; immediate (adv.), 38.7; 40.24;
42.1; 54.4; 66.26; 72.19, 21, 26, 28; 74.7, 11, 12, 18, 19, 24, 25, 30;
84.13, 17; 88.2; 102.12; 104.3, 7, 8, 11, 14, 18; 152.9–10; 154.11; 162.7,
20; 164.2
immensuratus, 36.10; *v.* cantus immensuratus
impar, *v.* locum impar, numerus impar
imperfectio, 228.21
imperfectus, 50.7–8, 9, 11–12; 52.1; 54.1; 88.5; 98.7; 100.9; 162.16, 17;
164.1, 14–15, 17; 200.16–17; 228.20; 242.15; imperfecte (adv.), 162.12,
32–33; *v.* tonus imperfectus
implere, 88.6, 7, 13; 90.5; 116.3
impletio modi, 90.3
importare, 40.20; 84.33; 86.31; 110.12, 14; 112.5; 118.8; 214.2; 238.16;
importari, 62.2 (bis); 102.13
impossibilis, 200.16, 25; 218.8; 224.19, 22; 234.34; 238.12; 240.25; 242.2
improprie (adv.), 236.8; 246.19
incipere, 38.2, 5; 40.7, 8 (bis), 9, 10, 11, 12; 66.8, 29; 76.6, 8, 17; 104.6, 11,
13, 17; 144.3; incipiens, 38.16; 58.24, 27; 60.1, 13; incipi, 42.16; 66.4, 5;
70.8, 15; 94.6
inclusive (adv.), 42.10, 11; 88.36
incohavere, 46.17
incompletus, 50.10, 12; 52.1; 162.16–17, 18, 33; 164.1, 15, 17; 200.17;
incomplete (adv.), 162.13
incurrere, 62.22
inde, 46.13; 52.3; 106.7
indebita, 54.1
indicatio, 56.31, 33; 98.5; 120.23
indictio, 40.3
indivisibilis, 190.3
inequalis, 52.3, 3–4; 160.22; 162.11, 23, 30; 164.5, 12; 166.7, 20; 168.3, 11,
18, 26, 33; 170.5, 18; 178.10, 11; 200.12, 13
infallanter, 104.9

materialiter, 234.33

maximus, *v.* magnus

mediari, 154.1, 7

medietas, 50.9; 162.14; 190.3–4, 8; 192.10; 194.2; 246.3–4; medietas semitonii minoris, 214.2–3; 222.28; 238.16–17, 17–18; mediatas toni, 200.23–24, 25, 26

mediatus, 162.31; 164.6, 13; 166.8, 21; 168.4, 12, 19, 27, 34; 170.6, 19

medium (n.), 40.22; 50.11; 52.2, 80.11; 110.18; 122.10; 162.15; 166.2; 172.20, 23; 192.5; 194.11, 16, 22, 26; 196.3, 12, 15, 20, 21 (ter), 22, 23; 198.9, 10, 13, 23 (bis), 24, 28, 31; 200.15; 222.17, 26, 32; medium continue proportionabile, 194.11–12, 17, 18–19, 20, 22, 24; 196.12–13, 15–16; medium continue proportionale, 198.29, medium non continue proportionabile, 198.33–34; 200.2–3, 5–6; *v.* positio in medio

medius, 38.3; 162.9, 14; 170.10; 208.10 (bis), 21; *v.* combinatio media, octava media

melius, *v.* bonus

membrum, 248.4, 5; *v.* proportiones membrorum consonantiarum

memorans, 66.29–30

memoria, 38.20; 60.26

mensura, 36.3, 10

mensuratus, *v.* cantus mensuratus

mentio, 164.30; 166.29; 168.1; 172.5, 8; 178.12; 196.6, 7

merito (adv.), 44.7; 54.21; 56.6; 58.3; 84.14; 86.1; 170.14; 172.24

methafora, 64.3

methaforice, 62.29

metricus, *v.* ars metrica

metrum, *v.* compositores metrorum

mi, 38.1, 13; 40.6, 22; 42.1, 3; 50.7 (bis); 54.2, 4, 6; 56.8, 11, 24, 27, 33; 60.16, 30; 64.9 (bis), 17; 66.11; 68.13; 72.3, 7, 11, 16, 17, 25; 74.3, 5 (bis), 6, 7 (bis), 9, 16, 21, 27; 82.1, 2, 8, 14; 112.21; 152.15, 16; 154.3 (bis), 5 (bis); 164.10; 168.24; 170.3; 210.20; 212.2, 3, 11, 14; 216.7, 8, 11, 12, 13, 14, 16, 17, 18; 230.23 (bis); mi contra fa, 72.31; mi fictum, 212.16 (bis), 17; *v.* ascensus a mi ad fa, descensus a fa ad mi

minimus, *v.* parvus

minor, –us, *v.* parvus

minoritas, 172.8; 208.30; 210.6; 214.14 (bis), 20; 216.10

minuere, 208.17, 24

miraculum, 64.14

mirari, 192.18; 238.8–9

mirus, 166.5

mixtus, 56.30; 88.5; 98.8; 100.10; *v.* tonus mixtus

moderni, 62.22, 24, 29; 64.1, 11, 13, 21; 110.10–11; 112.1; 118.5; 212.20; 214.9, 19, 22, 23; 216.10, 20, 22; 218.7; moderniores, 84.24; 84.15, 212.22; *v.* cantores moderni

modificare, 80.14

modus, 36.3, 7; 38.8, 9; 40.3; 46.7, 9, 10, 11; 54.16; 56.16; 60.19, 25; 64.3; 68.8; 70.7; 74.27; 76.6, 9, 12, 13; 80.7, 9, 13; 86.7; 88.2, 6, 7; 90.1, 5;

obtinere, 44.2, 4; 66.20; 76.16; 84.23, 31; obtinens, 46.21

occupare, 120.6–7; occupans, 120.5

occurare, 120.29

octava (n.), 46.22; 74.1; 88.7–8; 92.2; 94.12; 110.6; 170.1, 9, 22; 174.11; 208.8, 12, 17, 27, 30; octava consonans, 72.30, 33; 74.3, 26; 118.6; octava duplex, 208.9; octava maior, 170.1, 26, 26–27; 172.3, 6, 20, 22, 23, 24; 208.20, 23–24, 25–26, 31; 210.5; octava media, 170.9, 25, 28; 172.1, 4, 6, 19, 24; 208.20–21, 23, 23–24, 31–32 (bis); 210.2–3 (bis); octava minor, 170.22, 28; 172.3, 6, 20, 23; 208.23–24, 25, 31–210.1; 210.2, 7; octava triplex, 208.9

octavus, 44.2, 3; 46.20; 84.7, 22, 29–30; 100.14; 102.6; 116.10; 142.14, 15; 144.9; 152.14; 154.4; 170.2; 194.20 (bis); v. modus octavi toni, modus octavi toni alius novus, modus octavus, pars octava, tonus octavus

octenarius, 234.17, 20, 28; v. numerus octenarius, proportio numeri novenarii ad octenarium,

octo, 42.9, 18, 21; 44.1; 84.9, 14 (bis), 25, 27, 29; 86.4 (bis), 6, 9, 18; 88.1, 4; 92.9; 94.1, 2; 96.17; 98.7, 9; 100.8, 16, 21; 102.1; 104.4; 118.2, 7 (bis), 8, 10, 23; 120.20, 24; 122.3; 142.7, 11, 12, 13; 144.2; 234.2; 238.2

octodecim, 232.19

octupla (n.), 188.2; 190.1; octuple continue, 184.8

octuplus, 184.5–6; v. numerus octuplus, proportiones octuple continue

offertorium, 80.8

officium, 154.14, 15

olon, 246.2

omnis, 38.3, 5, 13; 40.2; 42.16, 17; 44.1, 3; 46.1 (bis); 56.8, 10, 26, 29; 58.24, 25, 26, 27, 28, 30 (bis); 60.1, 3, 5; 62.2; 66.5; 70.2, 9, 10; 76.2, 78.2; 84.2, 3, 14, 27, 29; 86.3; 88.1; 96.14, 16; 98.1, 4; 100.2; 104.1, 19; 106.1, 2, 6, 9, 14, 20, 21, 26, 29, 32; 108.4, 6; 114.9, 14, 18; 116.1; 120.6, 20, 21, 26, 27; 152.5, 16; 158.17; 162.7; 170.15, 27; 172.1, 27; 174.9; 176.9; 178.1, 3, 4 (bis), 5 (bis), 6 (bis), 7, 8, 9 (ter), 12, 14, 17, 18 (bis), 19, 192.23; 194.25; 206.9 (bis), 10, 12, 15, 17 (bis), 18, 10, 22; 208.7; 210.22; 214.15; 226.9; 234.1, 5, 8; 240.3; 242.15; 244.10; 246.2, 4, 13; 250.6; 252.3, 6; omnino, 34.6; 72.14; 158.5

omnipotens, 252.9

operari, 64.14, 17, 25; 78.3, 3–4, 5; 120.23; 154.18, 20, 21

operans, 212.23

operator, 154.19

opinio, 242.21

oportere, 88.11; 108.7; 210.29; 216.16

opportunus, 38.13; 68.3

oppositum, 180.8, 238.19

opus, 154.18, 24; 158.16; 160.5; 162.10; 176.11; 242.13

opusculum, 158.9

ordinare, 38.15, 22; 44.10; 222.11, 20–21, 27; ordinari, 68.19; 70.2; 76.12; 80.10; 86.31–88.1; 184.14, 28, 30; 186.15; 188.3; 190.9; 192.11; ordinatus, 38.2; 84.9; 154.13, 26; 184.21; ordinate (adv.), 38.3, 5, 16, 17; 46.17; 70.15 (bis); 72.2; 212.12

paucus, 56.2; 64.12; paucior, 74.1, 2; 120.30, 30–31; 236.14, 15, 16; 238.4, 5–6, 7, 23
paulatinus, 38.2, 4
paulo (adv.), 162.18; 164.18, 26; 166.25; 168.31; 170.10; 184.20; 212.8; 230.13
pausa, 120.5, 7, 8, 14, 17 (bis)
pausare, 120.2
pente, 112.3; 166.16
perduci, 212.9
perfectio, 94.15; 96.1; 228.21; 242.15–16
perfectus, 52.13; 88.4; 98.7; 100.9; 228.16 (bis), 19–20; 230.3; 248.7; perfecte (adv.), 160.23, 25, 26; perfectissime, 158.5; *v.* numerus perfectus, tonus perfectus
perficere, 200.23, 24; perfici, 218.5
permanere, 110.9
permitti, 94.11
permixtio, 34.5–6
permutari, 46.9, 11
pernotare, 118.16, 20, 22
perpendere, 64.10; 118.22
persuadere, 232.7, 16; 234.30, 35; persuadi, 224.11, 12; 232.12 (bis)
persuasio, 232.14–15
persuasive (adv.), 176.5–6, 16
pertinere, 210.23; pertinens, 34.14
pertractare, 34.15; 158.1
pervenire, 98.1; 114.4; 120.23; 154.16; 220.10; 228.14; perveniri, 42.16; 120.16, 19
pessime (adv.), 64.15, 25
physica, 78.9
Pitagoras ytalicus, 176.6, 9, 17; 220.6, 8, 10, 11, 13
plaga, 86.26, 28
plagalis, 36.4; 38.10; 84.30, 32; 86.1, 2, 25, 28, 29; 88.1 (bis), 11; 90.4; 92.2, 7; 94.7, 9, 10, 14, 16; 96.2, 4, 9, 11; 116.7, 9; 118.19, 22; plagalis deuteri, 86.5; plagalis proti, 86.5; plagalis tetrardi, 86.6; plagalis triti, 86.5; *v.* depositio plagalis, tonus plagalis
plagis, 84.32, 33; 86.30
planus, 36.7; *v.* Ars pratice cantus plani, cantus planus, musica plana
plena, 52.13; 54.1; plene (adv.), 160.23, 25, 26; 162.12; *v.* noticia plena
plures, *v.* multus
pluries, *v.* multus
plurimi, *v.* multus
plurimum, *v.* multus
plus, *v.* multus
plusquamperfectus, 88.5; 98.7; 100.9–10
polex, 70.8; 76.9, 17
policinius, 156.6

semidiptonus, 160.12; 162.30, 32, 34; 168.29; 172.17, 18; 186.18; 252.2; *v.*
   dyapason cum dyapente et semidiptono, dyapente cum semidiptono,
seminare, 218.8; 222.6; 236.10; seminari, 158.10–11; seminatus, 238.14, 21,
   22
semis, 50.10, 11
semitonium, 50.8, 10; 52.1, 2, 3, 4, 14 (bis); 54.2, 7; 58.5, 8; 72.31; 74.1, 2.
   80.5, 6; 88.13; 110.4, 11, 15, 17–18, 18, 20, 21–22; 112.2, 6, 7, 10, 12,
   14–15, 17, 18, 23, 24; 118.5, 9; 160.12; 162.2 (bis), 11, 13, 14, 16, 17,
   19, 31; 164.13, 16; 166.9, 22, 23; 168.5, 13, 14, 20, 28, 35; 170.7, 20,
   22; 172.13–14, 14, 15; 178.12, 14, 16, 21; 180.1, 3, 4; 186.1, 6; 200.20,
   22, 27, 30; 202.3; 204.12–13, 18, 20, 23, 24; 214.6, 8; 224.6, 7; 238.16,
   17, 24–25, 26, 28; 240.2, 4, 5, 13; 242.1, 7, 9, 11, 12, 17; semitonium
   cromaticum, 240.23; 242.3; semitonium maius, 200.14, 18, 26–27;
   204.26; 206.4, 9, 10, 11–12, 12, 18, 2, 3, 5; 208.8, 10, 11, 18, 18–19, 24,
   26; 210.11, 15, 17–18, 18, 20; 214.22; 216.18, 21–22; 242.5, 19 (bis);
   semitonium minus, 200.15, 18, 21, 24; 204.26; 206.3, 11, 17–18; 208.1,
   2, 3, 4, 4–5, 14–15, 16, 18–19, 22; 210.9–10; 212.13, 14, 17; 216.17;
   222.13, 17, 21; 242.5, 19 (bis); *v.* additio semitonii maioris, additio semitoniorum maiorum duorum, bisdyateseron cum semitonio, dyapason cum
   dyapente et semitonio, dyapason cum semitonio, dyapente cum semitonio,
   dyateseron cum semitonio, medietas semitonii minoris, nomina semitoniorum, numerus tonorum et semitoniorum, proportio semitonii, proportio
   semitonii maioris, proportio semitonii minoris, quarta trium semitoniorum,
   quinta quatuor semitoniorum, subtractio semitonii maioris, subtractio semitoniorum maiorum duorum, tercia duorum semitoniorum, tonus cum semitonio, tonus cum semitonio maiori
semitritonus, 160.12–13; 164.11, 14, 16, 28, 31; 166.1 (bis), 4, 6
semper, 42.17, 22; 56.13; 66.25, 26; 82.29; 84.8; 152.13; 172.5–6; 180.7, 9;
   196.8; 212.14; 216.3; 222.11; 228.30; 230.20; 232.26, 27; 234.4
semus, 50.9, 12; 52.1; 162.16, 17, 32; 164.14, 17; 200.17
senarius, 46.6; *v.* numerus senarius
sepissime (adv.), 118.11; 154.18
septem, 38.15; 42.11, 19, 21; 44.3; 46.16, 19; 66.5, 6, 14, 21, 25; 72.31–32;
   98.11; 238.2
septima (n.), 94.10; 110.5–6; 168.22, 30; septima maior, 168.22; septima
   minor, 168.30
septimus, 84.27; 90.2; 100.14; 102.6; 110.1; 152.16; 154.3; 168.23; *v.* modus
   septimi toni, tonus septimus
sequax, 86.1, 2; 214.12; 240.11; 242.6
sequentia, 96.19
sequi, 66.26; 94.13; 144.10; 164.30; 166.30; 172.5; 178.12, 17, 19, 20–21,
   23; 180.9; 186.4, 6; 194.21; 196.17, 24, 26; 206.14, 21; 208.3, 23, 25,
   26; 210.9; 224.3; 230.2; 234.33, 34; 242.17; sequens, 38.7; 40.24; 42.1,
   11, 12, 19; 44.3; 56.8, 11; 68.2; 72.12, 21, 28; 74.13, 20, 25; 164.30;
   172.27; 174.6, 10; 178.1, 23; 196.7
sequutio, 86.1
seriatim, 94.5

tercia (n.), 110.5; 164.2; 172.17; 194.2; 240.8, 9; tercia duorum semitoniorum, 174.19; tercia maior, 162.26; 172.18; 216.8, 14–15, 15, 19; tercia minor, 164.1; 172.18; 216.14–15; 240.16

tercius, 42.21, 48.20, 21, 22; 50:1; 60.8; 62.15, 25; 64.3; 72.3, 6–7; 76.4, 78.9; 80.22; 84.12 (bis), 18, 20 (bis), 27; 88.11; 92.5; 96.3; 100.12; 102.4; 104.6, 8; 112.23; 120.11; 152.14; 154.5; 162.28; 188.1, 3; 192.3; 202.24; 222.13, 14, 22 (bis), 28–29, 29; 232.21; 234.26, 31; 236.19; 238.21; 242.10, 15; 244.14; tercio (adv.), 196.19, 222.26; 226.3; 240.22; v. dyapente tercia species, dyateseron tercia species, modus tercii toni, pars tercia, tonus tercius

terminari, 40.7, 8, 9, 9–10, 10, 11, 12; 44.6

terminus, 160.8, 9; 186.13; 188.1; 190.1; 194.23; 196.2, 13, 15, 21–22; 202.21; 204.5; 234.13, 16, 22; terminus maior, 202.8, 14; 204.15, 16–17, 19; terminus minimus, 192.21; 198.23; 202.6, 10, 14, 18, 20, 26, 28, 29, 32, 33; 204.3, 6, 7, 8, 11, 13, 14; 234.10; terminus non minimus, 202.27; 204.2; terminus minor, 202.11, 12, 15 (bis); 204.17, 20; terminus ultimus, 190.7; v. proportio in terminis

ternarius, 46.3; 226.23; 244.5, 14; v. divisio ternaria, numerus supra ternarium, numerus ternarius

terra, 86.28

teseron, 110.12; 164.23

testis, 214.3, 4; 222.3, 4

tetra, 222.18

tetracordum, 222.15–16, 18, 19, 30; 224.1; 240.4; v. nomina tetracordorum

tetrardus, 80.21–22; 86.6, 21; v. plagalis tetrardi

textus, 232.3

Theorica musice, 214.5

theoricalis, 34.9; 156.12, 15; v. pars theoricalis

theoricus (n.), 52.6

theoricus (adj.), 34.5, 158.4

tonare, 160.25; tonans, 160.24; 162.13; tonari, 160.24

tonus, 80.4

tonus (interval), 50.6, 9, 10, 11, 12; 52.2 (bis), 11 (bis); 54.2, 8; 58.6, 7; 72.23; 74.1 (bis); 80.6; 82.21, 34; 88.8, 9; 110.3, 11, 15, 19, 20, 22; 112.2, 6, 9, 10 (bis), 11, 12, 13, 14, 15, 17, 24; 118.5, 9, 12; 160.12, 22, 24; 162.3, 4, 14, 15, 18 (bis), 20, 24, 25, 26, 31; 164.6, 7, 8, 13, 15; 166.8, 10, 21; 168.4, 6, 12, 19, 28, 34; 170.7, 16, 20; 172.13, 14, 15; 178.1, 8, 15, 21; 180.3, 5; 182.29; 186.1, 9, 23; 194.1, 5; 198.18, 20; 200.9, 11, 12, 23, 24, 26; 204.26; 206.3, 10, 11; 208.2, 5, 13, 18, 22; 212.11, 16; 214.15, 17; 216.17; 222.14; 224.10 (bis), 16, 18, 19, 21, 23; 230.6 (bis), 9, 15, 21, 23; 232.2, 8, 10, 17, 18, 22, 23, 27; 236.1, 2, 3, 5, 13, 16, 17; 238.4, 11, 19, 23, 24; 240.18; 242.9; toni continui, 184.2, 17; tonus cum semitonio, 82.21–22, 28; 88.9, 12; 94.8; 162.34; tonus cum semitonio maiori, 222.22, 25; v. Demonstratio partium toni, divisio toni, dyapason cum dyapente et tono, dyapason cum tono, dyapente cum tono, dyateseron cum tono, medietas toni, natura toni, numerus tonorum et semitoniorum, pars quinta toni, pars toni, proportio toni, ratio toni

ratios of the major and minor semitones are 17:16 and 18:17, 19, 248–49

Luc. 5.9, claim that 3 is a perfect number (whereas it is not) and proof (defective) thereof, 19, 248–51

Luc. 6.3, claim that ditone and semiditone do not consist in any ratio (whereas every interval consists in a ratio), 19, 252–53

Luc. 6.5, claim that no ratio is found between the duple and the triple (whereas there are an infinite number of ratios between them), 250–51

Martianus Capella, 19

McKinnon, James, 221n.

means:
    arithmetic, geometric, and harmonic, 17, 196–97
    consecutive proportionable, 194–201

meantone temperament, 4

mnemonic verses:
    C naturam dat ... , 57–58
    Primus, cum sexto, fa sol la semper habeto ... , 152–53
    Septimus et primus et sextus fa mi re mi sibi tenet ... , 154–55

mode, theory of, 8–14, 80–155;
    authentic and plagal, 8, 84–89, 80–155 *passim*
    classes of modes, 8, 88–93
        perfect, 8, 88–91
        imperfect, 8, 90–91
        pluperfect, 8, 92–93
        mixed or intermixed, 8, 13, 92–93
    diapason above final indicates chant authentic, 11, 118–19
    diapente above final, emphasized, indicates chant authentic, 11, 118–19
    diatessaron above final, emphasized, indicates chant plagal, 11, 116–19
    introits, modal characteristics in, 106–7
    irregular, 9n.
    Marchetto's and Prosdocimo's theories of mode compared, 8–14
    nine factors distinguishing one mode from another, 9–11, 94–121
        all to be taken into consideration, 96–99, 120–21
        chord, 9, 96–99; principal and secondary chord, 96–97
        differentiae of *Seculorum amen*, 10, 13, 102–5
        final, 9–10, 80–83, 97n., 100–103; cofinal, 9, 100–101, 108–9; *re, mi, fa, sol* as finals, 9–10, 102–3
        initial, 9, 98–101
        neume (characteristic melodic gesture), 9, 11, 116–19
        range (ascent and descent), 9, 94–95
        species, 10, 13, 110–17
            of diatessaron, 10, 110–11
            of diapente, 10, 112–13
            intermediation of species, 119n.
    distinction (end of phrase, rest), 11, 120–21

Studies in the History of Music Theory and Literature